I turned to look at her. She was older, about twenty-five maybe, and her face looked kind of sweet. She also didn't take her hand off my knee, which made me nervous, because the bad thing I do is a lot stronger when I'm actually touching a person, and so I mostly don't touch folks and I don't feel safe when they touch me. The fastest I ever killed a man was when he felt me up in a bathroom at a rest stop on I-85. He was coughing blood when I left that place, I really tore him up that time. So anyway that's why I felt real nervous her touching me there on the bus, even though there was no harm in it.

That was up till she smiles at me and says, "Mick, I want to help you." It took me a second to realize she spoke my name. I didn't know many people in Roanoke, and she sure wasn't one of them.

"Mick Winger," she says. "You got your first name from a note pinned to your blanket when you were left at the door of the sewage plant in Eden. You chose your last name when you ran away from the Eden Baptist Children's home, and you probably chose it because the first movie you ever saw was *An Officer and a Gentleman*. You were fifteen then, and now you're seventeen, and you've killed more people in your life than Al Capone."

—from *Eye for Eye* by Orson Scott Card

A Tor SF Double:

Eye for Eye by Orson Scott Card
The Tunesmith by Lloyd Biggle, Jr.

And a special essay by Orson Scott Card:
"How Lloyd Biggle, Jr., Changed My Life"

A Tom Doherty Associates, Inc. Book

Tor books by Orson Scott Card

The Folk of the Fringe
Hart's Hope
Saints
Songmaster
Wyrms

Ender's Game
Speaker for the Dead

The Tales of Alvin Maker:
   Seventh Son
   Red Prophet
   Prentice Alvin

Maps in a Mirror:
   The Short Fiction of Orson Scott Card

The Worthing Saga (forthcoming)

ORSON SCOTT CARD
EYE FOR EYE

THE TUNESMITH
LLOYD BIGGLE, JR.

WITH A SPECIAL ESSAY BY
ORSON SCOTT CARD
"HOW LLOYD BIGGLE, JR., CHANGED MY LIFE"

A TOM DOHERTY ASSOCIATES BOOK
NEW YORK

EYE FOR EYE

Copyright © 1987 by Orson Scott Card

THE TUNESMITH

Copyright © 1957 by Quinn Publishing Company, Inc.; copyright © 1985 by Lloyd Biggle, Jr.

Introduction and Afterword copyright © 1990 by Orson Scott Card

A Tor Book
Published by Tom Doherty Associates, Inc.
49 West 24th Street
New York, NY 10010

Cover art by Mark Ferrari

ISBN: 0-812-50854-8

First edition: November 1990

Printed in the United States of America

0 9 8 7 6 5 4 3 2 1

EYE FOR EYE
ORSON SCOTT CARD

JUST TALK, MICK. TELL US EVERYTHING. WE'LL listen.

Well to start with I know I was doing terrible things. If you're a halfway decent person, you don't go looking to kill people. Even if you can do it without touching them. Even if you can do it so as nobody even guesses they was murdered, you still got to try not to do it.

Who taught you that?

Nobody. I mean it wasn't in the books in the Baptist Sunday School—they spent all their time telling us not to lie or break the sabbath or drink liquor. Never did mention killing. Near as I can figure, the Lord thought killing

3

was pretty smart sometimes, like when Samson done it with a donkey's jaw. A thousand guys dead, but that was okay cause they was Philistines. And lighting foxes' tails on fire. Samson was a sicko, but he still got his pages in the Bible.

I figure Jesus was about the only guy got much space in the Bible telling people not to kill. And even then, there's that story about how the Lord struck down a guy and his wife cause they held back on their offerings to the Christian church. Oh, Lord, the TV preachers did go on about that. No, it wasn't cause I got religion that I figured out not to kill people.

You know what I think it was? I think it was Vondel Cone's elbow. At the Baptist Children's Home in Eden, North Carolina, we played basketball all the time. On a bumpy dirt court, but we figured it was part of the game, never knowing which way the ball would bounce. Those boys in the NBA, they play a sissy game on that flat smooth floor.

We played basketball because there wasn't a lot else to do. Only thing they ever had on TV was the preachers. We got it all cabled in—Falwell from up in Lynchburg, Jim and Tammy from Charlotte, Jimmy Swaggart looking hot, Ernest Ainglee looking carpeted, Billy Graham looking like God's executive vice-president—that was all our TV ever showed, so no wonder we lived on the basketball court all year.

Anyway, Vondel Cone wasn't particularly tall and he wasn't particularly good at shooting and on the court nobody was even halfway good at dribbling. But he had elbows. Other guys, when they hit you it was an accident. But when Vondel's elbow met up with your face, he like to pushed your nose out your ear. You can bet we all learned real quick to give him room. He got to take all the shots and get all the rebounds he wanted.

But we got even. We just didn't count his points. We'd call out the score, and any basket he made it was like it never happened. He'd scream and he'd argue and we'd all stand there and nod and agree so he wouldn't punch us out, and then as soon as the next basket was made, we'd call out the score—still not counting Vondel's points. Drove that boy crazy. He screamed till his eyes bugged out, but nobody ever counted his cheating points.

Vondel died of leukemia at the age of fourteen. You see, I never did like that boy.

But I learned something from him. I learned how unfair it was for somebody to get his way just because he didn't care how much he hurt other people. And when I finally realized that I was just about the most hurtful person in the whole world, I knew then and there that it just wasn't right. I mean, even in the Old Testament, Moses said the punishment should fit the crime. Eye for eye, tooth for tooth. Even Steven, that's what Old Peleg said before I killed him of prostate cancer. It was when Peleg got took to the hospital that I left the Eden Baptist Children's Home. Cause I wasn't Vondel. I *did* care how much I hurt folks.

But that doesn't have nothing to do with anything. I don't know what all you want me to talk about.

Just talk, Mick. Tell us whatever you want.

Well I don't aim to tell you my whole life story. I mean I didn't really start to figure out anything till I got on that bus in Roanoke, and so I can pretty much start there I guess. I remember being careful not to get annoyed when the lady in front of me didn't have the right change for the bus, And I didn't get angry when the bus driver got all snotty and told the lady to get off. It just wasn't worth killing for. That's what I always tell myself when I get mad. It isn't worth killing for, and it helps me calm myself down. So anyway I reached past her and pushed a dollar bill through the slot.

"This is for both of us," I says.

"I don't make change," says he.

I could've just said "Fine" and left it at that, but he was being such a prick that I had to do something to make him see how ignorant he was. So I put another nickel in the slot and said, "That's thirty-five for me, thirty-five for her, and thirty-five for the next guy gets on without no change."

So maybe I provoked him. I'm sorry for

that, but I'm human, too, I figure. Anyway he was mad. "Don't you smart off with me, boy. I don't have to let you ride, fare or no fare."

Well, fact was he did, that's the law, and anyway I was white and my hair was short so his boss would probably do something if I complained. I could have told him what for and shut his mouth up tight. Except that if I did, I would have gotten too mad, and no man deserves to die just for being a prick. So I looked down at the floor and said, "Sorry, sir." I didn't say "Sorry *sir*" or anything snotty like that. I said it all quiet and sincere.

If he just *dropped* it, everything would have been fine, you know? I was mad, yes, but I'd gotten okay at bottling it in, just kind of holding it tight and then waiting for it to ooze away where it wouldn't hurt nobody. But just as I turned to head back toward a seat, he lurched that bus forward so hard that it flung me down and I only caught myself from hitting the floor by catching the handhold on a seatback and half-smashing the poor lady sitting there.

Some other people said, "Hey!" kind of mad, and I realize now that they was saying it to the driver, cause they was on my side. But at the time I thought they was mad at *me*, and that plus the scare of nearly falling and how mad I already was, well, I lost control of myself. I could just feel it in me, like sparklers in my blood veins, spinning around my whole body and then throwing off this pulse that went and hit that bus driver. He was behind me, so I didn't see it with my eyes. But I could feel that sparkiness connect up with him, and twist him around inside, and then finally it came loose from me, I didn't feel it no more. I wasn't mad no more. But I knew I'd done him already.

I even knew where. It was in his liver. I was a real expert on cancer by now. Hadn't I seen everybody I ever knew die of it? Hadn't I read every book in the Eden Public Library on cancer? You can live without kidneys, you can cut out a lung, you can take out a colon and live with a bag in your pants, but you can't live without a liver and they can't transplant it either. That man was dead. Two years at the most, I gave him. Two years, all because he was in a bad mood and lurched his bus to trip up a smarthmouth kid.

I felt like piss on a flat rock. On that day I had gone nearly eight months, since before Christmas, the whole *year* so far without hurting anybody. It was the best I'd ever done, and I thought I'd licked it. I stepped across the lady I smashed into and sat by the window, looking out, not seeing anything. All I could think was I'm sorry I'm sorry I'm sorry. Did he have a wife and kids? Well, they'd be a widow and orphans soon enough, because of me. I could feel him from clear over here. The sparkiness of his belly, making the cancer grow and keeping his body's own natural fire from burning it out. I wanted with all my heart to take it back, but I couldn't. And like so many times before, I thought to myself that if I had any guts I'd kill myself. I couldn't figure why I hadn't died of my own cancer already. I sure enough hated myself a lot worse than I ever hated anybody else.

The lady beside me starts to talk. "People like that are so annoying, aren't they?"

I didn't want to talk to anybody, so I just grunted and turned away.

"That was very kind of you to help me," she says.

That's when I realized she was the same lady who didn't have the right fare. "Nothing," I says.

"No, you didn't have to do that." She touched my jeans.

I turned to look at her. She was older, about twenty-five maybe, and her face looked kind of sweet. She was dressed nice enough that could tell it wasn't cause she was poor that she didn't have bus fare. She also didn't take her hand off my knee, which made me nervous, because the bad thing I do is a lot stronger when I'm actually touching a person, and so I mostly don't touch folks and I don't feel safe when they touch me. The fastest I ever killed a man was when he felt me up in a bathroom at a rest stop on I-85. He was coughing blood when I left that place, I really tore him up that time, I still have nightmares about him gasping for breath there with his hand on me.

So anyway that's why I felt real nervous her touching me there on the bus, even though there was no harm in it. Or anyway that's half why I was nervous, and the other half was that her hand was real light on my leg and out of the corner of my eye I could see how her chest moved when she breathed, and after all I'm seventeen and normal most ways. So when I wished she'd move her hand, I only *half* wished she'd move it back to her own lap.

That was up till she smiles at me and says, "Mick, I want to help you."

It took me a second to realize she spoke my name. I didn't know many people in Roanoke, and she sure wasn't one of them. Maybe she was one of Mr. Kaiser's customers, I thought. But they hardly ever knew my name. I kind of thought, for a second, that maybe she had seen me working in the warehouse and asked Mr. Kaiser all about me or something. So I says, "Are you one of Mr. Kaiser's customers?"

"Mick Winger," she says. "You got your first name from a note pinned to your blanket when you were left at the door of the sewage plant in Eden. You chose your last name when you ran away from the Eden Baptist Children's Home, and you probably chose it because the first movie you ever saw was *An*

Officer and a Gentleman. You were fifteen then, and now you're seventeen, and you've killed more people in your life than Al Capone."

I got nervous when she knew my whole name and how I got it, cause the only way she could know that stuff was if she'd been following me for years. But when she let on she knew I killed people, I forgot all about feeling mad or guilty or horny. I pulled the cord on the bus, practically crawled over her to get out, and in about three seconds I was off that bus and hit the ground running. I'd been afraid of it for years, somebody finding out about me. But it was all the more scary seeing how she must have known about me for so *long*. It made me feel like somebody'd been peeking in the bathroom window all my life and I only just now found out about it.

I ran for a long time, which isn't easy because of all the hills in Roanoke. I ran mostly downhill, though, into town, where I could dodge into buildings and out their back doors. I didn't know if she was following me, but she'd been following me for a long time, or someone had, and I never even guessed it, so how did I know if they was following me now or not?

And while I ran, I tried to figure where I could go now. I had to leave town, that was sure. I couldn't go back to the warehouse, not even to say good-bye, and that made me feel real bad, cause Mr. Kaiser would think I just run off for no reason, like some kid who didn't care nothing about people counting on him. He might even worry about me, never coming to pick up my spare clothes from the room he let me sleep in.

Thinking about what Mr. Kaiser might think about me going was pretty strange. Leaving Roanoke wasn't going to be like leaving the orphanage, and then leaving Eden, and finally leaving North Carolina. I never had much to let go of in those places. But Mr. Kaiser had always been real straight with me, a nice steady old guy, never bossed me, never tried to take me down, even stuck up for me in a quiet kind of way by letting it be known that he didn't want nobody teasing me. Hired me a year and a half ago, even though I was lying about being sixteen and he must've known it. And in all that time, I never once got mad at work, or at least not so mad I couldn't stop myself from hurting people. I worked hard, built up muscles I never thought I'd have, and I also must've grown five inches, my pants kept getting so short. I sweated and I ached most days after work, but I earned my pay and kept up with the older guys, and Mr. Kaiser never once made me feel like he took me on for charity, the way the orphanage people always did, like I should thank them for not letting me starve. Kaiser's Furniture Warehouse was the first peaceful place I ever spent time, the first place where nobody died who was my fault.

I knew all that before, but right till I started running I never realized how bad I'd feel about leaving Roanoke. Like somebody dying. It got so bad that for a while I couldn't hardly see which way I was going, not that I out and out cried or nothing.

Pretty soon I found myself walking down Jefferson Street, where it cuts through a woody hill before it widens out for car dealers and Burger Kings. There was cars passing me both ways, but I was thinking about other things now. Trying to figure why I never got mad at Mr. Kaiser. Other people treated me nice before, it wasn't like I got beat up every night or nobody ever gave me seconds or I had to eat dogfood or nothing. I remembered all those people at the orphanage, they was just trying to make me grow up Christian and educated. They just never learned how to be nice without also being nasty. Like Old Peleg, the black caretaker, he was a nice old coot and told us stories, and I never let nobody call him nigger even behind his back. But he was a racist himself, and I knew it on account of the time he caught me and Jody Capel practicing who could stop pissing the most times in a single go. We both done the same thing, didn't we? But he just sent me off and then started whaling on Jody, and Jody was yelling like he was dying, and I kept saying, "It ain't fair! I done it too! You're only beating on him cause he's black!" but he paid no mind, it was so crazy, I mean it wasn't like I wanted him to beat me too, but it made me so *mad* and before I knew it, I felt so sparky that I couldn't hold it in and I was hanging on him, trying to pull him away from Jody so it hit him hard.

What could I say to him then? Going into the hospital, where he'd lie there with a tube in his arm and a tube in his nose sometimes. He told me stories when he could talk, and just squoze my hand when he couldn't. He used to have a belly on him, but I think I could have tossed him in the air like a baby before he died. And I did it to him, not that I meant to, I couldn't help myself, but that's the way it was. Even people I purely loved, they'd have mean days, and God help them if I happened to be there, because I was like God with a bad mood, that's what I was, God with no mercy, because I couldn't give them nothing, but I sure as hell could take away. Take it all away. They told me I shouldn't visit Old Peleg so much cause it was sick to keep going to watch him waste away. Mrs. Howard and Mr. Dennis both got tumors from trying to get me to stop going. So many people was dying of cancer in those days they came from the county and tested the water for chemicals. It wasn't no chemicals, I knew that, but I never did tell them, cause they'd just lock me up in the crazy house and you can bet that crazy house would have a *epidemic* before I been there a week if that ever happened.

Truth was I didn't know, I just didn't know it was me doing it for the longest time. It's just people kept dying on me, everybody I ever loved, and it seemed like they always took sick after I'd been real mad at them once, and you know how little kids always feel guilty about yelling at somebody who dies right after. The counselor even told me that those feelings were perfectly natural, and of course it wasn't my fault, but I couldn't shake it. And finally I began to realize that other people didn't feel that sparky feeling like I did, and they couldn't tell how folks was feeling unless they looked or asked. I mean, I knew when my lady teachers was going to be on the rag before *they* did, and you can bet I stayed away from them the best I could on those crabby days. I could feel it, like they was giving off sparks. And there was other folks who had a way of sucking you to them, without saying a thing, without doing a thing, you just went into a room and couldn't take your eyes off them, you wanted to be close—I saw that other kids felt the same way, just automatically liked them, you know? But I could feel it like they was on fire, and suddenly I was cold and needed to warm myself. And I'd say something about it and people would look at me like I was crazy enough to lock right up, and

I finally caught on that I was the only one that had those feelings.

Once I knew that, then all those deaths began to fit together. All those cancers, those days they lay in hospital beds turning into mummies before they was rightly dead, all the pain until they drugged them into zombies so they wouldn't tear their own guts out just trying to get to the place that hurt so bad. Torn up, cut up, drugged up, radiated, bald, skinny, praying for death, and I knew I did it. I began to tell the minute I did it. I began to know what kind of cancer it would be, and where, and how bad. And I was always right.

Twenty-five people I knew of, and probably more I didn't

And it got even worse when I ran away. I'd hitch rides because how else was I going to get anywheres? But I was always scared of the people who picked me up, and if they got weird or anything I sparked them. And cops who run me out of a place, they got it. Until I figured I was just Death himself, with his bent-up spear and a hood over his head, walking around and whoever came near him bought the farm. That was me. I was the most terrible thing in the world, I was families broke up and children orphaned and mamas crying for their dead babies, I was everything that people hate most in all the world. I jumped off an overpass once to kill myself but I just sprained my ankle. Old Peleg always said I was like a cat, I wouldn't die lessen somebody skinned me, roasted the meat and ate it, then tanned the hide, made it into slippers, wore them slippers clean out, and then burned them and raked the ashes, that's when I'd finally die. And I figure he's right, cause I'm still alive and that's a plain miracle after the stuff I been through lately.

Anyway that's the kind of thing I was thinking, walking along Jefferson, when I noticed that a car had driven by going the other way and saw me and turned around and came back up behind me, pulled ahead of me and stopped. I was so spooked I thought it must be that lady finding me again, or maybe somebody with guns to shoot me all up like on *Miami Vice*, and I was all set to take off up the hill till I saw it was just Mr. Kaiser.

He says, "I was heading the other way, Mick. Want a ride to work?"

I couldn't tell him what I was doing. "Not today, Mr. Kaiser," I says.

Well, he knew by my look or something, cause he says, "You quitting on me, Mick?"

I was just thinking, don't argue with me or nothing, Mr. Kaiser, just let me go, I don't want to hurt you, I'm so fired up with guilt and hating myself that I'm just death waiting to bust out and blast somebody, can't you see sparks falling off me like spray off a wet dog? I just says, "Mr. Kaiser, I don't want to talk right now, I really don't."

Right then was the moment for him to push. For him to lecture me about how I had to learn responsibility, and if I didn't talk things through how could anybody ever make things right, and life ain't a free ride so sometimes you got to do things you don't want to do, and I been nicer to you than you deserve, you're just what they warned me you'd be, shiftless and ungrateful and a bum in your soul.

But he didn't say none of that. He just says, "You had some bad luck? I can advance you against wages, I know you'll pay back."

"I don't owe no money," I says.

And he says, "Whatever you're running away from, come home with me and you'll be safe."

What could I say? You're the one who needs protecting, Mr. Kaiser, and I'm the one who'll probably kill you. So I didn't say nothing, until finally he just nodded and put his hand on my shoulder and said, "That's okay, Mick. If you ever need a place or a job, you just come on back to me. You find a place to settle down for a while, you write to me and I'll send you your stuff."

"You just give it to the next guy," I says.

"A son-of-a-bitch stinking mean old Jew like me?" he says. "I don't give nothing to nobody."

Well I couldn't help but laugh, cause that's what the foreman always called Mr. Kaiser whenever he thought the old guy couldn't hear him. And when I laughed, I felt myself cool off, just like as if I had been on fire and somebody poured cold water over my head.

"Take care of yourself, Mick," he says. He give me his card and a twenty and tucked it into my pocket when I told him no. Then he got back into his car and made one of his insane U-turns right across traffic and headed back the other way.

Well if he did nothing else he got my brain back in gear. There I was walking along the highway where anybody at all could see me, just like Mr. Kaiser did. At least till I was out of town I ought to stay out of sight as much as I could. So there I was between those two hills, pretty steep, and all covered with green, and I figured I could climb either one. But the slope on the other side of the road looked somehow better to me, it looked more like I just ought to go there, and I figured that was as good a reason to decide as any I ever heard of, and so I dodged my way across Jefferson Street and went right into the kudzu caves and clawed my way right up. It was dark under the leaves, but it wasn't much cooler than right out in the sun, particularly cause I was working so hard. It was a long way up, and just when I got to the top the ground started shaking. I thought it was an earthquake I was so edgy, till I heard the train whistle and then I knew it was one of those coal-hauling trains, so heavy it could shake ivy off a wall when it passed. I just stood there and listened to it, the sound coming from every direction all at once, there under the kudzu, I listened till it went on by, and then I stepped out of the leaves into a clearing.

And there she was, waiting for me, sitting under a tree.

I was too wore out to run, and too scared, coming on her sudden like that, just when I thought I was out of sight. It was just as if I'd been aiming straight at her, all the way up the hill, just as if she somehow tied a string to me and pulled me across the street and up the hill. And if she could do that, how could I run away from her, tell me that? Where could I go? I'd just turn some corner and there she'd be, waiting. So I says to her, "All right, what do you want?"

She just waved me on over. And I went, too, but not very close, cause I didn't know what she had in mind. "Sit down, Mick," says she. "We need to talk."

Now I'll tell you that I didn't want to sit, and I didn't want to talk, I just wanted to get out of there. And so I did, or at least I thought I did. I started walking straight away from her, I thought, but in three steps I realized that I wasn't walking away, I was walking around her. Like that planet thing in science class, the more I moved, the more I got nowhere. It was like she had more say over what my legs did than me.

So I sat down.

"You shouldn't have run off from me," she says.

What I mostly thought of now was to wonder if she was wearing anything under that shirt. And then I thought, what a stupid time to be thinking about that. But I still kept thinking about it.

"Do you promise to stay right there till I'm through talking?" she says.

When she moved, it was like her clothes got almost transparent for a second, but not quite. Couldn't take my eyes off her. I promised.

And then all of a sudden she was just a woman. Not ugly, but not all that pretty, neither. Just looking at me with eyes like fire. I was scared again, and I wanted to leave, especially cause now I began to think she really was doing something to me. But I promised, so I stayed.

"That's how it began," she says.

"What's how what began?" says I.

"What you just felt. What I made you feel. That only works on people like you. Nobody else can feel it."

"Feel what?" says I. Now, I knew what she meant, but I didn't know for sure if she meant what I knew. I mean, it bothered me real bad that she could tell how I felt about her those few minutes there.

"Feel that," she says, and there it is again, all I can think about is her body. But it only lasted a few seconds, and then I knew for sure that she was doing it to me.

"Stop it," I says, and she says, "I already did."

I ask her, "How do you do that?"

"Everybody can do it, just a little. A woman looks at a man, she's interested, and so the bio-electrical system heats up, causes some odors to change, and he smells them and notices her and he pays attention."

"Does it work the other way?"

"Men are always giving off those odors, Mick. Makes no difference. It isn't a man's stink that gives a woman her ideas. But like I said, Mick, that's what everybody can do. With some men, though, it isn't a woman's smell that draws his eye. It's the bio-electrical system itself. The smell is nothing. You can feel the heat of the fire. It's the same thing as when you kill people, Mick. If you couldn't kill people the way you do, you also couldn't feel it so strong when I give off magnetic pulses."

Of course I didn't understand all that the first time, and maybe I'm remembering it now with words she didn't teach me until later. At the time, though, I was scared, yes, because she knew, and because she could do things to me, but I was also excited, because she sounded like she had some answers, like she knew why it was that I killed people without meaning to.

But when I asked her to explain everything, she couldn't. "We're only just beginning to understand it ourselves, Mick. There's a Swedish scientist who is making some strides that way. We've sent some people over to meet with him. We've read his book, and maybe even some of us understand it. I've got to tell you, Mick, just because we can do this thing doesn't mean that we're particularly smart or anything. It doesn't get us through college any faster or anything. It just means that teachers who flunk us tend to die off a little younger."

"You're like me! You can do it too!"

She shook her head. "Not likely," she says. "If I'm really furious at somebody, if I really hate him, if I really *try*, and if I keep it up for weeks, I can maybe give him an ulcer. You're in a whole different league from me. You and your people."

"I got no people," I says.

"I'm here, Mick, because you got people. People who knew just exactly what you could do from the minute you were born. People who knew that if you didn't get a tit to suck you wouldn't just cry, you'd kill. Spraying out death from your cradle. So they planned it all from the beginning. Put you in an orphanage. Let other people, all those do-gooders, let them get sick and die, and then when you're old enough to have control over it, then they look you up, they tell you who you are, they bring you home to live with them."

"So you're my kin?" I ask her.

"Not so you'd notice," she says. "I'm here to warn you about your kin. We've been watching you for years, and now it's time to warn you."

Now it's time? I spent fifteen years in that children's home killing everybody who ever cared about me, and if they'd just come along—or you, or anybody, if you just said, Mick, you got to control your temper or you'll hurt people, if somebody just said to me, Mick, we're your people and we'll keep you safe, then maybe I wouldn't be so scared all the time, maybe I wouldn't go killing people so much, did you ever think of that?" Or maybe I didn't say all that, but that's what I was feeling, and so I said a lot, I chewed her up and down.

And then I saw how scared she was, because I was all sparky, and I realized I was just about to shed a load of death onto her, and so I kind of jumped back and yelled at her to leave me alone, and then she does the craziest thing, she reached out toward me, and I scream at her, "Don't you touch me!" cause if she touches me I can't hold it in, it'll just go all through her and tear up her guts inside, but she just keeps reaching, leaning toward me, and so I kind of crawled over toward a tree, and I hung onto that tree, I just held on and let the tree kind of soak up all my sparkiness, almost like I was burning up the

24

tree. Maybe I killed it, for all I know. Or maybe it was so big, I couldn't hurt it, but it took all the fire out of me, and then she *did* touch me, like nobody ever touched me, her arm across my back, and hand holding my shoulder, her face right up against my ear, and she says to me, "Mick, you didn't hurt me."

"Just leave me alone," says I.

"You're not like them," she says. "Don't you see that? They love the killing. They *use* the killing. Only they're not as strong as you. They have to be touching, for one thing, or close to it. They have to keep it up longer. They're stronger than *I* am, but not as strong as you. So they'll want you, that's for sure, Mick, but they'll also be scared of you, and you know what'll scare them most? That you didn't kill me, that you can *control* it like that."

"I can't always. That bus driver today."

"So you're not perfect. But you're trying. Trying not to kill people. Don't you see, Mick? You're not like them. They may be your blood family, but you don't belong with them, and they'll see that, and when they do—"

All I could think about was what she said, my blood family. "My mama and daddy, you telling me I'm going to meet them?"

"They're calling you now, and that's why I had to warn you."

"Calling me?"

"The way I called you up this hill. Only it

25

wasn't just me, of course, it was a bunch of us."

"I just decided to come up here, to get off the road."

"You just decided to cross the highway and climb this hill, instead of the other one? Anyway, that's how it works. It's part of the human race for all time, only we never knew it. A bunch of people kind of harmonize their bioelectrical systems, to call for somebody to come home, and they come home, after a while. Or sometimes a whole nation unites to hate somebody. Like Iran and the Shah, or the Philippines and Marcos."

"They just kicked them out," I says.

"But they were already dying, weren't they? A whole nation, hating together, they make a constant interference with their enemy's bioelectrical system. A constant noise. All of them together, millions of people, they are finally able to match what you can do with one flash of anger."

I thought about that for a few minutes, and it came back to me all the times I thought how I wasn't even human. So maybe I *was* human, after all, but human like a guy with three arms is human, or one of those guys in the horror movies I saw, gigantic and lumpy and going around hacking up teenagers whenever they was about to get laid. And in all those movies they always try to kill the guy only they can't, he gets stabbed and shot and burned up and he still comes back, and that's like me, I must have tried to kill myself so many times only it never worked.

No. Wait a minute.

I got to get this straight, or you'll think I'm crazy or a liar. I didn't jump off that highway overpass like I said. I stood on one for a long time, watching the cars go by. Whenever a big old semi came along I'd say, this one, and I'd count, and at the right second I'd say, now. Only I never did jump. And then afterward I dreamed about jumping, and in all those dreams I'd just bounce off the truck and get up and limp away. Like the time I was a kid and sat in the bathroom with the little gardening shears, the spring-loaded kind that popped open, I sat there thinking about jamming it into my stomach right under the breastbone, and then letting go of the handle, it'd pop right open and make a bad wound and cut open my heart or something. I was there so long I fell asleep on the toilet, and later I dreamed about doing it but no blood ever came out, because I couldn't die.

So I never tried to kill myself. But I thought about it all the time. I was like those monsters in those movies, just killing people but secretly hoping somebody would catch on to what was going on and kill me first.

And so I says to her, "Why didn't you just kill me?"

And there she was with her face close to

mine and she says, just like it was love talk, she says, "I've had you in my rifle sights, Mick, and then I didn't do it. Because I saw something in you. I saw that maybe you were trying to control it. That maybe you didn't want to use your power to kill. And so I let you live, thinking that one day I'd be here like this, telling you what you are, and giving you a little hope."

I thought she meant I'd hope because of knowing my mama and daddy were alive and wanted me.

"I hoped for a long time, but I gave it up. I don't want to see my mama and daddy, if they could leave me there all those years. I don't want to see you, neither, if you didn't so much as warn me not to get mad at Old Peleg. I didn't want to kill Old Peleg, and I couldn't even help it! You didn't help me a bit!"

"We argued about it," she says. "We knew you were killing people while you tried to sort things out and get control. Puberty's the worst time, even worse than infancy, and we knew that if we didn't kill you a lot of people would die—and mostly they'd be the people you loved best. That's the way it is for most kids your age, they get angriest at the people they love most, only you couldn't help killing them, and what does that do to your mind? What kind of person do you become? There was some who said we didn't have the right to leave you alive even to study you, because it would be like having a cure for cancer and then not using it on people just to see how fast they'd die. Like that experiment where the government left syphilis cases untreated just to see what the final stages of the disease were like, even though they could have cured those people at any time. But some of us told them, Mick isn't a disease, and a bullet isn't penicillin. I told them, Mick is something special. And they said, yes, he's special, he kills more than any of those other kids, and we shot *them* or ran them over with a truck or drowned them, and here we've got the worst one of all and you want to keep him alive."

And I was crying cause I wished they *had* killed me, but also because it was the first time I ever thought there was people arguing that I ought to be alive, and even though I didn't rightly understand then or even now why you didn't tell me, I got to tell you that knowing somebody knew what I was and still chose not to blast my head off, that done me in, I just bawled like a baby.

One thing led to another, there, my crying and her holding me, and pretty soon I figured out that she pretty much wanted to get laid right there. But that just made me sick, when I knew that. "How can you want to do that!" I says to her. "I can't get married! I can't have no kids! They'd be like me!"

She didn't argue with me or say nothing about birth control, and so I figured out later that I was right, she wanted to have a baby, and that told me plain that she was crazy as a loon. I got my pants pulled back up and my shirt on, and I wouldn't look at her getting dressed again, neither.

"I could make you do it," she says to me. "I could do that to you. The ability you have that lets you kill also makes you sensitive. I can make you lose your mind with desire for me."

"Then why don't you?" I says.

"Why don't you kill if you can help it?" she says.

"Cause nobody has the right," says I.

"That's right," she says.

"Anyway you're ten years older than me," I tell her.

"Fifteen," she says. "Almost twice your age. But that don't mean nothing." Or I guess she actually said, "That *doesn't* mean nothing," or probably, "that doesn't mean *anything*." She talks better than I do but I can't always remember the fancy way. "That doesn't mean a thing," she says. "You'll go to your folks, and you can bet they'll have some pretty little girl waiting for you, and she'll know how to do it much better than me, she'll turn you on so your pants unzip themselves, cause that's what they want most from you. They want your babies. As many as they can get, because you're the strongest they've produced in all the years since Grandpa Jake realized that the cursing power went father to son, mother to daughter, and that he could breed for it like you breed dogs or horses. They'll breed you like a stud, but then when they find out that you don't like killing people and you don't want to play along and you aren't going to take orders from whoever's in charge there now, they'll kill you. That's why I came to warn you. We could feel them just starting to call you. We knew it was time. And I came to warn you."

Most of this didn't mean much to me yet. Just the idea of having kinfolk was still so new I couldn't exactly get worried about whether they'd kill me or put me out for stud or whatever. Mostly what I thought about was her, anyway. "I might have killed you, you know."

"Maybe I didn't care," she says. "And maybe I'm not so easy to kill."

"And maybe you ought to tell me your name," says I.

"Can't," she says.

"How come," says I.

"Because if you decide to put in with them, and you know my name, then I *am* dead."

"I wouldn't let anybody hurt you," says I.

She didn't answer that. She just says to me, "Mick, you don't know my name, but you remember this. I have hopes for you, cause I know you're a good man and you never meant to kill nobody. I could've made you love me, and I didn't, because I want you to do what you do by your own choice. And most important of all, if you come with me, we have a chance to see if maybe your ability doesn't have a good side."

You think I hadn't thought of that before? When I saw Rambo shooting down all those little brown guys, I thought, I could do that, and without no gun, either. And if somebody took me hostage like the *Achille Lauro* thing, we wouldn't have to worry about the terrorists going unpunished. They'd all be rotting in a hospital in no time. "Are you with the government?" I ask her.

"No," she says.

So they didn't want me to be a soldier. I was kind of disappointed. I kind of thought I might be useful that way. But I couldn't volunteer or nothing, cause you don't walk into the recruiting office and say, I've killed a couple dozen people by giving sparks off my body, and I could do it to Castro and Qaddafi if you like. Cause if they believe you, then you're a murderer, and if they don't believe you, they lock you up in a nuthouse.

"Nobody's been calling me, anyway," I says. "If I didn't see you today, I wouldn't've gone nowhere. I would've stayed with Mr. Kaiser."

"Then why did you take all your money out of the bank?" she says. "And when you ran away from me, why did you run toward the highway where you can hitch a ride at least to Madison and then catch another on into Eden?"

And I didn't have no answer for her then, cause I didn't know rightly why I took my money out of the bank lessen it was like she said, and I was planning to leave town. It was just an impulse, to close that account, I didn't think nothing of it, just stuffed three hundreds into my wallet and come to think of it I really was heading toward Eden, I just didn't *think* of it, I was just *doing* it. Just the way I climbed up that hill.

"They're stronger than we are," she says. "So we can't hold you here. You have to go anyway, you have to work this thing out. The most we could do was just get you on the bus next to me, and then call you up this hill."

"Then why don't you come with me?" I says.

"They'd kill me in two seconds, right in front of your eyes, and none of this cursing stuff, either, Mick. They'd just take my head off with a machete."

"Do they know you?"

"They know *us*," she says. "We're the only ones that know your people exist, so we're the only ones working to stop them. I won't lie to you, Mick. If you join them, you can find us, you'll learn how, it isn't hard, and you can do this stuff from farther away, you could really take us apart. But if you join *us*, the tables are turned."

"Well maybe I don't want to be on either side in this war," I says. "And maybe now I won't go to Eden, neither. Maybe I'll go up to Washington, D.C. and join the CIA.''

"Maybe," she says.

"And don't try to stop me."

"I wouldn't try," she says.

"Damn straight," I says. And then I just walked out, and this time I didn't walk in no circles, I just headed north, past her car, down the railroad right of way. And I caught a ride heading up toward D.C., and that was that.

Except that along about six o'clock in the evening I woke up and the car was stopping and I didn't know where I was, I must have slept all day, and the guy says to me, "Here you are, Eden, North Carolina."

And I about messed my pants. "Eden!" I says.

"It wasn't far out of my way," he says. "I'm heading for Burlington, and these country roads are nicer than the freeway, anyway. Don't mind if I never drive I-85 again, to tell the truth."

But that was the very guy who told me he had business in D.C., he was heading there from Bristol, had to see somebody from a government agency, and here he was in Eden. It made no sense at all, except for what that woman told me. Somebody was calling me, and if I wouldn't come, they'd just put me to sleep and call whoever was driving. And there I was. Eden, North Carolina. Scared to death, or at least scared a little, but also thinking, if what she said was true, my folks was coming, I was going to meet my folks.

Nothing much changed in the two years since I ran off from the orphanage. Nothing much ever changes in Eden, which isn't a real town anyway, just cobbled together from three little villages that combined to save money on city services. People still mostly think of them as three villages. There wasn't nobody who'd get too excited about seeing me, and there wasn't nobody I wanted to see. Nobody living, anyway. I had no idea how my folks might find me, or how I might find them, but in the meantime I went to see about the only people I ever much cared about. Hoping that they wouldn't rise up out of the grave to get even with me for killing them.

It was still full day that time of year, but it was whippy weather, the wind gusting and then holding still, a big row of thunderclouds off to the southwest, the sun sinking down to get behind them. The kind of afternoon that promises to cool you off, which suited me fine. I was still pretty dusty from my climb up the hill that morning, and I could use a little rain. Got a Coke at a fast food place and then walked on over to see Old Peleg.

He was buried in a little cemetery right by an old Baptist Church. Not Southern Baptist, *Black* Baptist, meaning that it didn't have no fancy building with classrooms and a rectory, just a stark-white block of a building with a little steeple and a lawn that looked like it'd been clipped by hand. Cemetery was just as neat-kept. Nobody around, and it was dim cause of the thunderclouds moving through, but I wasn't afraid of the graves there, I just went to Old Peleg's cross. Never knew his last name was Lindley. Didn't sound like a black man's name, but then when I thought about it I realized that *no* last name sounded like a black man's name, because Eden is still just old-fashioned enough that an old black man doesn't get called by his last name much. He grew up in a Jim Crow state, and never got around to insisting on being called Mr. Lindley. Old Peleg. Not that he ever hugged me or took me on long walks or gave me that tender loving care that makes people get all teary-eyed about how wonderful it is to have parents. He never tried to be my dad or nothing. And if I hung around him much, he always gave me work to do and made damn sure I did it right, and mostly we didn't talk about anything except the work we was doing, which made me wonder, standing there, why I wanted to cry and why I hated myself worse for killing Old Peleg than for any of the other dead people under the ground in that city.

I didn't see them and I didn't hear them coming and I didn't smell my mama's perfume. But I knew they was coming, because I felt the prickly air between us. I didn't turn around, but I knew just where they were, and just how far off, because they was *lively*. Shedding sparks like I never saw on any living soul except myself, just walking along giving off light. It was like seeing myself from the outside for the first time in my life. Even when she was making me get all hot for her, that lady in Roanoke wasn't as lively as them. They was just like me.

Funny thing was, that wrecked everything. I didn't want them to be like me. I *hated* my sparkiness, and there they were, showing it to me, making me see how a killer looks from the outside. It took a few seconds to realize that they was *scared* of me, too. I recognized how scaredness looks, from remembering how my own bio-electrical system got shaped and changed by fear. Course I didn't think of it as a bio-electrical system then, or maybe I did cause she'd already told me, but you know what I mean. They was afraid of me. And I knew that was because I was giving off all the sparks I shed when I feel so mad at myself that I could bust. I was standing there at Old Peleg's grave, hating myself, so naturally they saw me like I was ready to kill half a city. They didn't know that it was me I was hating. Naturally they figured I might be mad at *them* for leaving me at that orphanage seventeen years ago. Serve them right, too, if I gave them a good hard twist in the gut, but I don't do that, I honestly don't, not anymore, not standing there by Old Peleg who I loved a lot more than these two strangers, I don't act out being a murderer when my shadow's falling across his grave.

So I calmed myself down as best I could and I turned around and there they was, my mama and my daddy. And I got to tell you I almost laughed. All those years I watched them TV preachers, and we used to laugh till our guts ached about how Tammy Bakker always wore makeup so thick she could be a nigger underneath (it was okay to say that cause Old Peleg himself said it first) and here was my mama, wearing just as much makeup and her hair sprayed so thick she could work construction without a hardhat. And smiling that same sticky phony smile, and crying the same gooey oozey black tears down her cheeks, and reaching out her hands just the right way so I halfway expected her to say, "Praise to Lord Jesus," and then she actually *says* it, "Praise to Lord Jesus, it's my boy," and comes up and lays a kiss on my cheek with so much spit in it that it dripped down my face.

I wiped the slobber with my sleeve and felt my daddy have this little flash of anger, and I knew that he thought I was judging my mama and he didn't like it. Well, I was, I got to admit. Her perfume was enough to knock me over, I swear she must've mugged an Avon lady. And there was my daddy in a fine blue suit like a businessman, his hair all blow-dried, so it was plain he knew just as well as I did the way real people are supposed to look. Probably he was plain embarrassed to be seen in public with Mama, so why didn't he ever just say, Mama, you wear too much makeup? That's what I thought, and it wasn't till later that I realized that when your woman is apt to give you cancer if you rile her up, you don't go telling her that her face looks like she slept in wet sawdust and she smells like a whore. White trash, that's what my mama was, sure as if she was still wearing the factory label.

"Sure am glad to see you, son," says my daddy.

I didn't know what to say, tell the truth. I *wasn't* glad to see them, now that I saw them, because they wasn't exactly what a orphan boy dreams his folks is like. So I kind of grinned and looked back down at Old Peleg's grave.

"You don't seem too surprised to see *us*," he says.

I could've told him right then about the lady in Roanoke, but I didn't. Just didn't feel right to tell him. So I says, "I felt like somebody was calling me back here. And you two are the only people I met who's as sparky as me. If you all say you're my folks, then I figure it must be so."

Mama giggled and she says to him, "Listen, Jesse, he calls it 'sparky.' "

"The word we use is 'dusty,' son," says

Daddy. "We say a body's looking dusty when he's one of us."

"You were a very dusty baby," says Mama. "That's why we knew we couldn't keep you. Never seen such a dusty baby before. Papa Lem made us take you to the orphanage before you even sucked one time. You never sucked even once." And her mascara just flooded down her face.

"Now, Deeny," says Daddy, "no need telling him everything right here."

Dusty. That was no sense at all. It didn't look like *dust*, it was flecks of light, so bright on me that sometimes I had to squint just to see my own hands through the dazzle. "It don't *look* like dust," I says.

And Daddy says, "Well what do *you* think it looks like?"

And I says, "Sparks. That's why I call it being sparky."

"Well that's what it looks like to us, too," says Daddy. "But we've been calling it 'dusty' all our lives, and so I figure it's easier for one boy to change than for f—for lots of other folks."

Well, now, I learned a lot of things right then from what he said. First off, I knew he was lying when he said it looked like sparks to them. It didn't. It looked like what they called it. Dust. And that meant that I was seeing it a whole lot *brighter* than they could see it, and that was good for me to know, especially because it was plain that Daddy *didn't* want me to know it and so he pretended that he saw it the same way. He wanted me to think he was just as good at seeing as I was. Which meant that he sure wasn't. And I also learned that he didn't want me to know how many kinfolk I had, cause he started to say a number that started with F, and then caught himself and didn't say it. Fifty? Five hundred? The number wasn't half so important as the fact that he didn't want me to know it. They didn't trust me. Well, why should they? Like the lady said, I was better at this than they were, and they didn't know how mad I was about being abandoned, and the last thing they wanted to do was turn me loose killing folks. Especially themselves.

Well I stood there thinking about that stuff and pretty soon it makes them nervous and Mama says, "Now, Daddy, he can call it whatever he wants, don't go making him mad or something."

And Daddy laughs and says, "He isn't mad, are you, son?"

Can't they see for themselves? Course not. Looks like *dust* to them, so they can't see it clear at all.

"You don't seem too happy to see us," says Daddy.

"Now, Jesse," says Mama, "don't go pushing. Papa Lem said don't you push the boy, you just make his acquaintance, you let him

41

know why we had to push him out of the nest so young, so now you explain it, Daddy, just like Papa Lem said to."

For the first time right then it occurred to me that my own folks didn't *want* to come fetch me. They came because this Papa Lem made them do it. And you can bet they hopped and said yes, knowing how Papa Lem used his—but I'll get to Papa Lem in good time, and you said I ought to take this all in order, which I'm mostly trying to do.

Anyway Daddy explained it just like the lady in Roanoke, except he didn't say a word about bio-electrical systems, he said that I was "plainly chosen" from the moment of my birth, that I was "one of the elect," which I remembered from Baptist Sunday School meant that I was one that God had saved, though I never heard of anybody who was saved the minute they was born and not even baptized or nothing. They saw how dusty I was and they knew I'd kill a lot of people before I got old enough to control it. I asked them if they did it a lot, putting a baby out to be raised by strangers.

"Oh, maybe a dozen times," says Daddy.

"And it always works out okay?" says I.

He got set to lie again, I could see it by ripples in the light, I didn't know lying could be so plain, which made me glad they saw dust instead of sparks. "Most times," he says.

"I'd like to meet one of them others," says

I. "I figure we got a lot in common, growing up thinking our parents hated us, when the truth was they was scared of their own baby."

"Well they're mostly grown up and gone off," he says, but it's a lie, and most important of all was the fact that here I as much as said I thought they wasn't worth horse pucky as parents and the only thing Daddy can think of to say is why I can't see none of the other "orphans," which tells me that whatever he's lying to cover up must be real important.

But I didn't push him right then, I just looked back down at Old Peleg's grave and wondered if he ever told a lie in his life.

Daddy says, "I'm not surprised to find you here." I guess he was nervous, and had to change the subject. "He's one you dusted, isn't he?"

Dusted. That word made me so mad. What I done to Old Peleg wasn't *dusting*. And being mad must have changed me enough they could see the change. But they didn't know what it meant, cause Mama says to me, "Now, son, I don't mean to criticize, but it isn't right to take pride in the gifts of God. That's why we came to find you, because we need to teach you why God chose you to be one of the elect, and you shouldn't glory in yourself because you could strike down your enemies. Rather you should give all glory to the Lord, praise his name, because we are his servants."

I like to puked, I was so mad at that. Glory!

Old Peleg, who was worth ten times these two phony white people who tossed me out before I ever sucked tit, and they thought I should give the *glory* for his terrible agony and death to *God*? I didn't know God all that well, mostly because I thought of him as looking as pinched up and serious as Mrs. Bethel who taught Sunday School when I was little, until she died of leukemia, and I just never had a thing to say to God. But if God gave me that power to strike down Old Peleg, and God wanted the glory for it when I was done, then I *did* have a few words to say to God. Only I didn't believe it for a minute. Old Peleg believed in God, and the God he believed in didn't go striking an old black man dead because a dumb kid got pissed off at him.

But I'm getting off track in the story, because that was when my father touched me for the first time. His hand was shaking. And it had every right to shake, because I was so mad that a year ago he would've been bleeding from the colon before he took his hand away. But I'd got so I could keep from killing whoever touched me when I was mad, and the funny thing was that his hand *shaking* kind of changed how I felt anyway. I'd been thinking about how mad I was that they left me and how mad I was that they thought I'd be proud of killing people but now I realized how brave they was to come fetch me, cause how did they know I wouldn't kill them? But they came anyway. And that's something. Even if Papa Lem told them to do it, they came, and now I realized that it was real brave for Mama to come kiss me on the cheek right then, because if I was going to kill her, she touched me and gave me a chance to do it before she even tried to explain anything. Maybe it was her strategy to win me over or something, but it was still brave. And she also didn't approve of people being proud of murder, which was more points in her favor. And she had the guts to tell me so right to my face. So I chalked up some points for Mama. She might look like as sickening as Tammy Bakker, but she faced her killer son with more guts than Daddy had.

He touched my shoulder and they led me to their car. A Lincoln Town Car, which they probably thought would impress me, but all I thought about was what it would've been like at the Children's Home if we'd had the price of that car, even fifteen years ago. Maybe a paved basketball court. Maybe some decent toys that wasn't broken-up hand-me-downs. Maybe some pants with knees in them. I never felt so poor in my life as when I slid onto that fuzzy seat and heard the stereo start playing elevator music in my ear.

There was somebody else in the car. Which made sense. If I'd killed them or something, they'd need somebody else to drive the car home, right? He wasn't much, when it came to being dusty or sparky or whatever. Just a little, and in rhythms of fear, too. And I could see *why* he was scared, cause he was holding a blindfold in his hands, and he says, "Mr. Yow, I'm afraid I got to put this on you."

Well, I didn't answer for a second, which made him more scared cause he thought I was mad, but mostly it took me that long to realize he meant *me* when he said "Mr. Yow."

"That's our name, son," says my daddy. "I'm Jesse Yow, and your mother is Minnie Rae Yow, and that makes you Mick Yow."

"Don't it figure," says I. I was joking, but they took it wrong, like as if I was making fun of their name. But I been Mick Winger so long that it just feels silly calling myself Yow, and the fact is it *is* a funny name. They said it like I should be proud of it, though, which makes me laugh, but to them it was the name of God's Chosen People, like the way the Jews called themselves Israelites in the Bible. I didn't know that then, but that's the way they said it, real proud. And they was ticked off when I made a joke, so I helped them feel better by letting Billy put on—Billy's the name of the man in the car—put on the blindfold.

It was a lot of country roads, and a lot of country talk. About kinfolk I never met, and how I'd love this person and that person, which sounded increasingly unlikely to me, if you know what I mean. A long-lost child is coming home and you put a *blindfold* on him. I knew we were going mostly east, cause of the times I could feel the sun coming in my window and on the back of my neck, but that was about it, and that wasn't much. They lied to me, they wouldn't show me nothing, they was scared of me. I mean, any way you look at it, they wasn't exactly killing the fatted calf for the prodigal son. I was definitely on probation. Or maybe even on trial. Which, I might point out, is exactly the way you been treating me, too, and I don't like it much better now than I did then, if you don't mind me putting some personal complaints into this. I mean, somewhere along the line somebody's going to have to decide whether to shoot me or let me go, because I can't control my temper forever locked up like a rat in a box, and the difference is a rat can't reach out of the box and blast you the way I can, so somewhere along the way somebody's going to have to figure out that you better either trust me or kill me. My personal preference is for trusting me, since I've given you more reason to trust me than you've given me to trust *you* so far.

But anyway I rode along in the car for more than an hour. We could have gotten to Winston or Greensboro or Danville by then, it was so long, and by the time we got there nobody was talking and from the snoring, Billy was even asleep. I wasn't asleep, though. I was watching. Cause I don't see sparks with my eyes, I see it with something else, like as if my sparks see other folks' sparks, if you catch my drift, and so that blindfold might've kept me from seeing the road, but it sure didn't keep me from seeing the other folks in the car with me. I knew right where they were, and right what they were feeling. Now, I've always had a knack for telling things about people, even when I couldn't see nary a spark or nothing, but this was the first time I ever saw anybody who was sparky besides me. So I sat there watching how Mama and Daddy acted with each other even when they wasn't touching or saying a thing, just little drifts of anger or fear or—well, I looked for love, but I didn't see it, and I know what it looks like, cause I've felt it. They were like two armies camped on opposite hills, waiting for the truce to end at dawn. Careful. Sending out little scouting parties.

Then the more I got used to understanding what my folks was thinking and feeling, toward each other, the easier it got for me to read what Billy had going on inside him. It's like after you learn to read big letters, you can read little letters, too, and I wondered if maybe I could even learn to understand people who didn't have hardly any sparks at all. I mean that occurred to me, anyway, and since then I've found out that it's mostly true. Now that I've had some practice I can read a sparky person from a long ways off, and even regular folks I can do a little reading, even through walls and windows. But I found that out later. Like when you guys have been watching me through mirrors. I can also see your microphone wires in the walls.

Anyway it was during that car ride that I first started seeing what I could see with my eyes closed, the shape of people's bio-electrical system, the color and spin of it, the speed and the flow and the rhythm and what-ever, I mean those are the words I use, cause there isn't exactly a lot of books I can read on the subject. Maybe that Swedish doctor has fancy words for it. I can only tell you how it feels to me. And in that hour I got to be good enough at it that I could tell Billy was scared, all right, but he *wasn't* all that scared of me, he was mostly scared of Mama and Daddy. Me he was jealous of, angry kind of. Scared a lit-tle, too, but mostly mad. I thought maybe he was mad cause I was coming in out of no-where already sparkier than him, but then it occurred to me that he probably couldn't even tell how sparky I was, because to him it'd look like dust, and he wouldn't have enough of a knack at it to see much distinction between one person and another. It's like the more light you give off, the clearer you can see other people's light. So I was the one with the blind-fold on, but I could see clearer than anybody else in that car.

We drove on gravel for about ten minutes, and then on a bumpy dirt road, and then sud-denly on asphalt again, smooth as you please, for about a hundred yards, and then we stopped. I didn't wait for a by-your-leave, I had that blindfold off in half a second.

It was like a whole town of houses, but right among the trees, not a gap in the leaves overhead. Maybe fifty, sixty houses, some of them pretty big, but the trees made them half invisible, it being summer. Children running all over, scruffy dirty kids from diapered-up snotnose brats to most-growed kids not all that much younger than me. They sure kept us cleaner in the Children's Home. And they was all sparky. Mostly like Billy, just a little, but it explained why they wasn't much washed. There isn't many a mama who'd stuff her kid in a tub if the kid can make her sick just by getting mad.

It must've been near eight-thirty at night, and even the little kids still wasn't in bed. They must let their kids play till they get wore out and drop down and fall asleep by themselves. It came to me that maybe I wasn't so bad off growing up in an orphanage. At least I knew manners and didn't whip it out and pee right in front of company, the way one little boy did, just looking at me while I got out of the car, whizzing away like he wasn't doing nothing strange. Like a dog marking trees. He needed to so he done it. If I ever did that at the Children's Home they'd've slapped me silly.

I know how to act with strangers when I'm

hitching a ride, but not when I'm being company, cause orphans don't go calling much so I never had much experience. So I'd've been shy no matter what, even if there wasn't no such thing as sparkiness. Daddy was all set to take me to meet Papa Lem right off, but Mama saw how I wasn't cleaned up and maybe she guessed I hadn't been to the toilet in a while and so she hustled me into a house where they had a good shower and when I came out she had a cold ham sandwich waiting for me on the table. On a plate, and the plate was setting on a linen place mat, and there was a tall glass of milk there, so cold it was sweating on the outside of the glass. I mean, if an orphan kid ever dreamed of what it might be like to have a mama, that was the dream. Never mind that she didn't look like a model in the Sears Catalog. I felt clean, the sandwich tasted good, and when I was done eating she even offered me a cookie. ✝

It felt good, I'll admit that, but at the same time I felt cheated. It was just too damn late. I needed it to be like this when I was seven, not seventeen.

But she was trying, and it wasn't all her fault, so I ate the cookie and drank off the last of the milk and my watch said it was after nine. Outside it was dusk now, and most of the kids were finally gone off to bed, and Daddy comes in and says, "Papa Lem says he isn't getting any younger."

He was outside, in a big rocking chair sitting on the grass. You wouldn't call him fat, but he did have a belly on him. And you wouldn't call him old, but he was bald on top and his hair was wispy yellow and white. And you wouldn't call him ugly, but he had a soft mouth and I didn't like the way it twisted up when he talked.

Oh, hell, he was fat, old, and ugly, and I hated him from the first time I saw him. A squishy kind of guy. Not even as sparky as my daddy, neither, so you didn't get to be in charge around here just by having more of whatever it was made us different. I wondered how close kin he was to me. If he's got children, and they look like him, they ought to drown them out of mercy.

"Mick Yow," he says to me, "Mick my dear boy, Mick my dear cousin."

"Good evening, sir," says I.

"Oh, and he's got manners," says he. "We were right to donate so much to the Children's Home. They took excellent care of you."

"You donated to the home?" says I. If they did, they sure didn't give *much*.

"A little," he says. "Enough to pay for your food, your room, your Christian education. But no luxuries. You couldn't grow up soft, Mick. You had to grow up lean and strong. And you had to know suffering, so you could be compassionate. The Lord God has given

you a marvelous gift, a great helping of his
grace, a heaping plateful of the power of God,
and we had to make sure you were truly worthy to sit up to the table at the banquet of the
Lord."

I almost looked around to see if there was
a camera, he sounded so much like the
preachers on TV.

And he says, "Mick, you have already
passed the first test. You have forgiven your
parents for leaving you to think you were an
orphan. You have kept that holy command-
ment, Honor thy father and mother, that thy
days may be long upon the land which the
Lord thy God hath given thee. You know
that if you had raised a hand against them,
the Lord would have struck you down. For
verily I say unto you that there was two rifles
pointed at you the whole time, and if your father and mother had walked away without
you, you would have flopped down dead in
that nigger cemetery, for God will not be
mocked."

I couldn't tell if he was trying to provoke
me or scare me or what, but either way, it was
working.

"The Lord has chosen you for his servant,
Mick, just like he's chosen all of us. The rest
of the world doesn't understand this. But
Grandpa Jake saw it. Long ago, back in 1820,
he saw how everybody he hated had a way of
dying without him lifting a finger. And for a

time he thought that maybe he was like those old witches, who curse people and they wither up and die by the power of the devil. But he was a god-fearing man, and he had no truck with Satan. He was living in rough times, when a man was likely to kill in a quarrel, but Grandpa Jake never killed. Never even struck out with his fists. He was a peaceable man, and he kept his anger inside him, as the Lord commands in the New Testament. So surely he was not a servant of Satan!''

Papa Lem's voice rang through that little village, he was talking so loud, and I noticed there was a bunch of people all around. Not many kids now, all grownups, maybe there to hear Lem, but even more likely they was there to see me. Because it was like the lady in Roanoke said, there wasn't a one of them was half as sparky as me. I didn't know if they could all see that, but *I* could. Compared to normal folks they was all dusty enough, I suppose, but compared to me, or even to my mama and daddy, they was a pretty dim bunch.

''He studied the scriptures to find out what it meant that his enemies all suffered from tumors and bleeding and coughing and rot, and he came upon the verse of Genesis where the Lord said unto Abraham, 'I will bless them that bless thee, and curse him that curseth thee.' And he knew in his heart that the Lord had chosen him the way he chose Abraham.

And when Isaac gave the blessing of God to Jacob, he said, 'Let people serve thee, and nations bow down to thee: cursed be every one that curseth thee, and blessed be he that blesseth thee.' The promises to the patriarchs were fulfilled again in Grandpa Jake, for whoever cursed him was cursed by God."

When he said those words from the Bible, Papa Lem sounded like the voice of God himself, I've got to tell you. I felt exalted, knowing that it was God who gave such power to my family. It was to the whole family, the way Papa Lem told it, because the Lord promised Abraham that his children would be as many as there was stars in the sky, which is a lot more than Abraham knew about seeing how he didn't have no telescope. And that promise now applied to Grandpa Jake, just like the one that said "in thee shall all families of the earth be blessed." So Grandpa Jake set to studying the book of Genesis so he could fulfill those promises just like the patriarchs did. He saw how they went to a lot of trouble to make sure they only married kinfolk—you know how Abraham married his brother's daughter, Sarah, and Isaac married his cousin Rebekah, and Jacob married his cousins Leah and Rachel. So Grandpa Jake left his first wife cause she was unworthy, meaning she probably wasn't particularly sparky, and he took up with his brother's daughter and when his brother threatened to kill him if he laid a hand on the girl, Grandpa Jake run off with her and his own brother died of a curse which is just exactly what happened to Sarah's father in the Bible. I mean Grandpa Jake worked it out just right. And he made sure all his sons married their first cousins, and so all of them had sparkiness twice over, just like breeding pointers with pointers and not mixing them with other breeds, so the strain stays pure.

There was all kinds of other stuff about Lot and his daughters, and if we remained faithful then we would be the meek who inherit the earth because we were the chosen people and the Lord would strike down everybody who stood in our way, but what it all came down to at the moment was this: You marry whoever the patriarch tells you to marry, and Papa Lem was the patriarch. He had my mama marry my daddy even though they never particularly liked each other, growing up cousins, because he could see that they was both specially chosen, which means to say they was both about the sparkiest there was. And when I was born, they knew it was like a confirmation of Papa Lem's decision, because the Lord had blessed them with a kid who gave off dust thicker than a dump truck on a dirt road.

One thing he asked me real particular was whether I ever been laid. He says to me, "Have you spilled seed among the daughters of Ishmael and Esau?"

I knew what spilling seed was, cause we got lectures about that at the Children's Home. I wasn't sure who the daughters of Ishmael and Esau was, but since I never had a hot date, I figured I was pretty safe saying no. Still, I did consider a second, because what came to mind was the lady in Roanoke, stoking me up just by wanting me, and I was thinking about how close I'd come to not being a virgin after all. I wondered if the lady from Roanoke was a daughter of Esau.

Papa Lem picked up on my hesitation, and he wouldn't let it go. "Don't lie to me boy. I can see a lie." Well, since *I* could see a lie, I didn't doubt but what maybe he could too. But then again, I've had plenty of grownups tell me they could spot a lie—but half the time they accused me of lying when I was telling the truth, and the other half they believed me when I was telling whoppers so big it'd take two big men to carry them upstairs. So maybe he could and maybe he couldn't. I figured I'd tell him just as much truth as I wanted. "I was just embarrassed to tell you I never had a girl," I says.

"Ah, the deceptions of the world," he says. "They make promiscuity seem so normal that a boy is ashamed to admit that he is chaste." Then he got a glint in his eye. "I know the children of Esau have been watching you, wanting to steal your birthright. Isn't that so?"

"I don't know who Esau is," says I.

The folks who was gathered around us started muttering about that.

I says, "I mean, I know who he was in the Bible, he was the brother of Jacob, the one who sold him his birthright for split pea soup."

"Jacob was the rightful heir, the true eldest son," says Papa Lem, "and don't you forget it. Esau is the one who went away from his father, out into the wilderness, rejecting the things of God and embracing the lies and sins of the world. Esau is the one who married a strange woman, who was not of the people! Do you understand me?"

I understood pretty good by then. Somewhere along the line somebody got sick of living under the thumb of Papa Lem, or maybe the patriarch before him, and they split.

"Beware," says Papa Lem, "because the children of Esau and Ishmael still covet the blessings of Jacob. They want to corrupt the pure seed of Grandpa Jake. They have enough of the blessing of God to know that you're a remarkable boy, like Joseph who was sold into Egypt, and they will come to you with their whorish plans, the way Potiphar's wife came to Joseph, trying to persuade you to give them your pure and undefiled seed so that they can have the blessing that their fathers rejected."

I got to tell you that I didn't much like hav-

ing him talk about my seed so much in front
of mixed company, but that was nothing compared to what he did next. He waved his hand
to a girl standing there in the crowd, and up
she came. She wasn't half bad-looking, in a
country sort of way. Her hair was mousy and
she wasn't altogether clean and she stood with
a two-bucket slouch, but her face wasn't bad
and she looked to have her teeth. Sweet, but
not my type, if you know what I mean.

Papa Lem introduced us. It was his daughter, which I might've guessed, and then he
says to her, "Wilt thou go with this man?"
And she looks at me and says, "I will go." And
then she gave me this big smile, and all of a
sudden it was happening again, just like it did
with the lady in Roanoke, only twice as much,
cause after all the lady in Roanoke wasn't
hardly sparky. I was standing there and all I
could think about was how I wanted all her
clothes off her and to do with her right there
in front of everybody and I didn't even care
that all those people were watching, that's
how strong it was.

And I liked it, I got to tell you. I mean you
don't ignore a feeling like that. But another
part of me was standing back and it says to
me, "Mick Winger you damn fool, that girl's
as homely as the bathroom sink, and all these
people are watching her make an idiot out of
you," and it was that part of me that got mad,
because I didn't like her making me do some-

thing, and I didn't like it happening right out in front of everybody, and I specially didn't like Papa Lem sitting there looking at his own daughter and me like we was in a dirty magazine.

Thing is, when I get mad I get all sparky, and the madder I got, the more I could see how she was doing it, like she was a magnet, drawing me to her. And as soon as I thought of it like us being magnets, I took all the sparkiness from being mad and I used it. Not to hurt her or nothing, because I didn't put it on her the way I did with the people I killed. I just kind of turned the path of her sparks plain upside down. She was spinning it just as fast as ever, but it went the other way, and the second that started, why, it was like she disappeared. I mean, I could see her all right, but I couldn't hardly *notice* her. I couldn't focus my eyes on her.

Papa Lem jumped right to his feet, and the other folks were gasping. Pretty quick that girl stopped sparking at me, you can bet, and there she was on her knees, throwing up. She must've had a real weak digestion, or else what I done was stronger than I thought. She was really pouring on the juice, I guess, and when I flung it back at her and turned her upside down, well, she couldn't hardly walk when they got her up. She was pretty hysterical, too, crying about how awful and ugly I was, which might've hurt my feelings except that I was scared to death.

Papa Lem was looking like the wrath of God. "You have rejected the holy sacrament of marriage! You have spurned the handmaid God prepared for you!"

Now you've got to know that I hadn't put everything together yet, or I wouldn't have been so afraid of him, but for all I knew right then he could kill me with a cancer. And it was a sure thing he could've had those people beat me to death or whatever he wanted, so maybe I was right to be scared. Anyway I had to think of a way to make him not be mad at me, and what I came up with must not've been too bad because it worked, didn't it?

I says to him, as calm as I can, "Papa Lem, she was not an acceptable handmaiden." I didn't watch all those TV preachers for nothing. I knew how to talk like the Bible. I says, "She was not blessed enough to be my wife. She wasn't even as blessed as my mama. You can't tell me that she's the best the Lord prepared for me."

And sure enough, he calmed right down. "I know that," he says. And he isn't talking like a preacher anymore, it's *me* talking like a preacher and him talking all meek. "You think I don't know it? It's those children of Esau, that's what it is, Mick, you got to know that. We had five girls who were a lot dustier than her, but we had to put them out into other families, cause they were like you, so strong they would've killed their own parents without meaning to."

And I says, "Well, you brought me back, didn't you?"

And he says, "Well you were *alive*, Mick, and you got to admit that makes it easier."

"You mean those girls're all dead?" I says.

"The children of Esau," he says. "Shot three of them, strangled one, and we never found the body of the other. They never lived to be ten years old."

And I thought about how the lady in Roanoke told me she had me in her gunsights a few times. But she let me live. Why? For my seed? Those girls would've had seed too, or whatever. But they killed those girls and let me live. I didn't know why. Hell, I still don't, not if you mean to keep me locked up like this for the rest of my life. I mean you might as well have blasted my head off when I was six, and then I can name you a dozen good folks who'd still be alive, so no thanks for the favor if you don't plan to let me go.

Anyway, I says to him, "I didn't know that. I'm sorry."

And he says to me, "Mick, I can see how you'd be disappointed, seeing how you're so blessed by the Lord. But I promise you that my daughter is indeed the best girl of marriageable age that we've got here. I wasn't trying to foist her off on you because she's my daughter—it would be blasphemous for me to try it, and I'm a true servant of the Lord. The people here can testify for me, they can tell you that I'd never give you my own daughter unless she was the best we've got."

If she was the best they got then I had to figure the laws against inbreeding made pretty good sense. But I says to him, "Then maybe we ought to wait and see if there's somebody younger, too young to marry right now." I remembered the story of Jacob from Sunday School, and since they set such store by Jacob I figured it'd work. I says, "Remember that Jacob served seven years before he got to marry Rachel. I'm willing to wait."

That impressed hell out of him, you can bet. He says, "You truly have the prophetic spirit, Mick. I have no doubt that someday you'll be Papa in my place, when the Lord has gathered me unto my fathers. But I hope you'll also remember that Jacob married Rachel, but he first married the older daughter, Leah."

The ugly one, I thought, but I didn't say it. I just smiled and told him how I'd remember that, and there was plenty of time to talk about it tomorrow, because it was dark now and I was tired and a lot of things had happened to me today that I had to think over. I was really getting into the spirit of this Bible thing, and so I says to him, "Remember that before Jacob could dream of the ladder into heaven, he had to sleep."

Everybody laughed, but Papa Lem wasn't satisfied yet. He was willing to let the marriage thing wait for a few days. But there was one thing that couldn't wait. He looks me in the eye and he says, "Mick, you got a choice to make. The Lord says those who aren't for me are against me. Joshua said choose ye this day whom ye will serve. And Moses said, 'I call heaven and earth to record this day against you, that I have set before you life and death, blessing and cursing: therefore choose life, that both thou and thy seed may live.'"

Well I don't think you can put it much plainer than that. I could choose to live there among the chosen people, surrounded by dirty kids and a slimy old man telling me who to marry and whether I could raise my own children, or I could choose to leave and get my brains blasted out or maybe just pick up a stiff dose of cancer—I wasn't altogether sure whether they'd do it quick or slow. I kind of figured they'd do it quick, though, so I'd have no chance to spill my seed among the daughters of Esau.

So I gave him my most solemn and hypocritical promise that I would serve the Lord and live among them all the days of my life. Like I told you, I didn't know whether he could tell if I was lying or not. But he nodded and smiled so it looked like he believed me. Trouble was, I knew *he* was lying, and so that meant he *didn't* believe me, and that meant I

64

was in deep poo, as Mr. Kaiser's boy Greggy always said. In fact, he was pretty angry and pretty scared, too, even though he tried to hide it by smiling and keeping a lid on himself. But I knew that he knew that I had no intention of staying there with those crazy people who knocked up their cousins and stayed about as ignorant as I ever saw. Which meant that he was already planning to kill me, and sooner rather than later.

No, I better tell the truth here, cause I wasn't *that* smart. It wasn't till I was halfway to the house that I really wondered if he believed me, and it wasn't till Mama had me with a nice clean pair of pajamas up in a nice clean room, and she was about to take my jeans and shirt and underwear and make *them* nice and clean that it occurred to me that maybe I was going to wish I had more clothes on than pajamas that night. I really got kind of mad before she finally gave me back my clothes—she was scared that if she didn't do what I said, I'd do something to her. And then I got to thinking that maybe I'd made things even *worse* by not giving her the clothes, because that might make them think that I was planning to skip out, and so maybe they weren't planning to kill me before but now they would, and so I probably just made things worse. Except when it came down to it, I'd rather be wrong about the one thing and at least have my clothes, than be wrong about the other thing and have to gallivant all over the country in pajamas. You don't get much mileage on country roads barefoot in pajamas, even in the summer.

As soon as Mama left and went on downstairs, I got dressed again, including my shoes, and climbed in under the covers. I'd slept out in the open, so I didn't mind sleeping in my clothes. What drove me crazy was getting my shoes on the sheets. They would've yelled at me so bad at the Children's Home.

I laid there in the dark, trying to think what I was going to do. I pretty much knew how to get from this house out to the road, but what good would that do me? I didn't know where I was or where the road led or how far to go, and you don't cut cross country in North Carolina—if you don't trip over something in the dark, you'll bump into some moonshine or marijuana operation and they'll blast your head off, not to mention the danger of getting your throat bit out by some tobacco farmer's mean old dog. So there I'd be running along a road that leads nowhere with them on my tail and if they wanted to run me down, I don't think fear of cancer would slow down your average four-wheeler.

I thought about maybe stealing a car, but I don't have the first idea how to hotwire anything. It wasn't one of the skills you pick up at the Children's Home. I knew the idea of it, somewhat, because I'd done some reading on

electricity with the books Mr. Kaiser lent me
so I could maybe try getting ready for the
GED, but there wasn't a chapter in there on
how to get a Lincoln running without a key.
Didn't know how to drive, either. All the stuff
you pick up from your dad or from your
friends at school, I just never picked up at all.

Maybe I dozed off, maybe I didn't. But I
suddenly noticed that I could see in the dark.
Not *see*, of course. Feel the people moving
around. Not far off at first, except like a blur,
but I could feel the near ones, the other ones
in the house. It was cause they was sparky, of
course, but as I laid there feeling them drifting here and there, in the rhythms of sleep
and dreams, or walking around, I began to realize that I'd been feeling people all along,
only I didn't know it. They wasn't sparky, but
I always knew where they were, like shadows
drifting in the back of your mind, I didn't even
know that I knew it, but they were there. It's
like when Diz Riddle got him his glasses when
he was ten years old and all of a sudden he
just went around whooping and yelling about
all the stuff he saw. He always used to see it
before, but he didn't rightly know what half
the stuff was. Like pictures on coins. He knew
the coins was bumpy, but he didn't know they
was pictures and writing and stuff. That's how
this was.

I laid there and I could make a map in my
brain where I could see a whole bunch of dif-

ferent people, and the more I tried, the better I could see. Pretty soon it wasn't just in that house. I could feel them in other houses, dimmer and fainter. But in my mind I didn't see no walls so I didn't know whether somebody was in the kitchen or in the bathroom, I had to think it out, and it was hard, it took all my concentration. The only guide I had was that I could see electric wires when the current was flowing through them, so wherever a light was on or a clock was running or something, I could feel this thin line, really thin, not like the shadows of people. It wasn't much, but it gave me some idea of where some of the walls might be.

If I could've just told who was who I might have made some guesses about what they was doing. Who was asleep and who was awake. But I couldn't even tell who was a kid and who was a grown-up, cause I couldn't see sizes, just brightness. Brightness was the only way I knew who was close and who was far.

I was pure lucky I got so much sleep during the day when that guy was giving me a ride from Roanoke to Eden. Well, that wasn't lucky, I guess, since I wished I hadn't gone to Eden at all, but at least having that long nap meant that I had a better shot at staying awake until things quieted down.

There was a clump of them in the next house. It was hard to sort them out, cause three of them was a lot brighter, so I thought they was closer, and it took a while to realize that it was probably Mama and Daddy and Papa Lem along with some others. Anyway it was a meeting, and it broke up after a while, and all except Papa Lem came over. I didn't know what the meeting was about, but I knew they was scared and mad. Mostly scared. Well, so was I. But I calmed myself down, the way I'd been practicing, so I didn't accidentally kill nobody. That kind of practice made it so I could keep myself from getting too lively and sparky, so they'd think I was asleep. They didn't see as clear as I did, too, so that'd help. I thought maybe they'd all come up and get me, but no, they just all waited downstairs while one of them came up, and he didn't come in and get me, neither. All he did was go to the other rooms and wake up whoever was sleeping there and get them downstairs and out of the house.

Well, that scared me worse than ever. That made it plain what they had in mind, all right. Didn't want me giving off sparks and killing somebody close by when they attacked me. Still, when I thought about it, I realized that it was also a good sign. They was scared of me, and rightly so. I could reach farther and strike harder than any of them. And they saw I could throw off what got tossed at me, when I flung back what Papa Lem's daughter tried to do to me. They didn't know how much I could do.

Neither did I.

Finally all the people was out of the house except the ones downstairs. There was others outside the house, maybe watching, maybe not, but I figured I better not try to climb out the window.

Then somebody started walking up the stairs again, alone. There wasn't nobody else to fetch down, so they could only be coming after me. It was just one person, but that didn't do me no good—even one grown man who knows how to use a knife is better off than me. I still don't have my full growth on me, or at least I sure hope I don't, and the only fights I ever got in were slugging matches in the yard. For a minute I wished I'd took kung fu lessons instead of sitting around reading math and science books to make up for dropping out of school so young. A lot of good math and science was going to do me if I was dead.

The worst thing was I couldn't see him. Maybe they just moved all the children out of the house so they wouldn't make noise in the morning and wake me. Maybe they was just being nice. And this guy coming up the stairs might just be checking on me or bringing me clean clothes or something—I couldn't tell. So how could I twist him up, when I didn't know if they was trying to kill me or what? But if he *was* trying to kill me, I'd wish I'd twisted him before he ever came into the room with me.

Well, that was one decision that got made for me. I laid there wondering what to do for so long that he got to the top of the stairs and came to my room and turned the knob and came in.

I tried to breathe slow and regular, like somebody asleep. Tried to keep from getting too sparky. If it was somebody checking on me, they'd go away.

He didn't go away. And he walked soft, too, so as not to wake me up. He was real scared. So scared that I finally knew there was no way he was there to tuck me in and kiss me good night.

So I tried to twist him, to send sparks at him. But I didn't have any sparks to send! I mean I wasn't mad or anything. I'd never tried to kill somebody on purpose before, it was always because I was already mad and I just lost control and it *happened*. Now I'd been calming myself down so much that I couldn't lose control. I had no sparks at all to send, just my normal shining shadow, and he was right there and I didn't have a second to lose so I rolled over. Toward him, which was maybe dumb, cause I might have run into his knife, but I didn't know yet for sure that he had a knife. All I was thinking was that I had to knock him down or push him or something.

The only person I knocked down was me. I

bumped him and hit the floor. He also cut my back with the knife. Not much of a cut, he mostly just snagged my shirt, but if I was scared before, I was terrified now cause I knew he had a knife and I knew even more that I didn't. I scrambled back away from him. There was almost no light from the window, it was like being in a big closet, I couldn't see him, he couldn't see me. Except of course that I *could* see him, or at least sense where he was, and now I was giving off sparks like crazy so unless he was weaker than I thought, he could see me too.

Well, he was weaker than I thought. He just kind of drifted, and I could hear him swishing the knife through the air in front of him. He had no idea where I was.

And all the time I was trying to get madder and madder, and it wasn't working. You can't get mad by trying. Maybe an actor can, but I'm no actor. So I was scared and sparking but I couldn't get that pulse to mess him up. The more I thought about it, the calmer I got.

It's like you've been carrying around a machine gun all your life, accidently blasting people you didn't really want to hurt and then the first time you really want to lay into somebody, it jams.

So I stopped trying to get mad. I just sat there realizing I was going to die, that after I finally got myself under control so I didn't kill people all the time anymore, now that I didn't really want to commit suicide, *now* I was going to get wasted. And they didn't even have the guts to come at me openly. Sneaking in the dark to cut my throat while I was asleep. And in the meeting where they decided to do it, my long lost but loving mama and daddy were right there. Heck, my dear sweet daddy was downstairs right now, waiting for this assassin to come down and tell him that I was dead. Would he cry for me then? Boo hoo my sweet little boy's all gone? Mick is in the cold cold ground?

I was mad. As simple as that. Stop thinking about being mad, and start thinking about the things that if you think about them, they'll make you mad. I was so sparky with fear that when I got mad, too, it was worse than it ever was before, built up worse, you know. Only when I let it fly, it didn't go for the guy up there swishing his knife back and forth in the dark. That pulse of fire in me went right down through the floor and straight to dear old Dad. I could hear him scream. He felt it, just like that. He felt it. And so did I. Because that wasn't what I meant to do. I only met him that day, but he was my father, and I did him worse than I ever did anybody before in my life. I didn't plan to do it. You don't plan to kill your father.

All of a sudden I was blinded by light. For a second I thought it was the other kind of light, sparks, them retaliating, twisting me.

Then I realized it was my eyes being blinded, and it was the overhead light in the room that was on. The guy with the knife had finally realized that the only reason not to have the light on was so I wouldn't wake up, but now that I was awake he might as well see what he's doing. Lucky for me the light blinded him just as much as it blinded me, or I'd have been poked before I saw what hit me. Instead I had time to scramble on back to the far corner of the room.

I wasn't no hero. But I was seriously thinking about running at him, attacking a guy with a knife. I would have been killed, but I couldn't think of anything else to do.

Then I thought of something else to do. I got the idea from the way I could feel the electric current in the wires running from the light-switch through the wall. That was electricity, and the lady in Roanoke called my sparkiness bio-electricity. I ought to be able to do something with it, shouldn't I?

I thought first that maybe I could short-circuit something, but I didn't think I had that much electricity in me. I thought of maybe tapping into the house current to add to my own juice, but then I remembered that connecting up your body to house current is the same thing other folks call *electrocution*. I mean, maybe I can tap into house wiring, but if I was wrong, I'd be real dead.

But I could still do something. There was a

table lamp next to me. I pulled off the shade and threw it at the guy, who was still standing by the door, thinking about what the scream downstairs meant. Then I grabbed the lamp and turned it on, and then smashed the light bulb on the nightstand. Sparks. Then it was out.

I held the lamp in my hand, like a weapon, so he'd think I was going to beat off his knife with the lamp. And if my plan was a bust, I guess that's what I would've done. But while he was looking at me, getting ready to fight me knife against lamp, I kind of let the jagged end of the lamp rest on the bedspread. And then I used my sparkiness, the anger that was still in me. I couldn't fling it at the guy, or well I could have, but it would've been like the bus driver, a six-month case of lung cancer. By the time he died of *that*, I'd be six months worth of dead from multiple stab wounds to the neck and chest.

So I let my sparkiness build up and flow out along my arm, out along the lamp, like I was making my shadow grow. And it worked. The sparks just went right on down the lamp to the tip, and built up and built up, and all the time I was thinking about how Papa Lem was trying to kill me cause I thought his daughter was ugly and how he made me kill my daddy before I even knew him half a day and that charge built *up*.

It built up enough. Sparks started jumping

across inside the broken light bulb, right there against the bedspread. Real sparks, the kind I could *see*, not just feel. And in two seconds that bedspread was on fire. *Then* I yanked the lamp so the cord shot right out of the wall, and I threw it at the guy, and while he was dodging I scooped up the bedspread and ran at him. I wasn't sure whether I'd catch on fire or he would, but I figured he'd be too panicked and surprised to think of stabbing me *through* the bedspread, and sure enough he didn't, he dropped the knife and tried to beat off the bedspread. Which he didn't do too good, because I was still pushing it at him. Then he tried to get through the door, but I kicked his ankle with my shoe, and he fell down, still fighting off the blanket.

I got the knife and sliced right across the back of his thigh with it. Geez it was sharp. Or maybe I was so mad and scared that I cut him stronger than I ever thought I could, but it went clear to the bone. He was screaming from the fire and his leg was gushing blood and the fire was catching on the wallpaper and it occurred to me that they couldn't chase me too good if they was trying to put out a real dandy house fire.

It also occurred to me that I couldn't run away too good if I was dead inside that house fire. And thinking of maybe dying in the fire made me realize that the guy was burning to death and I did it to him, something every bit as terrible as cancer, and *I didn't care*, because I'd killed so many people that it was nothing to me now, when a guy like that was trying to kill me, I wasn't even sorry for his pain, cause he wasn't feeling nothing worse than Old Peleg felt, and in fact that even made me feel pretty good, because it was like getting even for Old Peleg's death, even though it was me killed them both. I mean how could I get *even* for Peleg dying by killing somebody else? Okay, maybe it makes sense in a way, cause it was their fault I was in the orphanage instead of growing up here. Or maybe it made sense because this guy deserved to die, and Peleg didn't, so maybe somebody who deserved it had to die a death as bad as Peleg's, or something. I don't know. I sure as hell wasn't thinking about that then. I just knew that I was hearing a guy scream himself to death and I didn't even want to help him or even *try* to help him or nothing. I wasn't enjoying it, either, I wasn't thinking, Burn you sucker! or anything like that, but I knew right then that I wasn't even human, I was just a monster, like I always thought, like in the slasher movies. This was straight from the slasher movies, somebody burning up and screaming, and there's the monster just standing there in the flames and he *isn't burning*.

And that's the truth. I wasn't burning. There was flames all around me, but it kind of shied back from me, because I was so full of sparks from hating myself so bad that it was like the flames couldn't get through to me. I've thought about that a lot since then. I mean, even that Swedish scientist doesn't know all about this bio-electrical stuff. Maybe when I get real sparky it makes it so other stuff can't hit me. Maybe that's how some generals in the Civil War used to ride around in the open—or maybe that was that general in World War II, I can't remember—and bullets didn't hit them or anything. Maybe if you're charged up enough, things just can't *get* to you. I don't know. I just know that by the time I finally decided to open the door and actually opened it, the whole room was burning and the door was burning and I just opened it and walked through. Course now I got a bandage on my hand to prove that I couldn't grab a hot door-knob without hurting myself a little, but I shouldn't've been able to stay alive in that room and I came out without even my hair singed.

I started down the hall, not knowing who was still in the house. I wasn't used to being able to see people by their sparkiness yet, so I didn't even think of checking, I just ran down the stairs carrying that bloody knife. But it didn't matter. They all ran away before I got there, all except Daddy. He was lying in the middle of the floor in the living room, dou-bled up, lying with his head in a pool of vomit and his butt in a pool of blood, shaking like he was dying of cold. I really done him. I really tore him up inside. I don't think he even saw me. But he was my daddy, and even a monster don't leave his daddy for the fire to get him. So I grabbed his arms to try to pull him out.

I forgot how sparky I was, worse than ever. The second I touched him the sparkiness just rushed out of me and all over him. It never went that way before, just completely surrounded him like he was a part of me, like he was completely drowning in my light. It wasn't what I meant to do at all. I just forgot. I was trying to save him and instead I gave him a hit like I never gave nobody before, and I couldn't stand it, I just screamed.

Then I dragged him out. He was all limp, but even if I killed him, even if I turned him to jelly inside, he wasn't going to burn, that's all I could think of, that and how I ought to walk back into that house myself and up the stairs and catch myself on fire and die.

But I didn't do it, as you might guess. There was people yelling Fire! and shouting Stay back! and I knew that I better get out of there. Daddy's body was lying on the grass in front of the house, and I took off around the back. I thought maybe I heard some gunshots, but it could've been popping and cracking of timbers in the fire, I don't know. I just ran around the house and along toward the road, and if there was people in my way they just got *out* of my way, because even the most dimwitted inbred pukebrained kid in that whole village would've seen my sparks, I was so hot.

I ran till the asphalt ended and I was running on the dirt road. There was clouds so the moon was hardly any light at all, and I kept stumbling off the road into the weeds. I fell once and when I was getting up I could see the fire behind me. The whole house was burning, and there was flames above it in the trees. Come to think of it there hadn't been all that much rain, and those trees were dry. A lot more than one house was going to burn tonight, I figured, and for a second I even thought maybe nobody'd chase me.

But that was about as stupid an idea as I ever had. I mean, if they wanted to kill me before because I said Papa Lem's girl was ugly, how do you think they felt about me now that I burned down their little hidden town? Once they realized I was gone, they'd be after me and I'd be lucky if they shot me quick.

I even thought about cutting off the road, dangerous or not, and hiding in the woods. But I decided to get as much distance as I could along the road till I saw headlights.

Just when I decided that, the road ended. Just bushes and trees. I went back, tried to find the road. It must have turned but I didn't know which way. I was tripping along like a blind man in the grass, trying to feel my way to the ruts of the dirt road, and of course that's when I saw headlights away off toward the burning houses—there was at least three houses burning now. They knew the town was a total loss by now, they was probably just leaving enough folks to get all the children out and away to a safe place, while the men came after me. It's what *I* would've done, and to hell with cancer, they knew I couldn't stop them all before they did what they wanted to me. By the time their headlights got close enough to show the road, it'd be too late to get away.

I was about to run back into the woods when all of a sudden a pair of headlights went on not twenty feet away, and pointed right at me. I damn near wet my pants. I thought, Mick Winger, you are a dead little boy right this second.

And then I heard her calling to me. "Get on over here, Mick, you idiot, don't stand there in the light, get on over here." It was the lady from Roanoke. I still couldn't see her cause of the lights, but I knew her voice, and I took off. The road didn't end, it just turned a little and she was parked right where the dirt road met up sideways with a gravel road. I got around to the door of the car she was driving, or truck or whatever it was—a four-wheel-drive Blazer maybe, I know it had a four-wheel-drive shift lever in it—anyway the door was locked and she was yelling at me to get *in* and I was yelling back that it was *locked* until finally she unlocked it and I climbed in. She backed up so fast and swung around onto the gravel in a spin that near threw me right out the door, since I hadn't closed it yet. Then she took off so fast going *forward*, spitting gravel behind her, that the door closed itself.

"Fasten your seat belt," she says to me.

"Did you follow me here?" I says.

"No, I just happened to be here picnicking," she says. "Fasten your damn *seat belt.*"

I did, but then I turned around in my seat and looked out the back. There was five or six sets of headlights, making the jog to get from the dirt road onto the gravel road. We didn't have more than a mile on them.

"We've been looking for this place for years," she says. "We thought it was in Rockingham County, that's how far off we were."

"Where is it, then?" I says.

"Alamance County," she says.

And then I says, "I don't give a damn what county it is! I killed my own daddy back there!"

And she says to me, "Don't get mad now, don't get mad at me, I'm sorry, just calm down." That was all she could think of, how I might get mad and lose control and kill her, and I don't blame her, cause it was the hardest thing I ever did, keeping myself from busting out right there in the car, and it would've killed her, too. The pain in my hand was starting to get to me, too, from where I grabbed the doorknob. It was just building up and building up.

She was driving a lot faster than the headlights reached. We'd be going way too fast for a curve before she even saw it, and then she'd slam on the brakes and we'd skid and sometimes I couldn't believe we didn't just roll over and crash. But she always got out of it.

I couldn't face back anymore. I just sat there with my eyes closed, trying to get calm, and then I'd remember my daddy who I didn't even *like* but he was my daddy lying there in his blood and his puke, and I'd remember that guy who burned to death up in my room and even though I didn't care at the time, I sure cared now, I was so angry and scared and I hated myself so bad I couldn't hold it in, only I also couldn't let it out, and I kept wishing I could just die. Then I realized that the guys following us were close enough that I could feel them. Or no it wasn't that they was close. They was just so *mad* that I could see their sparks flying like never before. Well as long as I could see them I could let fly, couldn't I? I just flung out toward them. I don't know if I hit them. I don't know if my bio-electricity is something I can throw like that or what. But at least I shucked it off myself, and I didn't mess up the lady who was driving.

When we hit asphalt again, I found out that I didn't know what crazy driving was before.

She peeled out and now she began to look at a curve ahead and then switch off the headlights until she was halfway through the curve, it was the craziest thing I ever saw, but it also made sense. They had to be following our lights, and when our lights went out they wouldn't know where we was for a minute. They also wouldn't know that the road curved ahead, and they might even crash up or at least they'd have to slow down. Of course, we had a real good chance of ending up eating trees ourselves, but she drove like she knew what she was doing.

We came to a straight section with a crossroads about a mile up. She switched off the lights again, and I thought maybe she was going to turn, but she didn't. Just went on and on and on, straight into the pitch-black. Now, that straight section was long, but it didn't go on forever, and I don't care how good a driver you are, you can't keep track of how far you've gone in the dark. Just when I thought for sure we'd smash into something, she let off the gas and reached her hand out the window with a flashlight. We was still going pretty fast, but the flashlight was enough to make a reflector up ahead flash back at us, so she knew where the curve was, and it was farther off than I thought. She whipped us around that curve and then around another, using just a couple of blinks from the flashlight, before she switched on her headlights again.

I looked behind us to see if I could see anybody. "You lost them!" I says.

"Maybe," she says. "You tell *me*."

So I tried to feel where they might be, and sure enough, they was sparky enough that I could just barely tell where they was, away back. Split up, smeared out. "They're going every which way," I says.

"So we lost a few of them," she says. "They aren't going to give up, you know."

"I know," I says.

"You're the hottest thing going," she says.

"And you're a daughter of Esau," I says.

"Like hell I am," she says. "I'm a great-great-great-granddaughter of Jacob Yow, who happened to be bio-electrically talented. Like if you're tall and athletic, you can play basketball. That's all it is, just a natural talent. Only he went crazy and started inbreeding his whole family, and they've got these stupid ideas about being the chosen of God and all the time they're just *murderers*."

"Tell me about it," I says.

"You can't help it," she says. "You didn't have anybody to teach you. I'm not blaming you."

But I was blaming me.

She says, "Ignorant, that's what they are. Well, my grandpa didn't want to just keep reading the Bible and killing any revenuers or sheriffs or whatever who gave us trouble. He wanted to find out what we *are*. He also didn't want to marry the slut they picked out for him because he wasn't particularly dusty. So he left. They hunted him down and tried to kill him, but he got away, and he married. And he also studied and became a doctor and his kids grew up knowing that they had to find out what it *is*, this power. It's like the old stories of witches, women who get mad and suddenly your cows start dying. Maybe they didn't even know they were doing it. Summonings and love spells and come-hithers, everybody can do it a little, just like everybody can throw a ball and sometimes make a basket, but some people can do it better than others. And Papa Lem's people, they do it best of all, better and better, because they're breeding for it. We've got to stop them, don't you see? We've got to keep them from learning how to control it. Because now we know more about it. It's all tied up with the way the human body heals itself. In Sweden they've been changing the currents around to heal tumors. Cancer. The opposite of what you've been doing, but it's the same principle. Do you know what that means? If they could control it, Lem's people could be healers, not killers. Maybe all it takes is to do it with love, not anger."

"Did you kill them little girls in orphanages with love?" I says.

And she just drives, she doesn't say a thing, just drives. "Damn," she says, "it's raining."

The road was slick in two seconds. She slowed way down. It came down harder and harder. I looked behind us and there was headlights back there again. Way back, but I could still see them. "They're on us again," I says.

"I can't go any faster in the rain," she says.

"It's raining on them too," I says.

"Not with my luck."

And I says, "It'll put the fire out. Back where they live."

And she says, "It doesn't matter. They'll move. They know we found them, because we picked you up. So they'll move."

I apologized for causing trouble, and she says, "We couldn't let you die in there. I had to go there and save you if I could."

"Why?" I ask her. "Why not let me die?"

"Let me put it another way," she says. "If you decided to stay with them, I had to go in there and kill you."

And I says to her, "You're the queen of compassion, you know?" And I thought about it a little. "You're just like they are, you know?" I says. "You wanted to get pregnant just like they did. You wanted to breed me like a stud horse."

"If I wanted to *breed* you," she says, "I would have done it on the hill this morning. Yesterday morning. You would've done it.

87

And I should've made you, because if you went with them, our only hope was to have a child of yours that we could raise to be a decent person. Only it turned out you're a decent person, so we didn't have to kill you. Now we can study you and learn about this from the strongest living example of the phenomenon"—I don't know how to pronounce that, but you know what I mean. Or what she meant, anyway.

And I says to her, "Maybe I don't want you to study me, did you think of that?"

And she says to me, "Maybe what you want don't amount to a goldfish fart." Or anyway that's what she meant.

That's about when they started shooting at us. Rain or no rain, they was pushing it so they got close enough to shoot, and they wasn't half bad at it, seeing as the first bullet we knew about went right through the back window and in between us and smacked a hole in the windshield. Which made all kinds of cracks in the glass so she couldn't see, which made her slow down more, which meant they was even closer.

Just then we whipped around a corner and our headlights lit up a bunch of guys getting out of a car with guns in their hands, and she says. "Finally." So I figured they was some of her people, there to take the heat off. But at that same second Lem's people must have shot out a tire or maybe she just got a little careless for a second cause after all she couldn't see too good through the windshield, but anyway she lost control and we skidded and flipped over, rolled over it felt like five times, all in slow motion, rolling and rolling, the doors popping open and breaking off, the windshield cracking and crumbling away, and there we hung in our seat belts, not talking or nothing, except maybe I was saying O my God or something and then we smacked into something and just stopped, which jerked us around inside the car and then it was all over.

I heard water rushing. A stream, I thought. We can wash up. Only it wasn't a stream, it was the gasoline pouring out of the tank. And then I heard gunshots from back up by the road. I didn't know who was fighting who, but if the wrong guys won they'd just love to catch us in a nice hot gasoline fire. Getting out wasn't going to be all that hard. The doors were gone so we didn't have to climb out a window or anything.

We were leaned over on the left side, so her door was mashed against the ground. I says to her, "We got to climb out my door." I had brains enough to hook one arm up over the lip of the car before I unbuckled my seat belt, and then I hoisted myself out and stayed perched up there on the side of the car, up in the air, so I could reach down and help her out.

Only she wasn't climbing out. I yelled at her

and she didn't answer. I thought for a second she was dead, but then I saw that her sparks was still there. Funny, how I never saw she had any sparkiness before, because I didn't know to look for it, but now, even though it was dim, I could see it. Only it wasn't so dim, it was real busy, like she was trying to heal herself. The gurgling was still going on, and everything smelled like gasoline. There was still shooting going on. And even if nobody came down to start us on fire on purpose, I saw enough car crashes at the movies to know you didn't need a match to start a car on fire. I sure didn't want to be near the car if it caught, and I sure didn't want her *in* it. But I couldn't see how to climb down in and pull her out. I mean I'm not a weakling but I'm not Mr. Universe either.

It felt like I sat there for a whole minute before I realized I didn't have to pull her out my side of the car, I could pull her out the *front* cause the whole windshield was missing and the roof was only mashed down a little, cause there was a rollbar in the car—that was real smart, putting a rollbar in. I jumped off the car. It wasn't raining right here, but it *had* rained, so it was slippery and wet. Or maybe it was slippery from the gasoline, I don't know. I got around the front of the car, and up to the windshield, and I scraped the bits of glass off with my shoe. Then I crawled partway in and reached under her and undid her seat belt, and tried to pull her out, but her legs was hung up under the steering wheel and it took forever, it was terrible, and all the time I kept listening for her to breathe, and she didn't breathe, and so I kept getting more scared and frustrated and all I was thinking about was how she had to live, she couldn't be dead, she just got through saving my life and now she was dead and she couldn't be and I was going to get her out of the car even if I had to break her legs to do it, only I didn't have to break her legs and she finally slid out and I dragged her away from the car. It didn't catch on fire, but I couldn't know it wasn't going to.

And anyway all I cared about then was her, not breathing, lying there limp on the grass with her neck all floppy and I was holding on to her crying and angry and scared and I had us both covered with sparks, like we was the same person, just completely covered, and I was crying and saying, Live! I couldn't even call her by name or nothing because I didn't know her name. I just know that I was shaking like I had the chills and so was she and she was breathing now and whimpering like somebody just stepped on a puppy and the sparks just kept flowing around us both and I felt like somebody sucked everything out of me, like I was a wet towel and somebody wrung me out and flipped me into a corner, and then I don't remember until I woke up here.

What did it feel like? What you did to her?

It felt like when I covered her with light, it was like I was taking over doing what her own body should've done, it was like I was healing her. Maybe I got that idea because she said something about healing when she was driving the car, but she wasn't breathing when I dragged her out, and then she was breathing. So I want to know if I healed her. Because if she got healed when I covered her with my own light, then maybe I didn't kill my daddy either, because it was kind of like that, I *think* it was kind of like that, what happened when I dragged him out of the house.

I been talking a long time now, and you still told me nothing. Even if you think I'm just a killer and you want me dead, you can tell me about her. Is she alive?

Yes.

Well then how come I can't see her? How come she isn't here with the rest of you?

She had some surgery. It takes time to heal.

But did I help her? Or did I twist her? You got to tell me. Cause if I didn't help her then I hope I fail your test and you kill me cause I can't think of a good reason why I should be alive if all I can do is kill people.

You helped her, Mick. That last bullet

caught her in the head. That's why she crashed.

But she wasn't bleeding!

It was dark, Mick. You couldn't see. You had her blood all over you. But it doesn't matter now. We have the bullet out. As far as we can tell, there was no brain damage. There should have been. She should have been dead.

So I did help her.

Yes. But we don't know how. All kinds of stories, you know, about faith healing, that sort of thing. Laying on of hands. Maybe it's the kind of thing you did, merging the bio-magnetic field. A lot of things don't make any sense yet. There's no way we can see that the tiny amount of electricity in a human bio-electric system could influence somebody a hundred miles off, but they summoned you, and you came. We need to study you, Mick. We've never had anybody as powerful as you. Tell the truth, maybe there's never been any-body like you. Or maybe all the healings in the New Testament—

I don't want to hear about no testaments. Papa Lem gave me about all the testaments I ever need to hear about.

Will you help us, Mick?

Help you how?

Let us study you.

Go ahead and study.

Maybe it won't be enough just to study how you *heal* people.

I'm not going to kill nobody for you. If you try to make me kill somebody I'll kill you first till you have to kill me to save your own lives, do you understand me?

Calm down, Mick. Don't get angry. There's plenty of time to think about things. Actually we're glad that you don't want to kill anybody. If you enjoyed it, or even if you hadn't been able to control it and kept on indiscriminately killing anyone who enraged you, you wouldn't have lived to be seventeen. Because yes, we're scientists, or at least we're finally learning enough that we can start being scientists. But first we're human beings, and we're in the middle of a war, and children like you are the weapons. If they ever got someone like you to stay with them, work with them, you could seek us out and destroy us. That's what they wanted you to do.

That's right, that's one thing Papa Lem said, I don't know if I mentioned it before, but he said that the children of Israel were supposed to kill every man, woman, and child in Canaan, cause idolaters had to make way for the children of God.

Well, you see, that's why our branch of the family left. We didn't think it was such a terrific idea, wiping out the entire human race and replacing it with a bunch of murderous, incestuous religious fanatics. For the last

twenty years, we've been able to keep them from getting somebody like you, because we've murdered the children that were so powerful they had to put them outside to be reared by others.

Except me.

It's a war. We didn't like killing children. But it's like bombing the place where your enemies are building a secret weapon. The lives of a few children—no, that's a lie. It nearly split us apart ourselves, the arguments over that. Letting you live—it was a terrible risk. I voted against it every time. And I don't apologize for that, Mick. Now that you know what they are, and you chose to leave, I'm glad I lost. But so many things could have gone wrong.

They won't put any more babies out to orphanages now, though. They're not that dumb.

But now we have *you*. Maybe we can learn how to block what they do. Or how to heal the people they attack. Or how to identify sparkiness, as you call it, from a distance. All kinds of possibilities. But sometime in the future, Mick, you may be the only weapon we have. Do you understand that?

I don't want to.

I know.

You wanted to kill me?

I wanted to protect people from you. It was safest. Mick, I really am glad it worked out this way.

I don't know whether to believe you, Mr. Kaiser. You're such a good liar. I thought you were so nice to me all that time because you were just a nice guy.

Oh, he is, Mick. He's a nice guy. Also a damn fine liar. We kind of needed both those attributes in the person we had looking out for you.

Well, anyway, that's over with.

What's over with?

Killing me. Isn't it?

That's up to you, Mick. If you ever start getting crazy on us, or killing people that aren't part of this war of ours—

I won't do that!

But if you did, Mick. It's never too late to kill you.

Can I see her?

See who?

The lady from Roanoke! Isn't it about time you told me her name?

Come on. She can tell you herself.

THE TUNESMITH
LLOYD BIGGLE, JR.

Foreword

How Lloyd Biggle, Jr., Changed My Life, Part I

Orson Scott Card

I was always drawn to secrets, to mysterious hidden things. I learned to read from my older sister's copy of *The Hidden Staircase*, a Nancy Drew mystery. What I loved about it wasn't the writing or the characters, but rather the staircase itself. A hidden passage down into the darkness, a fearful place to go, yet if you followed it long enough it would lead back upward into the light. But it would be a new light, in a new place, and the only way you could get there was by those dark, hidden stairs.

Wait—did I find all that in a Nancy Drew novel? Sure. It's there, the hidden passage, the light. But I also brought something to the story. A memory of an apartment my family lived in when I was four. We had the upper story of an old Victorian house in the City Creek neighborhood in Salt Lake City. There were heavy outside stairs up to our apartment, and also an inside flight that had once been the main front stairs of the house.

What I didn't realize was that the house must have been built with another flight of stairs, the *back* stairs, for discreet passage by servants—and by members of the family who wished to remain invisible to company in the front parlor. I, unsuspecting, went rummaging one day in the coat closet just back of the kitchen. I burrowed into the heavy winter coats, worming my feet between the shoes and boots on the closet floor.

And then, to my horror, my probing feet suddenly reached a spot where there was no floor! If I had not been so tightly wedged among the jackets, I would have stumbled, would have fallen. As it was, I clung to the heavy fabric of my mother's cloth coat and reached my foot farther, farther, inch by inch. It was an agony of suspense for me. How did I know what might be lurking there in the darkness!

After several long, deep breaths, my foot touched floor again. Firm floor. I stepped down, and found another lip, another step. There was a stairway hidden in the back of the coat closet!

In the darkness at the back of the closet, I

imagined what might have happened if I *had* fallen. I might have rolled downward forever, or at least so far that I would never be found; and with the barrier of coats at the top of the stairs, my shouts for help would never be heard. Shuddering, my dread at last getting the better of me, I backed slowly out of the closet. I never spoke of it to my family. Better not to tell them that I knew the secret of the closet. Yet what if they didn't know? What if some night as we slept some terrible creature—man or monster—crept up those dark stairs into our house and murdered us in our sleep? I pictured such a creature killing me and carrying off my baby brother, while my parents and my older brother and sister slept on, oblivious. Many a sleepless hour I spent imagining such a terrible fate—or, when I was a bit more optimistic, imagining how I would leap heroically from my bed, crying out to alert my father, while in the meantime swinging some metal toy and striking the monster in the leg, causing it to double over in agony, dropping my baby brother, whom I would deftly catch. I, who would be ten years old before I ever caught a ball without cringing.

Now, being older, I'm sure that I must have stopped my exploration of the closet only inches from the back wall; the stairway would surely have been boarded up, and only the top few steps rescued from empty darkness by their use as a coat closet. But even knowing that doesn't stop that dark, hidden staircase from haunting me.

It was only a year later that my sister led me into the mysteries of reading my first grown-up book: *The Hidden Staircase*. Of course! That's why the book meant so much to me!

But that's too easy. Or rather, too incomplete. I'm not the only person who responds to stories in which the hero discovers a secret passage and creeps downward into the darkness. It's not just to please *me* that the descent to hell and the passage through a tunnel are two of the mythic motifs most common in storytelling in every society on Earth. Not *all* those people had a childhood experience with a secret stair!

No, I was responding to the real stairway in that Salt Lake apartment exactly the way that I responded to the imaginary staircase in the Nancy Drew mystery. Real or fictional, the passage in the darkness set me to dreaming, both of dangers that might arise out of the tunnel and of glorious things that might be discovered if I just went farther into the dark.

I feared it; I was fascinated by it. Maybe it's an unconscious memory of childbirth, but that, too, seems awfully neat. Besides, there's more to it than that, anyway. Why should I be so ambivalent toward it? Why, for that matter, should *all* human beings be so ambivalent toward strange, arcane, mysterious things? We are attracted, we are repelled—we slow down as we pass the accident scene, both hoping and dreading that death or maiming will leap out and imprint itself on our memory.

We see the black lumpy thing at the edge of the road. We must make *sure* that it isn't a baby or some other unbearable sight. Probably just a scrap of tire from some trucker's blowout. Or even a patch in the asphalt. But no, it's a dead dog, somebody's doberman, crushed and pulpy with blood, flies gloating as they swarm. We had to see—but now we turn our head away in revulsion. We're afraid to see, but also afraid to miss it.

A four-year-old version of myself had to flee from the dark closet stairway—but not until I had taken two steps along the downward path. Maybe you wouldn't have taken so many steps, overcome by fear earlier than I was. Maybe you would have stepped boldly on until you ran into the back wall and learned the truth about the closet, losing the mystery but also sparing yourself from the sleepless hours of fear in the night. We are all different. Some of us will do anything to avoid the unknown. Others can't avoid it, must explore it, understand it all, until there are no mysteries left.

In 1959 I turned eight. It was an innocent time; my parents let me hop on my bike and ride from our home on Las Palmas Drive all the way down Homestead Road to downtown Santa Clara, California. To the public library, a squat building in the middle of a circle of huge trees. A setting straight out of faerie, I realize now; then, though, I cared nothing for the trees. I parked my bike, sometimes even remembering to lock it, and plunged through the doors into the world of books.

It seemed such a large place then. Directly ahead as you came inside was the circulation desk, with a librarian always in attendance— always policing, I thought, since as an eight-year-old I had enough experience of life to know that all adults were always watching children to make sure they didn't get away with anything. When an unaccompanied child entered the library, there was only one permitted place to go: the children's section, to the right. The tall shelf units to the left, shadowy and forbidding with their thick, dark-spined books, were meant for adults only, and children were not to enter.

Not that anyone had *told* me that, of course. But the signs were clear. The children's section was for children—and that meant that the non-children's sections were *not* for children.

That year I read everything remotely interesting in the children's section. I prided myself, as a third-grader, on not reading anything aimed at any grade under sixth, and those books were soon read. What now? Nothing to read, nothing to check out with my library card and carry home in the basket on the front of my bike.

And then I realized: there were hundreds, thousands of books on the other side of the circulation desk. If I could just make my way over there, find a book, and then hide somewhere and read it . . .

I dared not. And yet that strange, forbidden territory lured me. I knew better than to *ask*—then I would be told *no* and would be watched all the more carefully because I had confessed my interest in forbidden places. So I watched, for all the world like a child hoping to shoplift and waiting for the clerks all to look the other way.

Finally they did. I moved swiftly and silently across the long space before the circulation desk, the no-man's-land between the bright-windowed children's section and the deep-shadowed adult section. No one called out for me to stop—it would have been a harsh, guttural "Halt!" I knew, for I had seen enough World War II movies on TV to know that unreasoning authority always spoke with a German accent. At last I ducked behind a shelf unit and found myself in the brave new land, safe for the moment.

Sheerest coincidence placed me directly in front of a single shelf entitled "Science Fiction." There were few books there—mostly story collections edited by people like Judith Merrill and Groff Conklin. *Best Science Fiction Stories of 1955.* That sort of thing.

But I was glad. After all, I was used to reading easier stuff. The letters in these books were all so small and close together. There were so many *words*. But at least the stories were short. And *science* fiction. That was like those time-travel stories in *Boy's Life*, right?

I took a couple of books and snuck off to a secluded table. There were some adults around, but they weren't official, and as long as I was quiet I figured they wouldn't tell on me. I opened the books and started to read.

Most of the stories were just too hard. I'd read a paragraph or two, maybe two pages, and then I'd flip on to the next story. Mostly it was because the stories were about things that I didn't care about. Sometimes I couldn't even figure out what was going on. Science fiction wasn't *meant* to be for eight-year-olds, I knew—but still, they didn't have to make it so darned hard, did they?

There were a few stories, though, that spoke clearly to me and captured my imagination from the start. One was the story of a man in a space station orbiting Jupiter, who was controlling a new artificial creature that had been designed to live on Jupiter's impossible surface. His own body had failed him, but as he controlled the powerful new body in a terrible, beautiful, inhuman world, he began to feel such new strength and hope that his consciousness—to my eight-year-old mind, his very soul—passed from the broken body in a tin can in space to the healthy new giant on the surface of Jupiter. I loved that story—the idea of changing in a moment from a weak, mortal man to a godlike being. Yet not a transcendent god, not an omnipotent, omniscient being, but rather a demigod that had a great hard work ahead of him—that rang true to me.

Now I see that the story was a new enactment of the almost-universal death-and-resurrection myth. The old, broken-down body must die, yet from it new life emerges. Yet it also partook of the myth of unmasking: in his new body, the man refused to keep his old name and identity. He might have the memories of the man he was, but he was something more now, and so he took the name they had causally used for the man-made creature. "Call me Joe," he said.

Of course I didn't understand the ending completely, not at first. I was too young; implications that adults would easily grasp eluded me until I had read the last page or so twice, three times. But the very gradualness of my understanding made it all the more powerful when it came. Ah, *that's* what it means! That's what happened!

How that story haunted me, a grand myth of becoming; and in that tale I learned that storytelling wasn't mere fun. There was a chance of magnificence when I opened the pages of a book. There was the possibility of catching a glimpse of grandeur.

Of course, being a child, I forgot at once the name of the story, and the author's name as well, if I ever noticed it. It wasn't until years later, reading a collection of great science fiction stories, that I realized that "Call Me Joe" by Poul Anderson sounded familiar. Familiar! It was the long-lost story of my childhood, the one that taught me what it felt like to read and understand a great myth.

There was another story among those I read in stolen hours in the Santa Clara Public Library. By far the longest one I was able to finish. But it held me. It began with the image of people visiting a great concert hall. Then it flashed back and told the story of how that great concert hall came to be.

You see, there was a time when people had forgotten the joy of music. It only survived in commercial jingles, short songs designed to sell something. Except that there was one jingle-writer who had a special gift, an ability that transcended the limitations of his craft.

I won't tell you the story because you're about to read it. But I'll tell you that the story struck me more deeply than any other I had ever read till then. I identified with the hero— he was all my best hopes and dreams. His pains were mine; his achievements would be mine as well. I, as a child, was too young to truly understand some of the concepts in the story. Intellectually I grasped them, but I had no experience to make the idea come to life. Nevertheless, the story itself, the hero's discovery of who he was and what he could do, the response of others around him, and what his actions led to—ah, that was the path of a great man's life, I thought. Anyone can be great when following in paths that others praise. But when you achieve solitary greatness, when you bend an unbending world and turn it into a new path, not because the world wanted to turn, not because anyone asked you to turn it or helped you, but rather because you walked that path yourself and showed the way, and having seen it, they could not help but follow: that became my lifelong measure of the true hero.

Or perhaps it already *was* my measure, and it took that story to make me aware of it—does that matter? At the time, as an eight-year-old child unschooled in philosophy, I found the story overwhelming. It remade me. I saw everything through new eyes afterward.

Will it do the same for you? Oh, I doubt it—though I hope it will. But I've found—being older than eight—that no two people respond to stories the same way. Perhaps you'll merely find it entertaining; perhaps literarily or historically interesting. Or perhaps you'll be moved by it, changed for having read it. Maybe even moved as much as I was—but not more. You could not be more changed than I was then, if only because you aren't as young and unformed as I was then, reading this story like forbidden fruit in the garden of literature.

Time passed. I read other books. I moved to another state. In Mesa, Arizona, the junior high library had books better suited to a youngster: Andre Norton's *Galactic Derelict* and *The Time Traders*; Robert Heinlein's *Citizen of the Galaxy* and *Tunnel in the Sky*; Nordhoff and Hall's *Mutiny on the Bounty*, *Men against the Sea*, and *Pitcairn's Island*. I discovered dozens, then hundreds of authors who could amuse me, teach me, touch me. I stopped thinking about those first stories I read as a little boy.

I grew up and learned to tell stories myself. First I was a playwright; then I turned to fiction, and when I did it was science fiction that I wrote, though I cared not overly much for science. It was the mythic story that I wanted to tell, though I couldn't remember when I had decided that. And it was in the genre of science fiction and fantasy that the mythic story could still be clearly, plainly told—I knew that, was deeply certain of it. I could not do with fiction what I knew I *had* to do, except in this realm of strangeness.

So I wrote science fiction, and eventually that came to be the mainsail of my writing career. And one day in the dealer's room in a science fiction convention I saw the name Groff Conklin on the spine of an old and weathered book and I remembered those old anthologies from my childhood, when I thought I had to sneak into the adult section in order to read. I stood there, my hands resting on the book, in reverie, trying to remember the stories that I had read, wondering if I might find them again and, if I did, whether I'd laugh at my childish taste.

I talked to the dealer, telling him the time period of the books I had read in the Santa Clara library. He showed me what he had; I scanned through the books. I couldn't remember title or author of the one story that meant most to me, but I remembered vaguely that it was the last story in the book. Or was it simply the last I read, because there was no point in reading any other? I couldn't remember even that.

Finally I struggled to tell him the tale, calling up more details with each one I spoke aloud. At last I had told him enough.

"That's 'The Tunesmith' you're looking for," he said. "By Lloyd Biggle, Jr."

Lloyd Biggle, Jr. Not one of the writers of that time who had made the transition into the seventies and eighties. His name was not a household word now, like Asimov, Clarke, Heinlein, or Bradbury, though all were his contemporaries. I felt a stab of regret; I also felt a tiny thrill of dread, because of course the same could happen to me. There's no guarantee, because your works have some following in one decade, that you'll still have an audience hungry for your stories in another. Let that be a lesson to you, I thought.

But it was a stupid lesson, and I refused to believe it. Because another thought came to mind. Lloyd Biggle, Jr. didn't become one of the rich and famous ones when science fiction became commercial in the seventies and eighties. He didn't have crowds of salesmen touting his works. He didn't have dumps of his novels near the checkout stand at every Waldenbooks in North America. But that had nothing to do with whether he had succeeded, whether his work had been worth doing, his tales worth telling. Because his story was alive in me. It had transformed me, though even then I did not yet understand how completely I had taken "The Tunesmith" into myself.

And I knew that if I could write a story that would illuminate some hitherto dark corner in someone's soul and live on in them forever, then it hardly mattered whether writing made me rich or kept me poor, put my name before the public or left me forgotten, for I would have bent the world's path a little. Just a little, yet all would be different from then on because I had done it.

Not every reader had to feel that way about my stories. Not even *many* readers. If only a few were transformed, then it would have been worth it. And some of those would go on to tell their own tales, carrying part of mine within them. It might never end.

The Tunesmith
by Lloyd Biggle, Jr.

Everyone calls it the Center. It has another name, a long one, that gets listed in government appropriations and has its derivation analyzed in encyclopedias, but no one uses it. From Bombay to Lima, from Spitsbergen to the mines of Antarctica, from the solitary outpost on Pluto to that on Mercury, it is—the Center. You can emerge from the rolling mists of the Amazon, or the cutting dry winds of the Sahara, or the lunar vacuum, elbow your way up to a bar, and begin, "When I was at the Center—" and every stranger within hearing will listen attentively.

It isn't possible to explain the Center, and it isn't necessary. From the babe in arms to the centenarian looking forward to retirement, everyone has been there, and plans to go again next year, and the year after that. It is the vacation land of the Solar System. It is square miles of undulating American Middle West farm land, transfigured by ingenious planning and relentless labor and incredible expense. It is a monumental summary of man's cultural heritage, and like a phoenix, it has emerged suddenly, inexplicably, at the end of the twenty-fourth century, from the corroded ashes of an appalling cultural decay.

The Center is colossal, spectacular, and magnificent. It is inspiring, edifying, and amazing. It is awesome, it is overpowering, it is—everything.

And though few of its visitors know about this, or care, it is also haunted.

You are standing in the observation gallery of the towering Bach Monument. Off to the left, on the slope of a hill, you see the tense spectators who crowd the Grecian Theater for Euripides. Sunlight plays on their brightly-colored clothing. They watch eagerly, delighted to see in person what millions are watching on visiscope.

Beyond the theater, the tree-lined Frank Lloyd Wright Boulevard curves into the distance, past the Dante Monument and the Michelangelo Institute. The twin towers of a facsimile of the Rheims Cathedral rise above the horizon. Directly below, you see the curious landscaping of an eighteenth-century French *jardin* and, nearby, the Molière Theater.

A hand clutches your sleeve, and you turn suddenly, irritably, and find yourself face-to-face with an old man.

The leathery face is scarred and wrinkled, the thin strands of hair glistening white. The hand on your arm is a gnarled claw. You stare, take in the slumping contortion of one crippled shoulder and the hideous scar of a missing ear, and back away in alarm.

The sunken eyes follow you. The hand extends in a sweeping gesture that embraces the far horizon, and you notice that the fingers are maimed or missing. The voice is a harsh cackle. "Like it?" he says and eyes you expectantly.

Startled, you mutter, "Why, yes. Of course."

He takes a step forward, and his eyes are eager, pleading. "I say, do you like it?"

In your perplexity you can do no more than nod as you turn away—but your nod brings a strange response. A strident laugh, an innocent, childish smile of pleasure, a triumphant shout. "I did it! I did it all!"

Or you stand in resplendent Plato Avenue, between the Wagnerian Theater, where the complete *Der Ring des Nibelungen* is performed daily, and the reconstruction of the sixteenth-century Globe Theatre, where Shakespearean drama is presented morning, afternoon and evening.

A hand paws at you. "Like it?"

If you respond with a torrent of ecstatic praise, the old man eyes you impatiently and only waits until you have finished to ask again, "I say, do you like it?"

But a smile and a nod is met with beaming pride, a gesture, a shout.

In the lobby of one of the thousand spacious hotels, in the waiting room of the remarkable library where a copy of any book you request is reproduced for you free of charge, in the eleventh balcony of Beethoven Hall, a ghost shuffles haltingly, clutches an arm, asks a question.

And shouts proudly, "I did it!"

Erlin Baque sensed her presence behind him, but he did not turn. Instead he leaned forward, his left hand tearing a rumbling bass figure from the multichord while his right hand fingered a solemn melody. With a lightning flip of his hand he touched a button, and thin treble tones were suddenly fuller, more resonant, almost clarinet-like ("But God, how preposterously unlike a clarinet!" he thought.)

"Must we go through all that again, Val?" he asked.

"The landlord was here this morning."

He hesitated, touched a button, touched several buttons, and wove weird harmonies out of the booming tones of a brass choir. (But what a feeble, distorted brass choir!)

"How long does he give us this time?"

"Two days. And the food synthesizer's broken down again."

"Good. Run down and buy some fresh meat."

"With what?"

Baque slammed his fists down and shouted above the shattering dissonance. "I will not rent a harmonizer. I will not turn my arranging over to hacks. If a Com goes out with my name on it, it's going to be composed. It may be idiotic, and it may be sickening, but it's going to be done right. It isn't much, God knows, but it's all I have left."

He turned slowly and glared at her, this pale, drooping, worn-out woman who'd been his wife for twenty-five years. Then he looked away, telling himself stubbornly that he was no more to be blamed than she. When sponsors paid the same rates for good Coms that they paid for hackwork . . .

"Is Hulsey coming today?" she asked.

"He told me he was coming."

"If we could get some money for the landlord—"

"And the food synthesizer. And a new visiscope. And new clothes. There's a limit to what can be done with one Com."

He heard her move away, heard the door open, and waited. It did not close. "Walter-

Walter called," she said. "You're the featured tunesmith on today's *Show Case*."

"So? There's no money in that."

"I thought you wouldn't want to watch, so I told Mrs. Rennik I'd watch with her."

"Sure. Go ahead. Have fun."

The door closed.

Baque got to his feet and stood looking down at his chaos-strewn worktable. Music paper, Com-lyric releases, pencils, sketches, and half-finished manuscripts were cluttered together in untidy heaps. Baque cleared a corner for himself and sat down wearily, stretching his long legs out under the table.

"Damn Hulsey," he muttered. "Damn sponsors. Damn visiscope. Damn Coms."

Compose something, he told himself. You're not a hack, like the other tunesmiths. You don't punch out silly tunes on a harmonizer's keyboard and let a machine complete them for you. You're a musician, not a melody monger. Write some music. Write a—a sonata, for multichord. Take the time now, and compose something.

His eyes fell on the first lines of a Com-lyric release. "If your flyer jerks and clowns, if it has its ups and downs—"

"Damn landlord," he muttered, reaching for a pencil.

The tiny wall clock tinkled the hour, and Baque leaned over to turn on the visiscope. A cherub-faced master of ceremonies smiled out at him ingratiatingly. "Walter-Walter again, ladies and gentlemen. It's Com time on to-day's *Show Case*. Thirty minutes of Commercials by one of today's most talented tunesmiths. Our Com spotlight is on—"

A noisy brass fanfare rang out, the tainted brass tones of a multichord.

"Erlin Baque!"

The multichord swung into an odd, dipsey melody Baque had done five years before, for Tamper Cheese, and a scattering of applause sounded in the background. A nasal soprano voice mouthed the words, and Baque groaned unhappily. "We age our cheese, and age it, age it, age it, age it, age it the old-fashioned way . . ."

Walter-Walter cavorted about the stage, moving in time with the melody, darting down into the audience to kiss some sedate housewife-on-a-holiday, and beaming at the howls of laughter.

The multichord sounded another fanfare, and Walter-Walter leaped back onto the stage, both arms extended over his head. "Now listen to this, all you beautiful people. Here's your Walter-Walter exclusive on Erlin Baque." He glanced secretively over his shoulder, tiptoed a few steps closer to the audience, placed his finger on his lips, and then called out loudly, "Once upon a time there was another composer named Baque, spelled B-A-C-H, but pronounced Baque. He was a real atomic propelled tunesmith, the boy with the go, according to them that know. He lived some five or six or seven hundred years ago, so we can't exactly say that that Baque and our Baque were Baque to Baque. But we don't have to go Baque to hear Baque. We like the Baque we've got. Are you with me?"

Cheers. Applause. Baque turned away, hands trembling, a choking disgust nauseating him.

"We start off our Coms by Baque with that little masterpiece Baque did for Foam Soap. Art work by Bruce Combs. Stop, look—and listen!"

Baque managed to turn off the visiscope just as the first bar of soap jet-propelled itself across the screen. He picked up the Com lyric again, and his mind began to shape the thread of a melody.

"If your flyer jerks and clowns, if it has its ups and downs, ups and downs, ups and downs, you need a WARING!"

He hummed softly to himself, sketching a musical line that swooped and jerked like an erratic flyer. Word painting, it was called, back when words and tones meant something. Back when the B-A-C-H Baque was underscoring such grandiose concepts as Heaven and Hell.

Baque worked slowly, now and then trying a harmonic progression at the multichord and rejecting it, straining his mind for some fluttering accompaniment pattern that would stimulate the sound of a flyer. But then—no. The Waring people wouldn't like that. They advertised that their flyers were noiseless.

Urgent-sounding door chimes shattered his concentration. He walked over to flip on the scanner, and Hulsey's pudgy face grinned out at him.

"Come on up," Baque told him. Hulsey nodded and disappeared.

Five minutes later he waddled through the door, sank into a chair that sagged dangerously under his bulky figure, plunked his briefcase onto the floor, and mopped his face. "Whew! Wish you'd get yourself a place lower down. Or into a building with modern conveniences. Elevators scare me to death!"

"I'm thinking of moving," Baque said.

"Good. It's about time."

"But it'll probably be somewhere higher up. The landlord has given me two days' notice."

Hulsey winced and shook his head sadly. "I see. Well, I won't keep you in suspense. Here's the check for the Sana-Soap Com."

Baque took the card, glanced at it, and scowled.

"You were behind in your guild dues," Hulsey said. "Have to deduct them, you know."

"Yes. I'd forgotten."

"I like to do business with Sana-Soap. Cash right on the line. Too many companies wait until the end of the month. Sana-Soap wants a couple of changes, but they paid anyway." He unsealed the briefcase and pulled out a folder. "You've got some sly bits in this one, Erlin my boy. They like it. Particularly this 'sudsy, sudsy, sudsy' thing in the bass. They kicked on the number of singers at first, but not after they heard it. Now right here they want a break for a straight announcement."

Baque nodded thoughtfully. "How about keeping the 'sudsy, sudsy' ostinato going as a background to the announcement?"

"Sounds good. That's a sly bit, that—what'd you call it?"

"Ostinato."

"Ah-yes. Wonder why the other tunesmiths don't work in bits like that."

"A harmonizer doesn't produce effects," Baque said dryly. "It just—harmonizes."

"You give them about thirty seconds of that 'sudsy' for background. They can cut it if they don't like it."

Baque nodded, scribbling a note on the manuscript.

"And the arrangement," Hulsey went on. "Sorry, Erlin, but we can't get a French horn player. You'll have to do something else with that part."

"No horn player? What's wrong with Rankin?"

"Blacklisted. The Performers' Guild nixed him permanently. He went out to the West Coast and played for nothing. Even paid his

122

own expenses. The guild can't tolerate that sort of thing."

"I remember," Baque said softly. "The Monuments of Art Society. He played a Mozart horn concerto for them. Their final concert, too. Wish I could have heard it, even if it was with multichord."

"He can play it all he wants to now, but he'll never get paid for playing again. You can work that horn part into the multichord line, or I might be able to get you a trumpet player. He could use a converter."

"It'll ruin the effect."

Hulsey chuckled. "Sounds the same to everyone but you, my boy. I can't tell the difference. We got your violins and a cello player. What more do you want?"

"Doesn't the London Guild have a horn player?"

"You want me to bring him over for one three-minute Com? Be reasonable, Erlin! Can I pick this up tomorrow?"

"Yes. I'll have it ready in the morning."

Hulsey reached for his briefcase, dropped it again, leaned forward scowling. "Erlin, I'm worried about you. I have twenty-seven tunesmiths in my agency. You're the best by far. Hell, you're the best in the world, and you make the least money of any of them. Your net last year was twenty-two hundred. None of the others netted less than eleven thousand."

"That isn't news to me," Baque said.

"This may be. You have as many accounts as any of them. Did you know that?"

Baque shook his head. "No, I didn't know that."

"You have as many accounts, but you don't make any money. Want to know why? Two reasons. You spend too much time on a Com, and you write it too well. Sponsors can use one of your Coms for months—or sometimes even years, like that Tamper Cheese thing. People like to hear them. Now if you just didn't write so damned well, you could work faster, and the sponsors would have to use more of your Coms, and you could turn out more."

"I've thought about that. Even if I didn't, Val would keep reminding me. But it's no use. That's the way I have to work. If there was some way to get the sponsors to pay more for a *good* Com—"

"There isn't. The guild wouldn't stand for it, because good Coms mean less work, and most tunesmiths couldn't write a really good Com. Now don't think I'm concerned about my agency. Of course I make more money when you make more, but I'm doing well enough with my other tunesmiths. I just hate to see my best man making so little money. You're a throwback, Erlin. You waste time and money collecting those antique—what do you call them?"

"Phonograph records."

"Yes. And those moldy old books about music. I don't doubt that you know more about music than anyone alive, and what does it get you? Not money, certainly. You're the best there is, and you keep trying to be better, and the better you get the less money you make. Your income drops lower every year. Couldn't you manage just an average Com now and then?"

"No," Baque said brusquely. "I couldn't manage it."

"Think it over."

"These accounts I have. Some of the sponsors really like my work. They'd pay more if the guild would let them. Supposing I left the guild?"

"You can't, my boy. I couldn't handle your stuff—not and stay in business long. The Tunesmiths' Guild would turn on the pressure, and the Performers' and Lyric Writers' Guilds would blacklist you. Jimmy Denton plays along with the guilds and he'd bar your stuff from visiscope. You'd lose all your accounts, and fast. No sponsor is big enough to fight all that trouble, and none of them would want to bother. So just try to be average now and then. Think about it."

Baque sat staring at the floor. "I'll think about it."

Hulsey struggled to his feet, clasped Baque's hand briefly, and waddled out. Baque closed the door behind him and went to the drawer where he kept his meager collection of old phonograph records. Strange and wonderful music.

Three times in his career Baque had written Coms that were a full half-hour in length. On rare occasions he got an order for fifteen minutes. Usually he was limited to five or less. But composers like the B-A-C-H Baque wrote things that lasted an hour or more—even wrote them without lyrics.

And they wrote for real instruments, among them amazing-sounding things that no one played anymore, like bassoons, piccolos, and pianos.

"Damn Denton. Damn visiscope. Damn guilds."

Baque rummaged tenderly among the discs until he found one bearing Bach's name. *Magnificat.* Then, because he felt too despondent to listen, he pushed it away.

Earlier that year the Performers' Guild had blacklisted its last oboe player. Now its last horn player, and there just weren't any young people learning to play instruments. Why should they, when there were so many marvelous contraptions that ground out the Coms without any effort on the part of the performer? Even multichord players were becoming scarce, and if one wasn't particular about how well it was done, a multichord could practically play itself.

THE TUNESMITH

The door jerked open, and Val hurried in.
"Did Hulsey—"

Baque handed her the check. She took it eagerly, glanced at it, and looked up in dismay.

"My guild dues," he said. "I was behind."

"Oh. Well, it's a help, anyway." Her voice was flat, emotionless, as though one more disappointment really didn't matter. They stood facing each other awkwardly.

"I watched part of *Morning with Marigold*," Val said. "She talked about your Coms."

"I should hear soon on that Slo-Smoke Com," Baque said. "Maybe we can hold the landlord off for another week. Right now I'm going to walk around a little."

"You should get out more—"

He closed the door behind him, slicing her sentence off neatly. He knew what followed. Get a job somewhere. It'd be good for your health to get out of the apartment a few hours a day. Write Coms in your spare time—they don't bring in more than a part-time income anyway. At least do it until we get caught up. All right, if you won't, I will.

But she never did. A prospective employer never wanted more than one look at her slight body and her worn, sullen face. And Baque doubted that he would receive any better treatment.

He could get work as a multichord player and make a good income—but if he did he'd have to join the Performers' Guild, which meant that he'd have to resign from the Tune-smiths' Guild. So the choice was between per-forming and composing, the guilds wouldn't let him do both.

"Damn the guilds! Damn Coms!"

When he reached the street, he stood for a moment watching the crowds shooting past on the swiftly moving conveyor. A few people glanced at him and saw a tall, gawky, balding man in a frayed, badly fitting suit. They would consider him just another derelict from a shabby neighborhood, he knew, and they would quickly look the other way while they hummed a snatch from one of his Coms.

He hunched up his shoulders and walked awkwardly along the stationary sidewalk. At a crowded restaurant he turned in, found a table at one side, and ordered beer. On the rear wall was an enormous visiscope screen where the Coms followed each other without interrup-tion. Around him the other customers watched and listened while they ate. Some nodded their heads jerkily in time with the music. A few young couples were dancing on the small dance floor, skillfully changing steps as the music shifted from one Com to another.

Baque watched them sadly and thought about the way things had changed. At one time, he knew, there had been special music for dancing and special groups of instruments to play it. And people had gone to concerts by the thousands, sitting in seats with nothing to look at but the performers.

All of it had vanished. Not only the music, but art and literature and poetry. The plays he once read in his grandfather's school books were forgotten.

James Denton's *Visiscope International* decreed that people must look and listen at the same time and that the public attention span wouldn't tolerate long programs. So there were Coms.

Damn Coms!

When Val returned to the apartment an hour later, Baque was sitting in the corner staring at the battered plastic cabinet that held the crumbling volumes he had collected from the day when books were still printed on paper—a scattering of biographies, books on music history, and technical books about music theory and composition. Val looked twice about the room before she noticed him, and then she confronted him anxiously, stark tragedy etching her wan face.

"The man's coming to fix the food synthesizer."

"Good," Baque said.

"But the landlord won't wait. If we don't pay him day after tomorrow—pay him everything—we're out."

"So we're out."

"Where will we go? We can't get in anywhere without paying something in advance."

"So we won't get in anywhere."

She fled sobbing into the bedroom.

The next morning Baque resigned from the Tunesmith's Guild and joined the Performers' Guild. Hulsey's round face drooped mournfully when he heard the news. He loaned Baque enough money to pay his guild registration fee and quiet the landlord, and he expressed his sorrow in eloquent terms as he hurried Baque out of his office. He would, Baque knew, waste no time in assigning Baque's clients to his other tunesmiths—to men who worked faster and not so well.

Baque went to the Guild Hall where he sat for five hours waiting for a multichord assignment. He was finally summoned to the secretary's office and brusquely motioned into a chair. The secretary eyed him suspiciously.

"You belonged to the Performers' Guild twenty years ago, and you left it to become a tunesmith. Right?"

"Right," Baque said.

"You lost your seniority after three years. You knew that, didn't you?"

"I did, but I didn't think it mattered. There aren't many good multichord players around."

"There aren't many good jobs around, either. You'll have to start at the bottom." He scribbled on a slip of paper and thrust it at Baque. "This one pays well, but we have a hard time keeping a man there. Lankey isn't easy to work for. If you don't irritate him too much—well, then we'll see."

Baque rode the conveyer out to the New Jersey Space Port, wandered through a rattletrap slum area getting his directions hopelessly confused, and finally found the place almost within radiation distance of the port. The sprawling building had burned at some time in the remote past. Stubby remnants of walls rose out of the weed-choked rubble. A walk curved toward a dimly lit cavity at one corner where steps led uncertainly downward. Overhead, an enormous sign pointed its flowing colors in the direction of the port. The LANKEY-PANK OUT.

Baque stepped through the door and faltered at the onslaught of extraterrestrial odors. Lavender-tinted tobacco smoke, the product of the enormous leaves grown in botdomes in the Lunar Mare Crisium, hung like a limp blanket midway between floor and ceiling. The revolting, cutting fumes of *blast*, a whisky blended with a product of Martian lichens, staggered him. He had a glimpse of a scattered gathering of tough spacers and tougher prostitutes before the doorman planted his bulky figure and scarred caricature of a face in front of him.

"You looking for someone?"

"Mr. Lankey."

The doorman jerked a thumb in the direction of the bar and noisily stumbled back into the shadows. Baque walked toward the bar.

He had no trouble in picking out Lankey. The proprietor sat on a tall stool behind the bar. In the dim, smoke-streaked light his taut pale face had a spectral grimness. He leaned an elbow on the bar, fingered his flattened stump of a nose with the two remaining fingers on his hairy hand, and as Baque approached he thrust his bald head forward and eyed him coldly.

"I'm Erlin Baque," Baque said.

"Yeah. The multichord player. Can you play that multichord, fellow?"

"Why, yes, I can play—"

"That's what they all say, and I've had maybe two in the last ten years that could really play. Most of them come out here figuring they'll set the thing on automatic and fuss around with one finger. I want that multichord *played*, fellow, and I'll tell you right now—if you can't play you might as well jet for home. There isn't any automatic on my multichord. I had it disconnected."

"I can play," Baque told him.

"All right. It doesn't take more than one Com to find out. The guild rates this place as Class Four, but I pay Class One rates if you can play. If you can really play, I'll slip you some bonuses the guild won't know about. Hours are six P.M. to six A.M., but you get plenty of breaks, and if you get hungry or

132

thirsty just ask for what you want. Only go easy on the hot stuff. I won't go along with a drunk multichord player no matter how good he is. Rose!"

He bellowed the name a second time, and a woman stepped from a door at the side of the room. She wore a faded dressing gown, and her tangled hair hung untidily about her shoulders. She turned a small, pretty face toward Baque and studied him boldly.

"Multichord," Lankey said. "Show him."

Rose beckoned, and Baque followed her toward the rear of the room. Suddenly, he halted in amazement.

"What's the matter?" Rose asked.

"No visiscope!"

"No. Lankey says the spacers want better things to look at than soapsuds and flyers." She giggled. "Something like me, for example."

"I never heard of a restaurant without visiscope."

"Neither did I until I came here. But Lankey's got three of us to sing the Coms, and you're to do the multichord with us. I hope you make the grade. We haven't had a multichord player for a week, and it's hard singing without one."

"I'll make out all right," Baque said.

A narrow platform stretched across the end of the room where any other restaurant would have had its visiscope screen. Baque could see the unpatched scars in the wall where the screen had been torn out."

"Lankey ran a joint at Port Mars back when the colony didn't have visiscope," Rose said. "He has his own ideas about how to entertain customers. Want to see your room?"

Baque was examining the multichord. It was a battered old instrument, and it bore the marks of more than one brawl. He fingered the filter buttons and swore softly to himself. Only the flute and violin filters clicked into place properly. So he would have to spend twelve hours a day with the twanging tones of an unfiltered multichord.

"Want to see your room?" Rose asked again. "It's only five. You might as well relax until we have to go to work."

Rose showed him a cramped enclosure behind the bar. He stretched out on a hard cot and tried to relax, and suddenly it was six o'clock and Lankey stood in the door beckoning to him.

He took his place at the multichord and fingered the keys impatiently. He felt no nervousness. There wasn't anything he didn't know about Coms, and he knew he wouldn't have trouble with the music, but the atmosphere disturbed him. The haze of smoke was thicker, and he blinked his smarting eyes and felt the whiskey fumes tear at his nostrils when he took a deep breath.

There was still only a scattering of customers. The men were mechanics in grimy work suits, swaggering pilots, and a few civilians who liked their liquor strong and didn't mind the surroundings. The women were—women; two of them, he guessed, for every man in the room.

Suddenly the men began an unrestrained stomping of feet accented with yelps of approval. Lankey was crossing the platform with Rose and the other singers. Baque's first horrified impression was that the girls were nude, but as they came closer he made out their brief plastic costumes. Lankey was right, he thought. The spacers would much prefer that kind of scenery to animated Coms on a visiscope screen.

"You met Rose," Lankey said. "This is Zanna and Mae. Let's get going."

He walked away, and the girls gathered about the multichord. "What Coms do you know?" Rose asked.

"I know them all."

She looked at him doubtfully. "We sing together, and then we take turns. Are you sure you know them all?"

Baque flipped on the power and sounded a chord. "Sing any Com you want—I can handle it."

"Well—we'll start out with a Tasty-Malt Com. It goes like this." She hummed softly. "Know that one?"

"I wrote it," Baque said.

They sang better than he had expected. He followed them easily, and while he played he kept his eyes on the customers. Heads were jerking in time with the music, and he quickly caught the mood and began to experiment. His fingers shaped a rolling rhythm in the bass, fumbled with it tentatively, and then expanded it. He abandoned the melodic line, leaving the girls to carry on by themselves while he searched the entire keyboard to ornament the driving rhythm.

Feet began to stomp. The girls' bodies were swaying wildly, and Baque felt himself rocking back and forth as the music swept on recklessly. The girls finished their lyrics, and when he did not stop playing they began again. Spacers were on their feet, now, clapping and swaying. Some seized their women and began dancing in the narrow spaces between the tables. Finally Baque forced a cadence and slumped forward, panting and mopping his forehead. One of the girls collapsed onto the stage. The others hauled her to her feet, and the three of them fled to a frenzy of applause.

Baque felt a hand on his shoulder. Lankey. His ugly, expressionless face eyed Baque, turned to study the wildly enthusiastic customers, turned back to Baque. He nodded and walked away.

Rose returned alone, still breathing heavily. "How about a Sally Ann Perfume Com?"

THE TUNESMITH

Baque searched his memory and was chagrined to find no recollection of Sally Ann's Coms. "Tell me the words," he said. She recited them tonelessly—a tragic little story about the shattered romance of a girl who did not use Sally Ann. "Now I remember," Baque told her. "Shall we make them cry? Just concentrate on that. It's a sad story, and we're going to make them cry."

She stood by the multichord and sang plaintively. Baque fashioned a muted, tremulous accompaniment, and when the second verse started he improvised a drooping countermelody. The spacers sat in hushed suspense. The men did not cry, but some of the women sniffed audibly, and when Rose finished there was a taut silence.

"Quick!" Baque hissed. "Let's brighten things up. Sing another Com—anything!"

She launched into a Puffed Bread Com, and Baque brought the spacers to their feet with the driving rhythm of his accompaniment.

The other girls took their turns, and Baque watched the customers detachedly, bewildered at the power that surged in his fingers. He carried them from one emotional extreme to the other and back again, improvising, experimenting. And his mind fumbled haltingly with an idea.

"Time for a break," Rose said finally. "Better get something to eat."

An hour and a half of continuous playing

had left Baque drained of strength and emotion, and he accepted his dinner tray indifferently and took it to the enclosure they called his room. He did not feel hungry. He sniffed doubtfully at the food, tasted it—and ate ravenously. Real food, after months of synthetics!

When he'd finished he sat for a time on his cot, wondering how long the girls took between appearances, and then he went looking for Lankey.

"I don't like sitting around," he said. "Any objection to my playing?"

"Without the girls?"

"Yes."

Lankey planted both elbows on the bar, cupped his chin in one fist, and sat looking absently at the far wall. "You going to sing yourself?" he asked finally.

"No. Just play."

"Without any singing? Without words?"

"Yes."

"What'll you play?"

"Coms. Or I might improvise something."

A long silence. Then—"Think you could keep things moving while the girls are out?"

"Of course I could."

Lankey continued to concentrate on the far wall. His eyebrows contracted, relaxed, contracted again. "All right," he said. "I was just wondering why I never thought of it."

Unnoticed, Baque took his place at the multichord. He began softly, making the music an unobtrusive background to the rollicking conversation that filled the room. As he increased the volume, faces turned in his direction.

He wondered what these people were thinking as they heard for the first time music that was not a Com, music without words. He watched intently and satisfied himself that he was holding their attention. Now—could he bring them out of their seats with nothing more than the sterile tones of a multichord? He gave the melody a rhythmic snap, and the stomping began.

As he increased the volume again, Rose came stumbling out of a doorway and hurried across the stage, perplexity written on her pert face.

"It's all right," Baque told her. "I'm just playing to amuse myself. Don't come back until you're ready."

She nodded and walked away. A red-faced spacer near the platform looked up at the revealed outline of her young body and leered. Fascinated, Baque studied the coarse, demanding lust in his face and searched the keyboard to express it. This? Or—this? Or—

He had it. He felt himself caught up in the relentless rhythm. His foot tightened on the volume control, and he turned to watch the customers.

Every pair of eyes stared hypnotically at his corner of the room. A bartender stood at a half crouch, mouth agape. There was uneasiness, a strained shuffling of feet, a restless scraping of chairs. Baque's foot dug harder at the volume control.

His hands played on hypnotically, and he stared in horror at the scene that erupted below him. Lasciviousness twisted every face. Men were on their feet, reaching for the women, clutching, pawing. A chair crashed to the floor, and a table, and no one noticed. A woman's dress fluttered crazily downward, and the pursued were pursuers while Baque helplessly allowed his fingers to race onward, out of control.

With a violent effort he wrenched his hands from the keys and the ensuing silence crashed the room like a clap of thunder. Fingers trembling, Baque began to play softly, indifferently. Order had been restored when he looked again, the chair and table were upright, and the customers were seated in apparent relaxation except for one woman who struggled back into her dress in obvious embarrassment.

Baque continued to play quietly until the girls returned.

At 6 A.M., his body wracked with weariness, his hands aching, his legs cramped, Baque climbed down from the multichord. Lankey stood waiting for him. "Class One rates," he said. "You've got a job with me as long as you

140

want it. But take it a little easy with that stuff, will you?"

Baque remembered Val, alone in their dreary apartment and eating synthetic food. "Would I be out of order to ask for an advance?"

"No," Lankey said. "Not out of order. I told the cashier to give you a hundred on your way out. Call it a bonus."

Weary from his long conveyer ride, Baque walked quietly into his dim apartment and looked about. There was no sign of Val—she would still be sleeping. He sat down at his own multichord and touched the keys.

He felt awed and humbled and disbelieving. Music without Coms, without words, could make people laugh and cry, and dance and cavort madly.

And it could turn them into lewd animals.

Wonderingly he played the music that had incited such unconcealed lust, played it louder and louder—

And felt a hand on his shoulder, and turned to look into Val's passion-twisted face.

He asked Hulsey to come and hear him that night, and later Hulsey sat slumped on the cot in his room and shuddered. "It isn't right. No man should have that power over people. How do you do it?"

"I don't know," Baque said, "I saw that young couple sitting there, and they were happy, and I felt their happiness. And as I played everyone in the room was happy. And then another couple came in quarreling, and the next thing I knew I had everyone mad."

"Almost started a fight at the next table," Hulsey said. "And what you did after that—"

"Yes. But not as much as I did last night. You should have seen it last night."

Hulsey shuddered again.

"I have a book about ancient Greek music," Baque said. "They had something they called *ethos*. They thought that the different musical scales affected people in different ways— could make them sad, or happy, or even drive them crazy. They claimed that a musician named Orpheus could move trees and soften rocks with his music. Now listen. I've had a chance to experiment, and I've noticed that my playing is most effective when I don't use the filters. There are only two filters that work on that multichord anyway—flute and violin—but when I use either of them the people don't react so strongly. I'm wondering if maybe the effects the Greeks talk about were produced by their instruments rather than their scales. I'm wondering if the tone of an unfiltered multichord might have something in common with the tones of the ancient Greek *kithara* or *aulos*."

Hulsey grunted. "I don't think it's the instrument, or the scales either. I think it's Baque, and I don't like it. You should have stayed a tunesmith."

"I want you to help me," Baque said. "I want to find a place where we can put a lot of people—a thousand, at least—not to eat, or watch Coms, but just to listen to one man play on a multichord."

Hulsey got up abruptly. "Baque, you're a dangerous man. I'm damned if I'll trust any man who can make me feel the way you made me feel tonight. I don't know what you're trying to do, but I won't have any part of it."

He stomped away in the manner of a man about to slam a door, but the room of a male multichordist at the Lankey-Pank Out did not rate that luxury. Hulsey paused uncertainly in the doorway, gave Baque a parting glare, and disappeared. Baque followed him as far as the main room and stood watching him weave his way impatiently past the tables to the exit.

From his place behind the bar, Lankey looked at Baque and then glanced after the disappearing Hulsey. "Troubles?" he asked.

Baque turned away wearily. "I've known that man for twenty years. I never thought he was my friend. But then—I never thought he was my enemy, either."

"Sometimes it works out that way," Lankey said.

Baque shook his head. "I'd like to try some Martian whisky. I've never tasted the stuff."

Two weeks made Baque an institution, and the Lankey-Pank Out was jammed to capacity from the time he went to work until he left the next morning. When he performed alone, he forgot about Coms and played whatever he wanted. He even performed short pieces by Bach for the customers, and received generous applause, but the reaction was nothing like the tumultuous enthusiasm that followed his improvisations.

Sitting behind the bar, eating his evening meal and watching the impacted mass of customers, Baque felt vaguely happy. He was enjoying the work he was doing. For the first time in his life he had more money than he needed.

For the first time in his life he had a definite goal and a vague notion of a plan that would accomplish it—would eliminate the Coms altogether.

As Baque pushed his tray aside, he saw Biff the doorman step forward to greet a pair of newcomers, halt suddenly, and back away in stupefied amazement. And no wonder—evening clothes at the Lankey-Pank Out!

The couple halted near the door, blinking uncertainly in the dim, smoke-tinted light. The man was bronzed and handsome, but no one noticed him. The woman's beauty flashed like a meteor against the drab surroundings. She moved in an aura of shining loveliness, with her hair gleaming golden, her shimmering, flowing gown clinging seductively to her voluptuous figure, and her fragrance routing the foul tobacco and whisky odors.

In an instant all eyes were fixed on her, and a collective gasp encircled the room. Baque stared with the others and finally recognized her: Marigold, of *Morning with Marigold*. Worshiped around the Solar System by the millions of devotees to her visiscope program. Mistress, it was said, to James Denton, the czar of visiscope. Marigold Manning.

She raised a hand to her mouth in mock horror, and the bright tones of her laughter dropped tantalizingly among the spellbound spacers. "What an odd place! Where'd you ever hear about a place like this?"

"I need some Martian whisky, damn it," the man said.

"So stupid of the port bar to run out. With all those ships from Mars coming in, too. Are you sure we can get back in time? Jimmy'll raise hell if we aren't there when he lands."

Lankey touched Baque's arm. "After six," he said, without taking his eyes from Marigold Manning. "They'll be getting impatient."

Baque nodded and started for the multichord. The tumult began the moment the customers saw him. They abandoned Marigold Manning, leaped to their feet, and began a stomping, howling ovation. When Baque paused to acknowledge it, Marigold and her escort were staring openmouthed at the nondescript man who could inspire such undignified enthusiasm.

Her exclamation rang out sharply as Baque seated himself at the multichord and the ovation faded to an expectant silence. "What the hell!"

Baque shrugged and started to play. When Marigold finally left, after a brief conference with Lankey, her escort still hadn't got his Martian whisky.

The next evening Lankey greeted Baque with both fists full of telenotes. "What a hell of a mess this is! You see this Marigold dame's program this morning?"

Baque shook his head. "I haven't watched visiscope since I came to work here."

"In case it interests you, you were—what does she call it?—a 'Marigold Exclusive' on visiscope this morning. Erlin Baque, the famous tunesmith, is now playing the multichord in a queer little restaurant called the Lankey-Pank Out. If you want to hear some amazing music, wander out to the New Jersey Space Port and listen to Baque. Don't miss it. The experience of a lifetime." Lankey swore and waved the telenotes. "Queer, she calls us. Now I've got ten thousand requests for reservations, some from as far away as Budapest and Shanghai. And our capacity is five hundred, counting standing room. Damn that woman! We already had all the business we could handle."

"You need a bigger place," Baque said.

"Yes. Well, confidentially, I've got my eye on a big warehouse. It'll seat a thousand, at least. We'll clean up. I'll give you a contract to take charge of the music."

Baque shook his head. "How about opening a big place uptown? Attract people that have more money to spend. You run it, and I'll bring in the customers."

Lankey caressed his flattened nose thoughtfully. "How do we split?"

"Fifty-fifty," Baque said.

"No," Lankey said, shaking his head slowly. "I play fair, Baque, but fifty-fifty wouldn't be right on a deal like that. I'd have to put up all the money myself. I'll give you one-third to handle the music."

They had a lawyer draw up a contract. Baque's lawyer. Lankey insisted on that.

In the bleak gray of early morning Baque sleepily rode the crowded conveyer toward his apartment. It was the peak rush load, when commuters jammed against each other and snarled grumpily when a neighbor shifted his feet. The crowd seemed even heavier than usual, but Baque shrugged off the jostling and elbowing and lost himself in thought.

It was time that he found a better place to live. He hadn't minded the dumpy apartment as long as he could afford nothing better, but Val had been complaining for years. And now when they could move, when they could have a luxury apartment or even a small home over in Pennsylvania, Val refused to go. Didn't want to leave her friends, she said.

Mulling over this problem in feminine contrariness, Baque realized suddenly that he was approaching his own stop. He attempted to move toward a deceleration strip—he shoved firmly, he tried to step between his fellow riders, he applied his elbows, first gently and then viciously. The crowd about him did not yield.

"I beg your pardon," Baque said, making another attempt. "I get off here."

This time a pair of brawny arms barred his way. "Not this morning, Baque. You got an appointment uptown."

Baque flung a glance at the circle of hard, grinning faces that surrounded him. With a sudden effort he hurled himself sideways, fighting with all of his strength. The arms hauled him back roughly.

"Uptown, Baque. If you want to go dead, that's your affair."

"Uptown," Baque agreed.

At a public parking strip they left the conveyer. A flyer was waiting for them, a plush, private job that displayed a high-priority X registration number. They flew swiftly toward Manhattan, cutting across air lanes with a monumental contempt for regulations, and they veered in for a landing on the towering

THE TUNESMITH

Visiscope International building. Baque was bundled down an anti-grav shaft, led through a labyrinth of corridors, and finally prodded none too gently into an office.

It was a huge room, and its sparse furnishings made it look more enormous than it was. It contained only a desk, a few chairs, a bar in the far corner, an enormous visiscope screen—and a multichord. The desk was occupied, but it was the group of men about the bar that caught Baque's attention. His gaze swept the blur of faces and found one that he recognized: Hulsey.

The plump agent took two steps forward and stood glaring at Baque. "Day of reckoning, Erlin," he said coldly.

A hand rapped sharply on the desk. "I take care of any reckoning that's done around here, Hulsey. Please sit down, Mr. Baque."

A chair was thrust forward, and Baque seated himself and waited nervously, his eyes on the man behind the desk.

"My name is James Denton. Does my fame extend to such a remote place as the Lankey-Pank Out?"

"No," Baque said. "But I've heard of you."

James Denton. Czar of Visiscope International. Ruthless arbiter of public taste. He was no more than forty, with a swarthy, handsome face, flashing eyes, and a ready smile.

He tapped a cigar on the edge of his desk and carefully placed it in his mouth. Men sprang forward with lighters extended, and he chose one without looking up, puffed deeply, and nodded.

"I won't bore you with introductions to this gathering, Baque. Some of these men are here for professional reasons. Some are here because they're curious. I heard about you for the first time yesterday, and what I heard made me want to find out whether you're a potential asset that might be made use of, or a potential nuisance that should be eliminated, or a nonentity that can be ignored. When I want to know something, Baque, I waste no time about it." He chuckled. "As you can see from the fact that I had you brought in at the earliest moment you were—shall we say—available."

"The man's dangerous, Denton!" Hulsey blurted.

Denton flashed his smile. "I like dangerous men, Hulsey. They're useful to have around. If I can use whatever it is Mr. Baque has, I'll make him an attractive offer. I'm sure he'll accept it gratefully. If I can't use it, I aim to make damned certain that he won't be inconveniencing me. Do I make myself clear, Baque?"

Baque, looking past Denton to avoid his eyes, said nothing.

Denton leaned forward. His smile did not waver, but his eyes narrowed and his voice was suddenly icy. "Do I make myself clear, Baque?"

THE TUNESMITH

"Yes," Baque muttered weakly.

Denton jerked a thumb toward the door, and half of those present, including Hulsey, solemnly filed out. The others waited, talking in whispers, while Denton puffed steadily on his cigar. Finally an intercom rasped a single word. "Ready!"

Denton pointed at the multichord. "We crave a demonstration of your skill, Mr. Baque. And take care that it's a good demonstration. Hulsey is listening, and he can tell us if you try to stall."

Baque nodded, and took his place at the multichord. He sat with fingers poised, timidly looking up at a circle of staring faces. Overlords of business, they were, and of science and industry, and never in their lives had they heard real music. As for Hulsey—yes, Hulsey would be listening, but over Denton's intercom, over a communication system designed to carry voices.

And Hulsey had a terrible ear for music.

Baque grinned contemptuously, touched the violin filter, touched it again, and faltered.

Denton chuckled dryly. "I neglected to inform you, Mr. Baque. On Hulsey's advice, we've had the filters disconnected."

Anger surged within Baque. He jammed his foot down hard on the volume control, insolently tapped out a visiscope fanfare, and started to play his Tamper Cheese Com. Denton, his own anger evident in his flushed face,

151

leaned forward and snarled something. The men around him stirred uneasily. Baque shifted to another Com, improvised some variations, and began to watch the circle of faces. Overlords of industry, science, and business. It would be amusing, he thought, to make them stomp their feet. His fingers shaped a compelling rhythm, and they began to sway restlessly.

He forgot his resolution to play cautiously. Laughing silently to himself, he released an overpowering torrent of sound that set the men dancing and brought Denton to his feet. He froze them in ridiculous postures with an outburst of surging emotion. He made them stomp recklessly, he brought tears to their eyes, and he finished off with the pounding force that Lankey called, "Sex Music."

Then he slumped over the keyboard, terrified at what he had done.

Denton stood behind his desk, face pale, hands clenching and unclenching. "Good God!" he muttered.

He snarled a word at his intercom. "Reaction?"

"Negative," came the prompt answer.

"Let's wind it up."

Denton sat down, passed his hand across his face, and turned to Baque with a bland smile. "An impressive performance, Mr. Baque. We'll know in a few minutes—ah, here they are."

THE TUNESMITH

Those who had left earlier filed back into the room, and several men huddled together in a whispered conference. Denton left his desk and paced the floor meditatively. The other men in the room, including Hulsey, gravitated toward the bar.

Baque kept his place at the multichord and watched the conference uneasily. Once he accidently touched a key, and the single tone shattered the poise of the conferees, halted Denton in midstride, and startled Hulsey into spilling his drink.

"Mr. Baque is getting impatient," Denton called. "Can't we finish this?"

"One moment, sir."

Finally they filed toward Denton's desk. The spokesman, a white-haired, scholarly-looking man with a delicate pink complexion, cleared his throat self-consciously and waited until Denton had returned to his chair.

"It is established," he said, "that those in this room were powerfully affected by the music. Those listening on the intercom experienced no reaction except a mild boredom."

"I didn't call you in here to state the obvious," Denton snapped. "How does he do it?"

"We can only offer a working hypothesis."

"So you're guessing. Let's have it."

"Erlin Baque has the ability to telepathetically project his emotional experience. When the projection is subtly reinforced by his multichord playing, those in his immediate presence share that experience intensely. The projection has no effect upon those listening to his music at a distance."

"And—visiscope?"

"He could not project his emotions by way of visiscope."

"I see," Denton said. A meditative scowl twisted his face. "What about his long-term effectiveness?"

"It's difficult to predict—"

"Predict, damn it!"

"The novelty of his playing would attract attention, at first. While the novelty lasted he might become a kind of fad. By the time his public lost interest he would probably have a small group of followers who would use the emotional experience of his playing as a narcotic."

"Thank you, gentlemen. That will be all."

The room emptied quickly. Hulsey paused in the doorway, glared hatefully at Baque, and then walked out meekly.

"Obviously you're no nonentity," Denton said, "but whatever it is you have is of no use to me. Unfortunately. If you could project on visiscope, you'd be worth a billion an hour in advertising revenue. Fortunately for you, your nuisance rating is fairly low. I know what you and Lankey are up to. If I say the word, you'll never in this lifetime find a place for your new restaurant. I could have the Lankey-Pank Out closed down within an hour, but it would hardly be worth the trouble. If you can develop a cult for yourself, why—perhaps it will keep the members out of worse mischief. I'm feeling so generous this morning that I won't even insist on a visiscope screen in your new restaurant. Now you'd better leave, Baque, before I change my mind."

Baque got to his feet. At that moment Marigold Manning swept into the room, radiantly lovely, exotically perfumed, her glistening blonde hair swept up into a new and tantalizing hairstyle.

"Jimmy, darling—oh!" She stared at Baque, stared at the multichord, and stammered, "Why, you're—you're—Erlin Baque! Jimmy, why didn't you tell me?"

"Mr. Baque has been favoring me with a private performance," Denton said brusquely. "I think we understand each other, Baque. Good morning."

"You're going to put him on visiscope?" Marigold exclaimed. "Jimmy, that's wonderful. May I have him first? I can work him in this morning."

Denton shook his head. "Sorry, darling. We've decided that Mr. Baque's talent is not quite suitable for visiscope."

"At least I can have him for a guest. You'll be my guest, won't you, Mr. Baque? There's nothing wrong with giving him a guest spot, is there, Jimmy?"

Denton chuckled. "No. After all the fuss you

stirred up, it might be a good idea for you to guest him. It'll serve you right when he bombs."

"He won't bomb. He'll be wonderful on visiscope. Will you come in this morning, Mr. Baque?"

"Well—" Baque began. Denton was nodding at him emphatically. "We'll be opening a new restaurant soon. I wouldn't mind being your guest on opening day."

"A new restaurant? That's wonderful! Does anyone know? I'll give it out this morning as an exclusive!"

"It isn't exactly settled, yet," Baque said apologetically. "We haven't found a place yet."

"Lankey found a place yesterday," Denton said. "He's having a contractor check it over this morning, and if no snags develop he'll sign a lease. Just let Miss Manning know your opening date, Baque, and she'll arrange a spot for you. Now if you don't mind—"

It took Baque half an hour to find his way out of the building, but he plodded aimlessly along the corridors and disdained asking directions. He hummed happily to himself, and now and then he broke into a laugh.

The overlords of business and industry—and their scientists—knew nothing about overtones.

"So that's the way it is," Lankey said. "You seem to have no notion of how lucky you were—how lucky we were. Denton should have made his move when he had a chance. Now we know what to expect, and when he finally wises up it'll be too late."

"What could we do if he decided to put us out of business?"

"I have a few connections myself, Baque. They don't run in high society, like Denton, but they're every bit as dishonest, and Denton has a lot of enemies who'll be happy to back us. Said he could close me down in an hour, eh? Unfortunately there's not much we could do that would hurt Denton, but there's plenty we can do to keep him from hurting us."

"I think we're going to hurt Denton," Baque said.

Lankey moved over to the bar and came back with a tall glass of pink, foaming liquid. "Drink it," he said. "You've had a long day, and you're getting delirious. How could we hurt Denton?"

"Visiscope depends on Coms. We'll show the people they can have entertainment without Coms. We'll make our motto *NO COMS AT LANKEY'S!*"

"Great," Lankey drawled. "I invest a thousand in fancy new costumes for the girls— they can't wear those plastic things in our new place, you know—and you decide not to let them sing."

"Certainly they're going to sing."

Lankey leaned forward, caressing his nose. "And no Coms. Then *what* are they going to sing?"

"I took some lyrics out of an old schoolbook my grandfather had. Back in those days they were called poems. I'm setting them to music. I was going to try them out here, but Denton might hear about it, and there's no use starting trouble before it's necessary."

"No. Save all the trouble for the new place—after opening day we'll be important enough to be able to handle it. And you'll be on *Morning with Marigold*. Are you certain about this overtones business, Baque? You really could be projecting emotions, you know. Not that it makes any difference in the restaurant, but on visiscope—"

"I'm certain. How soon can we open?"

"I got three shifts remodeling the place. We'll seat twelve hundred and still have room for a nice dance floor. Should be ready in two weeks. Baque, I'm not sure this visiscope thing is wise."

"I want to do it."

Lankey went back to the bar and got a drink for himself. "All right. You do it. If your stuff comes over, all hell is going to break loose, and I might as well start getting ready for it." He grinned. "Damned if it won't be good for business!"

* * *

THE TUNESMITH

Marigold Manning had changed her hair-styling to a spiraled creation by Zann of Hong Kong, and she dallied for ten minutes in deciding which profile she would present to the cameras. Baque waited patiently, his awkward feeling wholly derived from the fact that his dress suit was the most expensive clothing he had ever owned. He kept telling himself to stop wondering if perhaps he really did project emotions.

"I'll have it this way," Marigold said finally, waving a hand screen in front of her face for a last, searching look. "And you, Mr. Baque? What shall we do with you?"

"Just put me at the multichord," Baque said.

"But you can't just play. You'll have to say *something*. I've been announcing this every day for a week, and we'll have the biggest audience in years, and you'll just *have* to say *something*."

"Gladly," Baque said, "if I can talk about Lankey's."

"But of course, you silly man. That's why you're here. You talk about Lankey's, and I'll talk about Erlin Baque."

"Five minutes," a voice announced crisply.

"Oh, dear," she said. "I'm always so nervous just before."

"Be happy you're not nervous during," Baque said.

"That's so right. Jimmy makes fun of me,

but it takes an artist to understand another artist. Do you get nervous?"

"When I'm playing, I'm much too busy."

"That's just the way it is with me. Once my program starts, I'm much too busy."

"Four minutes."

"Oh, bother!" She seized the hand screen again. "Maybe I would be better the other way."

Baque seated himself at the multichord. "You're perfect the way you are."

"Do you really think so? It's a nice thing to say, anyway. I wonder if Jimmy will take the time to watch."

"I'm sure he will."

"Three minutes."

Baque switched on the power and sounded a chord. Now he *was* nervous. He had no idea what he would play. He'd intentionally refrained from preparing anything because it was his improvisations that affected people so strangely. The one thing he had to avoid was the Sex Music. Lankey had been emphatic about that.

He lost himself in thought, failed to hear the final warning, and looked up startled at Marigold's cheerful, "Good morning, everyone. It's *Morning with Marigold*!"

Her bright voice wandered on and on. Erlin Baque. His career as a tunesmith. Her amazing discovery of him playing in the Lankey-Pank Out. She asked the engineers to run the

Tamper Cheese Com. Finally she finished her remarks and risked the distortion of her lovely profile to glance in his direction. "Ladies and gentlemen, with admiration, with pride, with pleasure, I give you a Marigold Exclusive, Erlin Baque!"

Baque grinned nervously and tapped out a scale with one finger. "This is my first speech. Probably it'll be my last. The new restaurant opens tonight. Lankey's, on Broadway. Unfortunately, I can't invite you to join us, because thanks to Miss Manning's generous comments this past week all space is reserved for the next two months. After that we'll be setting aside a limited number of reservations for visitors from distant places. Jet over and see us!

"You'll find something different at Lankey's. There is no visiscope screen. Maybe you've heard about that. We have attractive young ladies to sing for you. I play the multichord. We know you'll enjoy our music. We know you'll enjoy it because you'll hear no Coms at Lankey's. Remember that—*no Coms at Lankey's*. No soap with your soup. No air cars with your steaks. No shirts with your deserts. *No Coms!* Just good food, with good music played exclusively for your enjoyment—like this."

He brought his hands down onto the keyboard.

Immediately he knew that something was wrong. He'd always had a throng of faces to watch, he'd paced his playing according to their reactions. Now he had only Miss Manning and the visiscope engineers, and he was suddenly apprehensive that his success had been wholly due to his audiences. People were listening throughout the Western Hemisphere. Would they clap and stomp, would they think awesomely, "So that's how music sounds without words, without Coms?" Or would they turn away in boredom?

Baque caught a glimpse of Marigold's pale face, of the engineers watching with mouths agape, and thought perhaps everything was all right. He lost himself in the music and played fervently.

He continued to play even after the pilot screen went blank. Miss Manning leaped to her feet and hurried toward him, and the engineers were moving about confusedly. Finally Baque brought his playing to a halt.

"We were cut off," Miss Manning said tearfully. "Who would do such a thing to me? Never, never, in all the time I've been on visiscope—George, who cut us off?"

"Orders."

"Whose orders?"

"My orders!" James Denton strode toward them, lips tight, face pale, eyes gleaming violence and sudden death. He spat words at Baque. "I don't know how you worked that trick, but no man fools James Denton more than once. Now you've made yourself a nuisance that has to be eliminated."

"Jimmy!" Miss Manning wailed. "My program—cut off. How could you?"

"Shut up, damn it! I just passed the word, Baque. Lankey's doesn't open tonight. Not that it'll make any difference to you."

Baque smiled gently. "I think you've lost, Denton. I think enough music got through to beat you. By tomorrow you'll have a million complaints. So will the government, and then you'll find out who really runs Visiscope International."

"*I* run Visiscope International."

"No, Denton. It belongs to the people. They've let things slide for a long time, and they've taken anything you'd give them. But if they know what they want, they'll get it. I gave them at least three minutes of what they want. That was more than I'd hoped for."

"How'd you work that trick in my office?"

"That wasn't my trick, Denton—it was yours. You transmitted the music on a voice intercom. It didn't carry the overtones, the upper frequencies, so the multichord sounded dead to the men in the other room. Visiscope has the full frequency range of live sound."

Denton nodded. "I'll have the heads of some scientists for that. I'll also have your head, though I regret the waste. If you'd played square with me I'd have made you a live billionaire. The only alternative is a dead musician."

He stalked away, and as the automatic door closed behind him, Marigold Manning clutched Baque's arm. "Quick! Follow me!" Baque hesitated, and she hissed, "Don't stand there like an idiot! He's going to have you killed!"

She led him through a control room and out into a small corridor. They raced the length of it, darted through a reception room and passed a startled secretary without a word, and burst through a rear door into another corridor. She jerked Baque after her into an anti-grav lift, and they shot upward. At the top of the building she hurried him to an air car strip and left him standing in the doorway. "When I give you a signal, you walk out," she said. "Don't run, just walk."

She calmly approached an attendant, and Baque heard his surprised greeting. "Through early this morning, Miss Manning?"

"We're running a lot of Coms," she said. "I want the big Waring."

"Coming right up."

Peering around the corner, Baque saw her step into the flyer. As soon as the attendant's back was turned, she waved frantically. Baque walked carefully toward her, keeping the flyer between the attendant and himself. A moment later they were airborne, and far below them a siren was sounding faintly.

"We did it!" she gasped. "If you hadn't got away before that alarm sounded, you wouldn't have left the building alive."

"Well, thanks," Baque said, looking back at the Visiscope International building. "But surely this wasn't necessary. Earth is a civilized planet."

"Visiscope International is not civilized!" she snapped.

He looked at her wonderingly. Her face was flushed, her eyes wide with fear, and for the first time Baque saw her as a human being, a woman, a lovely woman. As he looked, she turned away and burst into tears.

"Now Jimmy'll have me killed, too. And where can we go?"

"Lankey's," Baque said. "Look—you can see it from here."

She pointed the flyer at the freshly painted letters on the strip above the new restaurant, and Baque, looking backward, saw a crowd forming in the street by Visiscope International.

Lankey floated his desk over to the wall and leaned back comfortably. He wore a trim dress suit, and he'd carefully groomed himself for the role of a jovial host, but in his office he was the same ungainly Lankey that Baque had first seen leaning over a bar.

"I told you all hell would break loose," he said, grinning. "There are five thousand people over by Visiscope International, and they're screaming for Erlin Baque. And the crowd is growing."

"I didn't play for more than three minutes," Baque said. "I thought a lot of people might write in to complain about Denton cutting me off, but I didn't expect anything like this."

"You didn't, eh? Five thousand people—maybe ten thousand by now—and Miss Manning risks her neck to get you out of the place. Ask her why, Baque?"

"Yes," Baque said. "Why go to all that trouble for me?"

She shuddered. "Your music does things to me."

"It sure does," Lankey said. "Baque, you fool, you gave a quarter of Earth's population three minutes of Sex Music!"

Lankey's opened on schedule that evening, with crowds filling the street outside and struggling through the doors as long as there was standing room. The shrewd Lankey had instituted an admission charge. The standees bought no food, and Lankey saw no point in furnishing free music, even if people were willing to stand to hear it.

He made one last-minute change in plans. Astutely reasoning that the customers would prefer a glamorous hostess to a flat-nosed elderly host, he hired Marigold Manning. She moved about gracefully, the deep blue of her flowing gown offsetting her golden hair.

When Baque took his place at the multi-chord, the frenzied ovation lasted for twenty minutes.

Midway through the evening Baque sought out Lankey. "Has Denton tried anything?"

"Nothing that I've noticed. Everything is running smoothly."

"That seems odd. He swore we wouldn't open tonight."

Lankey chuckled. "He's had troubles of his own to worry about. The authorities are on his neck about the rioting. I was afraid they'd blame you, but they didn't. Denton put you on visiscope, and then he cut you off, and they figure he's responsible. And according to my last report, Visiscope International has had more than ten million complaints. Don't worry, Baque. We'll hear from Denton soon enough, and the guilds, too."

"The guilds? Why the guilds?"

"The Tunesmiths' Guild will be damned furious about your dropping the Coms. The Lyric Writers' Guild will go along with them on account of the Coms and because you're using music without words. The Performers' Guild already has it in for you because not many of its members can play worth a damn, and of course it'll support the other guilds. By tomorrow morning, Baque, you'll be the most unpopular man in the Solar System, and the sponsors, and the visiscope people, and the guilds are going to hate your guts. I'm giving you a twenty-four-hour bodyguard. Miss Manning, too. I want both of you to come out of this alive."

"Do you really think Denton would—"

"Denton would."

The next morning the Performers' Guild blacklisted Lankey's and ordered all the musicians, including Baque, to sever relations. Rose and the other singers joined Baque in respectfully declining, and they found themselves blacklisted before noon. Lankey called in an attorney, the most sinister, furtive, disreputable-looking individual Baque had ever seen.

"They're supposed to give us a week's notice," Lankey said, "and another week if we decide to appeal. I'll sue them for five million."

The Commissioner of Public Safety called, and on his heels came the Health Commissioner and the Liquor Commissioner. All three conferred briefly with Lankey and departed grim-faced.

"Denton's moving too late," Lankey said gleefully. "I got to all of them a week ago and recorded our conversations. They don't dare take any action."

A riot broke out in front of Lankey's that night. Lankey had his own riot squad ready for action, and the customers never noticed the disturbance. Lankey's informants estimated that more than fifty million complaints had been received by Visiscope International, and a dozen governmental agencies had scheduled investigations. Anti-Com demonstrations began to erupt spontaneously, and five hundred visiscope screens were smashed in Manhattan restaurants.

Lankey's finished its first week unmolested, entertaining capacity crowds daily. Reservations were pouring in from as far away as Pluto, where a returning space detachment voted to spend its first night of leave at Lankey's. Baque sent to Berlin for a multichordist to understudy him, and Lankey hoped by the end of the month to have the restaurant open twenty-four hours a day.

At the beginning of the second week, Lankey told Baque, "We've got Denton licked. I've countered every move he's made, and now we're going to make a few moves. You're going on visiscope again. I'm making application today. We're a legitimate business, and we've got as much right to buy time as anyone else. If he won't give it to us, I'll sue. But he won't dare refuse."

"Where do you get the money for this?" Baque asked.

Lankey grinned. "I saved it up—a little of it. Mostly I've had help from people who don't like Denton."

Denton didn't refuse. Baque did an Earth-wide program direct from Lankey's, with Marigold Manning introducing him. He omitted only the Sex Music.

Quitting time at Lankey's. Baque was in his dressing room, wearily changing. Lankey had already left for an early-morning conference with his attorney. They were speculating on Denton's next move.

Baque was uneasy. He was, he told himself, only a dumb musician. He didn't understand legal problems or the tangled web of connections and influence that Lankey negotiated so easily. He knew James Denton was evil incarnate, and he also knew that Denton had enough money to buy Lankey a thousand times over, or to buy the murder of anyone who got in his way. What was he waiting for? Given enough time, Baque might deliver a deathblow to the entire institution of Coms. Surely Denton would know that.

So what *was* he waiting for?

The door burst open, and Marigold Manning stumbled in half undressed, her pale face the bleached whiteness of her plastic breast cups. She slammed the door and leaned against it, sobs shaking her body.

"Jimmy," she gasped. "I got a note from Carol—that's his secretary. She was a good friend of mine. She says Jimmy's bribed our guards, and they're going to kill us on the way home this morning. Or let Jimmy's men kill us."

"I'll call Lankey," Baque said. "There's nothing to worry about."

"No! If they suspect anything they won't wait. We won't have a chance."

"Then we'll just wait until Lankey gets back."

"Do you think it's safe to wait? They know we're getting ready to leave."

Baque sat down heavily. It was the sort of move he expected Denton to make. Lankey picked his men carefully, he knew, but Denton had enough money to buy any man. And yet—

"Maybe it's a trap. Maybe that note's a fake."

"No. I saw that fat little snake Hulscy talking with one of your guards last night, and I knew then that Jimmy was up to something."

"What do you want to do?" Baque asked.

"Could we go out the back way?"

"I don't know. We'd have to get past at least one guard."

"Couldn't we try?"

Baque hesitated. She was frightened—she was sick with fright—but she knew far more about this sort of thing than he did, and she knew James Denton. Without her help he'd never have got out of the Visiscope International building.

"If you think that's the thing to do, we'll try it."

"I'll have to finish changing."

"Go ahead. Let me know when you're ready."

She opened the door a crack and looked out cautiously. "No. You come with me."

Minutes later, Baque and Miss Manning walked leisurely along the corridor at the back of the building, nodded to the two guards on duty there, and with a sudden movement were through the door. Running. A shout of surprise came from behind them, but no one followed. They dashed frantically down an alley, turned off, reached another intersection, and hesitated.

"The conveyer is that way," she gasped. "If we can reach the conveyer—"

"Let's go!"

They ran on, hand in hand. Far ahead of them the alley opened onto a street. Baque glanced anxiously upward for air cars and saw none. Exactly where they were he did not know.

"Are we—being followed?" she asked.

"I don't think so," Baque panted. "There aren't any air cars, and I didn't see anyone behind us when we stopped."

"Then we got away!"

A man stepped abruptly out of the dawn shadows thirty feet ahead. As they halted, stricken dumb with panic, he walked slowly toward them. A hat was pulled low over his face, but there was no mistaking the smile. James Denton.

"Good morning, Beautiful," he said. "Visiscope International hasn't been the same without your lovely presence. And a good morning to you, Mr. Baque."

They stood silently, Miss Manning's hand clutching Baque's arm, her nails cutting through his shirt and into his flesh. He did not move.

"I thought you'd fall for that little gag, Beautiful. I thought you'd be just frightened enough, by now, to fall for it. I have every exit blocked, but I'm grateful to you for picking this one. Very grateful. I like to settle a double cross in person."

Suddenly he whirled on Baque, his voice an angry snarl. "Get going, Baque. It isn't your turn. I have other plans for you."

Baque stood rooted to the damp pavement.

"Move, Baque, before I change my mind."

Miss Manning released his arm. Her voice was a choking whisper. "Go!"

"Baque!" Denton snarled.

"Go, quickly!" she whispered again.

Baque took two hesitant steps.

"Run!" Denton shouted.

Baque ran. Behind him there was the evil crack of a gun, a scream, and silence. Baque faltered, saw Denton looking after him, and ran on.

* * *

"So I'm a coward," Baque said.

"No, Baque." Lankey shook his head slowly. "You're a brave man, or you wouldn't have got into this. Trying something there would have been foolishness, not bravery. It's my fault for thinking he'd move first against the restaurant. I owe Denton something for this, and I'm a man who pays his debts."

A troubled frown creased Lankey's ugly face. He looked perplexedly at Baque. "She was a brave and beautiful woman, Baque," he said, absently caressing his flat nose. "But I wonder why Denton let you go."

The air of tragedy that hung heavily over Lankey's that night did not affect its customers. They gave Baque a thunderous ovation as he moved toward the multichord. As he paused for a halfhearted acknowledgment, three policemen closed in on him.

"Erlin Baque?"

"That's right."

"You're under arrest."

Baque faced them grimly. "What's the charge?" he asked.

"Murder."

The murder of Marigold Manning.

Lankey pressed his mournful face against the bars and talked unhurriedly. "They have some witnesses," he said. "Honest witnesses, who saw you run out of that alley. They have several dishonest witnesses who claim they saw you fire the shot. One of them is your friend Hulsey, who just happened to be taking an early-morning stroll along that alley—or so he'll testify. Denton would probably spend a million to convict you, but he won't have to. He won't even have to bribe the jury. The case against you is that good."

"What about the gun?" Baque asked.

"They'll have a witness who'll claim he sold it to you."

Baque nodded. Things were out of his hands, now. He'd worked for a cause that no one understood—perhaps he hadn't understood himself what he was trying to do. And he'd lost.

"What happens next?" he asked.

Lankey shook his head sadly. "I'm not one to hold back bad news. It means life. They're going to send you to the Ganymede rock pits for life."

"I see," Baque said. He added anxiously, "You're going to carry on?"

"Just what were you trying to do, Baque? You weren't only working for Lankey's. I couldn't figure it out, but I went along with you because I like you. And I like your music. What was it?"

"I don't know. Music, I suppose. People listening to music. Getting rid of the Coms, or some of them. Perhaps if I'd known what I wanted to do—"

"Yes. Yes, I think I understand. Lankey's will carry on, Baque, as long as I have any breath left, and I'm not just being noble. Business is tremendous. That new multichord player isn't bad at all. He's nothing like you were, but there'll never be another one like you. We could be sold out for the next five years if we wanted to book reservations that far ahead. The other restaurants are doing away with visiscope and trying to imitate us, but we have a big head start. We'll carry on the way you had things set up, and your one-third still stands. I'll have it put in trust for you. You'll be a wealthy man when you get back."

"When I get back!"

"Well—a life sentence doesn't necessarily mean life. See that you behave yourself."

"Val?"

"She'll be taken care of. I'll give her a job of some kind to keep her occupied."

"Maybe I can send you music for the restaurant," Baque said. "I should have plenty of time."

"I'm afraid not. It's music they want to keep you away from. So—no writing of music. And they won't let you near a multichord. They think you could hypnotize the guards and turn all the prisoners loose."

"Would they—let me have my record collection?"

"I'm afraid not."

"I see. Well, if that's the way it is—"

"It is. Now I owe Denton two debts."

The unemotional Lankey had tears in his eyes as he turned away.

The jury deliberated for eight minutes and brought in a verdict of guilty. Baque was sentenced to life imprisonment. There was some editorial grumbling on visiscope because life in the Ganymede rock pits was frequently a very short life.

And there was a swelling undertone of whispering among the little people that the verdict had been bought and paid for by the sponsors, by visiscope. Erlin Baque was framed, it was said, because he gave the people music.

And on the day Baque left for Ganymede, announcement was made of a public exhibition, by H. Vail, multichordist, and B. Johnson, violinist. Admission one dollar.

Lankey collected evidence with painstaking care, rebribed one of the bribed witnesses, and petitioned for a new trial. The petition was denied, and the long years limped past.

The New York Symphony Orchestra was organized, with twenty members. One of James Denton's plush air cars crashed, and he was instantly killed. An unfortunate accident. A millionaire who once heard Erlin Baque play on visiscope endowed a dozen conservatories of music. They were to be called the Baque

Conservatories, but a musical historian who had never heard of Baque got the name changed to Bach.

Lankey died, and a son-in-law carried on his efforts as a family trust. A subscription was launched to build a new hall for the New York Symphony, which now numbered forty members. The project gathered force like an avalanche, and a site was finally chosen in Ohio, where the hall would be within easier commuting distance of all parts of the North American continent. Beethoven Hall was erected, seating forty thousand people. The first concert series was fully subscribed forty-eight hours after tickets went on sale.

Opera was given on visiscope for the first time in two hundred years. An opera house was built on the Ohio site, and then an art institute. The Center grew, first by private subscription and then under governmental sponsorship. Lankey's son-in-law died, and a nephew took over the management of Lankey's—and the campaign to free Erlin Baque. Thirty years passed, and then forty.

And forty-nine years, seven months and nineteen days after Baque received his life sentence, he was paroled. He still owned a third interest in Manhattan's most prosperous restaurant, and the profits that had accrued over the years made him an extremely wealthy man. He was ninety-six years old.

* * *

THE TUNESMITH

Another capacity crowd at Beethoven Hall. Vacationists from all parts of the Solar System, music lovers who commuted for the concerts, old people who had retired to the Center, young people on educational excursions, forty thousand of them, stirred restlessly and searched the wings for the conductor. Applause thundered down from the twelve balconies as he strode forward.

Erlin Baque sat in his permanent seat at the rear of the main floor. He adjusted his binoculars and peered at the orchestra, wondering again what a contrabassoon sounded like. His bitterness he had left behind on Ganymede. His life at the Center was an unending revelation of miracles.

Of course no one remembered Erlin Baque, tunesmith and murderer. Whole generations of people could not even remember the Coms. And yet Baque felt that he had accomplished all of this just as assuredly as though he had built this building—built the Center—with his own hands. He spread his hands before him, hands deformed by years in the rock pits, fingers and tips of fingers crushed off, his body maimed by cascading rocks. He had no regrets. He had done his work well.

Two ushers stood in the aisle behind him. One jerked a thumb in his direction and whispered, "Now *there's* a character for you. Comes to every concert. Never misses one. And he just sits there in the back row watching people. They say he was one of the old tunesmiths, years and years ago."

"Maybe he likes music," the other said.

"Naw. Those old tunesmiths never knew anything about music. Besides—he's deaf."

Afterword

How Lloyd Biggle, Jr., Changed My Life, Part II

Orson Scott Card

Now you've read "The Tunesmith," and the story's had its chance to do to you whatever it's going to do. You know the ending now, so I won't be spoiling anything by talking freely about it. I only want to talk to you a few minutes more, to tell you exactly how this story influenced me.

It was only in the last few months, after I had worked out an agreement with TOR to publish my novella "Eye for Eye" in tandem with "The Tunesmith," that I began to think about how Biggle's story might have been showing up in my own work over the years.

In a way, the answer came almost by accident. Only a couple of months ago, I was talking to an audience about "The Tunesmith," telling them essentially the story I told you in my foreword. I began to speculate on influence. "Maybe that's why I kept writing so many stories about musicians early in my career," I said. "*Songmaster*, of course, and 'Unaccompanied Sonata.'"

Then I remembered that only a few minutes earlier I had mentioned that "Unaccompanied Sonata," probably the best short story I have ever written or will ever write, was one of the few works that came to me whole. That is, I 'sat down to write it (having made one abortive attempt a year or two before,) and it came out in one smooth draft in three or four hours. That draft was never revised, except for a little fiddling with punctuation and a word here or there. When other writers talked about stories being gifts from a Muse, I imagined that experience was the sort of thing they were talking about.

But now, thinking of "Unaccompanied Sonata" in that double context, as a story that came whole and also as a story about music, probably influenced by "The Tunesmith," it suddenly occurred to me that maybe "Unaccompanied Sonata" didn't come from a Muse at all (I've always been skeptical about such things anyway), but rather from Lloyd Biggle, Jr. After all, though the world in which "Unaccompanied Sonata" takes place is completely different from the milieu of "The

Tunesmith," the basic structure of both stories is almost identical.

My hero, Christian, has a phenomenal talent for music, but he is forbidden to compose or perform. The first time he breaks that proscription, playing piano in a bar after closing time, his fingers are surgically removed. Later, working on a road crew, he starts to sing, making up songs with his fellow workers. His songs begin to spread, and even though nobody reports him, the authorities recognize that this music could only be coming from Christian. They come to him and remove his voice—but then make him one of the authorities, knowing that his loss, both of music and of his voice and fingers, will make him reluctant to use his authority and compassionate in its use.

At the very end, retired, he walks into a diner and hears some teenagers singing a song he wrote. He listens, then writes notes to them, asking if they know who wrote the song. "Sugar," they say, using his nickname from road crew days. Their words show that they have great respect for the man who wrote the song, even though they haven't the faintest idea that he is the crippled man now standing before them. And as he leaves the diner, Christian takes a little bow, unnoticed, taking their words as his applause.

A musical genius, forbidden to perform, performs anyway, and his music has far-reaching effects, even though he is snatched away without ever having a chance to benefit personally from what he achieved. And at the end, he comes to the place where the music is being playing and takes his unrecognized bow.

Of course "Unaccompanied Sonata" came whole. I knew how the story had to go; I knew how it had to end. After all, when I was eight years old Lloyd Biggle, Jr. showed me how. The story felt so true to me and dwelt so deeply inside me that entirely without realizing it—at a time, in fact, when I didn't remember "The Tunesmith" consciously at all—I was reaching down into myself, finding the mythic elements of "The Tunesmith" that felt most true and right to me, and putting them into my strongest and truest tales.

And now a small coda about the way that storytelling works on people. I remember that when I was reading "The Tunesmith" for the first time, I thought, "Of course, *real* music could never have such an effect on people as this guy's Sex Music is having. Real music you just listen to—it doesn't change you."

But the story left me thinking—and dreaming—and I began to wonder if maybe music and art and stories *could* have such an effect. Or maybe they had that effect now, all the time, but since everybody felt it constantly, nobody noticed it.

I dropped the idea the way kids often drop their best thoughts, because they figure that since they aren't adults yet the ideas can't be worth much. But in later years I picked it up again, or something like it. I began to examine why it was that the storytelling arts are present in every human society, began to wonder whether it wasn't storytelling that made us human.

More particularly, couldn't it be storytelling that allowed communities to define individual identities in a way that explained such seeming anomalies as altruistic behavior and self-sacrifice. For instance, why should an individual ever consent to die for his country? Sociobiology's genetic explanation—that such behaviors enhance the survival chances of the genes of near kin—leaves me doubting. But storytelling explains for me what genetics cannot.

For there is no society that does not have a constantly repeated mythic element in its stories that declares over and over again that the noblest thing a person can do is give up his own personal interests for the sake of others' joy or survival—even if his society doesn't honor him for it.

Our stories—like "The Tunesmith" and "Unaccompanied Sonata"—teach people to value the good of others above their own. Indeed, having read such stories, the readers who identify strongly with heroes like these will remember *already having done it*. At the deepest levels, I don't believe our mind distinguishes between memories of powerful fiction and memories of real life; indeed, I think we turn our "true" memories into structured fiction in the process of remembering them. So any society that tells this mythic tale over and over again is likelier to have citizens who willingly sacrifice for the good of the group; obviously this would increase the chance of that society's survival, though at the cost of the survival of some individuals. In short, altruism is a device that works for the survival of the community over the individual, and storytelling is the primary means of encouraging altruism. Communities that don't have such stories don't survive. That's why all viable communities today tell that tale.

Because I read "The Tunesmith" (along with other pivotal stories in my life) and cared about it deeply, at an age when my identity was still unripe and unformed, Biggle's vision became incorporated into my own, perhaps to a greater degree than is possible for any story I read today.

Yet "The Tunesmith" carries its mythic message doubled. Not only is it *about* an artist whose art transforms and improves his community, it is in itself a work of art that also transforms and improves. It acts even as it describes. It has taught me twice, and I could not rest until I brought it to you, told you what it meant to me, and gave you a chance to read it for yourself.

THE BEST IN SCIENCE FICTION

THE BEST IN FANTASY

☐ 53954-0 SPIRAL OF FIRE by Deborah Turner Harris $3.95
    53955-9   Canada $4.95

☐ 53401-8 NEMESIS by Louise Cooper (U.S. only) $3.95

☐ 53382-8 SHADOW GAMES by Glen Cook $3.95
    53381-X   Canada $4.95

☐ 53815-5 CASTING FORTUNE by John M. Ford $3.95
    53826-1   Canada $4.95

☐ 53351-8 HART'S HOPE by Orson Scott Card $3.95
    53352-6   Canada $4.95

☐ 53397-6 MIRAGE by Louise Cooper (U.S. only) $3.95

☐ 53671-1 THE DOOR INTO FIRE by Diane Duane $2.95
    53672-X   Canada $3.50

☐ 54902-3 A GATHERING OF GARGOYLES by Meredith Ann Pierce $2.95
    54903-1   Canada $3.50

☐ 55614-3 JINIAN STAR-EYE by Sheri S. Tepper $2.95
    55615-1   Canada $3.75

Buy them at your local bookstore or use this handy coupon:
Clip and mail this page with your order.

Publishers Book and Audio Mailing Service
P.O. Box 120159, Staten Island, NY 10312-0004

Please send me the book(s) I have checked above. I am enclosing $_____
(please add $1.25 for the first book, and $.25 for each additional book to
cover postage and handling. Send check or money order only—no CODs.)

Name _____

Address _____

City _____ State/Zip _____

Please allow six weeks for delivery. Prices subject to change without notice.

Praise for

NAKED EDGE

continued . . .

UNLAWFUL CONTACT

"Powerful, sexy, and unforgettable, *Unlawful Contact* is the kind of story I love to read. Pamela Clare is a dazzling talent."
—Lori Foster, *New York Times* bestselling author

"A spellbinding, gut-wrenching page-turner with a gripping plot. This story is unique and creative with an imperfect hero you can't help getting sweaty palms over . . . Pamela Clare is a remarkable storyteller." —*Fresh Fiction*

"This is an exciting fast-paced romantic suspense thriller . . . Action packed." —*Midwest Book Review*

"A romantic suspense that has it all: gritty realism, edge-of-your-seat action, dynamic characterizations, surprising plot twists, and a scorching romance between two leads you won't soon forget."
—*BookLoons*

"A gripping and emotional story . . . An engaging tale that will have readers on the edge of their seats." —*Romance Reviews Today*

"A thrilling, captivating suspense novel . . . It has great characters, a wonderful story line with different connecting plots, and a happy ending for a couple that has many obstacles that they must surmount together." —*Romance Reader at Heart*

"Clare's impressive novel is rife with gripping suspense, secrets masterfully revealed, and characters in whom readers can become emotionally invested. The sexual tension between the protagonists is deliciously steamy, and the skillful plotting makes this thrilling book one readers won't be able to close until the final page." —*Romantic Times* (4 ½ stars)

HARD EVIDENCE

"A page-turner, a pulse-pounding thriller . . . Whether she is writing her incredible historicals or these great contemporaries, Ms. Clare proves, once again, she is one of the best storytellers today . . . It is a thriller, it is a treasure, and it is tremendous."
—*Fresh Fiction*

"Superb romantic suspense . . . Fans will appreciate this strong thriller."
—*Midwest Book Review*

"I cannot recommend this book highly enough. Pamela Clare's *Hard Evidence* is a powerful and, dare I say, flawless book, in my opinion. For those who love a good suspense or even just a good, satisfying read, it's a 'don't miss.'"
—*Romance Reader at Heart*

"This was a hard-to-put-down book with an exciting story line."
—*MyShelf.com*

"Clare adds a realistic edge to her suspenseful writing . . . [A] tight, gritty thriller . . . Clare definitely seems to have found her niche."
—*Romantic Times*

EXTREME EXPOSURE

"Investigative reporter turned author Clare brings a gritty realism to this intense and intricate romantic thriller. *Extreme Exposure* is the launch book for a sizzling new suspense series that promises to generate lots of intrigue, action, and romance. An author to keep an eye on!"
—*Romantic Times*

"A gem, *Extreme Exposure* has all the elements of great romance and is an entertaining summer read."
—*Romance Reviews Today* (Perfect 10)

"I really loved this book because it was so realistic. The characters were people I would love to know. Obviously, Ms. Clare knows this world and the nuances of investigative reporting. She communicates this in a terrific love story that grabs you and will not let you go. Believe me, I lost some sleep reading this book. I predict that Ms. Clare is an author to watch for the future and readers of romantic suspense are sure to love this excellent, well-written novel, one of the best I've read this year."
—*The Romance Readers Connection*

BREAKING POINT

PAMELA CLARE

BERKLEY SENSATION, NEW YORK

THE BERKLEY PUBLISHING GROUP
Published by the Penguin Group
Penguin Group (USA) Inc.
375 Hudson Street, New York, New York 10014, USA

Penguin Group (Canada), 90 Eglinton Avenue East, Suite 700, Toronto, Ontario M4P 2Y3, Canada
(a division of Pearson Penguin Canada Inc.)
Penguin Books Ltd., 80 Strand, London WC2R 0RL, England
Penguin Group Ireland, 25 St. Stephen's Green, Dublin 2, Ireland (a division of Penguin Books Ltd.)
Penguin Group (Australia), 250 Camberwell Road, Camberwell, Victoria 3124, Australia
(a division of Pearson Australia Group Pty. Ltd.)
Penguin Books India Pvt. Ltd., 11 Community Centre, Panchsheel Park, New Delhi—110 017, India
Penguin Group (NZ), 67 Apollo Drive, Rosedale, Auckland 0632, New Zealand
(a division of Pearson New Zealand Ltd.)
Penguin Books (South Africa) (Pty.) Ltd., 24 Sturdee Avenue, Rosebank, Johannesburg 2196,
South Africa

Penguin Books Ltd., Registered Offices: 80 Strand, London WC2R 0RL, England

BREAKING POINT

A Berkley Sensation Book / published by arrangement with the author

PRINTING HISTORY
Berkley Sensation mass-market edition / May 2011

Copyright © 2011 by Pamela Clare.
Excerpt from *Forgotten Sea* by Virginia Kantra copyright © by Virginia Kantra.
Cover art by Claudio Marinesco.
Cover design by Rita Frangie.

ISBN: 978-0-425-24051-9

BERKLEY® SENSATION
Berkley Sensation Books are published by The Berkley Publishing Group,
a division of Penguin Group (USA) Inc.,
375 Hudson Street, New York, New York 10014.
BERKLEY® SENSATION and the "B" design are trademarks of Penguin Group (USA) Inc.

PRINTED IN THE UNITED STATES OF AMERICA

10 9 8 7 6 5 4 3

This book is dedicated to the memory of the hundreds of murdered and missing women of Ciudad Juárez, Mexico. You were brutalized and discarded like you didn't matter. But the earth received your tears, your blood, your bones and, like a bereaved mother, the earth itself cries out for justice. May the violence end and those who stole your bodies and your lives be held to account.

ACKNOWLEDGMENTS

Special thanks to Tina Lewis Rowe, former U.S. Marshal for the District of Colorado, for her sense of humor, her insight, and her willingness to answer a thousand questions about the work of U.S. Marshals and DUSMs. You are one classy, smart, and impressive lady. I wish we could just hang out sometime.

Thanks, too, to retired Chief Deputy U.S. Marshal Larry Homenick for sharing his stories about catching fugitives in Mexico and working at EPIC. I'd love to have lunch with you and Tina again. And, yes, it's on me.

Much gratitude to Christine Bruce, whose life was changed by Hurricane Katrina and who graciously agreed to read the manuscript and help me get cultural aspects of Natalie's New Orleans background right.

Heartfelt gratitude to my mother, Mary White, an RN in cardiac rehab, who has kept many hearts beating, for her help with certain medical aspects of this story.

Many thanks to Natasha Kern, my friend and agent, for her encouragement, humor and support, and to Cindy Hwang, my editor, for her continued faith in my stories— and for getting Jed Hill, my mental image of Zach McBride, for the cover of this book.

Personal thanks and much love to my sister, Michelle, and to my son Benjamin, who've gone above and beyond to support my writing through the years.

Hugs and kisses to Sue, Kristi, and Libby for being such amazing bitchez and to Ronlyn, Jenn, Stef, Ruth, and Bo for their feedback on this story and support while I wrote it.

Thanks to Jefferson Dodge, managing editor at *Boulder Weekly*, for supporting my fiction career by being the world's best managing editor. What did I ever do without you?

And last but not least, thanks to my family for their love, encouragement, and understanding when I do things like ignore the phone and miss Thanksgiving dinner so that I can write. I love you.

CHAPTER 1

NATALIE BENOIT WATCHED the streets of Ciudad Juárez roll by outside the bus window, wishing the driver would turn up the air-conditioning. It wasn't yet noon and already the city was an oven. Even the palm trees seemed to wither in the July heat.

"With three other seasons in the year, why did SPJ have to choose summer for this conference?" She fanned herself with her copy of the day's program, perspiration trickling between her breasts.

"Don't tell me you think it's hot, *chula*." Joaquin Ramirez, the newspaper's best shooter, grinned at her from across the aisle, his camera still aimed out the window. "This can't be any worse than New Orleans in the summer."

"Is that where you are from, Miss Benoit—New Orleans?" Enrique Marquez, a journalist from Culiacán, glanced back from the seat in front of her, his Spanish accent making both her name and the name of her hometown sound exotic. In his fifties, he was still a handsome man, with salt-and-pepper hair, a well-trimmed mustache, and brown eyes that twinkled whenever he spoke of his grandchildren.

"Can't you tell by her accent?" Joaquin gave Natalie a wink.

Natalie ignored Joaquin, refusing to take the bait. "Yes, sir. I was born there and grew up in the Garden District." Which was why she did *not* have an accent, no matter what her colleagues might think. "I left Louisiana many years ago and live in Denver now."

She hoped Sr. Marquez would let it go, but was almost certain he wouldn't. Mention New Orleans, and people just had to ask about the storm. Given that journalists were far more curious than most people, Natalie supposed his next question was inevitable.

"Did you live there during Hurricane Katrina?"

She looked out the window, letting the words come with no thought and no emotion, as if what they represented meant nothing to her. "Yes, sir. It was a terrible time for so many of us. I moved to Denver after that."

She said nothing about where she'd been during the storm or what she'd endured or what had happened to her fiancé, Beau, and her parents in the aftermath.

"*Lo siento*. I am sorry, Miss Benoit."

"*No le gusta hablar de eso*," Joaquin said softly.

Natalie didn't speak Spanish well, but she understood that much. And Joaquin was right. She didn't like to talk about it. She'd left New Orleans in part so she wouldn't have to talk about it. Even six years later, it still hurt too much.

People told her she should move on, get over it, get on with her life. Oh, how she hated those words! They were easy to say, but no one had yet been able to explain to her exactly *how* she was supposed to "move on." Losing her parents had been hard enough, but losing Beau . . . How could she "get over" him?

How could she forget the man who'd died out of love for her?

It wasn't that she hadn't *tried* to move on. Selling her parents' home—the house at First and Chestnut where she'd grown up—had been a big step, as had moving to Denver. After a year, she'd stopped wearing her engagement ring. She'd even joined an online dating service and gone on several dates. But none of the men she'd met, no matter how intelligent, kind, or attractive, had sparked anything inside her.

It was as if some part of her had forgotten how to feel.

Banamex. Telcel. McDonald's. Lucerna. Pemex.

The names of banks, businesses, restaurants, and gas stations drifted before her, barely registering with her mind. What she *did* notice were the vibrant colors of the buildings.

Bright oranges. Vivid blues. Lush greens. Lemony yellows. And blazing blood reds. Everywhere reds. It was as if the residents of Juárez had decided to strike a blow on behalf of color in defiance of the drab brown landscape that surrounded them.

Natalie had signed up for the trip because she'd wanted to get away from the newsroom for a few days. She'd been working at the *Denver Independent* for almost three years now, and she felt stuck in some kind of professional ennui. Not that she didn't love her job. She did. Having a spot on the paper's award-winning investigative team—the I-Team—was every investigative journalist's dream. But journalism wasn't a low-stress profession even on the best of days. Burnout was a very real hazard of the job. Or maybe the lethargy that had taken over the rest of her life was affecting her job now, too.

Regardless, she'd needed a change of pace, and this trip had offered that.

She and thirty-nine other journalists—most American, some Mexican—had crossed the border from El Paso into Juárez early this morning, part of a three-day convention and tour put together by the Society of Professional Journalists and the U.S. State Department as a way of bringing Mexican and American journalists together to learn about the inter-mingled issues of immigration, the drug trade, and human trafficking. They'd started the day with breakfast at the U.S. consulate. Then, under the protection of two dozen armed *federales*, they'd toured a police station and the offices of *El Diario*, the local newspaper, where bullet holes in the walls reminded them just how dangerous it was to be a journalist in Mexico.

"And I thought *my* job sucked," one of the other American reporters had said, running his fingers over the scarred wall.

The sight of those bullet holes—and the empty desk of the journalist who'd been killed—had put a few things in perspective for Natalie, too. The worst thing she had to put up with during the course of the average workday was her editor's temper. But no amount of yelling from Tom Trent could compare to flying bullets.

Now they were on their way to the Museo de Historia—the beautiful Museum of History—where President Taft had once dined. After that, they'd visit a new five-star hotel in the downtown area for lunch. It was clear that Mexican officials were proud of their town and were making certain that the tour included a look at the beauty and culture of Juárez, and not just the violence for which the city was unfortunately known.

Natalie couldn't blame them for that. There were at least two sides to every story, and although the drug cartels made headlines, most people who lived here were decent men and women just trying to raise families and live their lives. Despite the poverty and the unremitting violence, Ciudad Juárez was a city that still dared to hope.

In the streets below, a young mother, her dark hair pulled back in a bouncy ponytail, pushed a baby in a stroller. A shopkeeper in a royal blue apron swept the stone steps of his store. Two teenage boys in bright white T-shirts and jeans walked past a gaggle of pretty girls, their heads craning for a better look as the girls passed them. The girls, well aware of this attention, covered their mouths with their hands and broke into giggles. Nearby, two elderly gentlemen sat on a bench, lost in conversation, straw fedoras on their heads, cigars in their hands.

Natalie felt the bus lurch to a stop but was so caught up in the tableau outside her window that she didn't realize something was wrong until the scene changed. The teenage boys stopped, then turned and ran up an alley. The shopkeeper dropped his broom and disappeared indoors. The woman with the stroller grabbed her baby and backed into a doorway, a look of fear on her face as she left the empty stroller to roll down the sidewalk. The two old men dropped to their knees and crouched behind the bench.

And then Natalie heard it—the grinding fire of automatic weapons.

Shattered glass. Screams. Staccato bursts of gunfire.

"¡Madre de Dios!"

"What the hell?"

"Natalie! Natalie, get down!"

Joaquin's shout of warning pierced Natalie's shock and disbelief. She ducked into the small space between her seat and the seat back in front of her, crouching against the floor, shards of glass falling around her like rain. Pulse pounding in her ears, she looked across the aisle, her gaze locking with Joaquin's as he reached out and closed his hand over hers.

IT WAS PAIN and thirst that woke him.

For a moment Zach McBride thought he was back in Afghanistan, lying on the rim of that canyon in the Hindu Kush mountains, an AK-47 round in his back. He opened his eyes to see pitch-black and then remembered. He wasn't in Afghanistan. He was in Mexico. And he was a captive—blindfolded and chained to a brick wall.

He raised his head and realized he was lying shirtless on his right side, his hands shackled behind his back, his bare skin resting against the filthy stone floor. His mouth was dry as sand. His wrists were blistered and bloody where the manacles had rubbed them raw. His cracked ribs cut into his left side like a blade.

He tried to sit, but couldn't.

Damn!

He was weaker than he'd realized.

Then something hard and multi-legged brushed his chest as it skittered by, bringing him upright on a punch of adrenaline. Pain slashed through his side, breath hissing between his clenched teeth as he bit back a groan. He wasn't afraid of the mice or the spiders, but they weren't the only creatures in here with him. The one time the Zetas had removed his blindfold, he'd seen scorpions. And the last damned thing he needed was a scorpion sting.

Dizzy from hunger, his heart pounding from sleep deprivation and dehydration, he leaned his right shoulder against the brick wall and tried to catch his breath, the chain that held him lying cold and heavy along his spine.

How long had he been here? Five days? No, six.

And where exactly was *here*?

Somewhere between Juárez and hell.

They were giving him only enough food and water to keep him alive, his hunger and thirst incessant, mingling with pain, making it hard to sleep. Only once in his life had he been this physically helpless. Only then it had been even worse.

If he survived, if he made it out of here alive, he would track down Gisella and kill her—or at least hand her over to D.C. The little bitch of a Mexican Interpol agent had set him up, betrayed him to the Zetas. She'd known what would happen to him—the Zetas were infamous for their brutality— and still she'd handed him over to them with a smile on her lying lips.

At least you didn't sleep with her, buddy.

Yeah, well, at least he could feel good about that. It would suck right now to have her taste in his mouth or her scent on his skin, knowing that she'd put him through this. Long ago he'd made it a rule never to get involved with women while on assignment, and despite Gisella's persistent attempts to get him to break that rule, he'd kept his dick in his pants.

Hell, they should carve that on your headstone, McBride.

If he got a headstone.

Would they put up a grave marker for him if they didn't have a body to bury? Barring one hell of a miracle, he'd soon be scattered across the desert in small pieces. A year or two from now, someone would spot a bit of bleached bone in the sand and wonder what it was. No one would ever know for sure what had happened to him.

Besides, who was there to buy a grave plot or erect a headstone? His fellow DUSMs? Uncle Sam? His closest friends were dead. His mother was gone, too. He hadn't spoken to his father since his mother's funeral four years ago. And there was no one else in his life—no girlfriend, no wife, no kids.

You're a popular guy.

He'd always thought he'd get married one day and do the family thing. He'd imagined a pretty wife, a couple of kids, a house near the ocean. But life hadn't turned out that way.

He'd met lots of girls in college, but none who'd held his interest. Then a confrontation with his father had sent him into the navy. He'd tackled Officer Candidate School and then two years of SEAL training. The only women who'd been available during his short periods of leave were either professionals or women who were so desperate to marry a Navy SEAL that they spread their legs for every frogman they met. Call him strange, but he'd never found the idea of paying for sex or being used appealing. He'd wanted a woman who loved

him for himself and not his SEAL trident. But war had inter-
fered, and he'd never found her.

Something tightened in his chest, a wave of regret passing
through him.

Feeling sorry for yourself?

No. He'd made his choices. He'd done what he thought
was right. And although his life hadn't turned out the way he
might once have hoped, it was better this way. He'd seen first-
hand what happened to women and children when the men
they loved and depended on were killed in action. At least he
wouldn't be leaving a grieving wife and children behind.

Okay, so no headstone.

Mike, Chris, Brian, and Jimmy were in Arlington resting beneath slabs of white marble, but for Zach it would be
saguaro and open sky. That was okay. He liked the desert. And
even if he didn't, it wouldn't make one damned bit of difference once he was dead.

Which will be soon if you can't find a way out of this.

Not that he was afraid to die. He'd expected his job would
catch up with him one day. In fact, some part of him had been
counting on it.

But not yet. And not like this.

He'd been about to wrap up the biggest covert operation
of his career when Gisella called him and asked him to meet
her at a nightclub in downtown Juárez, claiming to have intel
vital for catching Arturo César Cárdenas, the head of Los
Zetas, who was wanted in the United States for the murder
of Americans on U.S. soil. So Zach had grabbed his gun and
fake ID—he never carried revealing documentation when he
was working a black bag job like this—and headed straight to
the club, where he'd found Gisella, dressed to kill, sitting at
the bar. She'd bought him a Coke, walked with him to a table
near the rear exit, and started telling him something about a
shipment of stolen coke. And then . . .

And then—nothing.

The drink had been drugged. When Zach had awoken,
he'd found himself here, stripped of his gun and wallet and
surrounded by pissed off Zetas demanding to know whom
he worked for and where he'd hidden the cocaine. As for the
questions, Zach couldn't answer the first because it would

imperil the operation, putting the lives of others at risk. And he couldn't answer the second because he hadn't stolen any coke and had no idea where it was. But his refusal to talk had only angered the Zetas more.

So they'd brought in a specialist—a man who knew how to inflict pain while keeping his victims alive. Electric shock was his area of expertise. He'd gone to work on Zach two days ago, and so far the two of them were at an impasse. He'd been able to make Zach pass out. He'd made him bite his own tongue trying not to scream. He'd made him want to cry like a baby. But he hadn't made him talk.

Zach had the navy and SERE training to thank for that— Survival, Evasion, Resistance, and Escape. Designed to help SEALs survive behind enemy lines, his training had been a godsend, helping him through hour after excruciating hour. Even though he was no longer in the military, he'd instinctively fallen back on that training, silently reciting bits and pieces of the military code of conduct, using it to stay strong.

I am an American, fighting in the forces that guard my country and our way of life. I am prepared to give my life in their defense . . . I will never surrender of my own free will . . . If I am captured, I will resist by all means available . . . I will evade answering further questions to the utmost of my ability . . . I will make every effort to escape . . .

As weak as he was, he knew he didn't stand a chance of escaping. And that meant there was only one thing left for him to do—keep his mind together long enough for his body to give out, long enough for him to die as he ought to have done six years ago.

Killed in the line of duty.

It had a nice ring to it.

Strange to think there'd been a time when he'd thought of taking the coward's way out. He'd come home from the war and tried to return to civilian life. But then the nightmares had started. The doctors had said it was PTSD, but they didn't have any answers for him that didn't come in a pill. The navy had pinned a medal on his chest and called him a hero. But there was nothing heroic about him. He'd come back from Afghanistan, and his men had not.

Finally, it had overwhelmed him, and he'd spent a long

couple of months drinking and contemplating eating his own gun. But he hadn't been able to do it. How would he have been able to face Mike, Chris, Brian, and Jimmy if he'd committed suicide?

At least now when he met them, he wouldn't have to feel ashamed.

Raucous laughter drifted into his cell from across the courtyard, voices drawing nearer, boots crunching on gravel.

Zach stiffened, dread uncoiling in his stomach, rising into his throat.

They were coming for him again.

Jesus!

He drew as deep a breath as his broken ribs would allow, swallowing his panic with what was left of his spit.

I am an American, fighting in the forces that guard my country and our way of life. I am prepared to give my life in their defense. I will never surrender of my own free will.

"Padre nuestro que estás en los cielos, santificado sea tu Nombre."

Holding fast to Joaquin's hand, Natalie looked to her right, where Sr. Marquez crouched against the sliver-strewn floor, eyes closed, a rosary in his trembling hands, his whispered prayers barely audible over the pounding of her heart. She didn't understand everything he was saying, and it had been years since she'd been to Mass, but she recognized the cadence of the prayer, her mind latching on to the English words, speaking them along with him in her mind.

Thy kingdom come, Thy will be done, on Earth as it is in Heaven.

The door of the bus exploded inward in a spray of glass.

Too afraid even to scream, Natalie watched as three armed men in dark green military fatigues stomped up the stairs, pistols in hand, automatic weapons slung on straps over their shoulders. One stopped long enough to point a pistol at the bus driver, whose pleading cries were cut short with a *pop* that splattered blood across the windshield.

Screams. Black boots. Another *pop*.

Sr. Marquez prayed faster, his voice shaking. "*Danos hoy*

el pan de este día y perdona nuestras deudas como nosotros perdonamos nuestros duedores."

Then Natalie heard the mechanical click and buzz of Joaquin's camera. Somehow she'd let go of his hand, her face now buried in her palms. She looked up, saw him lying out in the aisle, his camera pointed toward their attackers, a look of focused concentration on his face as he did his job—documenting the news.

She whispered to him. "Joaquin, no! They'll kill—"

The boots drew nearer.

Joaquin kept shooting. *Click. Click. Click.*

"*¡No! Por favor, no—*" No, please don't—

Pop!

Screams.

And Natalie understood.

They were killing the Mexican citizens on the bus but leaving the Americans alive.

Pop! Pop!

She looked over at Joaquin, at his dark hair, his brown eyes, his brown skin, and was blindsided by fear for him. They would think Joaquin was Mexican. And they would kill him.

Pop! Pop! Pop!

Blood ran along the floor, pooled beneath the seats, the air stung by the smell of it.

Pop! Pop!

"*Y no nos dejes caer en la tentación sino que líbranos del malo. Amen.*" Sr. Marquez opened his eyes, his gaze meeting Natalie's, rosary still in his hands. "I am sorry, Miss Benoit."

And then the men in the boots were there.

Sweat trickling down his temples, Sr. Marquez looked up into his killer's face, pressing his lips to the cross.

Natalie cried out. "No, don't—!"

Pop!

Then he lay dead, his sightless eyes open, blood trickling from a bullet hole in his forehead.

Without thinking, Natalie threw herself into the aisle, shielding Joaquin with her body, struggling for the right words. "*Él no es mexicano! Él es americano!* He's a citizen of the United States! He's American!"

Cold brown eyes—a killer's eyes—watched her with apparent amusement, a pitiless smile spreading across a face too young to be so cruel. Then the teenage assailant's gaze shifted to his fellow killers, and he said something in Spanish that made them laugh.

Joaquin wrapped his arms around her and pulled hard, obviously trying to thrust her behind him, but constrained by the small space. "Natalie, stop! Don't do this!"

The young assailant raised his gun.

"He's American!" Natalie shouted the words. "*Es americano!* He's—"

Then she realized the gun was pointed at her.

Her breath caught in her throat.

He's going to shoot you, girl.

She wondered for a moment how much it would hurt—then gasped as the butt of the gun came down on her temple. Her head seemed to explode. Blinded by pain and limp as a rag doll, she fell forward and felt cruel hands wrench her away from Joaquin, who fought to hold on to her, shouting something in Spanish that she couldn't understand.

"He's American," she managed to say, her own voice sounding faraway, the world spinning as she was dragged down the bloody aisle and passed from one attacker to another. She struggled to raise her head and caught just a glimpse of the man who'd struck her aiming his pistol at Joaquin. "Joaquin!"

Pop!

And she knew he was dead.

CHAPTER 2

HER HEAD THROBBING, Natalie struggled to breathe in the strangling darkness, her heart beating so hard it hurt, the sweltering air suffocating her, breath catching in her throat before it reached her lungs. She had to get out of here. She had to get *out*!

God, please help me! Somebody help me!

She might have screamed the words, or she might only have thought them. She didn't know. But, regardless, no help came.

She twisted in the cramped space, tried to stretch out, desperate for room to breathe, but the trunk was too small. Gasping for air, she reached out with bound hands to find only inches between her face and the underside of the trunk lid.

It was like being buried alive.

A scream caught in her throat, panic driving her as she pushed on the trunk lid with her hands and feet, striking it, kicking it, trying to force it open.

It didn't budge.

And for a moment, she was back in New Orleans at the hospital, the storm raging.

Come see, darlin'. They were already dyin', them. I jus' made it easier. Ya get on in there now. Go on.

No! You can't shut me in here. I'll suffocate!

Hush, you! Have a good death, a peaceful death.

Darkness. Cold. No air to breathe. The endless howling of the storm.

The car hurtled around a corner, throwing Natalie against the side of the trunk, her face pressed against rough carpet that stank of exhaust, the violent motion jolting her past the worst edge of her claustrophobia and back to the present, the pitch-black of the morgue locker fading into the darkness of the closed trunk—and a reality just as horrible and terrifying.

Joaquin was dead.

He was dead, along with so many others. Dear Sr. Marquez, who'd loved his grandkids so much. Ana-Leticia Izel, who'd been about Natalie's age. Isidoro Fernandez, who'd survived being shot in the leg on his way home from work last year. Sergio de Leon, who'd spent eight months in hiding after exposing several corrupt government officials as pawns of the cartels.

All gone. All dead.

And she was a captive of the men who'd killed them.

The cold, hard truth brought her heartbeat to a near standstill.

Oh, God.

What were they going to do to her?

What do you think they're going to do?

The El Paso police had talked about it a lot on the first day—the unsolved murders of young women and girls in Juárez. Hundreds had gone missing, and those whose bodies had been found had been sexually brutalized and dismembered. At first, the police had believed there was a single serial killer to blame. Then they'd blamed copycat killers.

But now, years later, it was clear that rape and murder were just part of the violent landscape, with drug cartels, sex slavers, human traffickers, gangs, and serial killers from both sides of the border preying on the young women who flocked to Juárez hoping for a job in one of the *maquiladoras*. During the seminar, they'd shown photos of some of the victims, stark images of young women lying naked and dead in ditches, in garbage bins, in the open desert.

And suddenly Natalie found it hard to breathe again, her heart tripping hard and fast, her stomach threatening to revolt. But it wasn't claustrophobia this time.

It was straight-up terror.

She squeezed her eyes shut, trying to force the unbearable

images from her mind, the distress and sorrow she'd felt at seeing what had happened to those women becoming fear for herself. Is that what these men planned to do to her?

I don't want to die like that. Not like that.

She didn't want to die at all.

Maybe they would hold her for ransom. She was a U.S. citizen, after all, and they knew she was a journalist. Maybe they just wanted money. Oh, God, she hoped so.

God, help me!

It was so hot, so hot. Her entire body was sticky with perspiration, her mouth dry from thirst—or was that fear? Claustrophobia began to take hold again, the close air pressing in on her. She had to get out of here. They needed to open the trunk *now*.

Except that . . .

What would they do to her when they did?

Abruptly, the car swerved, then accelerated. Men's voices rose in shrill whoops and shouts, guns firing, the terrible sound making Natalie jump. Were they being pursued? Had someone come after them, hoping to free her? What if there was a firefight and someone accidentally fired into the trunk?

She held her breath and listened, desperately hoping to hear sirens.

More shouts. More gunshots. And now singing.

But no sirens.

And then it came to her.

They weren't being pursued. They were celebrating.

All those murders, the grief they would cause, the fear they'd created on that street—they had committed a massacre, and they were reveling in its aftermath.

What kind of men could enjoy killing like that?

No, not men. They were monsters.

And she was their prisoner.

ZACH LAY ON his side, no longer able to give a damn about scorpions. His body shivered uncontrollably from shock. His skin burned, seeming to shrink around his bones, every nerve ending on fire. His throat was raw from yelling—or whatever you called it when you screamed from between clenched teeth. He'd been through surf torture in BUD/S. He'd been hungry, cold, hot, sleep deprived. He'd lain half-dead in the dirt for hours with a round lodged in his back. But he'd never ever been through anything that could touch this for sheer pain.

What was it Jimmy used to say when they went into combat? *Hoka hey! It is a good day to die.*

Today *was* a good day to die. Yesterday had been good, too. The day before would have been even better.

Quit your whining, McBride. You're pathetic! On your feet!

"Hooya!" Zach answered aloud and raised his head before realizing that the voice he'd just heard had come from his own mind.

He was losing it. He'd hit the wall—hard. Time to rest. He needed rest.

He closed his blindfolded eyes and sank into oblivion.

Jack and Jill went up the hill to fetch a pail of water
Jack fell down and broke his crown
And poor Jill got stuck carrying the water by herself.

Natalie bit at the duct tape that bound her wrists, reciting nursery rhymes in her mind to keep her panic at bay. She spat out a little piece of tape and bit into it again, gratified when she realized she was down to the layer just above her skin. The tape was so strong and sticky that she'd had to nibble through it a layer at a time. Not that having the use of her hands would do her much good. There were more of them—and they had guns.

Hey-diddle-diddle
The cat and the fiddle
The cow jumped over the moon
The little dog laughed . . .

And she couldn't remember the rest.

She spat out another piece of tape and another, then twisted her wrists, the tape pulling apart where she'd weakened it and at last giving way. Biting back an exultant laugh, she tore off the strips that stuck to her skin and threw them aside, her hands finally free.

Then, careful not to bump anything or make a sound, she turned onto her side and brought her knees up toward her chest, reaching down to pull off the tape that bound her ankles. It was hard to maneuver, and it took more than a few tries before she was able to find the end, get a grip on it with her nails, and unbind her ankles.

For a while, she lay there in the stifling dark, breathing hard.

She was thirsty, so thirsty, the heat unbearable, the carpet itchy against her sweaty skin. She had no idea how many hours had gone by. Wherever they were taking her, it was far outside the city, far from any place where the police would think to look for her—if they were looking for her and not in cahoots with the men who'd kidnapped her.

Jack be nimble
Jack be quick
Jack jump over the candlestick

She reached out beside her, searching the darkness for something, anything she might be able to use as a weapon. A pair of boots. Bits of cord and what felt like burlap. A box of bullets. A roll of duct tape. Something cold and hard—a tire iron? No, it was too short to be a tire iron. Both ends had holes, as if it were meant to screw on to something. Was it a scope for a rifle or part of a gun barrel?

She closed her hand around it, then froze as smooth asphalt gave way to the crunch of gravel. The car slowed, turned, and then rolled to a stop. Loud music. Men's voices. A burst of automatic weapons fire.

Oh, God.

She drew deep breaths to steady herself, fear slick and cold in her belly.

Little Miss Muffet, sat on a . . . sat on . . . on a tuffet,

What the heck is a tuffet anyway?

Car doors opened and closed, scattering her thoughts, the sound of boots in gravel all but drowned out by the thundering of her own pulse. She clutched the metal rod, held it fast, rolled onto her back, every muscle in her body tense.

A key slipped into the lock.

The trunk opened, bright sunlight hurting her eyes.

She struck out blindly with the rod, kicking with both legs, her right foot connecting with something hard, hours of pent-up grief, fear, and fury rushing out of her in a long, strangled cry that sounded more animal than human.

She found herself on her knees, the rod still in hand, her breath coming in pants. Four men watched her from a safe distance, astonishment on their faces, assault rifles hanging from their shoulders. Another—the one who'd killed Joaquin and Sr. Marquez—stood doubled over, groaning and cupping a bleeding nose, the sight giving her a momentary sense of satisfaction.

Then the oldest one, a man with a thick mustache and a tattoo of a strange veiled skeleton on his left forearm, began to laugh. He said something in Spanish to the others, who also laughed—all except for the one still holding his bleeding nose.

The older one motioned for her to get out of the trunk. "Come, señorita."

What else could she do? Slam the trunk shut and stay inside?

Natalie climbed out, the rod in her right hand, ready to strike, a hot breeze catching her hair, the midday heat cool compared to the sweltering environment of the trunk. Her feet touched gravel, and she found herself standing on trembling legs in the center of an old, abandoned town. To her right stood what was left of a mission-style church, a satellite dish perched on its bell tower. To her left sat a small adobe brick shed with no windows. Rows of adobe brick houses fanned out around them, their walls crumbling into dust, unpaved roads reclaimed by scrub and cactus. Beyond was nothing but open desert.

Her stomach fell, a chill sliding up her spine.

There was no one here to help her, nowhere to run.

She looked to the oldest man, the one with the tattoo, thinking he might be the leader of the bunch, only to find him raking her with his gaze. They were all staring at her now, their astonishment turned to something much darker. They spoke to one another, stared at her breasts, made little telltale thrusts with their pelvises, grinning and laughing.

Natalie took an involuntary step backward, the car's bumper stopping her short.

They came closer, one of them reaching out to feel her hair.

Don't let them see how afraid you are, girl.

She raised her chin a notch. "*M-me llamo Natalie Benoit. Soy periodista. Mi periódico* Denver Independent *le pagará—*"

The blow took her by surprise, knocking her to the ground, the rod flying from her hand.

"*¡Puta estúpida!*" The one with the bloody nose glared down at her, then tossed his gun aside and reached down with bloodstained fingers to unzip his fly.

The man with the skeleton tattoo shouted something at him, gave him a shove, and the two of them began to argue, their words coming too fast for Natalie to understand anything.

Ra-ta-ta-ta-ta-tat!

The sudden burst of automatic gunfire made Natalie jump.

From the direction of the old church came a man's voice, shouting at the others. Looking startled and almost afraid, her captors quit arguing, and the one with the tattoo reached down and jerked Natalie to her feet.

In the church doorway stood a man with an assault rifle perched on his bicep. Tall and rangy, he had a jagged scar that ran beneath his jawline on the right, as if someone had tried to slit his throat but had missed, the right side of his mouth drooping. He looked at her through cold, brown eyes, then tossed a pair of handcuffs to the one with the tattoo, motioning with a jerk of his head toward the adobe shed.

Words poured out of her. "Please let me go! I don't know who you are or what you want, but my newspaper will pay ransom to get me back alive. Please call them! *Mi periódico pagará dinero para mí—mucho dinero.*"

But no one was listening to her.

In a heartbeat, her wrists were cuffed, and she was being shoved and dragged across the courtyard toward the shed. One of them opened the door, and the man with the skeleton tattoo shoved her inside.

It was a jail—or they'd turned it into a jail. Three cells

that might once have been horse stalls lined the back wall.
The stone floor was covered with mouse droppings, spiders
clinging to webs along the edges of the low ceiling. Then
something ran across the floor in front of her.

A scorpion.

Her empty stomach lurched.

One of the men opened the first cell—a dark, windowless
space, no bigger than the walk-in closet in her bedroom at
home and hemmed in along the front by thick iron bars.

Hush now! Have a good death, a peaceful death.

"Please don't put me in there! Please don't!" Her heart
pounded, panic buzzing in her brain. And as they closed the
door behind her and left her in the pitch-black, she heard herself scream. "*No!*"

IT WAS THE sound of her first strangled scream that had
woken him. It had been the feral scream of a woman trying
to survive. Then a moment later she'd spoken, her voice soft,
young, feminine, her accent unmistakably New Orleans.

Natalie Benoit was her name, and she was what the Zetas
hated most after honest cops and soldiers—a journalist.

Zach had found himself sitting upright, straining to hear
while Zetas whose voices he didn't recognize—newcomers—
joked about raping her, clearly enjoying the rush of having
her at their mercy, their laughter colored by lust. Rather than
crying or begging for her life, she'd tried to bargain her way
out of the situation. Either she had a lot of guts, or she hadn't
understood a word they'd said. Given how poorly she spoke
Spanish, he was willing to bet it was the latter.

Then one of the bastards had struck her—hard from the
sound of it—and two of the men had begun to argue.

"*¡La putita me rompió la nariz!*" *The little whore broke
my nose!*

Zach had found that remarkable. *Good for her.*

"*¡Deja tu verga en los pantalones o te corto los cojones!
El Jefe la quiere para si mismo—sin violación.*" *Leave your
prick in your pants, or I'll cut off your balls! The chief wants
her for himself—untouched.*

The words had hit Zach square in the chest.

If Cárdenas wanted her as his personal sex slave, she was as good as dead.

A burst of AK fire had ended the fight.

I don't know who you are or what you want, but my newspaper will pay ransom to get me back alive. Please call them! Mi periódico pagará dinero para mí—mucho dinero.

Her naiveté had been painful to hear. Clearly, it hadn't yet dawned on her that life as she knew it was over. But the men had long since quit listening to her. Instead, they'd talked casually about what they hoped Cárdenas would do to her, bile rising into Zach's throat at each graphic and brutal description.

Cárdenas had a reputation for abusing women. Zach had heard that he sacrificed women to *La Santa Muerte*—that macabre cult saint of *Narcotraficantes*, Holy Death—as a way of giving thanks for his success in the cartel wars. To think that Zach had been *this close* to taking him, to ending his reign of terror . . .

Gisella should be in that cell now, not Natalie, whoever she was.

Please don't put me in there! Please don't!

She'd become almost hysterical the moment they'd brought her in here, her scream when they'd closed the door and walked away laced with primal terror. And for good reason. This filthy, dark place was probably beyond her worst nightmares.

Now she was in the cell next to his, separated from him by a wall of adobe brick. From the sound of it, she was about to hyperventilate, her breathing shallow and rapid, each exhale a whimper. He thought he could just make out the words of a prayer.

Sorry, angel, God seems to have taken the week off.

Then he realized she wasn't praying. She was reciting a nursery rhyme.

"To market, to market, to buy . . . to buy a fat pig." Her voice was unsteady, and she was clearly having trouble remembering the words. "H-home again, home again . . . I want to go home again . . . jiggety-jig."

The sweetness of it hit Zach hard. He hung his head, the hopelessness of her situation tearing at him.

She might not be here if you'd done your job.

Men like him were supposed to *stop* bastards like Cárdenas and his Zetas from hurting people. But rather than putting Cárdenas away, Zach was going to have a front-row seat while Cárdenas raped and tortured this girl to death.

Son of a bitch! Damn it!

Zach didn't realize he was trying to break free of the manacles again until his hands were wet, water from broken blisters mixing with sticky, warm blood.

Who are you fooling, man? You can't save her. You can't even save yourself.

No, he couldn't. But he *could* reach out to her, let her know she wasn't alone.

He swallowed, then sucked in as deep a breath as he could, wincing at the pain in his ribs. "Natalie? Can you hear me? My name is . . . Zach."

CHAPTER 3

FOR A MOMENT, Natalie thought she'd imagined the voice.

Hold it together, girl. She sat on her heels and grasped the iron bars of the door for support, unable to stop her body from trembling, her gaze fixed on the floor, trying despite the darkness to spot any sign of eight-legged movement. *Hold it together.*

Then she heard it again—a man's voice, deep and rough, speaking to her out of the darkness. "Natalie? That is your name, isn't it?"

For a moment, she said nothing, astonished to realize she wasn't alone in this terrible place. "Who . . . who are you?"

"My name's Zach. I'm your new neighbor. Sorry if I startled you."

"H-how do you know my name?"

"I overheard you telling them."

For a second, she forgot about scorpions. "You're American, too."

"Yeah. Born in Chicago. You're from the South. New Orleans?"

"Yes." So maybe she *did* have an accent. "Where are we?"

"I have no idea. I was unconscious when they brought me in."

Something moved near her right foot. She shrieked, stood, felt something crunch beneath her shoe. She kicked it aside, her skin crawling. "Wh-who are those awful men?"

"They're mercenaries for Los Zetas. They work for Arturo César Cárdenas."

Natalie had never heard of them. "What would they want with me?"

"Why don't you tell me how you got here, and we'll try to figure that out."

So Natalie told him about the SPJ convention and how armed men had stormed the tour bus in downtown Juárez, killing the Mexican journalists—and Joaquin.

"He was a good friend, always watching out for the rest of us, especially the women. And he was the best photojournalist I've known. He kept shooting . . . While they were killing people, he kept shooting . . ." And for the first time since this whole nightmare began, Natalie found herself fighting tears, the all-too-familiar ache of grief in her chest. Why did the people she cared about always die? "I tried to stop them. I blocked the aisle. I told them he was American over and over again, but . . ."

Oh, Joaquin!

"I'm sorry, Natalie." He sounded like he truly meant it. "You did more than most people would have. Give yourself credit for that much."

"That's kind of you to say, but it doesn't change the fact that he's gone."

"I know."

And for a time neither of them spoke.

"So you were researching the cartels for an article and joined this tour?"

She wiped tears off her cheeks with her hands. "N-no. I just wanted to get away from the office for a while. I've never written about drug smuggling or cartels."

"Never?" He sounded surprised.

"Never." Something tickled her cheek. She gasped, brushed at it, her fingertips knocking what might have been a small spider off her face. She shrank against the bars, looking up to see what else might be about to drop down on her, but it was too dark.

"How about any big drug busts? Cartels growing dope on national forest land in Colorado? Mexican politics? Anything related to Juárez or the state of Chihuahua?"

"No. Not at all. I cover mostly local issues. Before I left, I started looking into the sheriff's handling of some sexual assaults that happened at a local boarding school. I don't imagine these Zetas care one whit about that."

"No, I don't imagine they do."

"Maybe I just caught their attention by trying to stop them from killing Joaquin."

"Maybe." He didn't sound convinced.

"Why are you here? Are you a journalist, too?"

Silence filled the darkness.

Then at last he answered. "The less you know about me, the better. Let's just say I made a bad decision and leave it at that."

So he'd done something to cross the Zetas. That meant he was probably a criminal, maybe even involved in the drug trade. "That's all you're going to tell me?"

"The Zetas have been . . . *interrogating* me for six days now. If they thought I'd spilled my guts to you, they'd start interrogating you, too, and believe me, that's not something either of us wants to see happen."

And Natalie understood. They weren't just asking Zach questions. They were torturing him. Then she noticed something she hadn't before. The way he spoke his words slowly, the strain in his voice, its rough timbre—he was in pain. "You're hurt."

"Don't worry about it."

"I . . . I'm sorry. I wish I could help—"

"You can't." The tone of his voice was starkly final.

Something brushed her arm, making her gasp and jump—and she realized it was a lock of her own hair. *Good grief, Benoit!* "You . . . You've been here for six days? I don't know how you've been able to stand it."

"Don't tell me you don't like the accommodations." He chuckled, then groaned, as if it hurt to laugh. "I know it's not five-star, and room service leaves a lot to be desired, but what this place lacks in comfort it more than makes up for in scorpions."

Natalie didn't find that funny. "I hate those things!"

"Yeah, I figured. I can hear you gasping and jumping around over there. I'm guessing you're afraid of the dark, too."

"No. I'm . . . I'm claustrophobic."

And then it dawned on her. She hadn't had to fight off panic since she'd heard Zach's voice.

ZACH CONCENTRATED ON Natalie's words as she told him what had happened to her to make her claustrophobic, the feminine sound of her voice calling him back from the brink, keeping him awake, helping him ignore his pain.

"Then he turned and saw me standing there. He knew I'd seen him inject that poor old man. I tried to run, but he moved so fast. He put his hand over my mouth and dragged me down the back stairs to the morgue. I fought as hard as I could, but he was so much stronger. He forced me into a morgue locker. He said the same thing to me that I'd overheard him say to the old man—'H-have a good death, a p-peaceful death.' And then he . . . he shut the door."

Her words quavered slightly, telling him that she was trembling, proof of how hard it was for her to relive what had happened to her during Hurricane Katrina—and no wonder. "Morgue lockers are airtight, aren't they?"

"Y-yes. It was cold, so cold. I tried to push the door open . . . but they don't open from the inside."

That made sense, as corpses rarely had a pressing reason to get out.

"I beat on the door, but that only used up air faster. Most of the staff had been evacuated, so no one was on the other side to hear." Her voice quavered again, something twisting in Zach's chest at the sound. "I started to fall asleep. I knew I was suffocating. I blacked out. Then a doctor was standing over me, pumping air into my lungs. They'd brought down the body of one of his victims and ended up finding me."

And none too soon from the sound of it.

"What happened to the intern?" It was bad enough that the bastard had decided to play God, murdering dying people, robbing them of their last days. But what he'd done to Natalie . . .

Have a good death, a peaceful death.

What kind of fucked up insanity was that? The son of a bitch was a sociopath, and Zach hoped someone had kicked his ass. And all at once it struck Zach as grotesquely unfair that Natalie had survived her ordeal during Katrina only to end up in the hands of the Zetas.

God has a sick sense of humor, McBride. You know that.

He sure as hell did.

"When I was fully conscious again, I told them what had happened. They arrested him. I wrote about it for the paper and testified at his trial. The jury sentenced him to life without parole. But I've been claustrophobic ever since. I . . . I just can't take feeling shut in."

Zach couldn't blame her for that. As he knew only too well, some experiences marked a person for life. But that was then. This was now.

"Listen to me, Natalie, and listen hard. Spiders won't kill you. These scorpions won't kill you—they're not the deadly kind. The dark sure as hell won't kill you, and no matter how it feels to you, this closed-in space won't kill you, either. But those men out there—there's not one of them who would think twice about taking your life."

For a moment she said nothing.

"What are they going to do to you, Zach?"

Wasn't that obvious? "You're talking to a dead man."

"Are you sure? Maybe, if you—"

"I'm sure."

"Aren't you . . . aren't you afraid?"

Hell, yeah, he was afraid—of breaking, of giving up intel that would get other people killed, of betraying his country, his fellow DUSMs, his mission. But he couldn't tell her that. "I'm not afraid of dying."

"You're braver than I am." She paused. "Wh-what do you think they'll do to me?"

Ah, hell.

How was he supposed to answer that question?

"Are you sure you want to go there?"

"I'm going to end up like the other girls who've gone missing from Juárez, aren't I?" She spoke the words calmly, but he knew she was terrified. What woman wouldn't be?

He wished he could tell her that everything would be okay, but he couldn't lie to her. "I don't think these guys are going to touch you. I heard them say they're saving you for their boss, for Cárdenas."

"B-but . . . why does he want me?"

Zach wished he could answer that question. He'd studied Cárdenas for years, knew him better than any other U.S. operative, and he found it strange that the bastard would kidnap an American journalist unless he had a reason. Then again, when it came to women, Cárdenas was a predator. "I've heard he has a thing for young women. Is your photo online?"

"Y-yes. It's on the newspaper's website and . . . and I think it's on the networking page for the SPJ conference, too. Do you think that's how he found out about me?"

"It's possible." Cárdenas had probably looked through the networking site to see which Mexican journalists would be on that bus, had seen Natalie's photograph, and had decided to take her. That meant Natalie had to be extremely attractive. Otherwise, Cárdenas wouldn't have bothered.

"What do you think Cárdenas will do with me?" She sounded so vulnerable.

Zach found it hard to answer her, regret at what he had to tell her forming a knot in his chest. "I imagine he'll . . . rape you repeatedly over a period of days or maybe even weeks and then . . . sell you . . . or kill you."

That's a hell of a thing to say to a woman, McBride.

She took it better than he'd imagined she would.

"*Oh, God!*" The words were whispered, a private expression of despair, not meant for him to hear. When she spoke again, her voice shook. "M-my mother always told me there'd come a day when I'd regret asking so many questions."

If she had fallen into hysterics, it might have been easier for him to bear because that's what he'd expected. But her attempt at humor left him feeling outraged at Cárdenas, at the Zetas, and most of all at himself for being helpless to stop them.

"Your mother must be very proud of you."

Not to mention worried out of her mind.

"My m-mother . . ." Natalie's voice broke. Tears at last. She'd held out a long time. "She and my father are . . . gone. They died with my fiancé in a car crash on the way to get me at the hospital."

It took a moment for Zach to realize what she was telling him. Her parents and her fiancé had been killed in a car accident on the way to the hospital to pick her up. *On the same day she'd almost been murdered.*

Behind his blindfold, he squeezed his eyes shut, the bottom dropping out of his stomach, pity for her momentarily overpowering his own suffering. She'd lost everything—everything but her life—thanks to a goddamned psychopath and Hurricane Katrina. And she'd survived all of that only to end up here.

"I'm so very sorry, Natalie." He didn't know what else to say.

In the darkness, he could hear her crying. "It's been a long time since I've talked about this with anyone."

"I'm glad you felt you could trust me." He knew it had nothing to do with him personally. Ordeals like the one she'd been through today had a way of stripping a person down to their core. And knowing what he now knew, Natalie's must be pure titanium.

She would need every bit of that strength before this was over.

Unable to do anything else to help her, Zach gave her the only advice he could. "I know it's hard, but you need to stay focused on what's happening now. Do whatever it takes to survive. Do you hear me, Natalie? Just survive."

NATALIE HUGGED HER arms around her legs and rested her chin on her knees, trying to calm her empty, churning stomach and pull herself back together. She hadn't meant to fall apart like that. She hadn't meant to dump her private pain into a stranger's lap. But being locked up like this had brought it all back for her, and it had come spilling out before she could contain herself, her grief as overpowering as it had been six years ago.

Oh, Mama. Daddy. Beau.

She wiped her tears away. Zach was right. She needed to focus on what was happening now, because her life depended on it.

I imagine he'll rape you repeatedly over a period of days or maybe even weeks and then sell you—or kill you.

It seemed strange to her that just this morning she'd had

little more on her mind than the heat and the day's itinerary. Now that world had been taken away from her. Soon her body would be stolen, too—and then her life. Would anyone know for sure what had happened to her? Would they find her body in a ditch one day, naked and broken?

> *Old Mother Hubbard*
> *Went to the cupboard*
> *To fetch the poor dog a bone*

Natalie's stomach growled, the sound loud enough to make her wonder if Zach had heard it. "Do they ever feed us?"

He didn't answer at first, and she thought he must have fallen asleep. When at last he answered, he sounded weaker, his words slower, his voice more strained. "Not so much. Don't . . . expect much to drink, either."

"Oh." Another wave of despair rolled through her. She fought to subdue it.

Zach wasn't whining and complaining. Neither should she.

"Zach, wake up! I think they're coming!"

Zach jerked awake.

Men's voices grew nearer.

Gritting his teeth, he dragged himself upright, more aware of Natalie's fear than his own discomfort or dread. He fought to catch his breath. "It's okay . . . Cárdenas isn't here yet. They're . . . coming for me . . . not for you."

"It's not okay! No matter what you've done to anger them, you don't deserve to be tortured or chained up like this. You are in chains, aren't you? I can hear them clinking when you move."

"I guess they figure . . . I'm more of a threat than you are." And then it hit him. She probably thought he was some kind of criminal. Not surprising, given their situation and how little he'd told her.

In that instant, the door was thrown wide, daylight spilling across his blindfold. Familiar voices joked in Spanish about Natalie.

"She *is* pretty—and shy. Look. She doesn't like it when I try to touch her."

Zach thought he heard Natalie gasp, her shoes scuffing on the floor as she backed away from the door to her cell.

The men laughed.

"I hope El Jefe shares her when he's done with her. Oh, she makes me hard."

"Do you think El Jefe would mind if we fuck only her mouth?"

Anger and disgust burned through Zach, reviving him, clearing his head. He spoke to them in their own language, hoping Natalie hadn't understood what they'd said. "Cárdenas will feed your dicks to his dogs, you stupid *chingaderos.*"

That got their attention.

Zach heard a key slip into the lock of his cell door.

"Eh, *cuñado*, are you ready to talk? Or do you want to die screaming?"

He ignored the taunt. "You should feed her and give her clean water. Do you think your Jefe wants a weak, half-starved bag of bones? And if these scorpions sting her and make her sick—I wonder what El Jefe will do to you then."

The stench of alcohol and sour sweat assaulted Zach's nostrils as someone leaned down and spoke directly into his face. "Shut your mouth before I cut out your tongue, you stinking son of a whore."

His manacles were unclipped from the chain, then he was hauled to his feet, one Zeta at each elbow. He stumbled blindly forward, wishing he had the strength to fight them. He'd tried on his first day here, but he hadn't been able to get his cuffed hands in front of his body fast enough to pull his blindfold off so that he could see the men he was trying to fight. That's when they'd kicked the shit out of him and broken his ribs.

Now he barely had the strength to stand upright.

"Zach!" Natalie's voice came from his right. "Leave him alone!"

He dug in his heels, fought to stand his ground for just another moment. "Listen to me, Natalie. Don't let Cárdenas get inside your head. Nothing he can do to you can change who you are. Remember that!"

Then he was shoved roughly forward, pain splitting his side, stealing his breath. Sunlight hit him full in the face, cool stone giving way to sharp, hot gravel beneath his bare feet. Every muscle in his body tensed.

I am an American, fighting in the forces that guard my country . . .

He started to recite the code of conduct, trying to prepare his mind for what was to come, but a different thought replaced it. It was nothing much—just a name—but it seemed to put steel back into his spine.

Natalie.

NATALIE BIT INTO the corn tortilla and chewed. It might as well have been sand. She swallowed, forcing it past the hard lump in her throat, eating only because she knew she must.

Do whatever it takes to survive. Do you hear me, Natalie? Just survive.

Overhead, vultures wheeled black against a blue sky, a hint of a breeze kicking up dust, the blazing disk of the sun moving toward a bank of clouds on the western horizon. The second worst day of her life was almost over, to be followed, she was sure, by an even worse day. Worse for her, but much worse for Zach.

There'd been a Zeta with a big rifle standing in front of her cell door when they'd dragged him out, so she hadn't been able to see his face. He'd been shirtless and barefoot, and she'd seen enough to know that he was tall, his body lean and muscular like an athlete's, his wrists in manacles behind his back, his hands covered with blood.

Another agonized cry.

She fought back tears.

God in heaven, what were they doing to him? It sounded like they were killing him. She'd never heard cries like this before—more animal than human, a cross between a scream and a roar. No wonder his voice was so rough. His throat must be raw after six days of this.

Six days.

God, help him! Please help him! Make them stop!

Her throat tight, she took another bite, chewed, then washed it down with the last of the cola, ignoring the Zeta with the skeleton tattoo, who stood within arm's reach, guarding her while she ate, a look of mingled amusement and lust on his face. Even from here she could smell the alcohol on his breath—and the stench of his unwashed body.

Not long after they'd come for Zach, a young Zeta had unlocked her cell door and led her out into the hot sunshine, where the one with the skeleton tattoo had been waiting with a plate of corn tortillas, an overripe banana, and a glass bottle of warm Coca-Cola. Then the younger one had disappeared inside the little prison with a broom, apparently sent to sweep it clean of scorpions and spiders. Why they'd suddenly decided to clean the hovel Natalie couldn't say, but she no longer cared about the spiders or the scorpions.

Another cry.

Long and drawn out, it ended on a high, desperate pitch that made her chest ache.

"Why are you doing this to him?" No answer. She tried again in Spanish. *"¿Por qué le haces esto a él?"*

"Se robó nuestra cocaína."

Zach had stolen cocaine from the Zetas.

Oh, my gentle Jesus! He called *that* a bad decision? Understatement of the century.

Still, he didn't deserve to be brutalized and chained like an animal. No one deserved to be treated like this.

Another cry.

The Zeta guarding her stepped closer. He reached out to caress her hair. She smacked his hand away.

He laughed. "Nice. *Le vas a gustar al Jefe." The boss will like you.*

Natalie ignored him.

Apparently thinking she hadn't understood him, he translated his words into English, this time thrusting with his pelvis to show exactly what he meant. "He will like you very much. And then . . . *Él te sacrificará a Santa Muerte."*

The words were close enough to English that Natalie understood.

He will sacrifice you to La Santa Muerte.

Saint Death?

Chills skittered down Natalie's spine. Was that his way of saying that this Cárdenas was going to kill her? She looked up to see the guard pointing to the strange skeleton tattooed onto his forearm. Then he drew his finger across his throat in a gesture that needed no explanation.

He smiled, exposing missing teeth. "*La Santa Muerte.*"

And Natalie understood. The image on his arm wasn't just a tattoo. It was an icon of sorts, like a dark saint, a saint of death. And he believed Cárdenas meant to sacrifice her to it.

Another long, strangled cry.

The last bit of tortilla that Natalie still held in her hand fell onto her plate.

Kidnapping. Torture. Human sacrifice to skeleton saints.

It might have been a hundred degrees in the shade, but Natalie felt ice-cold.

She hugged her arms around herself, shivering, her gazed locked on the macabre tattoo with its grinning skull. Then the door to the church burst open, and the Zeta whose nose she'd broken hurried over to them, shouting something in urgent tones to the one guarding her, both of his eyes blackened, his nose swollen.

Natalie was jerked to her feet, her plate and the empty Coke bottle falling to the ground. The one with the broken nose raised a hand, and she thought he was going to strike her again. Instead, his fingers dug into her arms and dragged her toward the church.

CHAPTER 4

ZACH HUNG LIMPLY from the manacles, unable even to hold up his head. His shoulders ached from supporting his deadweight, manacles biting into his bloody wrists. But none of that could compare to the residual pain of that last electroshock. His muscles seized in sharp spasms, his heart slamming erratically in his chest, his body shaking, his mouth filled with the coppery taste of his own blood.

Don't give in to the pain. Adjust for it.

He willed himself to relax, slowed his breathing.

Cold water splashed over his chest, making him jerk. It wasn't to revive him, he knew, but to make his skin more conductive to electricity. He waited for the next blast of agony, but instead felt a glass bottle against his lips. A hand fisted in his hair, tilting his head back, and he swallowed, warm cola sliding down his raw, parched throat.

Electrolytes. Caffeine. Calories.

All would help him stay alive.

Then his tormenter spoke to him, as always in Spanish. "You are dying, *cuñado*. And for what? You are alone now, forgotten, left without even a dog to bark at you. Tell us who has the cocaine and where we can find them. Then your torment will end. There will be no more pain, only sleep."

Zach fought off a wave of despair. "*¡Vete a la verga!*" *Fuck off!*

The bastard chuckled, but Zach knew he wasn't really

amused. They'd tried to break him and had failed. There'd be a price to pay when Cárdenas got the news.

Creaking hinges. Footsteps.

And Zach knew she was there. He could feel her presence, hear her rapid breathing. Hell, he could even smell her, something sweet in a world of filth.

Natalie.

"*Tráela aquí.*" *Bring her over here.*

What the hell?

Zach's head came up. Somehow, he drew himself to his feet, his hands clenched around the chains for support, his heart thudding hard in his chest. Why had they brought her in here? Were they going to torture her to get to him?

Over my dead body.

"Zach?" There was fear in her voice, but also sympathy, concern.

He shook his head, his sign to her to keep quiet, hoping she'd remembered what he'd told her earlier. If they thought he cared what happened to her, if they thought he'd told her anything . . .

An arm went around his shoulder. "You are a brave man. No one has ever lasted so long against my little stinger, so I'll offer you a better way out. Tell us where the coke is, and you can have the girl. We'll take off these chains, give you some food and a little coke to make you strong, *sí*? Then you can fuck her till your prick gives out. And when you're done, you get one bullet to the head. Fast, painless—and you die happy. If you do not, your suffering will be such that those who find what is left of your body will lie awake at night weeping for you."

Zach might have laughed if the situation hadn't been so serious. Having failed to break him with pain, they were now trying to bribe him with rape. They were only bluffing, of course. They had no intention of giving him their Jefe's prize. But if he played along with them, if he could persuade them to unchain him . . .

He pretended to consider the offer. "*¿Es bonita?*" *Is she pretty?*

Rough hands tore off his blindfold.

"*¡Mira sus tetas!*" *Just look at her tits!*

Unaccustomed to light he blinked, squinted—and quickly

assessed the situation. He was in a small room with a half-dozen armed Zetas. There were two small windows and only one door. Wooden chairs sat around an old table littered with dirty dishes and half-empty bottles of tequila. A couple of AKs leaned up against the wall to his right.

You'd give your left nut for one of those, wouldn't you, man?

He sure as hell would.

In front of him, a truck battery sat on a rolling cart, two electrical cables dropped on the floor near his feet. The sight made him shudder, dread mixing with rage in his gut.

Little stinger?

Beside the cart, two Zetas held a struggling young woman between them, while a third unbuttoned her blouse, laughing to himself. *Bastards.* Knowing he couldn't risk showing emotion, he met Natalie's gaze.

His heart seemed to stop. His mind went blank. And he stared.

She looked pleadingly up at him through the most beautiful eyes he'd ever seen, their irises an unusual shade of aqua blue. Her features were delicate, her otherwise flawless skin marred by dark bruises and smudges of dirt. Her dark brown hair—why had he imagined her as a blonde?—hung in thick tangles past her shoulders. She couldn't have been more than five-foot-four or an ounce over one-twenty.

The protective urge that welled up inside him took him by surprise, and he actually took a step toward her, until chains and pain reminded him where he was—and in what condition. Then her blouse fell to the floor, followed by a lacy, white bra, revealing two beautiful, natural breasts.

A low whistle. A groan.

"*¡Oye, mamacita, que buena estás!*" *Oh, baby, you are fine!*

The testosterone level in the room surged, and for a moment Zach was afraid the Zetas' lust for Natalie would overcome their fear of Cárdenas.

The one with a long scar—the electrical specialist who'd turned Zach's life into a living hell—walked over to stand behind Natalie, then reached around, drew her back against him, and grabbed her breasts, hands that enjoyed cruelty manhandling sensitive flesh.

"*¡Chécalo, güey—las chichis perfectas¡*" *Check it out, dude—perfect boobs.*

Zach felt his teeth grind, seeing only the emotion on Natalie's face—fear, revulsion, pain. Her gaze locked with his as if eye contact were the one thing keeping her shattered world together. She probably didn't understand what was happening or why they were doing this to her. He wished he could reassure her.

Instead, he was about to make it all much worse.

Stay strong, angel.

TRYING TO BLOCK out what was being done to her, Natalie clung to the encouragement in Zach's eyes. He had gray eyes, deeply set beneath dark brows and fringed with long lashes. Hollows in his cheeks accented high cheekbones, his square jaw and strong chin covered with a week's growth of dark stubble. His mouth was broad, his lips unusually full. They curved into a slight smile she knew was meant to bolster her.

But behind the smile, she could see he was suffering.

By far the tallest and most physically powerful man in the room, he stood with his arms chained to the ceiling, his wrists bleeding and raw from the manacles. His bare skin was wet, red blotches on his chest and abdomen where they'd shocked him. There was a dark bruise on his left side and dark circles beneath his eyes, his face bruised and lined with pain and exhaustion, his short, dark hair tousled. His bare feet were set wide apart for balance, water in a puddle beneath him, electrical cables dangerously near.

The Zeta who was groping her said something, his hands rough as he squeezed her, kneaded her, pinched her nipples.

Then Zach replied. "*No hay trato. Quítame las cadenas, y dame una hora para chingarla. Luego te diré dónde encontrar la cocaína.*"

Natalie understood only part of what he said, but it was enough to send blood rushing to her head.

Give me an hour to fuck her . . . I'll tell you where to find the cocaine.

He didn't mean it. He couldn't mean it.

Stunned, she stared into his eyes, looking for some sign that he was pretending, but seeing only lust.

He broke eye contact, licked his lips, his gaze raking over her, coming to rest on her breasts, his mouth twisting in a crude grin. *"Me gustaría jugar con esas."*

He was talking about her breasts.

Her heart gave a hard knock. "Wh-what are you saying?"

But Zach ignored her. He was arguing with Sr. Scar Face, who quit groping her—*thank God!*—and began shouting in rapid Spanish. Zach answered calmly, giving a little tug on his chains and motioning toward Natalie with a jerk of his head. And although Natalie couldn't understand more than a phrase or two, she knew their disagreement revolved around whether Zach would give up the location of the stolen cocaine before or after they unchained him and let him have her.

Then Sr. Scar Face reached up and grabbed Zach by the throat, his voice going cold and deadly quiet, each word enunciated clearly. *"¿Dónde está la cocaína?" Where is the cocaine?*

The room fell silent.

Zach laughed, winced as if laughing hurt, then answered in Spanish.

Sr. Scar Face glowered at him and shouted something to the other Zetas. As abruptly as her blouse and bra had been removed, they were shoved into her hands. She turned her back on the men to dress, her fingers fumbling as she tried to fasten her bra clasp and buttons, angry shouts filling the little room.

When she turned around again, Zach was blindfolded once more. Confused, afraid, she wanted answers. "Zach, what—"

He turned his face toward her, a black bandana tied tightly over his eyes. "Go, Natalie! Go, and don't ask questions!"

The Zeta with the skeleton tattoo grabbed her arm and pulled her toward the door, but not before she saw Sr. Scar Face pick up the electric cables and move in on Zach.

She heard her own voice shout in protest. "Stop it! Please don't—"

Then a hand closed roughly over her mouth, and she was dragged out the door, Zach's agonized cry following her back to her cell.

* * *

NATALIE PRESSED THE joint of her left handcuff against the mortar and scraped as hard as she could. It was so dark she couldn't see, but she knew she was making progress, mortar crumbling like sand and falling over her fingers to the floor. If she could scrape away the mortar and remove the bricks around the metal plate that held the latch, she might be able to open her cell door and escape. At the very least, she had to try.

If she didn't find a way out of here, she would have to endure a lot worse than just a man's filthy, repulsive hands on her breasts.

She scraped back and forth until her arms ached and she was out of breath, then rested for a few minutes and started again, oblivious to anything that crept or crawled in the darkness, a part of her listening for Zach's quiet moans—proof that he was still alive. They'd brought him back about twenty minutes ago, two Zetas dragging his unconscious body between them, and although she'd called his name, he hadn't responded.

What if he doesn't wake up?

He would wake up. He had to wake up.

She would never forget the sight of him, blindfolded and chained from the ceiling, his body twisting in agony as electricity shot through him. She couldn't fathom how he had endured that for a single hour, let alone six days.

All for some stupid cocaine.

His suffering dwarfed her own. Even so, she'd never felt more violated in her life, the sickening sensation of that man's hands cupping and squeezing her breasts leaving her nauseated. Even worse had been the expressions on the men's faces—even Zach's. They'd made her feel dirty, degraded, less than human, like a sexual toy to be played with and eventually broken. Oh, how she wanted a bath!

At least they didn't torture you, too.

That's what she'd thought they planned to do when they'd brought her into the church. She would probably never know exactly what had happened in that room—why they'd brought her in, why they'd stripped off her blouse and bra, why Sr.

Scar Face had groped her, displaying her to Zach like a piece of meat, why Zach had looked at her the way he had or said the things he'd said. They'd been trying to make a deal—information about the cocaine Zach had stolen in return for sex with her. Although part of her wanted to believe that Zach had been pretending, that he'd been playing along in hopes of escaping, she'd realized she knew nothing about him besides the fact that he'd stolen cocaine. And as she'd sat in the dark, unable to keep herself from hearing his cries, the stark reality of her situation had become clear.

If she wanted to live, she had to find a way to escape.

She certainly had nothing to lose by trying. The worst the Zetas could do was kill her, but Cárdenas was going to do that anyway. She might as well fight them with everything she had. At least then she'd have a chance.

That's when it had dawned on her that their little prison was made of the same crumbling adobe bricks as the houses. She'd tested it, scraping it with the edge of her handcuffs, her heart soaring when the mortar turned easily to dust. Then she'd looked around for the quickest and surest way out and had gone to work.

Why hadn't she thought of this sooner?

Though she *was* making progress, it was slow going. If they came for Zach again, if they caught her, if Cárdenas came for her before she was finished . . .

Don't go there, girl. Worrying won't help.

Her mind kept drifted back to Zach—and what it would mean for both of them if she left him behind.

You can't take him with you. You might not have time to break him out, too.

She might not. But to leave him here to suffer and die?

You don't know him. You can't trust him. He's a criminal.

Yes, he was. But could she turn her back on him? She knew from the way he'd tried to comfort her that there was kindness in him. Besides, no man deserved to suffer as he had.

He told you to do whatever you had to do to survive. He would understand.

He might understand, but would she be able to live with herself? Or would she hear those terrible cries for the rest of her life?

You could escape and tell the authorities about him. They could come and rescue him.

Yes, if he wasn't already dead by then.

Don't worry about it now. You have to get out of your cell first.

If she got through this, she was going to live her life to the fullest. She was going to go dancing and date and spend more time with her I-Team friends. She was going to take art classes and learn how to ski. She was going to learn to make beignets just like her Tante Evangeline had made them.

If she got through this.

She paused again to rest, her shoulders and neck aching, a thin layer of dust coating her skin, her teeth, her throat. "Zach? Can you hear me?"

Silence.

She went back to scraping.

NATALIE LOST ALL sense of time after that, though it seemed to her it must be after midnight. Loud music drifted across the courtyard together with the sound of men's and women's laughter. The Zetas had gone to town for some prostitutes—*those poor women!*—and were having a party.

She had managed to remove one small brick so far and was close to removing another, when the steel of her cuffs hit something hard. At first she thought it was the iron of the latch. Her pulse picking up, she ran her fingers over it, only to realize it had a different texture than the adobe—and was much harder.

Concrete.

Her stomach fell, and she sagged against the wall, fighting back a cry.

No! Please no!

As much as she didn't want to believe it, she knew it was true. When they'd installed the doors, they'd reinforced the wall with concrete because the original mortar was so weak. The latch, the hinges—they were probably all reinforced with concrete.

It's okay, girl. It's okay. It just means you have to take out more bricks.

She would have to remove all the bricks around the concrete, too. Which meant it would take much longer—perhaps longer than she had.

Fighting hopelessness and panic, she scraped furiously. Then she felt something catch, and her left elbow flew back, hitting the wall behind her. It wasn't until she reached over with her right hand to rub her funny bone that she realized her left wrist was free.

ZACH LAY WITH *his face in the dirt, thirsty and weak from blood loss, the pain in his back excruciating, the sat phone broken. But that didn't matter. He'd completed the call. Support was on its way—probably a chopper full of pissed-off SEALs and Army Night Stalkers.*

The guys would be okay. He might not get out alive, but his element would.

From down in the valley came the sound of three M4s and one HK MP5 firing.

Give 'em hell, boys.

Blood loss making him desperately thirsty, Zach raised his head, prayed to God his pack was within reach—and then he saw. His body went cold.

Oh, Christ, no!

At least eighty enemy combatants snaked down the mountainside across from him, headed straight for the valley, all of them armed. They would come up behind his team and catch the men by surprise. The guys would be caught in a cross fire by an enemy that outnumbered them and had the high ground.

By the time support arrived, it would be too late—for all of them.

He reached for his rifle, determined to send as many Taliban fighters to hell as he could, only to find his hands chained behind his back. He couldn't move.

Then Brian's wife, Debbie, walked up to him, dressed in black, tears streaming down her face, baby in her arms. "You should have died, not my husband. Not my husband!"

From the valley below came an explosion of gunfire and the cries of dying men.

"Zach? Can you hear me?"

Zach gasped, opened his eyes, and saw nothing, the taste of blood and horror in his mouth. Cold, dirty stone pressed against his skin, his left side aching.

Mexico. Not Afghanistan. Not Afghanistan.

"Zach? Are you awake?" It was Natalie.

He didn't bother trying to sit up, knowing it was beyond him. They'd put everything they had into breaking him, shocking him until he'd all but lost the ability to respond to pain. How his heart had held out, he wasn't sure. But he knew that the next sunrise would mark his last day on this earth. The Zetas were through with him.

"Tomorrow, I will fry you until you die, even if it takes all day and all night," his tormenter had hissed in his face just before they'd dragged him from the room.

All day and all night.

The leftover dread from his nightmare settled like lead in his belly.

"Zach, please wake up!"

He swallowed, his throat dry as sand. "I . . . I'm awake."

"Oh, thank God! I thought you . . ." She didn't finish the thought.

"No . . . I'm not dead." *Not yet.*

Her relief sounded sincere, and some part of him was touched that she cared enough to worry about him, especially after what he'd done. He knew she didn't understand what had happened in that room. He needed to explain. He could no more rape a woman than eat his own balls. But before he could tell her that, he was drifting again.

Her voice brought him back. "If I get us out of here, will you promise to help me get safely back to the States?"

"What?" What in the hell had she just said?

"If I can get us both out of here, will you promise to help me get safely home?"

It was then he noticed a scraping sound.

He opened his eyes. "Do you think you have a way out?"

"The mortar is really dry and soft. I've been digging at it all night, and I think I'm going to be able to open my cell door soon. My handcuffs broke, and the curved part is really good for scraping this stuff out."

"Your handcuffs broke?" Zach's mind raced, his pulse like thunder in his ears.

The scraping sound stopped.

"I hit concrete where they reinforced the wall," she answered, out of breath, "and it snapped the left one open."

"Natalie, I think you've got yourself a weapon."

CHAPTER 5

"IT'S NOT EASY to kill a man, but that's what you have to be ready to do." Zach leaned against the cool bricks, all of his senses focused on the young woman on the other side of the wall. Both of their lives now depended entirely on her. He'd been coaching her all night, talking her through this, his already battered voice worn to a hoarse whisper. "Once you start this, you have to finish it. If you don't, these bastards will take you apart piece by piece. Do you understand?"

"Yes."

Her answer didn't reassure him. How could she understand?

Killing was a brutal business. She didn't know what it was like to look into a man's panicked eyes, to smell his breath, to feel him fighting desperately to live—and to end his life. She wasn't trained to fight. She wasn't trained to kill.

Zach was. He should be the one getting ready to take on the Zetas, not Natalie. But until these chains came off, he was useless.

When she'd finally worked that last brick free and broken out of her cell, they'd realized there wasn't enough time for her to break him out, too. So he'd told her to focus instead on getting rid of any sign that the door to her cell had been tampered with. They didn't want an open cell door or displaced bricks to tip the Zetas off the moment they stepped inside. While she'd been busy settling bricks back into place, he'd tried to come up with a plan of attack that wouldn't get her killed, an unshakable sense of guilt gnawing at him.

He was supposed to protect the innocent, not the other way around.

He pushed the thought from his mind. "It's going to be tougher than you think. You have to inflict as much pain and do as much damage as you can as fast as you can. Go for their eyes, their balls. If you hesitate, if you don't put all your strength into it . . ."

Yet how much strength could a woman like Natalie bring to bear against men as ruthless as the Zetas? Zach had met women in the military who could kick ass, women who were ripped, women who were trained in martial arts and marksmanship. But even they didn't have the strength necessary to serve in Special Forces. Natalie had none of their training. She was soft, curvy, feminine—not the kind of woman who beat up paramilitary goons. When it came to fighting, her only assets were her intelligence and her courage.

That's why Zach had been trying all night to prepare her mind, channeling more than a decade of combat and law enforcement experience into a few stolen hours.

Would it be enough? It had to be.

"If you're trying to talk me out of this, it won't work. If I don't do *something*, we both die." There was determination in her voice, but also fear.

Fear was good. In the right amount, it could strengthen a person's resolve, sharpen his senses. But too much fear could paralyze.

"I *know* you can do it, Natalie." He wanted to build her up, not psych her out. "The way you tried to protect your friend Joaquin, the way you broke that Zeta's nose—that took guts. I'm just trying to prepare you for what you're about to face."

"I take it you've killed men before?" There was an edge to her voice.

Clearly, she didn't trust him. He couldn't blame her, not after last night.

He searched for an answer that would relieve her suspicion. He didn't want her thinking he was some kind of sociopath. "Yes, I've killed, but only when I had no choice. It's never easy taking another person's life, but sometimes it's necessary."

"Oh."

And for a time, neither of them spoke.

It was she who broke the silence. "You still haven't given me your word yet."

It took him a moment to figure out what she meant, his brain fogged by hunger, exhaustion, pain. "If you get me out of these chains, I promise I will do everything I can to get you home safely."

"Good, because I really don't want to leave you here."

He sure as hell didn't want to be left behind. But he knew what this was really about. If she wouldn't bring it up, he would. "What happened last night—how much of it did you understand?"

For a moment, she didn't answer. "Enough. You asked for an hour . . . with me in exchange for the location of the coke you stole."

Terrific. She thinks you're some kind of rapist and drug dealer, McBride.

If it hadn't been so serious, it might have been funny. He thought for a moment about setting her straight, but that would just make her ask more questions—questions he couldn't answer. So he kept his explanation simple.

"They used you to try to get to me. I was just playing along, hoping they would unchain me. I would never have gone through with it." When she didn't respond, he said the words he knew he needed to say. "I'm sorry, Natalie. You have no reason to be afraid of me. I would never hurt any woman like that. You haven't exactly caught me at my best."

That's one hell of an understatement.

He wanted to tell her the truth, but he'd be putting everything he'd worked for, everything he'd suffered for, at risk if he did.

"Apology accepted. But the next time you pull something like that, find a way to warn me first. I don't like being gawked at like I'm a *thing*."

Her scolding tone of voice, so out of place in this situation, made him grin. But he knew when he was being given a direct order. "Yes, ma'am."

"Okay, then. Now, can you please run through the plan one more time?"

*   *   *

"ONE PAIR OF boots. Do you hear that? Just one. You can do this, Natalie." Zach's voice reached out to her through the darkness, his confidence keeping her panic at bay.

Standing in the back corner of their little prison, diagonally across from her cell, Natalie fought to slow her breathing, her heart hammering against her breastbone, all but drowning out the approaching crunch of boots on gravel.

You can do this. You have to do this. If you don't . . .

Her right hand tightened around the chain of her handcuffs, her left hand clutching a brick, her palms sweating.

As they'd planned, Zach began to moan, his voice meant to cover any noise Natalie might make. A key slipped into the lock on the door—and a shaft of daylight spilled inside, followed by the dark shape of a man. His eyes weren't adjusted for the darkness, and she knew he couldn't see her. But she could see him.

It was the Zeta who'd killed Joaquin.

He was carrying something—a plate of food for her. He moved toward her cell, yelled at Zach. "*¡Cállate, cabrón!*" *Shut up, asshole!*

Moving as quickly and quietly as she could, she came up behind him, raised her broken left handcuff as if it were a mace and brought it crashing down on his head.

"*¡Ay!*" The plate clattered to the floor as he grabbed his skull.

"Again, Natalie! Hit him hard and fast!"

But Natalie didn't need Zach's encouragement. She swung the cuffs again and again, striking the Zeta's head and neck, beating him down, driving him to his knees.

He reached for her, but primed on adrenaline, she jumped backward, then swung again, leaving him on all fours.

She wasn't even afraid now, her actions fueled by pent-up rage. She thought of Joaquin and poor Sr. Marquez—and kicked the man who'd killed them in the stomach as hard as she could once, twice, three times, until he lay on the floor holding his middle. Then she brought the brick she'd held in her left hand down on the back of his skull.

The Zeta lay still, his body lying halfway in her cell, the door swinging open.

Had she killed him?

She stepped hesitantly forward, afraid he was just pretending.

"Make sure he's finished, Natalie, or all of this will have been for nothing!"

The Zeta groaned, raised an arm sluggishly to his head.

It's not easy to kill a man.

Now she knew what Zach meant.

From inside the church came the sound of men's voices.

"Oh, God!" She raised the brick and struck the semiconscious Zeta again with every ounce of her strength, pain shooting up her arm to her shoulder.

"If he's down, search him for weapons and keys." Zach sounded so calm, as if he were taking her through how to change a flat tire.

Natalie dropped the brick, knelt down beside the dead Zeta, and began to search his body with trembling hands. Touching the corpse of a man she'd just killed was beyond revolting. "There's a gun in his pocket . . . and a knife . . . but I can't find the keys!"

"Breathe, Natalie." Zach's voice wrapped around her again, shielding her from her own fear. "Forget what just happened. Forget those men's voices out there. Just breathe."

Natalie closed her eyes, drew a steadying breath. And when she opened her eyes, she saw the keys lying on the floor among scattered grapes. "I found them!"

"Hot damn! You did it, Natalie! Now, get me out of here!"

She tucked the gun in the back of her pants, grabbed the knife and the keys, and with trembling fingers searched for the one that unlocked the door to Zach's cell. Three keys were bigger than the rest and looked like they might fit the shape of the keyhole.

She hurried to his cell door and tried the first. It slid into the keyhole but didn't turn. "Oh, come on!"

Men's voices made her look over her shoulder.

"They're still inside." Zach's voice soothed her, only now she could see him—a dark silhouette hunched against the wall. "Don't think about them. Work the lock."

Heart thrumming, she tried the second key. It slid easily into the keyhole, and . . .

Click.

She opened the cell door, cringing as it squeaked on its hinges, then hurried inside and knelt down in front of Zach, looking at the smaller keys on the keychain. "One of these should open your cuffs . . ."

She lifted her gaze to look at him—and felt a hard lump in her throat.

Battered and bruised, he sat with his arms behind his back, his manacles locked to a thick chain that was bolted to the wall, his skin smudged with dirt and covered with burn marks. Had he sat like this all night? She couldn't imagine how uncomfortable he was, how much he had suffered.

"The key for the manacles will be small and very simple."

But Natalie wasn't looking at the keys. She was looking at his face with its thick growth of stubble, bruises, and streaks of dirt, pain, and exhaustion etched on every feature. Acting on instinct, she reached behind his head, untied the humiliating blindfold and let it fall.

Gray eyes stared intently into hers, and she forgot to breathe.

ZACH'S GAZE FIXED on Natalie's—and his mind went blank just as it had the first time he saw her. Her face only inches from his, she was even more beautiful than he remembered, her dark lashes long and thick, her pupils dilated by the darkness and adrenaline, the bruises on her face making her seem fragile. And out of nowhere, he felt an insane urge to kiss her.

Are you losing your fucking mind, McBride?

"Which . . . which key?" She looked down at the keys in her palm.

"The little one in the center."

He turned to give her access to his wrists, felt the key click, the bite of steel falling away, his wrists finally free. He tried to move his arms, only to be blindsided by pain.

Unable to stop himself, he let out a groan and slumped forward, his arms hanging, lifeless and aching, from shoulders that screamed.

She caught his weight, his head falling onto her shoulder. "I'm so sorry. What they did to you—it's terrible."

"Yeah. It sucked." He croaked out the words, fighting the

pain, willing himself to sit upright. Then he slowly rolled his shoulders and flexed his elbows to work the stiffness out of his joints and muscles. "Now it's payback time."

Big talk for a guy who can't get off his ass, McBride.

From across the courtyard came the sound of two Zetas arguing.

"How many men did you see last night?"

"Six, I think." She looked toward the half-open door. "They're coming."

"Not yet. They're arguing over who should drive the hookers back to town." He took the keys and unlocked the cuff that still held her right wrist, dropping both cuffs and keys to the floor. "Give me the pistol. Keep the knife, and don't hesitate to use it."

"Okay." She pressed cold steel into his right palm.

A Norinco M-77B—a Chinese military pistol. How it had ended up in Juárez, he could only guess. He turned the weapon over, testing its weight in his hand. Then he checked the magazine and found it fully loaded—nine 9mm rounds. "Listen to me, Natalie. From here on out, you'll do exactly what I tell you to do when I tell you to do it. Is that understood?"

She nodded.

It was the response he wanted, so he barely registered the surprise on her face at this abrupt change in his manner. "Good. Let's get out of here."

But that was easier said than done.

Pressing his left hand against the wall to brace himself, he rose unsteadily to his feet, his heart pounding at the effort, his head spinning, legs shaky. He thought for a moment he was going to fall on his face, then he felt her duck under his left arm, her slender arm encircling his waist, the feel of her solid beside him. "Damn."

Man up, McBride. Or maybe you're hoping she'll carry you back to Juárez.

"You can still aim the gun, right?"

Did he look that weak? "Of course I can aim the damned gun!"

They walked together toward the shaft of daylight that spilled through the door, Zach glancing over at the Zeta lying still on the floor in front of Natalie's cell.

Her gaze followed his. "I . . . I've never killed anyone before."

As if there were any doubt on that score, angel.

Trying not to look too much like his knees were giving out, which they more or less were, Zach sank down beside the unconscious man, felt for a pulse, and found one. "I hate to break it to you, but you still haven't killed anyone."

"He's . . . he's alive?"

"Not for long." Unwilling to risk the noise of gunfire, Zach tucked the gun into his pants, caught the Zeta's head between his left hand and right forearm, and gave it a quick twist, breaking the man's neck with an audible *crack*. He searched the body, finding a fistful of bills in one pocket and a sweet Ka-Bar rig on the man's ankle. He transferred the knife to his own ankle, stuffed the dinero into his pocket, then picked the scattered grapes up off the floor and, ignoring the dirt, tossed them into his mouth.

Electrolytes. Calories.

He was in dire need of both.

He rose unsteadily to his feet again, only to find Natalie watching him, a look of shock on her pretty face. Still chewing, he explained. "I didn't want him sneaking up behind us or warning the others, and we're going to need the money."

But she said nothing, still staring.

"Is this about the grapes? I should have saved some for you. Sorry."

She pressed a hand against her stomach as if she thought she might be sick, then shook her head. "N-no, that's fine."

"Stay behind me, and don't make a sound. Is that clear?"

"Yes."

Still shaken by what she'd just witnessed, Natalie followed Zach, her view blocked by his broad shoulders as he slowly nudged the door to their little prison wider and scanned the courtyard, pistol gripped in both hands. She half expected him to collapse, but somehow he stayed upright. Walking on bare feet, he crouched down, motioning for her to do the same. She followed him into the shadow of the car she'd arrived in, then behind the vehicle to the side of the old church, men's voices audible from inside. He drew her behind him, pressed himself up against the wall—then waited.

Standing so close to him, Natalie was struck by how tall and strong he truly was. Even weak and unsteady on his feet, he seemed dangerous. A few inches over six feet, he was muscular without being bulky, broad shoulders tapering to a narrow waist, slabs of lean muscle bisected by the groove of his spine. And she knew all that muscle wasn't just for show.

There was a scar that could only have been made by a bullet on his lower back, not far from his spine, proving that violence was nothing new in his life. And the way the pistol seemed to belong in his grasp, the way he moved, the way he'd broken that Zeta's neck without blinking—he'd obviously been trained to fight. He had even admitted to killing.

If she'd been sitting in a nightclub in Denver, he probably would have scared the hell out of her. But stranded in the Mexican desert with men who intended to hand her over to be raped and murdered, he was the closest thing she had to the cavalry. Maybe he was some kind of underworld criminal, but right now he was on *her* side.

Heavy hinges squeaked, and boots hit gravel, bringing her thoughts to a halt.

"*¡Eh, Diego! ¿Qué demonios estás haciendo?*" *What the hell are you doing?* A man in military fatigues started across the courtyard, clearly trying to figure out what was taking his friend so long.

In front of her, Zach silently retrieved the knife he'd strapped to his ankle, still a bit wobbly on his feet. Then he rose to his full height, steadied himself, and with a speed that amazed her, threw it, hitting the Zeta just below the base of his skull, the knife sinking to the hilt.

The man's legs turned to water beneath him, and he fell lifeless to the ground.

Zach held up four fingers, his meaning clear.

Four Zetas remained.

Motioning for her to stay where she was, he hurried out into the open and stripped the body of its weapons, including the knife, which he wiped clean on the dead man's pants and returned to its sheath. When he reached her side, he had two more pistols, one of which he handed to her, the other of which he tucked into the waistband of his pants. He bent down and whispered, "Do you know how to use one of these?"

She looked at the weapon in her hands. It was heavier than she'd imagined—and cold. "You point it and pull the trigger."

The look on his face told her there was more to it than that. "This is the safety. As long as it's in this position, the gun won't fire. Flick it down like this before you pull the trigger. Aim for the chest."

"Can't we just hot-wire the car and go?"

But Zach was already moving, walking on silent feet around the corner and toward the church's front door. Made of thick planks of weathered wood with iron hinges that opened outward, it had no windows to enable them to see if anyone was standing on the other side—which is why it took her by surprise when it began to swing outward toward them.

Natalie found herself thrust back against the wall behind Zach, the door concealing them both as it opened. She saw Zach raise his pistol, then heard him swear beneath his breath as two scantily clad young women—prostitutes, not Zetas—stepped outside. They didn't see Zach or Natalie, but they did see the dead body.

And they screamed.

CHAPTER 6

ONE MINUTE THINGS had been under control, and the next they'd gone straight to hell. Two women—girls no older than eighteen—stared at the man Zach had just killed, their screams and incoherent babbling blowing to bits any hope Zach had of taking the rest of the Zetas by surprise. That was the bad news.

The good news was that the girls hadn't yet seen him or Natalie.

"*¡Está muerto! ¡Santa Madre de Dios, está muerto!*" *He's dead! Holy Mother of God, he's dead!* One of the young women turned toward the door, clearly planning to run for help. She saw Zach—and froze.

Zach spoke quietly but with enough menace to make sure the women knew he meant business. "*Si quieres vivir, véte con tu amiga al coche y acuéstense.*" *If you want to live, you and your friend go get in the car and lie down.*

Brown eyes that had already seen too much went wide, and without another word the girl took her friend's hand and dragged her to the car, an ugly brown Nissan Tsuru, then opened the back door, pushed her inside, and piled in behind her, their two heads disappearing from view just as heavy footfalls sounded from inside the church—another pair of boots.

Zach whispered over his shoulder to Natalie. "Get down!"
She crouched behind him.

"¡Putas estupidas! ¿Qué problemas les están causando ahora?" Stupid whores! What trouble are you causing now?

Zach recognized the voice as belonging to one of the Zetas who'd kidnapped Natalie. The bastard stepped out through the open door—an older man with a tattoo of La Santa Muerte on his forearm—and Zach dropped him with a single shot.

A gasp from Natalie. Muffled screams from the prostitutes. Men's shouts.

And then all was silent.

The Zetas knew they'd been taken by surprise, and they were regrouping.

Zach tried to put himself in their place, tried to see the situation from their point of view. They knew they were under attack, but they didn't know by whom. They would probably assume their attackers were members of a rival cartel, and they would call for support. Then, when they realized there were only three of them left alive, they would take up defensive positions and wait for the fight to come to them.

Zach would hate to disappoint them.

Hoping adrenaline would keep him upright, he motioned to Natalie to get to her feet, then led her through the open doorway behind him, stopping just inside the threshold to clear the foyer and let his eyes adjust to the dim interior.

He took it all in at a glance.

It was a small mission church, the interior divided by fat stone pillars that rose from floor to roof. To his left, a crumbling flight of stairs led upward toward the bell tower. Directly ahead where there should have been pews sat a dozen unmade cots, posters of naked women in pornographic poses stuck to pitted walls, makeshift shelves holding magazines and clothes, weapons lying carelessly about.

What had once been the altar was now a shrine to outlaw narco-saints Jesús Malverde and La Santa Muerte, a portrait of Cárdenas hanging on the wall above it as if he were Christ himself. Off to the right, the baptismal nook appeared to have been converted into a junk heap. The sacristy stood to the left of the Malverde/Muerte shrine, its door half-open.

That was their little torture chamber. And that's where they were hiding.

Or maybe not.

From somewhere nearby he heard the telltale *ka-chunk* of someone working the bolt on an AK-47, slipping a new magazine into place.

Zach shoved Natalie behind a pillar, shielding her with his body as the first volley exploded, sending up a spray of stone around them.

Ra-ta-ta-ta-ta-ta-tat!

He watched the bullets hit, trying to discern their attacker's location.

At least four meters away and to the right.

He leaned down, whispered. "*Stay here. Stay down.*"

He turned his back to Natalie, dropped to one knee, pivoted to his right, and looked around the pillar, catching a glimpse of an AK muzzle and the top of a man's head peeking up from behind a cot. He fired, aiming low, knowing the 9mm rounds would penetrate the mattress.

Bam! Bam! Bam!

A man in BDUs and a white T-shirt rose clumsily to his feet, aiming his weapon unsteadily at Zach, blood spreading down the front of his shirt. Then he pitched forward and lay still, AK at his side.

Four down, two to go.

Zach's hands itched to get ahold of that weapon, but he couldn't cross the room to retrieve it without exposing himself to fire from that back room, and he didn't want to leave Natalie alone or—

A shadow fell across the floor, framed by the doorway.

Forgetting his broken ribs, Zach had no time to do anything but react. He threw himself onto his left side, sliding out from behind the pillar and aiming toward the Zeta who stood in the doorway pointing his weapon toward Natalie.

Bam!

But it wasn't Zach who'd pulled the trigger.

Son of a bitch!

His heart ricocheted against his breastbone as he squeezed off three quick shots.

Bam! Bam! Bam!

The Zeta slumped against the door, firearm slipping from his hand and landing with a clatter as he sank lifeless to the stone floor.

Ignoring the pain in his side, Zach scrambled on all fours around the pillar, hoping to God the bastard had missed, only to find Natalie on her knees staring at the dead Zeta, pistol in hand, a shocked expression on her face. It took three hard beats of Zach's heart to comprehend that she *hadn't* been shot, that she *wasn't* wounded. He looked from her to the Zeta and back again, stunned to realize that it had been *her* shot he'd heard.

He stared at her, more than a little amazed. That was the second time today she'd saved their asses. "I think I'm in love."

"I think I'm going to be sick." She dropped her weapon and pressed her hand against her stomach, a look of shock and distress on her face.

But there wasn't time for that.

"Save the puking for later." He rose to his feet, gritting his teeth as the pain in his ribs caught up with him. "This isn't over yet."

He collected the dead Zeta's weapon—a Glock 17 9mm— and led her quietly from pillar to pillar toward the back room, the old church silent apart from their breathing. Then from outside came the roar of an engine. But it wasn't the car in which the prostitutes were hiding. The sound came from *behind* the church.

"Shit!" Digging for some buried reserve of strength, Zach ran as fast as his legs could carry him toward the front of the church, reaching the front door just as a battered RAV4 cleared the courtyard and hit the highway, spitting gravel.

Aiming for the driver, he fired off his two remaining rounds, shattering the vehicle's window and leaving a hole in the driver's door. But it was too late. "Damn it!"

Tires squealed as the SUV swerved, then sped away to the south.

Adrenaline spent, legs shaking, it was all Zach could do to walk back inside.

Natalie finished washing her hands and face in the filthy little bathroom at the back of the church, the need to be clean overwhelming—if a person could truly get clean washing in the water that poured from that tap. She'd found an unopened toothbrush and had claimed it, brushing her teeth with bottled water and Colgate from an almost used-up tube, the idea of sharing toothpaste with the Zetas repulsive—but not quite repulsive enough to stop her.

She dried her hands on a paper towel and walked back out into the sanctuary, to find Zach still hard at work pillaging the place.

"Eat."

She caught the banana he tossed to her, watching as he peeled his second and consumed it in three bites. "I don't feel hungry."

All she wanted in the entire world was to leave this place.

"Your body needs fuel." He tossed his banana peel aside. "Eat."

"Yes, sir!" Who did he think he was? She gave a mock salute, then sat on a cot and forced herself to peel the banana, slowly eating it while he systematically searched through the dead Zetas' belongings, looking for things he thought they might need.

He was no longer the reassuring voice in the darkness, the man with whom she'd shared her darkest memories and deepest fears, the man who had encouraged her and helped her fight back. Now he was a stranger to her, a man who barked out orders, who killed with skill and efficiency—but who had killed to protect her.

He held up a black T-shirt with a green marijuana leaf on the front, then slipped it over his head, breath hissing between his teeth as he drew it down over the dark bruises on his rib cage. It was too small, the fabric stretched tightly across the muscles of his chest and abdomen, the sleeves riding high on his shoulders, but he didn't seem to care. He went back to his search, moving with a businesslike efficiency through the room, piling anything he thought they might need onto one of the cots.

Keys to the car. Tortillas. Boxes of bullets. Socks. Pesos. Potato chips. Duct tape. Big guns. Little guns. Pocketknife. First-aid kit. Candy bars. Sunglasses.

"Well, I'll be damned." He held up a black leather billfold. "My wallet. The cash is gone, but my driver's license and credit card are still here."

He tucked it in the back pocket of his jeans and kept moving. It didn't seem to bother him that he'd just killed four men. And why should it? Those men had beaten him, tortured him, starved him, and they would have killed *both* of them if they'd had the chance.

Natalie didn't feel a bit sorry for the Zetas either. But that didn't mean she could sit here surrounded by blood and dead bodies and not want to run away screaming.

Zach hardly seemed to notice. He'd gone from body to body, taking their money and weapons. She knew he'd been angry to discover that Sr. Scar Face—the Zeta who'd tortured him and molested her—was the one who'd gotten away. Zach hadn't said anything to her, but his jaw had gone rigid when he'd checked the last body, and she'd heard him swear.

As for the money, he'd stuffed most of it in his pocket and had given the rest to the terrified prostitutes. The gesture had touched Natalie—until he'd told the girls to get out of the car and head back to whatever town they'd come from on foot.

"It's must be a hundred and ten degrees out here. They'll roast!"

He'd met her gaze, not the least bit of sympathy in his eyes. "Either we walk, or they walk. Which would you prefer?"

That had simplified things.

Feeling more than a little guilty, Natalie had given the two girls bottled water and then watched them hurry down the highway in high heels. She'd wanted to leave, too, but that's when Zach had come back into the church and started searching the place. She'd followed him. "Shouldn't we get out of here?"

His voice was cold when he answered. "If we leave now, are you prepared for whatever might happen out there? If the Zetas catch up with us or show up in a helicopter, are you ready to fight back? If the car breaks down and we need to cross the desert on foot, are you prepared to handle it? I made you a promise, and I'm trying to keep it."

Realizing he knew what he was doing and she didn't, she'd gotten out of his way, the adrenaline from earlier wearing away, leaving her feeling numb, images of what had happened skulking in her mind. A man appearing out of nowhere at the church door. The barrel of his pistol pointing at her. His body jerking when she'd pulled the trigger.

Then Zach was there beside her. "Here."

She gasped, jumped.

In his hand was a bottle of water. "So, you're afraid of me now?"

"No." She unscrewed the cap and drank, unable to meet his gaze. She wasn't afraid of him, exactly—but she didn't necessarily trust him. "It's just that . . . Before yesterday, I'd never seen anyone get shot and killed, and now . . ."

She'd beaten one man unconscious and shot another.

"Don't dwell on it." Zach turned, grabbed an empty military duffel bag and dropped it on the cot beside her. "On your feet. Let's load up and get the hell out of here."

Natalie helped him pack everything he'd set aside into a couple of duffel bags, then followed him out the church's door, ignoring bodies and flies that buzzed at pools of drying blood, and looking up into the bright blue sky instead.

"You drive." Zach tossed her the keys, then opened the back door and shoved the duffel bags onto the backseat, pulling out a big gun and several spare magazines. "I'll ride shotgun."

Natalie climbed into the car in which she'd once been a prisoner, started the engine, and cranked the AC. She waited for Zach to climb in beside her, then hit the gas, a lump forming in her throat as she watched the ghost town, and the hell that lay within its crumbling walls, disappear in the rearview mirror.

She was going home.

JOAQUIN COULDN'T LOOK up from his beer, unable to stand the pity he knew he'd see on his friends' faces. "I let her down. Natalie saved my life, and I let her down. Whatever she's going through right now is my fault. *Christ!*"

He took a drink, swallowed beer together with the rock that seemed to be lodged in his throat, a glass full of stout not nearly strong enough to make him forget the sound of her voice crying out to him as they'd dragged her from the bus—or to keep him from thinking about what might be happening to her now.

He'd been home for four hours. He and the other American journalists—every single Mexican reporter had been killed—had been taken under escort to the U.S. consulate, where they'd been questioned by Mexican and U.S. authorities, before being packed into a couple of choppers and flown across the border to El Paso. This morning, he'd caught his flight home from Texas, the empty seat next to him a constant, unbearable reminder of the friend who should have been there beside him.

The airport had been a madhouse, reporters and TV cameras waiting for him. But for the first time in his life, Joaquin had found himself trying to avoid the media, his emotions too ragged to share with strangers. And yet every journalist there had wanted to interview and photograph him because *his* colleague had been the only American taken from the bus. When he'd refused to comment, they'd assumed he was saving the details for his own newspaper. But everything he had to say had already run in today's paper, in an article written by Tom, the editor in chief, together with his photographs of the massacre, which Joaquin had e-mailed to the paper from El Paso. The only people he could talk to about this were his *abuelita* and his brothers—and the people sitting around him right now.

He hadn't asked the I-Team staff, past and present, to come over. In fact, part of him had dreaded seeing them, knowing he'd have to tell them what had happened and that he'd see the same contempt in their eyes that he'd seen in the eyes of the federal agents who'd questioned him—a look that told him Natalie would be back home now if only he'd been more of a man.

But they loved Natalie, too. He owed it to them to face them.

Matt Harker, the only other man on the I-Team and one of Joaquin's best buddies, had shown up first, carrying a case of Yeti Imperial Stout, their favorite Colorado microbrew. Kara McMillan, an old friend and former I-Team reporter, had arrived next, her arms full of groceries, her three kids at swimming lessons with her schoolteacher husband, Reece Sheridan. Tessa Darcangelo, another former I-Team reporter and her husband, Julian, a vice cop and former FBI special agent, had followed. Then Kara and Tessa had taken over Joaquin's little kitchen making lunch, while Julian had grabbed a beer and joined him and Matt on the back deck.

Sophie Alton-Hunter, the I-Team's criminal justice reporter, and her husband Marc Hunter, a SWAT sniper, had brought soft drinks and paper plates, ringing the bell only minutes ahead of Holly Bradshaw, an entertainment writer, and Kat James, the paper's environmental reporter, who came with her husband Gabe Rossiter and their baby girl, Alissa. Tom had come last, his arrival a surprise, as he almost never left the newsroom in the middle of the day.

Only after everyone had gotten their fill of tacos and salad had Joaquin found the will to tell them the entire story. Sophie and Kat, who'd known Natalie best, were now in tears, the men silent. And still Joaquin couldn't take his gaze off his beer.

"This isn't your fault, Joaquin." Kara broke the silence. "Don't even go there."

"If I had stopped her from trying to protect me, she might not have caught their attention. They might have walked right past her—"

"And shot you in the head." Matt's voice dripped with sarcasm. "Yeah, that would've made everything better."

"Kara's right, Joaquin." Tessa took his hand. "We know you did everything you could."

"Yeah." Joaquin let out a bitter laugh. "I'm a fucking hero."

Tessa leaned in closer. "The only ones to blame are the murdering bastards who kidnapped her."

"You said it, Tess." Sophie dabbed her eyes with a tissue. "I still can't believe they killed all those poor people in cold blood."

Joaquin ignored his friends' reassurances and willed himself to look up and meet the gazes of the three men in the room he most respected. How pitiful he must seem to them. "Would they have been able to take her from you, Darcangelo? Or from you, Hunter? And how about you, Rossiter? If you'd been on that bus with Natalie—"

"Knock it the hell off, Joaquin." Julian stood in the back against the wall, his arms crossed over his chest. "I might know a few more tricks than you do, but that doesn't mean I'm invincible. I've gotten my ass kicked plenty of times."

Gabe reached over and adjusted the blanket that Kat had draped over herself for modesty's sake while nursing the baby. "If you'd fought them any harder, they probably would've shot you just like they shot the others. Then they'd have taken Natalie anyway."

Heads nodded.

"If I thought you'd been a coward, I'd tell you to your face." Marc's gaze bored into Joaquin's from across the kitchen table. "But without some kind of weapon, there's really nothing more you could've done."

Kat looked up from her baby, tears still on her cheeks. "It's right to feel sick about Natalie. We all do. But you're going to have to quit feeling guilty for being the one who came home. It's not your fault, Joaquin."

Joaquin squeezed his eyes shut, fighting the turmoil inside him. He *hated* feeling this helpless, this angry, this afraid for someone he cared about.

Then Tom spoke. "I've been in touch with the flack at the State Department. They say they're doing all they can to help Mexican authorities find her."

Darcangelo gave a snort. "Yeah, trust the State Department diplomats to get the job done. I've been in touch with some of my old contacts down there. If what they say is true and Los Zetas is responsible for the attack on the bus, then the State Department isn't going to be able to do a damned thing for her. The Zetas hate journalists—as you saw, Joaquin—and they've got as much firepower as the *federales*—probably more."

And Joaquin felt an unexpected ray of hope. Darcangelo had worked for the FBI in Mexico and knew more about the country and its underworld than most. He met the big man's gaze. "Is there any chance you can go down there and help them find her?"

Tessa glared at him. "I do *not* want to lose my friend *and* my husband, thank you very much. Julian is *not* going to Mexico."

"I can't go—not now anyway." Darcangelo squeezed his wife's hand. "I'm not going to leave Tessa alone."

Joaquin had forgotten. Tessa was three months pregnant and having problems. "No, of course not."

"Why do you think they took her? What will they do with her?" Holly asked the question that Joaquin hadn't been able to bring himself to ask.

Julian seemed to hesitate. "Natalie represents two things that interest the Zetas. She's a reporter, and she's a pretty young female. It makes me sick to say it, but if the Mexican AFI—that's their FBI—doesn't get a lead soon, there's a good chance we'll never see her again."

The beer in Joaquin's stomach turned to acid.

CHAPTER 7

THE CAR'S AC didn't work well, but it did use up gasoline, so Zach had turned it off. Now open windows offered the only relief from the scorching midday heat. It was like driving through a blast furnace.

It still beats being outside in eighty percent humidity.

Natalie wasn't so sure she believed herself on that point. But then it had been a long time since she'd spent a summer in New Orleans.

Sweat trickled down the back of her neck and between her breasts, the discomfort making her cross. Or maybe that was lack of sleep. Or fear.

Somewhere out there, killers were hunting for them.

She drew up to a stop sign, the word "ALTO" spelled out in big white letters against a red background that had been bleached by the sun. She stopped, looked both ways, then pressed on the gas again, not another car in sight.

Beside her, Zach loaded bullets one by one into a magazine, his fingers moving with a speed that clearly came from experience, sweat beading on his temples. A gun he'd said was an AK-47 rested between his legs, its business end pointing toward the floor. As she watched him, she knew he'd been in situations like this before—up to his neck in trouble and ready to fight. With his thick stubble, dirty, torn jeans, skintight marijuana T-shirt, and hardened physique, he certainly *looked* like a man who lived his life armed and dangerous.

Yet no matter how dangerous he might be, she couldn't help but worry about him. Given how tired *she* was, she knew he must be exhausted, not to mention in pain, the lines of strain on his face and the dark circles beneath his eyes more noticeable in naked daylight. She'd half expected him to fall asleep the moment the car started moving, but he hadn't closed his eyes once. He was alert, his body radiating tension, his mind sharp. Still, no man could hold out forever, no matter how strong or hardened he was.

"Your driver's ed teacher would be proud. Not another car as far as the eye can see, but still you come to a complete stop." His gaze met hers over the top of mirrored sunglasses, the glint of humor in his gray eyes making her pulse skip.

Oh, no, girl! You are not *attracted to him.*

"You told me not to draw people's attention."

How could she find him attractive? He was a crook, a criminal, a man who stole cocaine and shot people and ate dirty grapes off the floor of an arachnid-infested cell—not a gentleman like Beau. The fact that he was also tall, strong, brave, and still had enough goodness left inside him to help her escape the Zetas didn't matter.

"That was back on the highway. I didn't want you to attract attention from the cops because some of them work for the Zetas." He glanced around. "But I doubt you'll find any cops lurking behind these old saguaros."

And just like that, she felt like an idiot.

Her cheeks burned. "Sorry. I didn't think . . . I'm not used to . . . I guess I'm just tired and not thinking clearly. I'm doing the best I can."

"Do you know what happens if our best isn't good enough?" His gaze met hers again, any hint of humor gone. "We die."

Fear made her snap at him. "I know that!"

She hadn't forgotten that they were running for their lives, but she hadn't thought of it quite like that either, his stark words making her stomach knot.

"I'm not saying this to try to scare you, Natalie. We both need to do better than our best if we're going to survive."

If they were going to survive?

Natalie didn't like the uncertainty of that. "Do you really think they'll come after us with a helicopter?"

"Cárdenas is the ultimate narcissist. We escaped from him, killed five of his men, stole arms, ammunition, and a car from him. His ego won't be able to stand it. Hell, yeah, he'll come after us with a helo. He'll send ground troops. He'll alert the cops and *federales* who work for him. By leaving the highway, we've bought ourselves some time. But his men are out there, Natalie, and they're hunting for us."

She pushed on the gas, nudging the needle past seventy.

Outside the window, drab, parched hills rose from drab, parched plains that stretched as far as the eye could see, stands of tall cactus and scraggly shrubs dotting a brown landscape that shimmered with heat. Other than the occasional jackrabbit that darted across the road, Natalie hadn't seen any sign of life. It certainly didn't seem possible that they were on the outskirts of a big city, but Zach insisted that Chihuahua wasn't far ahead and that the only way to reach it safely was to take the back roads.

They'd been making good time on Mexico 45 when he pulled out one of the Zetas' cell phones and called someone named Carlos, his Spanish sounding like gibberish to her—something about new houses, bridges, and goat horns. All he'd told her afterward was that they needed to get off the highway and ditch this car. Then he'd pulled out the phone's SIM card, tossed the phone out the window, and told her to take the next exit.

Only later had it dawned on her that his phone call might have had less to do with getting her safely home and more to do with the stolen cocaine.

She'd been on the brink of asking him once or twice about the coke but had thought the better of it. She couldn't afford to have him dump her by the side of the road out here in the middle of the desert. The landscape was every bit as deadly as the Zetas. And with nothing stronger than a promise to keep him from abandoning her, she needed his goodwill. She wouldn't say anything.

Not yet.

"THIS ISN'T WORKING!"

Zach raised his head and glanced up to where Natalie was bent over a mesquite branch, trying to rub out the car's left tire tracks, her hair tied back, the AK she'd insisted on carrying slung over her shoulder like an ugly purse. "Put more muscle into it."

"Easy . . . for *you* . . . to say."

It *was* hard work, and he supposed having two X chromosomes made it tougher. Then again, none of this had been easy for her.

You've been hard on her, too, McBride.

Yeah, he had been.

He'd done well enough when he'd been in chains and needed her help, but for the past few hours all he'd done was issue orders. But she wasn't a SEAL. She wasn't a deputy U.S. marshal either. And she sure as hell wasn't an enemy combatant or a fugitive. She was an innocent civilian, a young woman who'd suffered more than her share of tragedy, who'd witnessed a massacre, who'd been kidnapped and assaulted, who'd been forced to kill. She deserved his respect—and some damned human kindness, if he could manage it.

Yet his first priority was getting her safely home again. And that meant staying focused on the objectives, which, at the moment, were evasion and escape.

Driving the Tsuru down into the arroyo had been a bitch. Zach had made Natalie get out of the car just to be safe, and for a few seconds he'd thought he was going to roll the damned thing or get stuck in the sandy, dry bottom. But the vehicle was now concealed beneath a concrete bridge, hidden from anyone who might drive by or fly overhead. Once its tire tracks were wiped out, it would take an expert in cutting sign to know they were there.

Or that was the theory, anyway.

He walked slowly backward, swishing the branch across the sandy soil as he went, careful not to fall down the steep bank as the ground became softer and less stable. He was about to warn Natalie to watch her step, when he heard her gasp. He looked up in time to see her tumbling toward him.

He reached out and stopped her fall. "You okay?"

She sat up, nodding. "I'm a little dizzy, but I'm fine."

He took one look at her face and knew that wasn't true. She was flushed, but she wasn't sweating. "You're dehydrated."

She looked puzzled. "I'm not thirsty."

Not good.

He'd seen men die from the heat in Afghanistan as medics struggled in vain to save their lives. He knew that dizziness and lack of thirst were *not* good signs.

"Let's get you into the shade." He drew her to her feet, slid an arm around her waist, and guided her over to the car and into the passenger seat, taking the AK from her. He propped the rifle against the car, then reached into the backseat for a bottle of water, ripped off the cap, and pressed it into her hands. Too bad there were no powdered electrolytes to go with it. "Drink. A few gulps, then regular sips."

While she drank, he touched his palm to her forehead, and was relieved to feel that her skin was neither clammy nor feverishly hot. She was definitely dehydrated and on her way to overheating, but she didn't have heatstroke. Not yet.

You pushed her too hard, you dumb shit.

She looked up at him. "Were you a paramedic in your past life or something?"

"No." He dug through the crap in the backseat for the first-aid kit, then pulled out a cotton washcloth. "But I do know a few things about first aid."

"That's a good skill for someone in your, um . . . line of work."

"You got that right." He would've loved to hear what line of work she thought he was in, but this wasn't the time. "Quit talking, and keep drinking."

You're giving orders again.

He grabbed another bottle of water and dropped to his knees beside her, then poured out enough water to thoroughly wet the washcloth and pressed it against her forehead and cheeks, hoping to bring down her core temp.

She sighed, her eyes drifting shut. "Oh, that feels good."

A bolt of heat shot through his belly straight to his groin.

His mind knew her response hadn't been sexual, nothing seductive intended, but his body apparently didn't. He drew his hand back, knowing he was in trouble. But then she turned her head, exposing the side of her throat, and he couldn't resist.

He pressed the cool cloth against that sensitive area, watched goose bumps appear on her soft skin. She sighed again, the sweet sound making his own temperature rise. Slowly, she tilted her head back to allow his hand to pass beneath her chin, then turned her face toward him, her eyes still closed, her mouth relaxed.

By the time she opened her eyes, his lips were almost touching hers. And for a single, slow heartbeat, he stayed that way, unable to speak, his mouth so close to hers that he could nearly taste her, his gaze fixed on hers.

What the . . . ?

He jerked back, dropped the wet washcloth in her lap, his brain searching for words. "I . . . You . . . You can probably handle this yourself."

She looked up at him. "Thank you. For helping me."

"I need to get back to hiding our tracks." He stood and walked away, his abrupt retreat startling a few swallows out of the mud nests they'd built in the bridge's life-giving shade. "Keep drinking."

He walked back into the blazing sunshine, grabbed his mesquite branch and rubbed furiously at the tracks—which now included the soil disturbed by her fall down the embankment.

What the fuck was wrong with him?

That Zeta bastard must have shocked him one too many times, because only fried brain cells could explain what had just happened. He'd almost kissed a woman he was charged with protecting—while administering first aid, no less.

That kind of mouth-to-mouth is against the rules, and you know it.

Okay, so he hadn't technically been *assigned* to protect her, which meant that the rules didn't technically apply. In fact, her being with him was purely coincidence and had nothing to do with this case. But he did *not* get mixed up with women while on the job. He did *not* develop feelings for them, and he certainly did *not* get physical with them. That wasn't marshal service policy; that was his own personal policy. And he *never* broke his own rules.

Maybe it was just the situation—the two of them being thrown together like this, forced to work together to stay alive, sharing the dangers of a survival situation, his being injured, her being vulnerable. He knew from his years in combat how walking that line between life and death could make two people bond. A bit of pheromone had probably gotten mixed in with all the adrenaline. Simple enough to explain.

And how many of your SEAL teammates did you try to kiss?

Ignoring that stupid question, he stood back, his gaze moving over the embankment, searching for any sign he might have missed—a shoe print, an overturned rock, obvious swish marks. Satisfied, he walked backward under the bridge, rubbing out his footprints as he went and assuring himself that he'd done just as thorough a job of rubbing out any inappropriate impulses he might have had toward Natalie.

When he reached the car, she was sound asleep, her lashes dark on her cheeks, her lips relaxed, an empty water bottle perched in her slender fingers. A sensation of warmth spread inside his chest.

Oh, McBride, you are in such deep shit.

He slid quietly into the driver's seat, felt her forehead and was relieved to find it cooler. Then he settled his rifle at his side, took the empty bottle from her, and, helpless to stop himself, watched her sleep.

HELL, YEAH, HE'LL come after us with a helo.

His men are hunting us. They'll come after us in a helo.

Hell, yeah, he'll come after us.

In a helicopter.

A helicopter.

Natalie jerked awake on a jolt of adrenaline, only to find that she hadn't been dreaming. From somewhere overhead came the deep whir of chopper. And it was getting nearer.

"Easy, Natalie." Zach sat beside her in the driver's seat. "They don't know we're here. They're just coming in for a closer look."

Heart thudding, she sat upright. "How do you know it's the Zetas?"

"They passed over once already at a higher altitude. I can't imagine anyone else wanting to circle back to get a closer look at this bridge. Time to move. Come on."

Her mind fogged by sleep, Natalie had no idea what he meant. "Where are we going?"

"We're getting out of the car and into position just in case they land." AK-47 in hand, he climbed out, then retrieved a bag of gear from the backseat.

She followed him, scrambling up the embankment to where it met the underside of the bridge, crouching down beside him and watching as he opened the duffel bag and drew out weapons one at a time. He checked each one as he went, talking quickly, his hoarse voice taking on an almost businesslike tone.

"If they land, we'll have no choice but to engage them. I'll be at that side of the bridge, trying to take them out as they disembark." He pointed to his right. "Your job is to stay here and keep an eye on the other side in case someone escapes my fire and tries to circle around that way. The objective is simple—shoot to kill. There could be as many as seven of them, so we're outnumbered. But we have the tactical advantage."

There wasn't time to ask what he meant by that.

He handed her an AK-47 and a pistol. "The AK is on full auto. Just hold down the trigger and spray back and forth. And you remember how to use the pistol?"

Natalie stared down at the heavy weapons in her hands, a sense of unreality coming over her. Was this ever going to end? "Yes, but I . . ."

The helicopter seemed to beat down on them now.

Zach tucked a finger beneath her chin and lifted her gaze to meet his. "You didn't bring this on yourself, Natalie, but you're in it now. You're going to have to stand strong if you want to get home again. Understand?"

There was no reproach in his eyes, only concern, his dark eyebrows knit together in a frown, his voice as reassuring as it had been when she'd been locked in that cell.

She drew a deep breath, tried to force her fear aside. "Go. I'll be fine."

But he didn't go. Instead, he lowered his head—and kissed her.

It was barely a brushing of lips, and it lasted for only a second. But for that brief second the world disappeared. There was no helicopter. There were no Zetas. There was only Zach and the shock of his lips against hers. And then it was over. Astonished, Natalie stared after him as he hurried away, his head bent low, duffel bag in hand.

He kissed you, girl.

So she *hadn't* imagined it earlier. When he'd been helping her to cool off, she'd opened her eyes to find him leaning over her, his lips so close to hers and . . .

But now the helicopter was on top of them, and there was time to think of nothing else. To her right, Zach got into position, lying on his belly, his head toward the top of the embankment, his legs spread wide, toes dug into the dirt. He adjusted something on his AK-47, another rifle at his side, spare magazines tucked in the back of his jeans.

The seconds crept by.

The metallic whirring of the chopper's propeller.

The thrumming of her own heartbeat.

The cold weight of a gun in her hand.

Then the helicopter lifted into the sky, the deep pulse of its rotors disappearing into the distance.

CHAPTER 8

THE SUN WAS setting by the time Carlos finally arrived, the western horizon turning a pale shade of yellow. The pavement radiated heat from a day of relentless sun. In the distance, a pack of coyotes yipped and howled.

Zach had managed to make it through the past few hours without doing anything dangerously stupid—like kissing Natalie again. Not that it had been easy. He could still feel her on his lips, the raw current that had arced between them unlike anything he'd felt before. His body seemed to think that the only cure for this problem was another kiss, but he knew better. He should never have touched her in the first place.

It's sexual attraction, McBride.

And it had him by the balls.

He cleared his mind, focused on the present, watching as Carlos climbed out of a white VW Jetta Europa and walked toward him.

"Do you trust him?" The tone of Natalie's voice told Zach she didn't.

Smart woman.

"Carlos knows better than to double-cross me." The two pistols Zach had tucked in the back of his jeans were his insurance in case Carlos had forgotten that fact.

Zach had saved the kid's life a few years back when Carlos had gotten himself in over his head with a couple of drug smugglers. Since then, Carlos had given up the narco trade and now ran a couple of chop shops. At times, he also served as Zach's eyes and ears on the streets, a fact that was known only to Zach.

Wearing a few more gold chains around his neck than the last time Zach had seen him in person, Carlos stopped a good six feet away, his gaze shifting from Zach to Natalie. "*¿Quién es la mamacita? ¿Está a la venta, también?*" *Who's the babe? Is she for sale, too?*

It was a joke, but it wasn't a funny one.

Clearly having understood, Natalie moved sideways to stand behind Zach, her anxious reaction at being discussed like merchandise sparking an almost violent protective response inside Zach. His voice took on a warning tone. "*Cuidado, Carlos. Ella está conmigo.*" *Watch yourself, Carlos. She's with me.*

Carlos stood up straighter, his gaze snapping back to Zach again, a hint of fear in his eyes. He'd fucked up, and he knew it. "*Es exactamente lo que pidió. Las placas son legales. El tanque de gasolina está lleno. Déjeme ver las armas.*" *It's exactly what you asked for. The plates are legal. The gas tank is full. Show me the guns.*

Carlos held up the car keys like bait, his gaze drifting to Natalie again.

Zach dropped the duffel bag of firearms at Carlos's feet, knowing that if anything could take the bastard's eyes off her it would be weapons. "*Hay seis pistolas y cuatro cuernos de chivo, además de amuniciones.*" *There are six pistols and four goat horns, plus ammunition.*

Carlos knelt down, opened the bag, then drew out an AK, admiring it and smiling like a kid on Christmas morning, a gold tooth catching what was left of the light. "*Me encantan estos pequeños cuernos de chivo.*" *I just love these little goat horns.*

"Goat horn" was a strange thing to call an assault rifle, but given the curved shape of the magazine, Zach could understand it. Mexican slang was nothing if not colorful.

"*¿Quieres decirme qué está pasando?*" *Want to tell me what's going on?*

"No." Zach glanced at the black Chevy Silverado that idled in the distance, waiting to drive Carlos back to town. "*Es tu hermano?*" *Is that your brother?*

"*Sí.*" Carlos nodded, catching the strap of the duffel bag with his shoulder and starting to rise. "*Puedes confiar en él.*" *You can trust him.*

"*No lo hago.*" *I don't.* Zach put his foot down on the duffel bag, holding it to the ground, almost pulling Carlos off balance in the process. "*Las llaves.* The keys. Give them to her. Natalie, take the keys, and start the engine."

Natalie stepped out from behind him, took the keys from Carlos, whose gaze followed her as she ran to the car.

Zach lowered his voice and switched back to Spanish. "Get your eyes off her if you want to keep them, amigo."

The car's engine started with a roar.

Zach lifted his foot off the bag. "*Muchísimas gracias.*"

Carlos stood, a grin on his face. "*Te debo una.*" *I owe you big-time.*

Zach knew that the moment he and Natalie were gone, Carlos and his brother would take the Tsuru apart, salvaging everything they could and selling it at a handy profit. If the Zetas came back tomorrow, all they would find was an empty, unrecognizable shell.

"*Gracias.*" Zach shouldered the other duffel bag. "*Hay te wacho.*" *See you later.*

Carlos hoisted the bag of arms, turned, and hurried toward his brother's truck, calling farewell over his shoulder. "*Sale y vale.*"

Zach opened the passenger side door, shoved his gear into the back, and climbed into the car. "Turn the car around and head into town."

She did as he asked, Carlos and his brother craning to get a look at her as she drove past. "That was illegal. You gave guns to a man who is almost certainly a criminal. How do you know he won't use them against—"

Zach didn't have the energy for this. "I traded weapons for this car because driving around in *that* one would've eventually gotten us both killed. Do you know why the Zetas are called Zetas?"

"No."

"The license plates on all their vehicles start with the letter Z." He gave that a moment to sink in. "Yes, we could have ditched the plates, but driving around with stolen plates or no plates at all will get you pulled over in Mexico just like it will in the U.S. You might not like my methods, but now we can drive on the highway without getting shot. Any more questions?"

She shook her head.

"Good. Drive."

"WHEN WE GET to the junction of 45 and Carretera Federal 10, take the exit and turn west—that's left."

"But that will take us away from Juárez."

"We're not going to Juárez. We're going to Nuevos Casas Grandes."

"Why aren't we going to Juárez?"

"Do you ever stop with the questions? We're not going there because your photograph will have been all over the news. Because the Zetas control much of the city. And because Cárdenas expects us to go there. Anything else you'd like to ask?"

"Can we stop at the next Pemex? I need to use the ladies' room."

"Oh, for God's sake!"

ZACH DROPPED THE duffel bag, unlocked the door to their hotel suite, and drew out a handgun, motioning for Natalie to stay put. He'd said the Zetas wouldn't look for them in an upscale place like this, but clearly he wasn't taking any chances. He disappeared inside, and she caught a glimpse of him moving quickly through the rooms, gun ready. After a minute or two, he called to her. "It's okay."

She shut the door behind her, locked it, then slipped the door guard into place. Then she walked a few steps to an armchair and sank into it, too tired even to think.

Zach tucked the gun into his jeans and walked over to her. "Hey, there's a shower in the next room with your name on it—hot water, soap, towels."

A shower.

Hadn't she been longing for a shower all day?

Natalie willed herself to stand, the appeal of being clean barely enough to break through the exhaustion and numbness that had taken hold of her. For the past twelve hours all she'd done was run. Now she could barely move.

She walked into the bathroom, flicked on the light, then locked the door behind her and began to undress, letting her filthy clothes fall to the tile floor. She never wanted to wear them again; though, of course, she had no choice. Then she turned toward the shower, stopping short when she caught a glimpse of herself in the mirror.

She barely recognized herself. Her hair was a tangled mess, her face smudged with dirt. A tender goose egg stood out on her scalp where she'd been struck by the butt of the gun. A big, dark bruise marred her left cheek, and there were fainter bruises on her breasts, an unwelcome reminder of Sr. Scar Face's rough hands. But her eyes were what she noticed most—they were a stranger's eyes. Shadowed by dark circles, they stared back at her, haunted by her own panic and the dying screams of others.

Feeling like she was made of wood, she turned away from her reflection and turned on the shower, then stepped beneath the spray, letting it carry away two days' worth of sweat, dirt, and fear. She shampooed her hair three times, massaged in conditioner, then scrubbed her body with a soapy washcloth till her skin glowed pink. She wanted to be clean again, needed to feel clean again. Then she rinsed her hair and her body, watching the bubbles swirl down the drain.

It's over. I'm alive. I'm going home.

The thought hit her, putting a lump in her throat—but close on its heels came another. So many people *weren't* going home.

Joaquin.

Tears spilled down her face. How many had died on that bus? A dozen? Fifteen? All of them journalists, all of them there because they wanted to make the world a better place. Killed without mercy. Shot down.

Screams. Flying glass. Blood.

I am sorry, Miss Benoit.

The bathroom seemed to dissolve, and she was on the bus again. She didn't hear Zach's knock at the door, didn't hear him call her name, didn't know he was there until he turned off the water, wrapped a towel around her, and lifted her into his arms.

IGNORING HIS OWN exhaustion and the sharp pain in his ribs, Zach carried Natalie toward the bed, her body shaking, her heart beating so hard he could feel it against his chest. He sat, held her, stroking her wet hair, wishing to God he knew how to help her. He couldn't tell her everything was okay, because it wasn't. Her friend was dead, along with so many others. She was still in danger—and she had enough bad memories to feed a lifetime of nightmares.

"I'm sorry, Natalie."

He'd seen that haunted look in her eyes all evening, and he'd known she would break sooner or later. It was the same haunted look he'd sometimes seen in the eyes of young SEALs back from their first taste of real combat.

He knew how to help his fellow seamen. He'd slap them on the back and tell them what a great job they'd done, welcoming them into the brotherhood of men who understood what it meant to fight and kill. Most snapped out of it quickly. But they had chosen that lifestyle. For whatever reason— patriotism, a thirst for adventure, family tradition—they had *chosen* to face the ugliness of war.

Natalie hadn't chosen any of this.

Goddamn you, Cárdenas!

Her naked body covered only by the bath towel, she was huddled against him, her fists clenched around his filthy ganja T-shirt, her face buried against his chest, her body wracked with sobs. The soft scents of shampoo and clean female skin filled his head, both arousing and comforting, reminding him of a part of life he'd nearly forgotten. And as he held her, helpless to do anything for her, he realized that he hadn't been this intimate with a woman in years.

Slowly, her tears subsided, and she seemed to realize where she was. She scooted off his lap onto the bed, drawing the towel tight around her. "I . . . I'm sorry."

He handed her a tissue. "You have no reason to apologize."

She sniffed, dabbed her eyes. "It was wrong of me to fall apart like that."

"No." He brushed a strand of wet hair from her cheek. "It wasn't. There aren't many women who could've done what you did today, Natalie. For a sweet little magnolia from Louisiana, you're pretty damned tough."

She met his gaze, a look of doubt in her eyes. "You don't mean that. I—"

"Yeah, I do." He did.

She took his hand. "Thank you for getting me away from that place."

"You played a pretty big role in that yourself." He closed his fingers around hers, her hand so small compared to his, her skin soft.

Careful, McBride. You're treading on thin ice here.

Oh, was he ever.

Then her lips curved in a shaky smile, dimples appearing in her cheeks, her vulnerability making something twist deep inside his chest. "I guess it was lucky for me that I ended up locked in a cell next to you."

He gave her hand a squeeze. "That was lucky for both of us."

And for a moment, neither of them said anything.

She broke eye contact first, withdrawing her hand and hugging her arms around herself as if she suddenly felt exposed. "I . . . I suppose I should get dressed and call someone—the consulate, SPJ, the paper. They'll want to know I'm safe."

"No. Not yet. I don't think what happened to you was random, and until we know for certain why Cárdenas wanted you, we need to lie low."

She looked confused. "Why—"

Feeling suddenly exhausted, he cut her off, not willing to waste time answering more damned questions. "You want to get home safely? Do what I tell you to do. You have no idea what you're dealing with here."

She balked as if he'd yelled at her.

He stood, needing air. "We can talk about it in the morning. I'm going down to the shops in the lobby to buy some clothes and personal supplies. What size do you wear?"

"Six." She stood, a wary expression on her face. "You won't leave me here."

She phrased it as a statement, but he knew it was a question.

He met her gaze, held it. "I made you a promise, Natalie, and I'm going to keep it."

He left the room, making sure the door locked behind him, then went down to the lobby and used his encrypted government credit card to withdraw five grand from the hotel's bank. No one outside the Marshal Service would be able to detect his use of the card, and even the Marshal Service wouldn't see the withdrawal until this time tomorrow. But by then, he and Natalie would be long gone.

He grabbed the basics, like ibuprofen for his broken ribs and toothbrushes and toothpaste, then picked out clothes for himself. But he must have been more exhausted than he'd realized. When it came to choosing clothes for Natalie, he found himself grabbing whatever he thought might look pretty on her, including a silky white nightgown that looked like it was meant for honeymooners. He dismissed the voice that told him he was out of his mind, assuring himself that this had nothing to do with his desire to see her in pretty clothes. After all she'd been through, he just wanted her to have some new things to take home with her.

As mementos of the wonderful time she had in Mexico? Great idea, McBride.

He paid with the credit card, then carried three bags stuffed with purchases back to the elevator and up to their room. There he found Natalie sound asleep, still wearing only her towel. It looked as if she'd simply collapsed on the bed and fallen asleep the moment he'd left. He couldn't blame her.

He dropped the bags on the floor, locked and bolted the door. Then, barely able to stay on his feet, he propped an AK against the wall next to the headboard, put the Glock on the bedside table, and stretched out on the bed beside her.

NATALIE AWOKE FROM a dreamless sleep to the sound of someone taking a shower. She opened her eyes, and for a moment, she couldn't figure out where she was. It was the sight of the hunter green duffel bag—and the weapons inside—that brought it all back to her.

She sat bolt upright, only to realize she was wearing nothing but a towel. The indentation in the pillow next to hers told her that Zach had slept beside her all night. Slept beside her—and apparently hadn't touched her.

Still sleepy, she rose, wondering where she'd left her clothes. Then she spotted a pile of women's clothing on a chair in the corner and remembered Zach saying he was going down to the lobby to buy them a few things. A *few* things?

A small wardrobe sat there, the tags still on—panties, skirts in a rainbow of colors, blouses, T-shirts, a pair of linen pants, and a white silk nightgown. She reached out, touched the different fabrics, surprised that he'd bought so many things for her. Even without looking at the prices, she knew this must have cost him a few hundred U.S. dollars. This was a lot more clothing than she'd need for the single day it would take to drive to the border, unless . . .

Unless he doesn't plan on driving to the border.

Her heart gave a hard knock. She looked over at the closed bathroom door and wondered for a moment if she should take this chance to call the paper and tell them where she was or perhaps run downstairs and take a cab to the U.S. consulate. Did Nuevos Casas Grandes even have a consulate? She had no idea.

Even if it does, you can't go there naked, can you, girl?

No, she couldn't.

She slipped into a pair of lacy white panties and a tiered cotton skirt in turquoise blue, then searched through the pile of clothing for a bra, only to realize he hadn't bought one. Consigned to going without, at least until she could wash her old one, she pulled a white tank top over her head, then dug through a pile of newly purchased hygiene supplies for a hairbrush and began to brush her hair, quickly working through the tangles.

By the time she was presentable, she had decided against making a run for it. She didn't know whom to trust here in Mexico. But she knew she could trust her friends at the paper. She could call them, tell them where she was, and they could contact the State Department for her without risking giving her away to the Zetas. She hurried around the bed to the phone, picked up the receiver, and dialed 0 for the operator, trying to remember her Spanish.

"Natalie, don't!"

She whirled toward the bathroom to see Zach standing in the bathroom doorway wearing nothing but a towel, his hair wet and ruffled, water beaded on the skin of his chest and trickling down his belly. He crossed the room in three long strides, took the handset, and slammed it down. He leaned in, his face inches from hers. "I said no phone calls—not yet."

But it wasn't the face she knew.

Gone was the thick stubble, the dirt, and the grime. The dark circles were gone, too. His skin was tanned and smooth, the hollows in his cheeks seeming deeper, his lips somehow fuller. And she found herself remembering how he'd kissed her and battling an unexpected urge to reach up and run her thumb along his lower lip just to see what it felt like.

Then those lips pressed together in a hard line.

He stood back and glared at her, his gray eyes hard as steel. "Do you want to tell me what in the hell you were just doing?"

CHAPTER 9

ZACH KNEW HE should have ripped the damned phone out of the wall. "Did you give them your name or location?"

"Wh-what?"

He stepped closer. "Did you tell the operator who you are?"

She shook her head. "No, of course not. I . . . I was trying to call the paper to let them know I'm okay."

It was then that Zach noticed she wasn't wearing a bra. The soft fabric of her tank top clung to her breasts, accentuating her curves, the dark circles of her nipples just visible through the thin white cotton.

His mouth watered, blood rushing to his groin.

He jerked his gaze back to her face, but it was too late. He was already on the brink of embarrassing himself, the towel he'd tied around his hips not enough to hide his growing hard-on. Silently cursing his dick, he turned his back to her, walked over to the table, grabbed a pair of boxer briefs, and slid them on beneath his towel.

"I told you not to call anyone yet." He reached for the gray Dockers he'd bought, tucking his half-hard penis inside. "We need to agree on what you can say and whom you can call *before* you start dialing."

He turned to face her, determined to treat her like he would any other woman on any other case. But one look at those big aqua eyes, and he knew he was screwed.

Whatever this was between them—he could feel it from across the room.

What the hell is wrong with you? You didn't react this way to Gisella.

Then again Gisella was half porn star, half barbed wire. Natalie was one hundred percent woman.

He willed himself to focus. "Listen, Natalie, you weren't taken from that bus randomly. Cárdenas wanted you for some reason. Now he wants revenge. He's probably turning Juárez upside down to find you. If you call the State Department or the consulate, there's a chance that word will get to Cárdenas through wiretaps, moles, dirty agents—you name it. I won't take that risk—not when both our lives are at stake."

"So you don't even think it's safe for me to tell my friends? I can assure you that none of them have ties to Cárdenas." The arch of a graceful brow and the cool tone of her voice told him she thought he was being ridiculous.

"If you call the paper, they'll want to write an article—"

"They won't write anything if I tell them to keep it secret." Then her eyes narrowed. "Do you know what I think this is really about?"

"Do tell." *This ought to be good.*

"You don't want to go anywhere near U.S. authorities or the media because you're afraid you might be arrested." There was defiance on her face, but beneath it was a hint of fear. "Or maybe you don't intend to take me home at all."

That last bit took a moment to sink in. When it did, he didn't know whether to laugh out loud—or go ballistic.

"Last night you were afraid I was going to abandon you here, and now you think I'm—what?—kidnapping you or some shit?"

She said nothing, but her chin rose a notch.

"Please tell me—if I don't plan on taking you home, what *do* I plan to do with you?" He closed the space between them in slow strides, then caught her chin between his finger and thumb and let his gaze travel over her. "Maybe I want to sell you and turn a profit off your sweet body and pretty face. Or maybe I'm just greedy and planning to keep you for myself."

Watch yourself, McBride. She's been through hell.

He let go of her, stepped back, turned away, fighting to

regain control of his temper. "When did you get the impression I was kidnapping you? Was it when I saved you from dehydration? Was it when I carried you out of the bathtub? Or was it last night when I slept beside you and you were half-naked and I didn't so much as touch you?"

"All I know is that I could be safely home tonight." There was a slight quaver in her voice as if she were fighting tears. "But you won't let me call any of the people who could help me get there. And then I wake up to find all kinds of pretty clothes—far more than I could possibly wear in the few hours it would take to reach the border. It seems to me that you plan on keeping me around."

When she put it like that, he couldn't blame her for being suspicious. What the hell had he been thinking? He'd needed to buy her practical clothing—a pair of boots, BDUs, heavy socks, a few T-shirts. Pretty skirts and a silk nightgown were *not* going to help her escape the Zetas.

This is what happens when you let your dick do the shopping.

He saw the doubt in her eyes, and once again he wished he could tell her the truth about himself, but that wasn't an option until they were safely across the border—for her sake as well as his own. No, he couldn't tell her what he was.

But maybe . . .

Maybe he could tell her what he was *not*.

"I bought the clothes because I was trying to make up for some of what you've been through and I thought you'd look pretty in them." And he was paying the price for that now, wasn't he? She *did* look pretty. Next time he was stuck with a naked woman in a hotel room, he'd buy her old lady clothes—polyester pants with elastic waistbands and long-sleeved shirts with big flowers on them. "As for the rest—I'd love to explain it, but I can't. But I *can* tell you that I'm not whatever you think I am."

His stomach growled.

"Can we talk about this over breakfast?"

NATALIE TOOK A sip of coffee, studying Zach over the top of her porcelain cup as he devoured what was left of his breakfast. Most of the time when she interviewed someone, she had a good sense of whether that person was telling her the truth. Today, however, her intuition seemed to be taking a vacation.

Maybe the stakes were too high this time. Maybe she was too caught up in her own emotions and too close to the situation to focus clearly. Or maybe Zach was just harder to read than most people.

If only he would put on a shirt!

It wasn't right for any man to be so dangerous and so sexy at the same time. Her adrenal gland and her ovaries were locked in a shouting match now, the former insisting she needed to run away fast, the latter wishing he'd kiss her again.

And that's why you need to think with your brain.

She set her cup down. "How did you get shot? I've seen the scar."

"A man aimed an AK-47 at my back and fired." He shoveled the last bite of hash browns into his mouth and chewed.

Okay, so he wasn't going to answer that one.

"What's your last name?"

He set down his fork and napkin. "Smith. No, Jones. No, wait—it's Black. I like that better. Zach Black. It rhymes."

He wasn't going to answer that one either.

"If you didn't steal the cocaine, Zach *Black*, why didn't you just tell me that right away? Why let me believe you're some kind of criminal if you're not?"

"I was afraid you'd start asking a lot of questions, like you always do, and we both had more important things to deal with." His plate clean, he reached for his coffee, then leaned back in his chair, his long legs stretched out in front of him, his pants riding low enough on his hips to expose a trail of dark hair that disappeared behind his zipper. "Besides, it's not like you were going to say, 'Please leave me with the Zetas.'"

He took a sip.

"Why did the Zetas think you'd stolen the drugs if you didn't?"

He seemed to think about this, as if deciding whether or not to answer. "The person I believe stole the shipment drugged me, then handed me over to them and told them I'd stolen it, making me the scapegoat for her actions."

A woman? "She *drugged* you?"

He nodded. "She called, asked me to meet her at a bar in Juárez, and the next thing I knew, I was a guest in Hotel Zeta."

Hotel Zeta?

More like hell on earth.

Natalie couldn't fathom how he could make light about his captivity after what he'd been through. "Didn't she care what they would do to you?"

"I guess she cared more about money." He took another sip.

"That's terrible."

Proof of how much he'd suffered was still visible on his body—from the dark purple bruise on his rib cage to the faint pink electrical burns on his chest and belly to the gauze bandages on his raw, blistered wrists. If what he'd said was true, this person had turned him over to the Zetas, knowing full well he would be tortured and killed.

How could any woman be so heartless?

The next question that popped out of Natalie's mouth was not the one she'd been about to ask. "Was she your lover?"

How incredibly rude! That's none of your business!

Zach didn't answer right away, his lips curving in a smile. "Now, why, oh why would you ask me that, Ms. Benoit?"

"No reason." She felt herself blush. "Just curious."

"Ah, I see." He set his coffee cup down on the tray, the amused expression on his face telling her that he *did* see right through her. "No, she wasn't my lover—though not for lack of trying on her part."

So Zach didn't sleep with every woman who threw herself at him. That was good to hear. "Are you married?"

He shook his head. "No."

Natalie couldn't seem to stop herself. "Divorced?"

"No!"

"Gay?"

He came face-to-face with her in one smooth motion, so close that she could see flecks of gold in the gray of his irises, the spicy-clean scent of his skin filling her lungs. "Oh, angel, I think you know the answer to that one, but if you need proof . . ."

A big hand slid into her hair, cradling the back of her skull, angling her face upward. Pulse tripping, she found herself looking into his eyes, wondering if he was really going to do it, if he was really going to kiss her.

And then he *did* kiss her.

Slowly.

He brushed his lips over hers, the mere whisper of a touch sending shudders through her, making her breath catch. Then he slipped his other arm around her and drew her against his bare chest, the hard feel of his body making her go weak. But still he didn't kiss her full on, teasing her mouth with his, nipping her lips, tracing their outline with his tongue, until her lips tingled and ached and she was trembling.

She shouldn't let him do this. Zach was a dangerous man, a killer. She knew next to nothing about him, not even his last name. All she had was his promise that he wasn't a criminal. But it had been so long since a man had touched her, so long since she'd *wanted* a man to touch her.

She slid her arms around his neck, arched into him, desperate for more.

He groaned, and the hand in her hair became a fist. And in a heartbeat the kiss transformed, his lips pressing hard and hot against hers, his tongue thrusting deep.

Oh, my stars!

Heat lanced through her, striking deep in her belly. With a whimper, she kissed him back, welcoming his tongue with her own, breathing in the male scent of him, her insides going liquid as his hand moved slowly down her spine.

And then it was over.

He drew back, his gaze meeting hers, his brows furrowed. He was breathing as hard as she was, his lips wet, his eyes dark. "I'm . . . I'm sorry. I shouldn't have done that."

He's sorry.

Natalie tried to still her body's trembling, tried to catch her breath, fighting to understand how he could mean what he'd just said. He'd been the one to start it. "So . . . you . . . you didn't actually mean to kiss me?"

She didn't believe that.

"Ah, hell." He stood, took a few steps back, ran a hand through his hair. "Of course, I did. You're a beautiful woman, Natalie, but this isn't the time or place for . . . I can't afford to get distracted."

"Oh." Natalie hugged her arms around herself, feeling

rejected despite his attempt at a compliment, her body still thrumming.

He sat down in the chair again and leaned forward. "Here's the bottom line. You need to trust me. We need to be able to trust each other. If we're going to get home safely, we need to work as a team, just like we did yesterday. I need to know that you'll do what I tell you to do, and you need to believe that I'm acting in your best interests. I may not have time to explain everything, but I won't tell you to do something if it isn't very important."

"Why is it important that I not call my friends? I trust them with my life."

"We're still deep in the state of Chihuahua. All it would take is one wiretap, one intercepted e-mail, one weak link in the chain of communication to bring the Zetas crashing through that door." He pointed, his words leaching the heat from her blood. "It's better for your friends and family to worry about you for a few extra days than it is for them to hear you're okay, only to have you killed on the way home."

She hadn't realized they were still so vulnerable—or that the Zetas were so connected. "What is your plan for getting us home again?"

"We can't go to the consulate. I'm sure they've staked those out. We'd probably get ambushed and shot trying to walk in. Same thing with the police stations. We can't just drive across the border—his men are probably watching the highways up to the ports of entry, too. Traffic comes to a stop there, making it very easy to close in on a vehicle and carry out a hit. So we're going to do the last thing Cárdenas expects us to do."

"And what's that?"

"We're going to head northwest to a little town called Altar. We're going to buy supplies there, and then we're going to sneak across the border on foot. By the time Cárdenas has any clue what has happened, you'll already be back in Denver."

ARTURO KNELT IN his private chapel, blood rushing to his head at the news. "What do you mean they got away?"

His sister's youngest son knelt in the aisle, gaze focused on the chapel's marble floor, his arm bandaged where a bullet had struck it. "Forgive me, Jefe, but we did all you asked and more, and we cannot find them. They have vanished like two wisps of smoke."

Hands clasped piously, Arturo bent his head as if in prayer, not wanting José-Luis to see his fear. Arturo César Cárdenas feared nothing. It was he who made others fear. Those who served him well, he rewarded. Those who failed him, those who betrayed him, he killed, their blood, their pain, their lives an offering to the one saint who ruled over all—*La Huesuda*, the Bony Lady, his grandmother had called her. He called her *Santa Muerte*.

Holy Death.

He raised his head, looked at the carved image of her that sat upon the altar, the candle he'd lit flickering at her feet. He'd had her carved from ivory and crowned with gold, her white hood and robes made of cloth taken from a priest's robes. In one skeletal hand, she held a carved human skull, in the other a scythe used for harvesting human lives. And she was his protector.

She would protect him now.

His heartbeat slowed, fear cooling to anger. "Two people kill five of my men, escape in one of our cars, shoot you, my own nephew—and you cannot find them? I think you must not be trying. He is nothing but a thief and a liar, and she is just a woman, just another whore."

An image of Natalie Benoit came into his mind. Young. Beautiful. Her strange blue eyes full of life. He'd been looking forward to having her for weeks. He enjoyed nothing more than dominating a woman until she broke, until her own suffering no longer mattered to her if it meant she could please him. Some of his women had walked willingly into the hands of Death for his sake. Others had fought him until the moment their souls had left their bodies, the fear on their young faces transforming to peace with their last breath. At that moment, they were more beautiful to him than they'd ever been.

Natalie Benoit would have made the perfect sacrifice. But now this *chingadero* who'd stolen his shipment of cocaine had also stolen her. And his men had failed to bring them back.

He crossed himself, wanting to set a good example for José-Luis, ugly scarred bastard that his nephew was. Then slowly he rose to his feet. "This man who stole the shipment— the man you could not break. He has taken the girl for himself. He probably has her in a hotel somewhere and is even at this moment fucking what is mine. Get our police officers into the hotels with her photograph. Check every hotel in every town in the state of Chihuahua if you must, but find them. Then bring them to me."

"*Sí, Jefe.*" José-Luis started to rise.

Arturo caught him by his injured arm and squeezed, ignoring his nephew's gasp of pain. "You have lost me a sacrifice. I swear on *La Santa Muerte* that if you do not find her, you will pay in blood. *¿Comprende?*"

"*Sí! Sí, Jefe.*"

CHAPTER 10

NATALIE THOUGHT ABOUT the kiss while she took another shower and shaved her legs. She thought about it while she slathered lotion on her skin. She thought about it while she blew her hair dry. She was still thinking about it as she started to dress.

The teasing brush of his lips over hers. The possessive way he'd clenched his fist in her hair. The steel-hard feel of his body against hers.

It had been so long since she'd felt the rush of desire that she'd almost forgotten what it was like—the racing pulse, the flutter in the belly, the urgent need to touch and be touched. In those few seconds, she'd felt more alive than she had since . . .

Since before Beau died.

Guilt, thick and greasy, spread through the pit of her stomach, leaving her cold. What was she thinking? Had she just compared Zach to Beau?

No, of course she hadn't. There was no comparison. Zach was a stranger, a man she'd known for little more than forty-eight hours, a man who didn't even trust her enough to tell her his last name.

Beau was the man she'd loved. He'd been her first date, her first real kiss, her first and only lover. He'd meant so much to her that she'd happily agreed to marry him and had worn his engagement ring proudly on her finger. She'd spent almost five years with him, never imagining that their life together would end so soon. How could she compare the way he'd made her feel to one silly kiss from a man she barely knew?

Except that the kiss hadn't been silly. It had been passionate and hot and . . . *real*. Not just a memory. It had stirred something to life within her, making her blood run again, penetrating the numbness inside her. It had made her *feel*.

And for those few seconds, she'd been herself again.

A woman could get addicted to that.

What was she thinking? Was she actually hoping Zach would kiss her again?

She was out of sorts. That's all. She'd just survived a horrible ordeal and was confusing the gratitude she owed Zach with desire. The fact that he was as handsome as sin wasn't helping. But she wasn't really interested in him, no matter how good-looking or courageous he was. How could she be when she still loved Beau?

Beau has been dead for six years, girl. Isn't six years long enough?

Refusing to acknowledge the question or the direction of her own thoughts, she tugged on her panties, drew her tank top over her head, and stepped into the skirt, tucking the tank top into its elastic waistband. Then, too furious with herself to look at her own reflection, she opened the bathroom door.

She found Zach sitting on the edge of the bed cleaning one of the AK-47s, watching a television newscast. At least he was wearing a shirt now.

"Check this out." He gave a jerk of his head toward the TV, his hands busy.

On the screen a pretty young woman spoke in rapid Spanish that was hard for Natalie to understand. But running across the bottom were English subtitles, white letters spelling out news that made her stomach knot.

Two American couples were attacked in their hotel rooms in Cd. Juárez last night with eyewitnesses blaming members of Los Zetas cartel.

"ARE YOU SURE you understand?"

Natalie nodded. "Yes."

Zach sat and leveled his gaze at her, a warning look in his eyes. "No slipups."

She pushed the button for speaker phone so that he could hear the conversation, then dialed the direct line for her editor's desk, feeling both excited and nervous. Zach had grilled her about her coworkers and her boss, asking questions about each and every one of them. When he'd heard that Kat was Navajo, he'd seemed especially interested in her. He'd written out a script for Natalie, warning her that he would end the call if she deviated from it. Then he'd made her wait until they were packed and ready to go, so that the moment she hung up, they could leave the hotel.

Now it was finally time.

The phone rang once, twice, three times.

"Tom Trent."

Natalie's throat grew tight at the sound of Tom's grouchy voice, and she had to swallow before she could speak. "Hi, Tom. It's me. Please don't say my name."

There was a pause and some noise in the background. "I'm listening."

She knew he was doing more than listening. He was recording the call, too, as they all did when an important call came in. "Nothing I say, not even the fact that I called, can go in the paper or online."

"Understood. If it's okay with you, I'd like to put you on speaker phone."

Natalie looked over to Zach, who nodded. "That's fine. Go ahead."

From the background came gasps, and Natalie knew Tom had quickly summoned the rest of the I-Team into his office. They were all there, standing around his desk—everyone except Joaquin. And again her throat grew tight.

She looked down at her notes, fought to keep from tearing up. "This vacation got off to a bad start. I met some people I didn't like. Then things turned around. I met another tourist, and we're traveling together. We're trying to avoid crowds because we don't want to be bothered."

"Can we call someone? Can we help in any way?"

A part of her wanted to cry, "Yes!" and beg Tom to call the State Department, the White House, the CIA, and the

Marines. But Zach was sitting right next to the phone. Though she still wasn't convinced that he hadn't stolen that cocaine, he had proved that he was willing to risk his life to protect her. Besides, it was obvious that he knew Mexico much better than she did. Given the situation, she had little choice but to trust him.

"No, thanks." It hurt to say those words.

"What's next on your itinerary?" Tom was playing along.

"We're not sure." She only hoped what she had to say next would make sense to someone, because it made no sense to her. "I have a message for Kat."

"She's here. Go ahead."

Natalie began to read from the notes Zach had written, careful to annunciate each nonsense syllable. "A-zeh-ha-ge-yah. Bi-tsan-dehn. Wol-la-chee. Ah-jad. A-woh. Be-la-sana. Dah-nes-tsa."

She went on, hoping Kat understood what she was saying, because she certainly didn't. The words must be Navajo—why else would Zach want the message to go to Kat? But when Natalie had asked Zach where he'd learned to speak Navajo, he told her that he didn't speak Navajo at all.

She finished reciting the message, then waited, wondering how Kat would respond. But there was only silence. "Should I say that again?"

"No," Tom answered. "I think we got it."

Zach motioned for her to end the call.

But she didn't want to hang up. Hearing Tom's voice, knowing her friends were there—it felt like a lifeline. A link to home.

Then Tom spoke. "Before you go, there's someone who wants to say hello."

Natalie looked over to Zach, who frowned, tapping the face of his new watch and whispering, "Only if it's really quick."

"Is that really you, *chula*?"

Joaquin!

Blood rushed from Natalie's head, the room seeming to spin. She found herself on her knees. But how? "I thought . . . I thought you were dead!"

Zach stood, shaking his head.

Joaquin's voice came through strong. "Thanks to you, I'm still here."

Zach whispered in her ear, "Time to go."

"Good-bye! I miss you all so—"

But Zach had already hung up the phone.

"ARE YOU GOING to explain all that gibberish you had me say over the phone? Obviously it was a code of some kind."

"Navajo code talk." Zach left the city's midday traffic behind and merged onto Carretera Federal 10 northbound, glad to be safely away from the hotel. "Some buddies and I memorized it, used to send messages to each other."

He and his teammates had studied a code-talker dictionary, memorizing it during their early days as SEALs, figuring that it might come in handy behind enemy lines. Mostly, they'd just used it to irritate other SEALs and play pranks on people.

"Do you think Kat will be able to figure it out?"

"If she does, she'll know exactly where we're going. If not, I'll still get you home." But this time Zach had a few questions of his own. "So . . . '*chula*,' huh? Sounds to me like Joaquin thinks the two of you are more than just friends."

Maybe Natalie felt the same way. The look on her face when she'd heard Joaquin's voice had been one of overwhelming relief and happiness.

Are you jealous, McBride?

No, of course he wasn't jealous. Why should he care if Natalie and this photographer had a thing for each other? Good for them.

Natalie shook her head. "That's just Joaquin. He calls all the women in the newsroom '*chula*.' He says it means 'pretty woman.' "

And some part of Zach felt relieved. "It's the Mexican Spanish equivalent of calling a woman 'baby,' as in, 'Hey, baby.' But if you're okay with that . . ."

"I'm not going to file a sexual harassment lawsuit or burn my bra over it."

At the word "bra," Zach's gaze jerked reflexively to the amazing sight of her braless breasts. He dragged it back to the highway.

Jesus, McBride! You should've beat one out in the shower.

He hadn't been this horny since he'd first arrived at college and found himself surrounded by equally horny eighteen-year-old women.

It's your own fault, you big idiot. You light a match, you get burned. If only you'd kept your mouth to yourself . . .

Yeah, but he hadn't, had he?

She'd been asking him very personal questions, pretending that it was only journalistic curiosity driving her, when he knew damned good and well that she was every bit as attracted to him as he was to her.

So you had to go and prove that, didn't you? Now what?

Now he needed to keep his mind on the job and his hands—and lips—off the woman. Her life depended on his keeping a cool head. Besides, she was more than a little vulnerable. Whatever attraction she felt toward him was surely colored by the fact that he was in the act of saving her life—and that she was alone and entirely dependent on him. He'd be lower than a snake's ass if he took advantage of that.

He glanced over to find her smiling, the AK looking out of place on her lap.

"I'm just so glad he's alive." Her smile slowly faded. "I thought for sure they'd shot him, but I guess they killed someone else. It feels wrong to be happy about that."

"The world is a crazy place, Natalie." He reached over, took her hand, and gave it a squeeze. "Sometimes you have to take happiness where you find it. Your friend is alive, in part because of what you did to save him, and that's a good thing."

She looked up at him through big beautiful eyes, her slender fingers lacing through his. "Thanks for understanding."

And for a while they drove in silence.

"Those couples who were attacked in their hotel rooms—the Zetas were looking for the two of us, weren't they?"

"Yeah."

The cops had called the incidents "robberies," but Zach knew better.

"Was anyone hurt?" There was a hint of worry in her voice, as if she'd been wondering about this for the past couple of hours but had been afraid to ask.

"They roughed them up a bit but didn't kill anyone." He didn't tell her that one of the women had been raped. She'd probably take the weight of that on her own slender shoulders.

Why are you shielding her from the truth all of sudden, McBride?

He started to make up some excuse in his mind about not wanting to deal with her when she got emotional, but then gave up. Truth was, he didn't want to burden her with information that she didn't need. She'd been traumatized enough already.

"Oh, thank goodness for that! I hate to think of anyone suffering because the Zetas mistook them for us." She seemed to relax.

"Why don't you have a boyfriend?" The question must have come out of some other guy's mouth, because Zach hadn't planned on asking her anything about her love life.

Her voice took on a tone of artificial calm. "What makes you so sure I don't have a boyfriend?"

"You've never mentioned him." It seemed logical to Zach. "Given your situation, if there were some special man in your life, you probably would have tried to call him rather than your boss at the newspaper."

"You know why." She looked at her hands. "I lost my fiancé and—"

"That was six years ago, Natalie. *Six years.*"

What a loss it would be for the male race if she spent her life pining away for a corpse. Then again, he had no idea what it was like to lose a lover. He'd never been in love—not seriously anyway.

"I guess I haven't met the right man." Then she turned the question around, her face a carefully composed mask. "Why is there no one in *your* life?"

This was an easy question to answer. "As you've seen, my life isn't exactly the sort of existence a man shares with a woman."

"Maybe you should do something about that—like quit being a crook."

He chuckled, but his reply died before it reached his tongue.

When he looked in the rearview mirror again, a military jeep bristling with assault rifles passed a slower-moving pickup and swerved into their lane, gaining ground fast.

The first letter on its license plate was a big, black Z.

Adrenaline punched through him. "Get down!"

Natalie turned to look over her shoulder. "Wha—"

"I said get down, damn it!" Zach forced her head down, hoping the men behind them hadn't seen that there was a woman in the vehicle. He drew the AK onto his lap, working the bolt with one hand. "There's a jeep full of Zetas on our tail."

Steady, McBride. Don't rabbit. Just because they're behind you doesn't mean they know they're behind you.

He glanced down at the speedometer to make certain he wasn't speeding, then did his best to drive casually, the jeep now right on their tail. "Reach for the Glock. It's on the floor near your feet. Hold on to it. If they start shooting—"

With a roar of its engine, the jeep swerved to the left, passing them in a plume of exhaust and heading up the highway.

Zach let out a long, slow breath, adrenaline subsiding. "You can sit up now."

Slowly, Natalie sat upright, peering over the dashboard with wide eyes, Glock in her hand. "They're gone?"

"Yeah."

"Oh, thank God!"

Zach didn't share her sense of relief. The Zetas were headed straight for the junction at Janos, where Mexico 10 intersected with the Carret and connected Janos to Juárez. Anyone headed west from Juárez would have to pass that intersection, as would any driver heading north on Mexico 10. It was the perfect place to screen traffic leaving the state of Chihuahua for Sonora.

That's where Zach was taking Natalie, and now the Zetas would reach the intersection before they did.

ZACH GLANCED OVER at his sleeping passenger, feeling a tug in his chest. Her long hair spilled over her cheek, her lips slightly parted, her breathing deep and even. The bruise on her cheek was the only indication of the hell she'd been through these past couple of days—well, that and the Glock resting in her lap.

What was it about her that got to him? Sure, she was pretty. Okay, she was beautiful. But he'd met lots of beautiful women, and none of them had gotten inside him like Natalie had. Maybe it was the combination of grit and vulnerability that was so much a part of her. Or maybe it was just their situation. Hell, he didn't know.

And now isn't the time to try to figure it out.

Besides, it didn't matter. His job was to get her home safely. Then she would go back to her life, and he would get on with his mission. They wouldn't see each other again.

He glanced in the rearview mirror, then over at Natalie again.

It would be better for both of them if she stayed awake. If another jeep full of Zetas were to come up behind them now, he'd lose precious seconds waking her and waiting for her to get her bearings before she'd be of any use to him. And for a moment, he considered rousing her. But he couldn't bring himself to do it. The peaceful expression on her face told him she'd found forgetfulness in sleep, and the last damned thing he wanted to do was to rob her of that, not when ugly reality lay just up the highway.

Let her sleep, McBride.

He took one hand off the wheel, opened the plastic bottle of ibuprofen he'd left on the dash, and popped a couple of pills, then washed them down with bottled water. Then he put his gaze back where it should be—on the road.

IT WAS ALMOST midnight by the time they reached Altar. The streets were still busy, but, apart from a couple of street vendors, most of the stores were closed, making it impossible to buy everything they'd need for their journey. They had no choice but to stay the night.

Zach had been forced to leave the highway to avoid roadblocks the Zetas had set up outside Janos, Agua Prieta, and Nogales. But he hadn't seen a single Z on a license plate since they'd passed the outskirts of Nogales. Oh, the Zetas were here, all right. All the cartels had a presence in Altar, which served as a starting point for many of the trafficking routes into the U.S. But Altar was in the grasp of the Sinaloa Cartel.

The Zetas were lying low.

Beside him, Natalie stared out the window in apparent fascination at a vendor who was doing a brisk business in bottled water, canned food, and sunhats with American flags on them. "Is there a drought coming on? Look at how many gallons of water that man in the cowboy hat just bought."

"Keep your head down, Natalie. Someone might recognize you."

She did as he asked, her dark hair falling down like a curtain, concealing her face. "Sorry. I'm just curious by nature, I guess."

Really? I hadn't noticed.

"He's selling water to people who are going to start out for the border tonight."

"Tonight?"

"It gets up to a hundred and fifteen degrees out there in the desert. Traveling by day puts a person at greater risk not only of being seen by traffickers, but also dying of heatstroke or dehydration. If you've got the cash to pay a good coyote who knows the way, you can travel when it's cool, and then rest during the heat of the day."

She nodded thoughtfully as if thinking this through, then slowly turned to look up at him, wariness on her face. "Is that what we're going to do—walk across the desert at *night*?"

So she didn't like the idea. He couldn't say he blamed her.

"That's the plan." He drew up to a stop sign, then made a left. "Oh, don't worry. We aren't leaving tonight. I need to buy supplies. Our objective now is to lie low—get a room in a safe hotel, buy supplies tomorrow, and then get out of town."

"I suppose you'll be shopping around for a 'coyote,' too." She spoke the word with distinct—and understandable—contempt.

"No need, angel." He glanced over at her and smiled. "You've already got a guide."

He tilted his head back and let loose his best coyote howl. Chuckling, he glanced down again, his laughter ending abruptly when he saw the expression on her face.

Clearly, she was *not* amused.

CHAPTER 11

NATALIE COULDN'T BELIEVE she was doing this, her heart already pounding. She squirmed and tried to make herself smaller, her body bent in a fetal position and crammed into the military duffel bag that had held their guns. Then her hair caught on the zipper. "Ouch!"

"Sorry." Zach's fingers freed the strands, then tugged the corner of the bag up over her right shoulder, encasing all but her face in thick canvas.

"You promised. Just a few minutes."

"I'll get you out of here as fast as I can." Zach reached down, cupped her cheek, his features invisible, his head a shadow against the darkness. "I'm sorry, Natalie, but it's the only way. Are you ready?"

She wanted to shout at him to get her out, but then how would he sneak her into the hotel room? The Zetas were searching for American *couples*. If anyone saw her, if anyone recognized her . . .

She drew a deep breath, steeled herself. *You can do this.* "Yes."

Then he closed the trunk.

Darkness. Heat. The duffel bag tighter than a coffin.

Her pulse picked up, panic closing in.

Snap out of it! Two days ago, you spent hours in a trunk in the hands of killers. You're safer in here than out there.

She heard the driver's door shut, heard the engine start,

and drew a steadying breath. It was only a few blocks from the edge of town, where Zach had pulled off the road, to the hotel. He would drive to the front entrance, where everyone could see that he was alone. He would go in, pay in cash, speaking only Spanish, then drive the car around to the door of their room—and sneak her inside.

No one would know that she was there. If the Zetas showed up looking for an American man and woman, the front desk would tell them there weren't any.

She closed her eyes, kept her breathing slow and steady as the car slowed and came to a stop at the traffic light.

Only two blocks to go.

The seconds dragged by, the heat inside the duffel bag sweltering, her body cramped, her skin slick with sweat.

The car began to move again, then slowed and turned left.

One block.

The darkness seeped in on her, so slowly that at first she didn't realize it.

Have a nice death, a peaceful death.

She swallowed, her mouth dry, those hated words running unwelcome through her mind. She tried to force them aside, unwilling to be held hostage by the horror of that day.

The car rolled to a stop.

Above the rush of her own pulse, she heard the door open. She would be alone now while Zach went inside and got a room.

You can do this. You can do this.

After a brief eternity, the driver's side door opened again, and the engine started. Moments later, she felt the car slow, turn, and roll to a stop.

Not long now. Not long.

The door opened and closed, and then . . .

Nothing.

What was he doing? Where had he gone? Had something happened?

She strained to listen but could hear nothing. The seconds became minutes which seemed to stretch into hours, until the only sound Natalie could hear was the hammering of her own heart.

Something's wrong. Something's gone wrong.

Her breath came in shallow pants, adrenaline making her heart beat harder.

What if something had happened to him? No one would know where she was. She would be stuck here, just like she'd been stuck in that morgue cooler.

Oh, where is he?

She should be home by now, not trying to sneak into her own country across the desert, where hundreds of people died every year. Why had she gone along with this? Why had she let herself be locked in this trunk by a man who wouldn't tell her his last name, who insisted he wasn't a criminal but knew smuggling routes well enough to guide her through them? Who else knew smuggling routes besides drug smugglers, men who bought, sold and stole drugs and carried guns and traded guns for cars and killed people without blinking?

She choked back a sob.

Jack Sprat could eat no fat.

Footsteps. A key in the lock. Cool night air spilling in around her.

ZACH KNEW SHE was in trouble the moment he opened the trunk. She was hyperventilating, her eyes wide. He bent down, as if searching for something in the trunk, aware that they were surrounded by windows, alleys, streets where anyone would be lurking, watching. He lowered his voice to a whisper. "It's almost over. Stay quiet. Stay still. I have to zip it."

He pushed the zipper up carefully over her panicked face, then lifted the duffel bag with her inside it and slung it over his left shoulder like a sack of potatoes, her weight causing a tug of pain in his ribs. Trying to act casual, he walked with long but unhurried strides toward the unlocked door of their room. He opened the door, walked inside, and locked it behind him, then hurried to lower his trembling human baggage gently to the bed, where it wriggled and whimpered.

He reached for the zipper, tugged. "Sorry that took so long. There were cops on the street out front. I wanted to make sure the place was safe before I—"

Natalie's pale face emerged from the duffel bag. "Get me out!"

"That's what I'm trying to do. Hold still for just—"

But she didn't hold still. She wiggled and twisted, shrugging her shoulders out of the bag, then flipping onto her hands and knees and crawling the rest of the way out, as Zach pulled the bag from beneath her with a few strong tugs. She turned and sat on the bed facing him, out of breath and shaking, her eyes wild, her skirt pushed up around her hips, her hair a dark, tangled mane. There were beads of sweat on her forehead and an angry red scratch on her left arm, probably from the zipper.

He sat beside her, drew her into his arms. "Easy, Natalie. Shhh. It's over."

For a moment she let him hold her, her body trembling. Then her spine went stiff, and she drew away from him, sliding off the bed and smoothing her skirt into place. "No. No, it's not over. It won't be over till I'm home."

Well, she was right about that.

But why did he get the feeling he'd done something wrong? "I wouldn't have left you in there so long, but with three cop cars parked on the street, I had to make certain the place was clear before I brought you in."

Her gaze bored through him as if she hadn't heard a word he'd said, one hand absentmindedly rubbing the scratch on her arm. "If you're not a drug thief or trafficker, how do you know the smuggling routes well enough to travel through the desert without a guide?"

So, it had come back to that, had it? Why couldn't she just trust him?

Would you trust you, McBride?

Hell, no.

"We'll talk in a minute." He turned and walked toward the door. "Stay out of sight, and stay quiet. I need to get the rest of our shit out of the car."

He waited until she'd backed into the bathroom, then grabbed the empty duffel bag and walked out to the vehicle. Scanning the scene for any sign that he was under surveillance, he opened the trunk and quickly loaded the firearms and ammo into the bag. Then he grabbed the rest of their stuff and carried it with the weapons into their room, locking the door behind him.

What in the hell was he going to tell her this time—that he'd earned the rank of Eagle Scout by helping little old ladies cross the desert?

Damn it!

She reappeared at the bathroom door. "Are you going to answer my question?"

"I said we'll talk." He tucked a Glock into the back of his jeans, then searched one of the bags for the first-aid kit. "But first we're going to take care of that scratch. I don't want it getting infected while we're out in the desert."

"PLAY THAT BACK and amplify the background. Listen."

Joaquin watched as Julian and Marc used fancy police equipment to dissect the recording of Natalie's phone call, picking up a man's voice in the background. Julian scrolled back through the digital version of the recording, then hit play again.

"Before you go, there's someone who wants to say hello." That was Tom.

A slight hesitation from Natalie. Joaquin wouldn't have noticed it if Julian and Marc hadn't pointed it out.

That's why they're the cops, and you're the photographer, amigo.

And then a man's voice whispering. "*Only if it's really quick.*"

"Is that really you, *chula*?" Joaquin heard the emotion in his own voice, the rush of relief he'd felt at the sound of her voice so overwhelming he'd found it almost impossible to speak.

Then Natalie's voice, her surprise and relief every bit as strong as his. "I thought . . . I thought you were dead!"

"Thanks to you, I'm still here."

And then a faint whisper. "*Time to go.*"

"Good-bye! I—"

Then the line went dead.

Twice Julian replayed it, adjusting the computer, making the whispered words even clearer. "The accent's American. My guess is he's standing right beside her."

Marc nodded. "Whoever he is, he's calling the shots. That's for damned sure."

Joaquin didn't like it. "Is she his prisoner?"

Julian leaned back in his chair, crossed his arms over his chest, a frown on his face. "Anything is possible, but unless that secret message turns out to be some kind of ransom demand, I don't think so. She called him 'another tourist' and said they were traveling together, which could be their way of telling us they're on the same side. And he's not threatening her. He lets the call go to speaker phone, and when Tom tries to bring you into the call, this guy's response is 'Only if it's really quick.' Seems to me he's being understanding, trying to accommodate her."

"That's my take on it, too." Marc took a slug of coffee. "Somehow this guy helped her escape—how we don't know—and now they're on the run. Do you think he's an operative?"

"No idea. The key is in that message." Julian sat upright, pushed a few buttons on the computer, and popped out a CD. "She called so we'd know she was alive. He *let* her call so she could deliver that message."

Joaquin didn't understand. "Why would they call us? If she escaped, why not call the U.S. consulate or the State Department or the police? Why is she hanging out with this loser?"

Marc met his gaze. "This *loser* may have saved her life."

"There are lots of reasons they might be lying low rather than contacting the authorities." Julian powered down the computer. "The cartels have infiltrated law enforcement and government at all levels in Mexico, and it's hard to trust—"

The door opened, and Kat appeared, her long dark hair tied in a knot on the back of her head, a look of excitement on her face, a notebook and pen in her hand. "It's Navajo code talk."

"Have you deciphered it?" Marc pulled out a chair for her.

Kat shut the door behind her, shaking her head. "Only partly. It's more complicated than that. I used a code-talker dictionary, but it still makes no sense."

Julian cleared a space on the table. "Show us what you've got."

She sat and looked at her notes. "Here's the first part: 'Escape from ant leg tooth apple ram.'"

Joaquin shook his head. "What the hell does that mean?"

"Well, 'escape from' is clear enough, but the rest of it . . ."

Julian shrugged. "Do the words have any significance in code talk beyond their literal meaning?"

"Yes, but that didn't make any sense either." There was an apologetic tone in Kat's voice, as if she felt she'd failed them, her pretty face lined with stress and fatigue.

It was almost one in the morning, and she had a baby at home.

Joaquin reached out, gave her hand a squeeze. "Hey, it's okay."

For a moment no one spoke.

Then Julian grabbed a notebook and a pen. "Give us everything you've got. Let's go over every word, look at every possible meaning."

An hour later, they'd made no progress, the message just as incomprehensible as it had been when Kat first read out the strange list of words.

"Maybe we should call it a night." Julian leaned back, rubbing his eyes. "I don't know about the rest of you, but my mind's not getting any sharper."

"I hear that," Marc muttered. Then he frowned. "What if these aren't just words. What if they're a mix of words and words that stand for letters that spell other words?"

Kat looked confused. "What do you mean?"

"Well, 'Escape from' makes sense. Then it turns into gibberish. What if the other words *spell* words?"

"But how do we know which letters to use?"

Marc turned to a new sheet of paper. "They wanted us to be able to figure this out, so let's make it simple and use the first letter of each word to start with."

"So that's 'Escape from a-l-t-a-r.'" Kat frowned. "Are they in a church?"

And then Joaquin knew.

He looked up, met Julian's gaze. "No, not an *altar* like inside a church. *Altar.*"

He saw understanding dawn in Julian's eyes. "That's it."

Marc shook his head. "All-tar? What's 'all-tar'?"

Joaquin answered. "It's a town not far from the border, a jumping off place for drug smugglers and others trying to cross illegally into the U.S."

"Way to go, Joaquin." Julian raised an eyebrow and looked

at Marc as if impressed. "Well, I'll be damned, Hunter. You might earn your paycheck this week."

"Fuck you, Dickangelo."

"Not gonna happen, Hunter. Sorry."

Joaquin knew they weren't really angry at each other. For all their insults, they were as tight as brothers.

To his right, Kat was working furiously, scribbling words. Then she looked up, eyes wide. "I think I have it."

Julian's head whipped around. "Let's hear it."

"Escape from Altar. Then the words 'infiltrate,' 'shadow' and 'wolf.' Then 'Tohono.'" She looked around the room at them, the expression on her face telling Joaquin these words meant something to her.

Julian's face went dark like a thundercloud. He stood. "Son of a bitch!"

Joaquin looked at Marc. Marc looked at Joaquin.

They both looked at Julian and Kat.

"So do either of you feel like filling us in, or are you having a private moment here?" Marc asked, clearly irritated and as much in the dark as Joaquin.

"Escape from Altar. Infiltrate Shadow Wolf. Tohono." Kat put the message together, worry on her face. "I think it means they're going to try to make a desert border crossing from Altar onto the land of the Tohono O'Odham."

"The toe-ho-no oh-damn . . . what?" Marc looked at Joaquin as if to see whether this made any sense to him.

But Joaquin was too appalled at the thought of Natalie trying to cross the unforgiving desert in the heat of high summer to say anything. People died out there every year, their lives lost to hunger, dehydration, heatstroke, not to mention cartel violence. As Joaquin had learned during the SPJ conference, the Sonoran Desert along the border was a no-man's-land of cartels, coyotes, and fugitives.

It was Kat who answered Marc's question. "The Tohono O'Odham—an Indian nation whose land extends into Mexico. They have a border guard unit known as the Shadow Wolves, Indian federal agents who are the best trackers in the world."

"So he's bringing her across the desert?" There was an edge to Marc's voice now.

"If he doesn't get her killed first." Joaquin swallowed the bile that rose in his throat, anger like acid in his stomach.

Marc looked over at Julian. "They didn't just tell us this to say, 'Hey there. Having a great time. Call you when we get there.' They told us this so that we can meet them, get them out of the desert, act as backup, be a welcome wagon."

"Agreed." Julian met first Joaquin's gaze and then Marc's, letting out a long, slow breath. "I can't go. Tessa needs me. If she loses this baby . . ." He dropped his gaze to the floor. "We lost one six months ago. It tore her apart. I won't leave her."

Stunned silence.

"I'm sorry." Marc stood, rested a hand on Julian's shoulder. "I didn't know."

Joaquin thought back six months and realized that Tessa had dropped out of the picture for several weeks. At the time, he'd thought nothing of it. "*Lo siento.* I'm so sorry."

"That must have been so hard for both of you." Kat's hand rested on her lower belly, a woman's empathy for another woman's loss.

"We hadn't yet told anyone she was pregnant. She didn't want anyone to know about the miscarriage. She thought she'd be able to deal with it better if no one knew."

More silence.

"I'll go." Kat stood. "I have a friend in Sells whose brother is a Shadow Wolf."

"You don't have to go, Kat." Marc stood, pushing his chair in. "You've got a baby girl at home who needs you. If you can help me connect with these Shadow Wolves, I'll head down and—"

"You're not going without me." Joaquin rose to his feet, the words out before he realized he'd spoken.

Marc and Julian looked over at him as if sizing him up. Then Marc nodded. "Sure, Joaquin. You can come along."

And Joaquin found himself feeling like someone's kid brother. Marc would allow him to tag along but wasn't expecting anything from him.

And why would he? What can you do besides get in the way?

Kat picked up her things. "I'll call my friend first thing in the morning."

Julian leaned back against the wall, crossed his arms over his chest, his brows furrowed, clearly trying to puzzle something out. "A man comes out of nowhere, connects with Natalie, maybe even helps her escape from cartel thugs. He's familiar with Navajo code talk, knows Mexico, believes he can get her across the desert." Then Julian looked up at Marc. "Who *is* this guy?"

CHAPTER 12

"IF YOU'D STARTED screaming, those cops would've heard. They'd have come over to investigate. That would've drawn a crowd, and our lives would suck right now."

As Zach opened the first-aid kit, Natalie watched, heat rushing into her cheeks, mortified to the core by the way she'd just lost it. He'd been in the process of getting her out of the duffel bag, but some wild, terrified, frantic part of her had taken over, and she hadn't been able to bear it a second longer.

"But I didn't scream." At least she could say that much for herself.

He motioned her to come over to the little table where the light was best. "I know you didn't, and I know it couldn't have been easy. But you weren't far from it, either. Another few minutes and . . ."

He shrugged, his unspoken words left to hang in the air.

"Believe it or not, I was okay at first." She felt some strange need to defend herself. "Then you were gone so long. I started wondering if something had happened, if you'd gotten arrested or hurt or if you'd forgotten about me—"

"*Forgotten* about you?" He caught her chin, forced her to make eye contact, his gaze flashing anger, then slowly going gentle. "That would never happen. *Never.*"

And Natalie got the sense that she'd hurt him.

He released her, then tore open an antiseptic swab, the

scent of rubbing alcohol wafting through the air. "You still don't trust me."

"I *want* to trust you, but . . ." There was no point in keeping her thoughts from him. "There's a preponderance of evidence to suggest that you're mixed up in drug dealing, Zach Black. Your conflict with the Zetas. Your refusal to answer questions. Your skill with guns and knives. Your ability to draw thousands in cash out of the thin air. I *watched* you hand weapons over to a criminal. And now you tell me you can smuggle me through the desert as well as a human trafficker. Tell me I'm wrong to worry about how those pieces fit together."

She watched his face, but he gave away nothing.

He held out his hand. "Give me that arm."

"It's just a scratch." She did as he asked anyway.

"The skin is broken. An infection in the desert could be fatal." His fingers were gentle, awareness skittering up her arm.

Stop it! You shouldn't think of him that way.

No, she shouldn't. But she couldn't seem to help it.

"Isn't it enough to know that you're safe with me, that I would never do anything to hurt you?" He dabbed at the scratch on her arm with the alcohol swab.

The sting made her gasp. "People die in the desert, Zach. I still can't help but believe that we're risking our lives to sneak across the border, not because that's the only way, but because you want to avoid the authorities. The last thing in the world I want to do is make trouble for you. Even if you *are* a drug dealer or an arms trader or some kind of cartel mercenary, I don't think I could bring myself to turn you in. But I don't want to die out there just because you're afraid you'll go to prison."

Drug dealer? Arms trader? Cartel mercenary?

Zach looked up to find Natalie watching him, a pleading look in her eyes, and a part of him wanted to laugh at the utter absurdity of the situation.

A preponderance of evidence. How do you like that, McBride?

He saw now that it had been a strategic mistake to keep everything from her. How could he expect her to trust him when connecting the dots created such a damning picture of

him? She was an intelligent woman, an investigative reporter.
Of course she would put it together like that. If Zach had
met someone under these circumstances, he'd probably have
reached a similar conclusion.

It was time for a new strategy. He would tell her enough
of the truth to alleviate some of her fears, but not enough to
endanger his mission—or her life.

A freaking preponderance of evidence!

Shit.

"I served in Iraq and Afghanistan." It wasn't the whole
truth, but it was the truth and more than Zach ought to tell her.

He could almost *see* the little wheels in her mind spinning.

"So you're a veteran."

"Yeah."

"Are you still active duty or in the reserves?"

He almost smiled at how quickly she'd gone from thinking
of him as a criminal to wondering if he were some kind of
undercover military operative. That's exactly why he hadn't
told her before. She was too damned smart.

*Next time a chick saves your life, make sure she's not a
reporter.*

"Neither. I was honorably discharged six years ago."

Let's see what you make of that, angel.

He dropped the swab into the trash and reached for the
antibiotic ointment, aware that she was studying him.

"That's where you learned how to use guns and fight the
way you do."

"Learned how—and got lots of practice." He rubbed ointment on the scratch, then put the cap back on the tube and
picked up a large adhesive bandage.

"Is that how you got shot?" Her voice had lost its inquisi-
tive edge and taken on a softer tone, but she was still testing
him, still probing, still looking for loose threads to pull.

"Yeah." He peeled the paper strips off the bandage and
pressed it over the abrasion. "We were ambushed by Taliban
fighters in the Hindu Kush mountains in the Nuristan province of Afghanistan. I caught a round in the back."

"That must have been terrible." She rubbed her hand over
the bandage, her eyes filling with concern. "I'm sorry. I can't
imagine—"

"I'm not looking for sympathy." Memories he didn't care to relive made his voice colder than he'd intended, the screams of dying friends echoing in his mind. He crumpled the bandage wrapper in his fist, tossed it in the trash, then closed the first-aid kit. "I told you so that you'll understand why we don't need a guide."

Her brows settled into a delicate frown. "I know I'm not a geography whiz, but my recollection is that Iraq and Afghanistan lie somewhat to the east, while the desert we intend to cross is in a more northerly direction."

Why did her accent have to make every damned thing she said seem charming, even when she was being a smartass?

It was time to get to the point.

He looked her straight in the eyes. "I know how to survive in the wild, Natalie. I can get you safely through the desert. I can protect you from Cárdenas and his men. But I can't protect you from the consequences of your mistrust or your stubbornness or your curiosity. If you do anything reckless or desperate or stupid, we will *both* pay."

She opened her mouth as if to object, but he pressed a finger to her lips.

"Listen to me. There are things you can't know about me, things I can't tell you for *your* sake. But I promised you I'd do everything I could to get you home safely, and I will. Please quit asking so damned many questions and trust me."

He held her gaze, hoping she understood.

She studied him, as if she were measuring him against his words. "Okay, Zach Black, I'll trust you. I'll quit asking questions—or at least I'll try."

He couldn't help but grin at that last bit. "Thank you."

She looked down, a troubled expression darkening her face. "After all you saw in the war, you must really think I'm a wimp to freak out like that."

He reached out and ran a knuckle over the curve of her cheek. "After all I saw in war, Natalie, I understand." He understood more than she would ever know. "You are *not* a wimp. There are people who have claustrophobia for no reason. After all you've been through . . ."

She met his gaze again. "Please don't let me down, Zach. I do *not* want to die out there in the desert."

He drew her into his arms and held her close, partly to reassure her and partly because he couldn't help himself. "If *you* die, angel, it means I'm already dead."

NATALIE CLOSED THE bathroom door behind her, then turned and met her own gaze in the mirror, exhaling in a long, slow sigh of relief.

What Zach had told her was the truth. She'd seen it in his eyes.

He was ex-military, a war veteran who'd been badly wounded in combat and then honorably discharged. Even if he was somehow mixed up in drug trafficking now, he'd once served his country and had almost lost his life. That didn't absolve him of any wrongdoing in the present, but it helped her understand why he was willing to put his life on the line for hers—and why she could count on him to keep his word.

Deep inside, he had a strong sense of duty.

But what had brought him to the life he led now? How could a man go from serving his country to breaking its laws? And what exactly did he do? She couldn't imagine him participating in human trafficking. The men who stole, bought, and sold people had no respect for human life. But drugs, guns . . . She could imagine him being involved in either. Or did he work as a hired gun for someone else?

She might have agreed to quit asking him questions, but that couldn't keep them from popping into her mind.

She set her toiletries down on the counter, hung the white silk nightgown he'd bought for her on the hook on the back of the door, then undressed and stepped into the shower, wanting to rinse the sweat from her skin.

It all made sense now. Zach's super-fit physique. His knowledge of first aid. His skill with weapons. His talent for strategy and staying one step ahead of the Zetas. His tendency to bark at her as if giving orders. His resilience in resisting torture. His ability to kill—precisely, cleanly, without hesitation.

Yes, I've killed, but only when I had no choice. It's never easy taking another person's life, but sometimes it's necessary.

Now she knew what he'd meant by that.

She'd be lying if she denied that what he'd told her had made her feel safer. A short trek across the desert into the U.S. was surely a cakewalk for a man who'd fought in the deserts of Iraq and the mountains of Afghanistan. He'd probably had lots of outdoor survival training. He would know what supplies to bring. He would know how to navigate with GPS so they wouldn't get lost. And if they ran into armed traffickers in the middle of nowhere, he would know how to deal with them, too.

She finished rinsing her skin, then stepped out and patted herself dry with a fluffy white towel, her gaze fixing on her reflection. The bruises on her cheek and temple were now a dull color of purple. She ran her fingers over them—proof of how close she'd come to dying. If it hadn't been for Zach . . .

He'd already done so much for her. More than once he'd put himself between her and danger, even shielding her with his own body.

If you die, angel, it means I'm already dead.

He'd spoken those words to reassure her, but they struck her differently now, stirring something uneasy inside her. She clutched the towel to her chest, dread gathering cold behind her breastbone.

Oh, God, she didn't want that. No, she didn't want that.

She'd already lost her parents, already lost Beau. They'd been trying to help her, too. She didn't want anyone else to die.

No, that wouldn't happen. That couldn't happen. She wouldn't let it happen. She would do exactly what Zach told her to do. She would carry her own weight. She would do her best not to slow them down. And she wouldn't complain. He'd told her he didn't think she was a wimp, and she would do her best to prove him right.

They would make it. They would *both* make it.

Trying to draw comfort from her resolve, she draped the towel over the nearest towel bar, then reached for the silk nightgown, the fabric cool against her skin as she slipped it over her head. Then she set about brushing her teeth. It was only when she'd finished rinsing her mouth that she saw her reflection again.

Oh, my stars!

The nightgown made her look beautiful—like a bride on her wedding night. But this wasn't the sort of nightgown a woman wore in the presence of a man unless she wanted very much to have sex with him. White silk clung to her breasts, her belly, her hips, leaving almost nothing to the imagination. The swells of her breasts were covered only by lace, her nipples dark against the shimmering fabric, the thin stripe of her pubic hair a shadow.

Had Zach bought this hoping to see her in it?

Rather than making her angry, the thought made her breath catch, sent a trill of excitement into her belly. She found herself wanting to *let* him see her in it, wanting to see how he would react, wanting to see where that would take them. He was such an intense man. Kissing him had shaken her to her core. Making love with him would be . . .

Did she actually want it? Did she truly want to sleep with a man she'd known for all of three days, a man with secrets, a man who might be a criminal? Did she truly want to have sex with Zach?

Would it be so wrong if she did?

For six long years, she had grieved for Beau, missing him, holding on to his memory, hating herself for calling him from the hospital and asking him to come get her. That phone call had cost him his life. She'd wept for him until there was nothing left inside her, until the pain of losing him had left her numb, until she'd begun to think that she had died, too.

But Zach's kiss had brought her back to life. He had awakened something inside her, made her feel things she hadn't felt in years. She couldn't help but want him.

Would it be so wrong if she let herself live again?

The question jabbed at her conscience, but her body had a very different response. Even the *idea* of sex with Zach aroused her, the wetness between her thighs having nothing to do with her shower. She couldn't help but want him. Besides, hadn't she promised herself that if she got away from the Zetas she would live her life to the fullest?

Yes, she had.

Who have you become, Natalie?

She met her own gaze, unable to answer. She didn't appear any different, not on the outside. But something inside her had changed. During the course of these past few days, something had definitely changed.

Her gaze dropped to the nightgown.

No, of course, she couldn't wear this. She couldn't. It wouldn't be right.

But she couldn't seem to get herself to take it off either.

ZACH READ OVER the list of supplies he'd just written, checking to make certain he hadn't forgotten anything. Handheld GPS. Batteries. Compass for when the GPS fucked up. Wristwatch. Night vision goggles. Infrared binoculars. Night scope for the AK. Box of 115 grain +P jacketed hollow point rounds for the Glocks. Cartridges for the AKs. Double shoulder holster. Flashlight. Two backpacks. Sturdy trail shoes, athletic socks, BDU pants and jackets for both of them. Thick leather gloves. Bandanas. A heavy wool blanket. Duct tape. Sunscreen. Lip balm. Hats. Rope. Powdered electrolytes. Moleskin for blisters. Antihistamine. Insect repellant. Snakebite kit. Codeine-caffeine tablets. Hard candy. MREs if he could find them. Canned food and a can opener if he couldn't. Hand wipes. And eight gallons of water—enough to last three or four days if they traveled at night.

As a supply town that served everyone from poor families planning to cross the border illegally in search of work to wealthy drug lords, Altar had pretty much everything on the list. To avoid attracting attention, Zach would pay in cash, wear sunglasses, speak only Spanish. Shopkeepers in Altar had long ago learned not to ask questions, and there was almost no chance that Zach would be recognized. There was only one Zeta still alive who knew what he looked like.

But Natalie was a different matter. Her photo had been in the papers and on the news. As striking as she was, she'd be recognized immediately. What was he going to do with her?

He stood, stretched, pain in his ribs stopping him short. He looked over at the bed, his body desperately in need of sleep. He was still in combat mode, exhaustion kept at a distance by adrenaline. But he'd had only one full night of sleep since being taken by the Zetas. Eventually, it was going to catch up with him.

He dragged one of the chairs over to the door, jammed it beneath the doorknob—an extra obstacle just in case—and had just started checking the weapons when the bathroom door opened and Natalie walked out. He glanced up—and his mouth went dry.

Sweet Jesus!

She was wearing it. She was wearing the nightgown.

And damned if she wasn't the most beautiful thing he'd ever seen—virginal, achingly feminine, seductive as hell. The fabric seeming to slide over her skin like a whisper, breasts that had teased him all day from beneath her tank top now daring him to touch them, kiss them, suck their velvety tips. And that dark stripe where her thighs came together . . .

Not a triangle, a *stripe*.

She waxes.

The thought of smooth, bare labia knocked the breath from his lungs, heat rushing to his groin, his cock already half-hard and getting harder, his jeans uncomfortably tight.

You are such a fucking idiot, McBride! Why did you buy the thing? Haven't you been tortured enough lately?

Oh, but this was a completely different kind of torture, as sweet as it was unbearable—and much more likely to break him.

Through a testosterone fog, he realized she was watching him.

"Thank you." Her cheeks glowed a delectable shade of pink. "It's beautiful."

He wanted to tell her that the gown was only beautiful because she was wearing it, but he was too caught up defending himself from the part of him that wanted to kick his own ass. "I was half-asleep when I grabbed it. I think it was all they had."

"Oh." Her cheeks flushed crimson, and she turned away from him, her hands suddenly busy drawing down the covers and plumping pillows.

The sight of her hips and sweet ass swathed in silk shorted out his brain, so it took him a moment to realize that he'd hurt her. Well, it had been years since he'd spent any real time with a woman. Obviously, he'd forgotten everything he'd learned about dealing with females—which probably hadn't been much in the first place.

Son of a bitch!

Sexually frustrated, irritated with himself, he went back to what he'd been doing. But there'd been a change of plans. Rather than setting the Glock on the nightstand, he carried it to the table together with the duffel bag of weapons and ammo. He drew one of the chairs into the corner beneath the AC and leaned an AK against the wall beside the chair. He told himself this position would enable him to look out the window and keep an eye on the parking lot. But the truth was that it would keep him from lying in bed beside Natalie.

You handled it last night, and she was only wearing a towel.

Yes, but last night he'd been half-dead. Tonight, he was half-hard.

He turned to face her, found her crawling beneath the covers. He grabbed one of the Glocks, and set it on the nightstand next to her. "At the first sign of trouble, run into the bathroom and lie down in the tub. And take this with you. Understand?"

"Yes." Her face expressionless, she looked up at him, then glanced over at the chair. "Are you sleeping there? It doesn't look very comfortable."

"I want to keep an eye on the parking lot."

She propped herself up on an elbow, raised a graceful brow. "While you sleep?"

"I'll catnap." He took off his shirt, tossed it onto the table, then clicked off the light, neon from outside flickering red through white curtains. "Get some rest."

He went and sat in the chair, crossed his arms over his chest, and kicked his feet up onto the table, settling in for the night. Overhead, the AC rattled.

It was going to be one long damned night.

CHAPTER 13

GRITTING HIS TEETH against agony, Zach switched his M4 into full auto mode and fired, spraying the hillside, trying to take out as many damned Taliban as he could before they could reach his element. He hoped the men would hear his shots and recognize the sharper retort of his M4 over the AK fire echoing through the canyon. Hopefully, they'd turn and see the fighters coming up behind them. If they didn't . . .

Rat-ta-ta-ta-ta-tat! Rat-ta-ta-ta-ta-tat! Rat-ta-ta-ta-ta-tat!

Sweat stinging his eyes, he emptied his magazine, the recoil making the pain in his back that much more unbearable. But he didn't give a damn about pain, not when his team was depending on him for their survival. Across on the opposite hillside, bodies dropped, wounded men crying out, others running for cover as the Taliban fighters realized they were under fire. One walked in mindless circles, clutching the stump of his arm, as if looking for the rest of it.

Zach needed more ammo, but the spare ammunition was in his pack a good three feet away. He dragged himself inch by inch across the ground, the pain in his back tearing through him. He reached with bloody fingers, grabbed a full magazine and a fistful of stripper clips, then shoved the magazine into place and raised the weapon. But by then most of the Taliban fighters had already disappeared down the side of the hill, out of his sight. He opened fire again, taking down a handful of stragglers, including the man whose arm he'd shot off.

Then from down in the valley he heard it—the frenzy of metallic AK-47 fire as the Taliban who'd made it down the hill—the ones he hadn't gotten—started shooting. Beneath it, he could just hear the steady fire of three M4s and Jimmy's HK MP5.

And then . . .

The explosion of an IED and a cry.

Brian?

Fuck! Fuck, no!

His element, his team, his friends—they were dying.

Zach tried to crawl to the edge of the cliff, inching his way forward, but he'd lost too much blood, black spots swimming before his eyes. He looked skyward, hoping to hear the sound of a Blackhawk. "Come on, goddamn it!"

Another cry.

A woman's high-pitched scream of terror.

Natalie?

How in the hell had she gotten here?

Jesus, no!

He clawed at the dirt, trying to pull himself forward, trying to reach her, calling for her, AK fire drowning out his voice, only one M4 firing now.

"Zach, wake up!"

Zach jerked upright, choking on terror, his eyes flying open to find Natalie kneeling beside him. Still lost in his nightmare, he reached for her, his fingers sliding through her thick hair, feeling their way over her face and down her neck to her shoulders, searching for injuries.

She caught one of his hands, held it. "It's okay. It was just a dream."

Just a dream.

He stood, pushed past her, his heart hammering, his lungs hurting for breath. But there was nowhere to go. He crossed the small room, turned, walked to the other side of the bed, then back to the table again. He slammed it with a closed fist, making Natalie jump, a strangled cry working its way loose from his throat. He turned, crossed to the other side of the bed again, and, adrenaline finally spent, sat on the corner of the bed, his back to her, no sound in the room but his own rapid breathing and the rattle of the AC. He closed his eyes, tried to slow his breathing, his insides shredded, his stomach churning, the taste of death fresh in his mouth.

It had seemed so real, so goddamned real. It always did.

You are such a fuckup, McBride.

He sensed her behind him, felt her hand rest against the nape of his neck, her cool fingers caressing his hair in soothing strokes. A part of him wanted to shout at her to get the hell away from him. He didn't want her compassion. He didn't need her compassion.

Oh, but he did. Jesus, yes, he did.

Her touch was a lifeline, the only one he had. A light in the darkness, it called him back from the abyss. She started to pull away, but he couldn't let her go.

He caught her hand with his, drawing her around the corner of the bed to stand in front of him, needing . . . Needing what? Hell, even he didn't know.

He felt empty, broken, defeated.

He wrapped his arms around her, refusing to let go, his head dropping to rest against her chest.

Without a word, she enfolded him in her embrace, holding him to her breast like a mother comforting a child, her fingers curling in his hair, her heartbeat steady in his ear. And he clung to her.

Natalie felt the tension roiling inside Zach, and wished she knew what to do for him. She'd heard him cry out and had been out of bed and on her way to the bathtub before she'd realized that they weren't being attacked, that he was asleep and caught in a nightmare. Covered in sweat, his face had been a tormented mask, red neon spilling across his features like blood. She'd never seen such anguish on a human face before.

The nightmare had clearly shaken him to his soul. And although she didn't know him well, she knew without a doubt that he rarely asked for help or accepted comfort from others. He wasn't the kind of man who let himself be vulnerable.

But he was vulnerable now.

She pressed her cheek against the crown of his head, offering him what solace she could. And for a while they stayed that way.

Then something began to change. Zach's breathing deepened, his head coming up just enough that his lips touched her skin. He slowly turned his face, one big hand feeling its way up her spine as he kissed first her breastbone, then the swell of her left breast, the unexpected contact making her shiver.

Confused at the shift in him, she said nothing. But her hands had ideas of their own. Hungry for the feel of him, they slid through his hair, working their way to his nape then on to his bare shoulders, hard muscle shifting beneath her palms, his skin soft.

He pulled back, and for a moment she thought it was over. She bit her lip, torn between relief and disappointment.

Then she felt his fingertips skimming their way up her arms, his touch raising bumps on her skin. Only when his thumbs caught the slender straps of the nightgown did she realize what he meant to do. She tensed, anticipation twined with nervousness inside her, making it hard to breathe.

With agonizing slowness, he drew the straps over her shoulders and down her arms, baring her to her waist. She looked down to find his gaze fixed on her breasts, a strained expression on his face. She felt—and saw—her nipples tighten under the heat of his perusal, heard the breath leave his lungs in a long, slow exhale. Then he reached up with both hands and cupped her.

Without warning, her mind flashed back to the Zeta hellhole, rough hands squeezing and pinching her. She closed her eyes, forced the unwanted memory away, unwilling to be robbed of this moment. This was Zach, not the Zetas, and he wasn't hurting her. Far from it.

He ran circles over her nipples with the pads of his thumbs, teasing their sensitive tips, sending sparks of pleasure skittering into her belly. She arched into his touch, her fingers sliding into his hair again, urging his head forward, her breasts longing for his mouth. He groaned, held her tighter, gave each nipple a flick of his tongue, then drew one into his hot, slick mouth—and suckled.

"Oh!" She gasped, her head falling back, the delicious sensation making her inner muscles clench, the heat inside her turning to honey.

He went greedily back and forth from one breast to the other, tugging at her nipples with his lips, tasting them with his tongue, teasing them with the sharp edges of his teeth, his hands cupping her, holding her for his mouth.

Had her breasts always been this sensitive? She couldn't remember. All she knew was that she felt every touch, every tug, every flick of his tongue all the way to her core. Drenched in sensation, she dug her fingers into his shoulders, her breath coming hard and fast, need for him a raw ache inside her.

This is what it felt like to want and be wanted, to be a woman, to be alive.

Feeling almost euphoric, she let the nightgown fall to the floor, climbed onto his lap, and wrapped her legs around him. Then she took his face between her hands, drew his mouth down to hers, and kissed him.

A groan. His fist in her hair. His tongue thrusting deep.

He forced her head back and took control of the kiss with an intensity that left her breathless, plundering her mouth, nipping and sucking her lips, crushing her to him.

Oh, yes!

And then she was beneath him.

Zach was breaking the rules, but he didn't give a goddamn, her impatient hands spreading fire over his skin as she explored his shoulders, chest, abdomen. Blood roaring in his ears, he tasted her mouth, cradling her head with one arm, his free hand skimming over the puckered velvet of her nipples, down the silky skin of her belly to that little landing strip of dark curls that had been driving him insane. He wasted no time, feeling his way through those trimmed curls to cup her, his dick nearly splitting his jeans when he discovered that her labia really were waxed bare—and that she was wet. He looked, took in the erotic sight of her vulva, and almost freaking lost it.

Holy God in heaven.

The musky scent of her arousal urging him on, he parted those soft, naked lips, gave the swollen bud of her clitoris a few teasing strokes, then slowly nudged first one finger, then two, into her slippery heat.

She whimpered his name, her sharp little nails digging into his shoulders, her thighs parting to give him better access.

He found a rhythm, his thumb rubbing circles over her clit, while his fingers stroked her deep inside. He swiped at a puckered nipple with his tongue, tugged at it with his lips. "Does that feel good, angel?"

A long, breathless moan.

God, she was responsive. As badly as he wanted to get inside her, he couldn't get enough of watching her, of watching what his touch did to her. He sucked a nipple and felt her vagina clench, kissed her throat and saw goose bumps rise across her chest, thrust his fingers deeper inside her and watched her belly jerk. And her scent . . .

Jesus!

She was close, so close. Her eyes were squeezed shut, her head rolling back and forth, her dark hair lying in thick tangles across her pillow. Her breath came in pants, each exhalation a ragged moan, the sound of a woman lost in the ache and ecstasy of sex. Her nails dug deeper, her entire body tense, her inner muscles drawing tighter.

Then her breath broke, and she came, bliss bright on her face, her back arching, her vagina contracting tightly around his fingers. He caught her cry with his mouth, riding through the orgasm with her, keeping his rhythm steady until the quaking inside her subsided. And then he could hold back no longer.

He reached down to unzip his jeans, but her hands were already there, impatiently tugging at his fly. He freed his cock, guided himself to her cleft. Then with a single, slow thrust, he slid inside her, her moan mingling with his.

Tight. Hot. Slick.

She felt *so . . . damned . . . good*.

For a moment, he held himself still inside her, letting her get used to the feel of him. Then his gaze locked with hers, and he began to move, pushing himself into her again and again, the hot, slippery friction already driving him toward the breaking point. He willed himself to relax, shifted his position so that he was riding her high, his cock rubbing over her clit with each deep thrust.

Her response was instantaneous. Her eyes went wide, and she arched beneath him. "Ooh! I never . . . I never . . . *Again?*"

And through a haze of pheromone he realized she'd never come twice in a row before. "As much as you can take, angel."

And he meant it. He hadn't been a SEAL for nothing. He'd learned to control his body in extreme situations so that he could use it as a weapon. Now he was going to use it to please her—to please Natalie.

Guided by her response, he sharpened the angle, thrust into her faster, harder, fighting to keep his own climax at bay. Then he propped himself up on one arm and used his free hand to play with those exquisitely sensitive nipples of hers.

She whimpered, every exhalation a moan, her nails digging like talons into his hips, as if to draw him deeper inside her, her head going back as a second orgasm claimed her, her body shuddering beneath him, clenching around him.

He was on fire now, burning . . . burning for Natalie . . . His hips a piston, driving into her . . . Her slick vagina gripping him like a fist . . . He wanted, needed her . . . Her mouth on his skin . . . Her hips rising to meet his . . . "You're so . . . damned . . . beautiful!"

With his last ounce of control, he pulled out of her, his entire body screaming in protest. His wet cock hovered above her for just a second before erupting into spasms, white ribbons of cum shooting onto her belly, a frustrated climax stuttering through him.

That's what you get for not having a condom handy, McBride.

With that thought, he sank onto her, sweaty and spent.

HAPPILY EXHAUSTED, NATALIE watched Zach wipe semen off her belly with a hot, wet washcloth, his lips trailing little kisses across her clean, wet skin. She let her fingers wander through his hair and along his stubble-rough jaw, trying to ignore a growing sense of guilt, desperate to hold on to this feeling—the languid afterglow of great sex.

But the guilt was there, niggling at her, refusing to go away.

She didn't feel bad that she'd had sex with Zach. And she certainly didn't feel guilty for enjoying it. And she had enjoyed it, every unbelievable minute of it.

But what she'd realized—and what had begun to gnaw at her—was the fact that not once during the time she and Zach were making love had she thought of Beau.

* * *

ZACH HELD NATALIE, watched her sleep, his own eyelids heavy, a warm knot of emotion in his chest. He knew he should kick his own ass, but he wasn't going to. He'd broken his own rules—and he didn't give a damn. There was no way to undo what he'd done tonight, and he wouldn't undo it even if he could.

He'd broken down in front of her, let the weakness inside of him show. But she hadn't turned away from him. She hadn't judged him. Instead, she'd accepted him, comforted him, given herself to him.

He'd never known a woman like Natalie.

But he didn't want to hurt her. He was going to have to be honest so she'd understand. Just because they'd had sex didn't mean they had a future. He hadn't been joking when he'd said his life wasn't the kind of life a man shared with a woman. He was rarely home. He spent most of his time on assignment. And unless he was very careful, he'd wind up in a body bag. He didn't want to put any woman through that.

But it wasn't just the dangerous and demanding job.

It was *him*.

He'd spent a good nine months trying to get back in the swing of everyday civilian life after his discharge from the navy, but it hadn't worked. His nightmares had gotten so bad that he'd eventually come to dread sleeping. He'd taken up drinking, hoping to knock himself out, to drown his demons in scotch. But that hadn't worked. As for gainful employment, he hadn't been able to find, much less keep, a decent job. How was a man supposed to go from fighting in a war to sitting at a damned desk all day?

It hadn't been long after that that he'd seen a recruitment ad for the U.S. Marshal Service. And he'd known that was the answer—going back to war. Granted, the war the Marshal Service fought was very different than the one he'd fought while in the navy. But it was the same basic principle—find the bad guys and deal with them. Zach had embraced that mission and never looked back.

But the bottom line was that he didn't know how to live a civilian life any longer. He could never be the family man with the house in the suburbs, the wife, the two kids, and the dog. The only way he knew how to go on was to keep fighting.

Natalie deserved a full and happy life with a man who wasn't fucked up or in the line of fire, and he aimed to see she got her chance at it. He would get her safely home even if it cost him every last drop of his blood. But then they would go their separate ways. It sucked for him, really, because if ever he'd met a woman who made him feel . . .

No, he couldn't let himself go there.

He glanced over to make sure the Glock was on the night-stand, then closed his eyes, held her closer, and let sleep take him. This time, he didn't dream.

CHAPTER 14

NATALIE WOULD NEVER again take for granted the simple pleasure of waking up in a man's embrace. Her body floating, she opened her eyes to find her head resting on Zach's chest, their legs twined together, one strong arm wrapped protectively around her. He was still asleep, his breathing deep and even. She closed her eyes and dozed, savoring the feeling of lying skin to skin beside him, refusing to let herself think.

When she awoke again, he was still asleep, one arm around her, the other stretched over his head. Somehow the two of them had kicked off the sheet, which was now tangled around their knees, leaving them both exposed. Though they'd made love last night, she hadn't gotten so much as a glimpse of *that* part of him. But now with daylight filtering through the curtains, all she could do was stare.

Oh . . . my . . . stars!

To say he was well endowed was an understatement. Soft but not small, his penis lay across the upper part of his right thigh, the glans pointing toward her, veins visible just beneath the skin of the shaft. It was rooted in a thatch of dark hair, his testicles relaxed against his thighs, the left one lower than the right. She found the sight of him primal, erotic, beautiful.

She let her gaze travel upward, over his six-pack and up to his chest, with its well-defined pecs and dark, flat nipples. Although she didn't want to wake him, she couldn't resist touching him, her fingers trailing through the dark curls on his chest, her thoughts returning to last night.

She didn't regret it—having sex with him. She'd gone so long without a man's touch. And Zach's touch was magic, giving her back a part of herself that she'd thought she'd lost. Yes, sex with Beau had been wonderful. But sex with Zach had been wonderful, too—and very intense.

Just like the man.

Everything about last night had been perfect. The way he'd kissed her as if his life depended on it. The way he'd taken his time with her, not rushing things. The way he'd held himself back, bringing her to that second astonishing climax. The way he'd met her gaze as he'd come, a pleading look in his eyes, an expression akin to pain on his face, every muscle in his body straining.

You're so . . . damned . . . beautiful!

Although she'd entirely forgotten about contraception, he hadn't. He'd pulled out in good time, sacrificing some of his own pleasure for her. She wouldn't have expected that kind of thoughtfulness from a man who lived on the dark side.

Signs of the life he lived were still on his body—bruises, scrapes, faded burn marks. The sound of his tortured cries echoed in her mind—and she found herself wanting somehow to erase that pain, to give him pleasure.

She let her fingers have their way with him, following an irresistible line of hair down his belly to his groin. Then, she took him in hand and began to stroke the soft length of him, gently moving her hand down to the base, then back up again to the tip.

He groaned in his sleep, his hips shifting as his penis began to fill, growing thick and firm in her hand. She stroked him harder now, excited by the feel of him, a little bead of moisture pearling at the tip. Then he gasped, his abdominal muscles jerking, and she glanced up to find him looking down at her, an expression of astonishment on his handsome face, his gray eyes smoky with arousal.

"*Jesus!*" He reached down, closed a hand over hers to guide her, increasing the pressure, his hips rocking so that he thrust smoothly into her fist.

She kissed his chest, ran her tongue over a tight, flat nipple, then nibbled him, her heart racing. It felt right to give him pleasure. After all he'd suffered . . .

His rhythm quickened until his hips bucked wildly, his fingers clenched in her hair, his body strung tight, muscles straining. She increased the pressure slightly and felt him stiffen. Then he arched and shuddered, a deep groan tearing itself from his throat as he came in her hand.

It was she who went for the hot washcloth this time, his gaze following her as she climbed back into bed and carefully wiped him clean, the friction and heat of the washcloth making the muscles of his belly jerk. Then she snuggled up against him, his arm going around her, holding her close.

He made a contented sound deep in his throat, his fingertips stroking lazy lines down the skin of her back. "That's one hell of a way to wake a man up, angel. I thought all you Cajun girls were good little Catholics."

She laughed, then gave him her most innocent smile. "Why, yes, we are. But you're forgetting—we're French."

"Ah. In that case . . ." He bit the tip of his tongue, then drew it back into his mouth, slowly pushing her onto her back, a grin on his face, his eyes full of mischief, a playfulness about him she'd never seen before.

She felt a hard flutter in her belly, pretty certain she knew what he meant to do.

He rolled on top of her, then slowly slid down her body. "I want to taste—"

Thumpthumpthump!

Someone beat on the door.

In an instant, Zach was out of bed, gun in his hand. He hissed at her in a whisper. "*Get to the bathroom!*"

Thumpthumpthump!

Heart thudding, Natalie jumped out of bed, ran to the bathroom, and stepped into the tub, drawing the shower curtain into place, suddenly feeling very naked. If she had to deal with those Zeta bastards again, she'd rather do it with her clothes on.

Thumpthumpthump!

"*¡Servicio de mucama!*" A woman's voice. The house-keeper?

"*Por favor no me molestes. No necesito servicio de limpieza. Quiero dormir tranquilo.*"

Natalie understood most of that. Zach had just asked the woman not to disturb him and said he wanted to sleep in peace. The rest of it had gotten by her.

"*Sí, señor. Gracias.*"

"You can come out. It's just the maid."

Natalie heaved a sigh of relief and stepped out of the shower. But the interruption had broken the fragile bubble that had surrounded them since last night. Reality had intruded.

Zach glanced at the clock, the playfulness gone. "It's noon already? *Shit.*"

"You needed the sleep." Natalie sat on the bed, covering herself with the sheet.

"We've got a big day ahead of us." He walked toward the bathroom, small gun in one hand, AK-47 in the other, clearly in military mode again. "I'm going to take a quick shower, grab us some breakfast, and then we need to talk. If anyone knocks at the door, come straight into the bathroom. Don't respond in any way."

She watched, puzzled. "You're going to take a shower—with your guns?"

"I'm not actually going to take them into the shower. I just want them close by." Then he turned, a grin on his face, some of the playfulness returning. "You know, if you're going to hang with me, you need to learn the correct terminology."

He held up the AK-47, the muscles of his arm bunching against the weight. "This is an assault rifle."

Then he held up the handgun. "This is a semi-automatic pistol."

Then he gave a little thrust of his hips and looked down at his penis. "*That* is my gun. As you've discovered, it's pump-action like a shotgun, but it doesn't fire bullets."

Then he shut the door behind him, leaving Natalie to giggle into her pillow.

ZACH RAN THE soap over his skin, working up a lather, his body still strung out from that unexpected orgasm. Strange to think that three days ago he'd been in the worst pain of his life and close to dying. Today, he'd awoken in heaven.

He'd been dreaming that he was making love to Natalie, his dick buried deep inside her. It had felt so real. His heart had almost stopped when he'd opened his eyes to find that what he was feeling *was* real, the sight of her hand on his cock shocking him wide awake. He wouldn't have guessed she'd do something as bold as that, but then she was full of surprises.

French, huh?

Too bad he hadn't had the chance to show her what he'd learned to do with his tongue when he was on shore leave in France.

This isn't what you should be thinking about right now, man.

No, it wasn't. He needed to get them some breakfast and then go shopping for supplies, which would mean either leaving Natalie alone in the hotel or locking her in the trunk for hours. He didn't like either option, so he needed to find another.

He also needed to find a way to explain that just because they'd had sex didn't mean they had a relationship. He wanted to do this right, to find a way to tell her without hurting her. She was without a doubt the most amazing woman he'd ever met—smart, strong, sweet, sexy.

He mulled this problem over while he washed his hair and rinsed himself off, thinking about what he would say, how he would say it. And as he turned off the water it hit him in a way that it hadn't before—and he didn't like it.

In four days at the most, Natalie would be out of his life.

ZACH FINISHED OFF his third breakfast burrito and started in on a banana. "If I leave the backseats down, the trunk won't be dark, and you'll be able to see out. I'll pile the supplies in the backseat, so it will get crowded. And it *will* get hot. You'll be in the car with the windows rolled up. Do you think you can handle it?"

"It's better than being left in this room alone." She dabbed her lips with a paper napkin, not yet finished with her first breakfast burrito. "I'd feel like a sitting duck."

"That's not what I asked." He leaned forward, his gaze locked with hers. "Do you think you can handle it?"

She looked away, nibbling her lip, clearly thinking it through and clearly worried. Then she nodded. "Yes, I can. Can you check on me from time to time?"

"I will as often as I can, but I still have to buy a lot of things and stand in line in the checkout lane. I have no control over how long that will take."

"I understand."

"There's something else we need to talk about." Zach tossed the banana peel in the trash, took a moment to line his words up in the right order. He reached out, ran a finger over her cheek. "Last night was incredible. We didn't plan it, but it happened. I can't bring myself to regret it, and I hope to God you don't either."

She looked away, a shadow passing quickly over her face. Then she met his gaze through clear blue eyes. "I don't regret it. It was . . . perfect."

Perfect.

She sure as hell was.

Maybe that's why what he had to say next didn't come easily. "When we get back to the U.S., you and I will go our separate ways. That's just how it is. My life—it's not the kind of life a man shares with a woman. I don't want to mislead you, and I don't want to hurt you, so—"

"Relax. It was just sex." Natalie stood, turned her back to him, and carried her paper plate and burrito wrapper to the trash. "It's not like I could get serious with a man who lives the way you do."

"Right." That was exactly Zach's point.

Good. She understood.

So why did he suddenly feel like shit?

THEY LEFT ALTAR after supper—and after Zach had given Natalie some basic firearms instruction for both the Glock and the AK. Her hair still damp from one last shower, she sat in the passenger seat, wearing brown camo fatigues, a tan T-shirt, and a brown camo jacket. A fully loaded semi-auto Glock 17 sat in her lap, an AK-47 leaning against her thigh, her gaze drawn to every license plate in search of the dreaded Z as Zach drove the car north along the rutted dirt road to a place he called El Sasabe.

"Don't forget to breathe." Looking every bit the military man, he wore camo fatigues, too, his eyes concealed behind new sunglasses, two semi-autos hidden beneath his jacket in a shoulder holster. "Do as I say, and we'll get through this."

She drew in a deep breath, her stomach swarming with butterflies. It was bad enough to think that they were going to spend the next four days walking through this inhospitable landscape. But knowing that the Zetas were on this road and looking for them made things much worse.

Zach had overheard a couple of *federales* talking about it outside the Pesquiera Hermanos, Altar's big grocery store. He'd played the role of gringo tourist and chatted with them about it. They'd told him that the Zetas had put up roadblocks on every road leading to a U.S. port of entry from Tijuana to Loredo and were searching cars at gunpoint. That included El Sasabe. No one knew why the Zetas were doing this, but word on the street was that a shipment of cocaine had been stolen and Cárdenas was trying to catch the thieves—and make them pay.

The good news was that the Zetas clearly had no idea where he and Natalie were. Zach's plan for evading them had worked—so far.

The car bounced over the rough dirt road, the washboard bumps making her teeth rattle. "How far are we going to be walking total?"

"I'm guessing it will be about forty miles."

"That's not so bad." She'd run in a few 10K races. That was six miles.

He glanced over at her, his eyes concealed behind sunglasses. "If you say so."

Despite the rough condition of the road, traffic was heavy, kicking up plumes of dust that made it hard to see. "There are so many vans and trucks. It's like rush hour."

"Drug traffickers mostly. Some human traffickers. They're trying to reach El Sasabe before sundown and get set for tonight."

It unnerved Natalie to be surrounded by them. "I hope one day you'll tell me how you know that."

He said nothing.

His plan was to leave the highway on the outskirts of El Sasabe and drive as far as the car could take them along the dirt roads that fanned out like tentacles around the town and ran across the desert toward the border. Once the car died—which Zach had assured her would be sooner rather than later—they'd put on the enormous backpacks that sat in the backseat and go on foot.

He'd spent what seemed like forever adjusting the straps on her pack and trying to balance the weight. "You'll thank me later," he'd promised.

Her pack weighed about thirty pounds, his at least twice that.

And then there were the weapons.

She was going to be carrying both an AK-47 and the Glock, together with two spare magazines and extra ammunition, while he carried two semi-autos in shoulder holsters, as well as two AKs, extra magazines, and most of their ammunition.

The brake lights on the van ahead of them came on.

Traffic was slowing.

ZACH DIDN'T LIKE this.

If this slowdown was the result of the Zetas' roadblock, then the bastards had chosen their position well. A gully big enough to swallow a Humvee ran perpendicular to the road just ahead, making it impossible for vehicles to avoid the roadblock by simply going off the road and driving around it.

He searched for options.

He didn't want to try fighting his way through the roadblock, because he had no idea how many Zetas were there or what kind of weapons they had. All it would take to end Natalie's life was one bullet. No, Zach wouldn't risk it.

They could head back to Altar and hole up until the Zetas left. But there was no guarantee that the Zetas would leave—or that they wouldn't raid the hotels. Besides, the longer he and Natalie were missing, the greater the risk to other Americans in Mexico.

The only option was to backtrack along the road, find a good place to head cross-country, and travel north—on foot if necessary.

Ahead of them, the van drew to a stop.

"Maybe it's just an accident." Hope failed to conceal the fear in Natalie's voice.

"I doubt it." He leaned his head out the window, looking around the van for oncoming traffic. "It's time to leave this party."

He was about to flip a U-turn and head back the way they'd come, when he caught sight of three black vans hurtling north in the southbound lane. He slammed on the breaks as the vans streaked by, catching just a glimpse of a man with a grenade launcher—and a license plate without a Z.

The roadblock was about to become a bloodbath.

"Get down!" He checked again for oncoming vehicles, then made a quick and dirty U-turn, just as the sound of AK fire exploded behind them. "Hang on!"

And then—*BAM!*—a grenade exploded.

He hit the gas, knowing that the plume of dust behind them would conceal the make of the car and its license plate. No one was paying attention to them anyway. The car bounced over ruts, pebbles and rocks hitting the undercarriage as Zach tried to put a fast mile between them and the shoot-out. Then he saw what he'd been looking for—tire tracks leading off the highway and north into the desert.

He hit the breaks again, then cranked the wheel and drove off the road, the car fishtailing in loose gravel. Beside him, Natalie was still bent down. "It's okay. You can sit up now."

She sat up, glanced around them, blue eyes wide. "What just happened?"

"I think the Sinaloa boys got pissed off at the Zetas for holding up traffic and decided to take down the roadblock by force." He stopped the car, waited for the dust to settle, then pointed. "Look."

In the distance, black smoke rose into the air, the report of automatic weapons sounding like firecrackers. But even at this distance, stray rounds were a danger.

He took Natalie's hand, gave it a squeeze, hoping to reassure her. "You ready? This ride is bound to get rough."

She nodded, the fear in her eyes giving way to determination.

He nudged the car forward, and they were off.

CHAPTER 15

NATALIE STARED AT the charred remains of a minivan as they drove slowly by. It was not the first abandoned vehicle they'd passed, but it was the first to look like it had come through a war zone. "What happened to them?"

"Looks like they came under fire, and the fuel tank blew up."

"A fight between drug smugglers?" She noticed dozens of bullet holes in the doors, shivers sliding down her spine.

"Maybe. Or it could have been *bajadores.*"

She'd never heard that word before. "*Bajadores?*"

"Thieves who hide out along both sides of the border and steal drugs, money, and sometimes even human cargo from anyone who passes by."

"Great. So we have to worry about desert pirates, too." She looked around them, saw a landscape rich with opportunities for ambush.

"You let me worry about them. You worry about yourself."

"I *am* worrying about myself."

"That's not what I mean." He chuckled, the sound warm and masculine, the smile on his handsome face making her pulse skip.

Stop it, you!

She needed to quit feeling so drawn to this man. He might be with her at this moment, but he wasn't actually a part of her life. He'd said himself that his wasn't the kind of life a man shared with a woman. She certainly didn't want to get mixed up with a man who lived on the edge the way he did. She and Zach were headed in very different directions. The fact that they'd met was nothing more than an accident—a very lucky accident.

Natalie knew this, and yet . . .

When we get back to the U.S., you and I will go our separate ways.

His words had sent her spirits plummeting. She'd tried to cover her emotions by pretending not to care. But how could what she and Zach had experienced together have been nothing more than casual sex when it had touched her so deeply?

Maybe you're making it out to be more than it was.

Perhaps she'd been so starved for a man's touch that she was overreacting to what had been nothing more than good sex. How would she know? She'd never had casual sex before. She'd never been with anyone besides Beau, and they'd been deeply in love and committed to each other before they'd crossed that line.

And then her spirits sank further, weighted down by a sense of guilt. How could she have had sex without once thinking of Beau?

She didn't want to think about this any longer, not here, not now.

She met Zach's gaze, her tangled emotions making her words sharper than she'd intended. "I *know* what you mean."

She was supposed to tell him immediately if she felt dehydrated, dizzy, disoriented. She was supposed to tell him if her feet hurt, even if it was nothing more than the beginnings of a blister. She was even supposed to tell him if she got a headache or felt too exhausted to go on.

"Anything that slows you down can be deadly out here," he'd explained.

Not that they were making great time now.

They'd been following these dirt tracks for almost an hour. The front left tire had gone flat, shredded by three-inch-long thorns, less than twenty minutes after they'd left the road. Zach had quickly changed it. Ten minutes later, the rear right tire had blown. Now they were limping along, driving on two tires, the donut and one rim.

But Natalie was grateful for every mile they put behind

them. The terrain was nothing like she'd imagined. She'd thought it would be flat, like the desert that had surrounded the Zeta compound. Tiptoeing through the cactus for forty miles over flat terrain hadn't seemed like such a big deal.

But the landscape here wasn't flat at all. There were steep hills, rocky ridges, deep gullies, and sandy washes everywhere she looked, all of them covered by dense stands of saguaro and other strange desert plants, most of which looked like they'd sprung from some dark Dr. Seuss fantasy. She understood why Zach believed it would take four days to cover forty miles.

"Shit." Zach looked into his rearview mirror.

Natalie's pulse spiked. From behind them came the sound of engines.

"I don't think they've been following us, or I'd have noticed them before now. Whoever they are, we don't want to run into them."

He left the tracks, steered the car down a sandy embankment into a stand of mesquite, and cut the engine. For a moment they waited, the roar of engines drawing nearer. Then a convoy of three battered vans rumbled by them in a cloud of dust.

THE CAR GAVE out a few klicks south of the border.

"So we walk from here." Natalie didn't look excited at the prospect.

"No." Zach unbuckled his seat belt. "We get our gear, take up a defensive position nearby, lie in, and wait for dark. Then we walk."

"Why not just wait here?"

"You'll see." Zach slipped into his pack, then helped Natalie with hers. "Make sure the hip band rests in the right place. It will take some of the weight off your shoulders. How does that feel?"

She looked up at him, sliding her small hands into thick leather gloves, her hair turned auburn by the sunlight. "I think it's good."

He gave her a once-over. She was by far the hottest thing he'd ever seen in camo. That was for damned sure.

Get your mind out of the gutter, man.

"This is the tube to your hydration pack. Keep it clipped right here so you can reach it when you need it. I gave us just enough water to get us through the night, so drink when you need to, but don't overdo it. Steady sips, no long gulps."

"Got it."

He checked once more to make sure the AK was easily accessible, grabbed his infrared binoculars, then took a look at the surrounding area, getting the lay of the land. There—a quarter mile to the northwest. They'd settle in on that rocky hilltop, watch for traffickers below and wait for the sun to set. "Let's go—and watch where you step."

This was the first time Zach had ever done anything like this with a civilian, let alone a woman. He knew that if he moved at his normal pace he'd exhaust her and leave her in the dust. He tried to set a pace she could manage and was pleased to find her matching it easily.

But reaching the hilltop wasn't a simple matter of walking directly toward it. Dense stands of saguaro and thorny ocotillos combined with boulders and hidden washes to complicate things, forcing them to snake their way along.

"Watch out for the ocotillos." Speaking just loud enough for Natalie to hear him, he grabbed a branch with a gloved hand to show her the thorns hidden among bright green leaves, his gaze shifting to scan their surroundings for any sign of other humans. "The thorns can shred both clothing and skin."

They moved forward again, their approach flushing a desert cottontail out of a clump of grasses, the creature disappearing in a flash.

"The night shift is about to come on."

"The night shift?"

He'd known she would ask. "The nocturnal fauna. You see the lizards, pronghorns, deer, raptors, rabbits, and maybe a herd of javelinas during the day. And then at twilight the hunters appear—tarantulas, scorpions, rattlesnakes, coyotes, owls, bobcats, cougars."

"I think I like the day shift better."

He couldn't help but chuckle. "Just look before you sit and watch where you walk. You'll be fine."

By the time they reached the hilltop, the sun was an

orange disc on the horizon, the clouds above it scorched pink. He found a safe place for them to sit, empty water bottles, tuna cans, and other trash proof that this place had been used before. He dropped his pack and turned to help Natalie out of hers, only to find her watching the sunset, a smile on her face, those sweet dimples back in her cheeks.

"It's beautiful." Her face was flushed from exertion, the last rays of sunlight wrapping her in gold.

He felt a hitch in his chest. "Yeah. Beautiful."

Four days max, McBride. And then she's gone.

He pushed aside a sense of gloom. That was how it should be. He'd been so worried this morning that he would hurt her, but she understood as well as he that whatever this was between them was a temporary thing.

Relax. It was just sex.

He had to admit that he'd been surprised to hear her put it like that. He'd bet cold, hard cash that she'd never had "just sex." Zach had. Having "just sex" was like going jogging side by side with a stranger. You exchanged polite greetings, got sweaty, tried to pace yourself so that you could finish the run with some dignity, then you waved good-bye, went home, and took a shower. What had happened last night between him and Natalie didn't feel anything like "just sex."

Then again, maybe his brain was fried. Or maybe those long hours he'd spent chained in the darkness alone had showed him exactly how empty his life was. Not that he could change it now. But if there'd ever been a woman who—

Out of the corner of his eye, in the distance, he saw movement. "*Get down!*"

He peered through the infrared binoculars, the device offering clarity of vision through the desert's deepening shadows. And there, where they'd been a mere twenty minutes ago, he saw exactly what he thought he'd see—*bajadores* closing in on their abandoned vehicle with weapons drawn.

He handed Natalie the binoculars, motioning for her to look through them. She did as he asked, her little gasp proof that she'd seen what he wanted her to see. He readied the AK-47 with its new night scope just in case the *bajadores* tried to track them. "That's why we didn't stay with the car."

* * *

NATALIE FOLLOWED ZACH, doing her best to keep up and to step where he stepped so as to avoid stepping on a rattlesnake or anything else with fangs. She trusted him—and the night vision goggles he wore—to find a safe path through the darkness. He looked a bit like a character from a *Terminator* sequel with the headgear on and the goggles over his eyes, but she wasn't in the mood to joke about it.

The *bajadores* hadn't tried to track them—thank God!—but Natalie couldn't shake the jittery feeling she'd gotten as she'd watched those terrible men move in on the car, ready to steal and kill. If she and Zach had stayed at the car, as she'd suggested . . .

She shuddered.

Zach had watched through the scope on his rifle until the men disappeared, his finger near the trigger. If he'd felt any anxiety at all, he hadn't showed it. She had no doubt that he would have shot and killed every single one of those five men if he'd felt it was necessary to keep them both safe.

Darkness had come quickly after that. It was the most complete and total darkness Natalie had ever experienced—no flashlight or headlamps to light their path or to give their position away to others. And although her eyes had adjusted somewhat, human eyes just weren't meant for this. The desert as she knew it had disappeared, leaving in its place a world of sinister shadows and strange sounds.

Saguaros stood all around them, gray shades against the darkness, looking strangely human, like people who stood frozen with their arms raised in surrender. Hills rose in the distance, black against the starlit sky. Ocotillos floated like black coral in a dark undersea realm. And all around them came the noises of night creatures.

It was the strangest symphony Natalie had ever heard—crickets chirping, coyotes yipping and yowling, and countless frogs belching, ribbeting, and croaking out love songs, hoping to attract mates. As for the other creatures of the night shift, Natalie hoped to see and hear nothing.

"Watch your step." Zach turned and gave her his gloved

hand, helping her down the side of a steep gully. "It gets rocky down here. Don't trip."

She tripped anyway, but he caught her, strong arms steadying her.

"How are you doing?"

She took a sip of water, the electrolyte powder he'd added giving it a disgusting fake lemonade taste. "Fine. A little chilled."

The temperature had dropped quickly.

"The best way to fight that is just to keep moving."

On they went for most of an hour, Zach guiding her across the landscape, headed roughly northwest. She'd begun to feel the weight of her backpack, not only in her shoulders, but also in her thighs. Forty miles was beginning to feel like a thousand. But she wasn't about to complain. She would gladly walk a thousand miles barefoot on broken glass if that's what it took to get safely home again.

Then Zach took her hand, turned her, and pointed. "There it is."

Natalie looked where Zach pointed off to their right but couldn't see anything.

He drew the goggles off his head and handed them to her.

She held them up to her eyes—and the world reappeared, the desert cast in a strange green hue. And there in the distance she saw what he'd wanted her to see—the U.S.-Mexico border. She felt a swell of emotion behind her breastbone.

Home.

"Thank God!"

Two fences ran parallel across the land, separated by a space of about twenty feet. The first was made of steel H-beams that ranged in height from about four feet to well over her head. The second was shorter and made of steel posts and cables. Between them was a no-man's-land devoid of plant life. It looked like a road.

"Once we cross that border, we're safe, right?" She scanned the area around them, amazed at what she could see—including a large, hairy tarantula crawling across the ground, moving in the other direction. "Oh, yuck!"

"A scorpion?"

"A hairy, disgusting tarantula."

"Yeah, they're out in force tonight."

She took the goggles down, the world going black again, her eyes just able to make out the features of Zach's face. "How many have you seen?"

"Probably six or seven."

Her skin crawled. She handed the goggles back to him. "I think it's best if I'm kept in the dark."

He chuckled, and fixed the goggles back into his headgear. "Oh, yeah, I see her. She's a big one. As for being safe again— we won't be safe until you're out of the desert and in the hands of border patrol agents. Forget eight-legged creatures. It's the ones who walk on two legs that are dangerous out here. I've tried to steer us far enough to the west of the main Sasabe smuggling routes that we'll miss most of the cartel traffic, but make no mistake—there are plenty of dangers on *both* sides of the border."

With those words in her mind, she followed Zach, the darkness pressing in on her.

They reached the first fence fifteen minutes later.

Zach climbed it with no problem, then turned back to her, his gaze searching the landscape behind her. "Give me your pack."

Natalie unbuckled the hip band, slipped out of the shoulder harness, and handed it to him. He dropped it onto the sandy ground and reached for her, helping her over.

His hands lingered at her waist. "That's it. That's the U.S. border. You're back in the States now, angel."

And some part of Natalie wanted to cry.

"YOU SHALL HAVE a First Communion worthy of a true princess, *sí*?" Arturo gave his granddaughter a good-night kiss, her sweet smile taking the edge off his nerves at least for a moment. He switched off her bedside lamp. "Sleep with the angels, Isabella."

"Good night, Grandpa."

He left the child to his daughter's care, then walked to the other wing of the house, to his private study, where no one, not even his wife, would dare to bother him. He poured himself a shot of tequila. It would hurt his stomach, but he needed it.

He tossed it back, grimaced at the razor-sharp pain in his gut, poured another.

The news today had not been good. The men José-Luis had set to watch the U.S. consulate had opened fire on a car in which they thought Natalie Benoit was riding, only to learn later that they had wounded the wife of a U.S. official. Then several of his men had been killed when the roadblock they'd set up at Altar was attacked by those goat-fucking Sinaloa bastards.

Arturo didn't give a horse's ass for the American woman who'd been shot or for the men he'd lost at Altar. He didn't even care about the shipment of cocaine. All he cared about now was getting his hands on that bitch of a reporter and killing her.

If he failed . . . If she survived . . .

He hadn't built an empire out of nothing only to lose it now. La Santa Muerte wouldn't allow it. Then again it had been a long time since the Bony Lady had been fed. He had promised her Natalie, but both he and the Lady had been denied.

Perhaps that was the problem—or part of it. Bad things happened in threes. Everyone knew that. But now the count was full. The bitch and the gringo who'd stolen Arturo's cocaine had disappeared. Next, his men had shot the wife of a U.S. diplomat. And then they'd been attacked at Altar. Three pieces of bad luck.

Could the tide be turned with blood?

He drew his mobile phone out of his pocket and dialed José-Luis. His nephew had failed him miserably, so perhaps it ought to be *his* blood Arturo spilled. But La Santa Muerte would want nothing to do with his ugly, scarred face. She preferred sweeter-tasting blood.

José-Luis answered after the third ring.

He started to speak, but Arturo cut him off. "I want you to find that bitch Gisella. I want to know everything she knows about the American who stole our cocaine. Perhaps she knows more about him than she told us before. Perhaps she can lead us to him again."

CHAPTER 16

A WANING HALF moon peeked out from behind banks of fast-moving clouds, providing at least some light, but the wind had picked up, a sign that a monsoon was brewing. Getting caught in a downpour was not high on Zach's list of things to do tonight. Not only would it put them at risk for hypothermia, but it would make walking more dangerous and difficult—and leave a trail of prints that anyone could follow.

He glanced behind him, trying to gauge how Natalie was holding out. Damn, she was tough. She hadn't complained once, though he knew this had to be hard for her, both physically and mentally. Combat-style sleep deprivation, a forced night march, the ever-present threat of violence—she'd never been through anything like this before.

Then again, neither had he.

In the past when he'd been in circumstances like these, he'd been with other men who'd undergone the same training he had. They'd had his back, and he'd had theirs. Or he'd tried.

Which doesn't explain why they're dead and you're not, does it, McBride?

He forced the thought aside, refusing to let it distract him.

Natalie had no military or law enforcement training. She was dependent on him in a way that his SEAL team and fellow DUSMs had never been. He'd never felt so entirely responsible for another person's life as he had these past few days—and it scared the hell out of him.

He found himself listening to her breathing, the tread of her boots against the sand, his gaze drawn over his shoulder time and again as he tried to determine whether she needed to rest, eat something, or drink more. But so far, so good.

They'd been walking for almost five hours now, the terrain steeper as they moved into the foothills south of Baboquivari Peak, which would serve as their guidepost. By dawn, they ought to be able to see its rocky summit jutting into the sky like a giant tooth. They would keep it on their right, heading diagonally—

"Ooh!" A gasp of pain.

Zach turned to find Natalie holding her arm, an ocotillo branch snagged on the collar of her jacket. "Hold still."

"Sorry," she whispered. "I was watching my feet. I didn't see it."

He took the branch and pulled it free, careful to keep the thorns away from her face. But there on the right side of her neck was a deep, nasty scratch. "Let's take a break, and I'll look at that."

He drew her to some nearby rocks, sent a scorpion flying with his boot before she could spot it, then shucked his backpack and helped her out of hers. Then he opened his pack, drew out the first-aid kit and a couple of energy bars. "Eat. How are your feet?"

She took one of the bars and tore open its wrapper. "The left one is just a little sore on the heel."

"Let's look at that, too." Figuring the moonlight would be enough, he shed the night vision goggles and his gloves, set them on the pack where nothing was likely to crawl inside them, then opened the first-aid kit and drew out a Betadine swab. "Tilt your head to the left. Perfect. This is pretty deep, so the antiseptic is going to sting."

She gasped, squeezed her eyes shut, the energy bar stopped just short of her lips.

He worked quickly, spreading antibiotic ointment on it, and then covering the scratch with an adhesive bandage. "Okay, now the foot."

"Yes, Mom." She gave him a teasing look, then reached to unlace her left boot.

He beat her to it. He drew off her boot and sock and set

them in her lap. Then he grabbed the moleskin out of the first-aid kit. "Were you and your mother close?"

What's the matter with you, McBride? Now you're asking the nosy questions.

Natalie nodded. "I was an only child, so, yes, she and I were close. I was close to my father, too. They were the best parents in the world."

"They'd be incredibly proud if they could see you now—the way you've handled this, how much you've done for yourself."

"Do you really think so?"

"I know so."

"I miss them. Every day of my life, I miss them." Her voice was filled with sadness.

He took a piece of moleskin, tore off the adhesive strip, and wrapped the protective flannel around her heel where he could just feel the beginning of a blister. "I'm sorry. I shouldn't have—"

She looked up at him, rested a hand on his arm. "No, don't be. I don't m—"

He clamped a hand over her mouth and listened.

Men's voices.

WITHOUT ZACH NEEDING to tell her what to do, Natalie drew on her sock, crammed her foot into her boot, and began lacing. By the time she was finished, Zach had her pack ready. She slipped into the shoulder straps and fastened the hip belt.

He pointed toward the hillside, whispering. *"Go! Fast as you can."*

Fast as she could was pretty damned fast if there were bad guys on their tail.

Fueled by adrenaline, she attacked the hillside with quick strides, ignoring the burn in her thighs and the ache in her lungs, watching for rocks, branches, snakes. Which is why she happened to see the rattlesnake coiled up a few feet ahead of her.

She froze.

"This way." Strong hands grabbed the back of her pack and jerked her to the right just as the telltale rattle started.

Moving as fast as her feet could carry her, she continued in the direction Zach had steered her. She was wondering how she was going to get around the stand of mesquite in their path, when he halted her.

"*Down.*"

Grabbing the rifle off her pack, she crawled beneath the mesquite, her breath coming hard. Zach raised his goggles, then lifted his AK, sighting on the valley below, his finger shifting the weapon into full-auto mode. She did the same, just as he'd showed her back at the hotel in Altar. Through the rifle's night scope, the desert glowed green again.

Some thirty feet away, the rattlesnake had fallen silent. Or maybe her heart was beating too loudly for her to hear it.

And then off to the south, she saw them—a line of about fifteen men carrying strange burlap backpacks. Judging from the way the men walked, stooping forward, the packs were extremely heavy.

Zach pressed his lips against her ear. "*Drug runners.*"

Three of them had what looked like AK-47s. Moving slowly, they scanned the hillside, weapons raised. They must have heard her and Zach talking—or heard their gear rattling during their hasty uphill escape.

"*Don't fire. Don't move.*" Zach's voice was barely a whisper.

None of the men below were wearing night vision goggles, which gave Natalie some hope. One hissed something to another in Spanish. That one hissed back. It sounded to her like they were arguing, though she couldn't make out the words.

Slowly, so slowly, they passed by, Natalie watching through the night scope until they disappeared in the distance.

She let out the breath she'd been holding and leaned her cheek against the cold steel of the rifle, her heart still racing, her body starting to tremble.

"You are without a doubt the most amazing woman I've ever known."

Adrenaline still hot in her veins, she looked over to find Zach watching her, his teeth white in the darkness as he smiled down at her. Without even thinking, she let go of the rifle, planted her palms on either side of his face—and kissed him.

He made a little groan in his throat, leaned into the kiss,

his tongue meeting hers halfway, his hands removing first his backpack, then hers. Then his arms were around her, crushing her against him, the kiss now a brutal clash of lips and teeth and tongues.

She reached down, unbuttoned the top button of his pants, slid her hand beneath his T-shirt, feeling the ridges of his muscles before unzipping his fly and freeing his erection. She took him in hand, working the length of him, as his hand fought with her zipper, slid inside her panties, and stroked her.

Then all at once she was on her hands and knees, Zach jerking her pants down with such force that he dragged her backward. He nudged his knee between her legs, parting her thighs as wide as they could go, then pushed into her—hard.

Again and again he drove himself into her, stretching her, filling her, the slippery friction igniting a fire deep in her belly. She arched her back, his thrusts so wonderfully hard that they rocked her, his testicles slapping against her. Then he reached around, his fingers delving between her thighs, finding her clitoris, stroking her inside and out.

It felt so good, so good . . . Thrust after thrust . . . Deeper, harder . . . *Zach!* Piercing her, penetrating her . . . *Oh, Zach!* She needed him, ached for him . . . Her gloved fingers dug into the sand . . . Digging in, holding on, as the heat inside her drew into a tense, shimmering knot—and exploded.

She bit her lip, held back a cry as pleasure blazed through her, a firestorm of sensation, Zach's deep thrusts prolonging her climax until the flames had burned themselves out, her body nothing but ashes floating on the night wind.

Then she heard him suck in a breath, felt him pull out, his fingers digging into her hips as he came on her bare derriere, ejaculate hitting her in hot, wet spurts, his bare thighs pressed against her. Then for a moment he collapsed over her, breathing hard, pressing kisses to her shoulder, his hand resting beside hers in the sand.

"You are the most amazing woman . . . Don't move." One big hand rubbed circles onto the skin of her lower back, while the other rummaged around in his pack. Then something cold and wet touched the skin of her behind as he wiped her clean. "If I told you your bare ass looks fantastic in the moonlight, would you hold that against me?"

* * *

Zach helped Natalie to her feet, fighting the urge to hold her. "You okay?"

"I'm fine." She fastened her hip belt. "I'm not that fragile, for goodness' sake."

"Let's go. We've got some catching up to do." He slipped into the night vision goggles, then led her down the hillside, regret taking some of the glow out of his postorgasmic high.

He didn't regret having sex with her. What red-blooded, heterosexual man would? True, shagging in the middle of the desert in the middle of the night in the middle of what was essentially a war zone was not an act of tactical genius. In fact, it had been flat-out irresponsible. Still, he couldn't bring himself to regret it. But he was sorry for the way he'd handled it.

She deserves tenderness, McBride. You just shoved her onto her hands and knees and fucked her.

To be fair, she *had* started it, and she *had* come. It was not as if she hadn't enjoyed it. But he'd been so rough with her. After everything she'd been through . . .

If you had waited until it was safer, until you had more time . . .

He would make it up to her when they reached Sells. In the meantime, he was going to find where he'd put the damned condoms he'd bought and make sure he kept one where he could easily grab it. The chemistry between them was combustible. If he wasn't careful, he was going to lose control and come inside her, and he did *not* want to do that to her.

He glanced back to make sure she truly was okay, then focused his mind on footprints in the sand, not because he wanted to track the drug runners who'd passed by them, but because he wanted to avoid them. He'd watched them disappear beyond the draw just ahead. If he and Natalie followed the draw west, they might be able to avoid them and still stay on course. The traffickers had clearly heard them and knew someone else was in the area. They would be ready and waiting.

He crouched down as they neared the draw, his gaze searching through thick stands of mesquite, looking for any sign of movement. *Nada.* "This way."

They traveled west along the draw until it vanished into a tangle of tamarisk and ocotillo, then made their way carefully northward again, flushing a small herd of javelinas out of a patch of prickly pear where they'd been feasting.

"Look!" She pointed, a smile on her face. "Wild pigs!"

"They have razor-sharp tusks, so don't try to hug one."

Zach kept his gaze on the sand, wishing he had Jason Chiago's skill with cutting sign. But Jason had been born to it. He could read the desert like no one Zach had ever seen. Zach had trained with him for a couple of weeks during his first year with the Marshal Service. He'd learned a lot, but not enough to match even the least skilled Shadow Wolf.

They stopped at 0300 hours to rest and refuel, Zach introducing her to the joys of MREs.

"That's a fudge brownie?" She stared down at the food in her hand. "It tastes more like—"

"Chocolate-flavored cardboard? Eat the entire thing. You need it."

"Yes, sir!" She gave him a mock salute, but dutifully took another bite, washing it down with a sip from her hydration pack.

She still hadn't uttered a single word of complaint, but Zach could see the exhaustion on her face. "I had planned to go on past dawn. Are you up to that?"

She nodded again.

But two hours later it was clear that she wasn't going to hold out. Dead on her feet, she stumbled after him, misery and fatigue etched in every feature of her pretty face.

"We're going to find a place to camp and stop for the night."

"Okay." She started to sit.

He grabbed her shoulder harness and drew her back to her feet. "Not here, angel. We need to find someplace sheltered. Stay with me, okay?"

"Okay."

Thirty minutes later he'd found a rock ledge overhanging a space wide enough for the two of them. It was protected on one side by a gully and hidden on the other by a thick stand of mesquite. Best of all, it faced west—away from the rising sun.

He took Natalie's pack and sat her down on a nearby rock

with orders to eat another so-called brownie. He made sure the area under the overhang was arachnid and snake free, then set out the wool blanket he'd brought. Grabbing two ibuprofen from his pack, he carried them to her. "Take these, then drink the rest of your water."

She didn't even ask what the pills were, but swallowed them with several gulps from her hydration pack.

"It's bedtime."

"Thank God." She stood, took his hand, and let him lead her to the little camp he'd made, her movements wooden. She stopped and glanced upward, speaking in a sleepy voice. "I never knew there were so many stars."

He sat on the blanket. She sat beside him, her head falling against his chest. And he realized that she was already sound asleep.

Chuckling to himself, he lowered her to the blanket, removed his jacket, and draped it over her to ward off the nighttime chill. Then he grabbed the AK and leaned back against the rock to keep watch, his gaze returning again and again to her face.

Natalie was sound asleep when something jabbed her on the butt—hard. She opened her eyes, found herself lying on her stomach on a thick wool blanket, the sun already up. And for a moment she thought she'd imagined being poked.

Then it happened again—a painful, sharp jab.

She rolled over, saw something big and black standing beside her, and screamed.

Whatever it was—a big ugly bird—screamed, too, flapping its wings and jumping away from her. Then it spread its wings and, with a few hops, took to the sky.

Heart hammering, she watched it fly away, big black wings flapping.

Then off to her left she heard what sounded like a choking sound. Zach stood there, biting his lower lip, clearly trying very hard not to laugh.

"It's not funny!" She sat up, feeling more than a little surly. "What was it? And what was it trying to do?"

"That was a turkey vulture." He'd quit laughing, but there was a broad grin on his face. "I think it thought it had found some very fresh meat for breakfast."

Hot now, Natalie pulled off her jacket. "It scared me to death."

"You scared *it* to death. Imagine how you'd feel if you stuck your fork in a nice, juicy steak only to have it moo and jump off your plate." He started laughing again.

"What if it had taken a chunk out of my . . . ? Where were you?"

"I was over there taking a leak." He squatted down next to his pack, drew out sanitizing hand wipes and wiped his hands. "Go back to sleep, Little Miss Grumpy. I promise, I won't let the mean birdies eat your behind, though I can't blame them for wanting a piece of it. It is pretty damned delicious."

His playful words stirred memories of last night's crazy sex in the bushes, breaking through her bad mood and making her smile. She'd never experienced anything like it. It had been animal sex—primal, rough, out of control, and with just a hint of real danger. Though she'd had sex with Beau in that position before, she'd never been able to climax. But with Zach, it had been so easy, so natural, so—

No. Don't compare them. You can't compare them. Beau was your fiancé, the man you would have married. Zach is just . . .

What was he?

Her protector with benefits? Her temporary lover? A desert fling?

Too tired to think about it and in dire need of her own bathroom break, she crawled across the blanket, then stood, careful not to bump her head on the rock overhang. Every muscle in her body screamed. "Ooh . . . God."

"Sore?"

She whimpered, in too much pain to care how undignified it was.

"Let's get some breakfast in you, and then more ibuprofen. And then you really do need to sleep."

"What time is it?"

"About seven thirty. You've been asleep for a little over two hours."

No wonder she felt like death.

And then it hit her.

He hadn't slept at all.

CHAPTER 17

AWAKENED BY THE oppressive midday heat, Zach opened his eyes to see a small blue and tan lizard doing what looked like push-ups about a foot away from his face. Up and down it moved, then froze and looked at him in what was clearly a territorial display. It pumped out a few more, then froze again. "Yeah, you're bad."

Zach glanced at his new watch for the time and temp—1320 hours and 114 degrees. He sat up, frightening the lizard away. Then, leaving Natalie to sleep, he grabbed his rifle and binoculars and did a perimeter scout, looking for any sign of human beings nearby. Baboquivari Peak rose to the northeast, reigning over the parched landscape. Apart from insects, lizards, birds, and a few pronghorns off in the distance, nothing was moving in this heat. Everyone was pinned down until sunset.

By the time he returned to their little haven of shade, his hair was damp, his T-shirt stained with sweat. He set the rifle down, munched a handful of nuts, then washed them down with a long drink from his hydration pack.

Beside him, Natalie lay sleeping, her face turned toward him, cheeks flushed from the heat, strands of hair sticking to her damp skin. He didn't think he could ever get enough of looking at her. Her creamy, almost translucent skin. Her thick, dark lashes. Those graceful, dark brows. Her sweet little nose. Those high, delicate cheekbones. The dimples that showed when she smiled. Her soft, full lips.

Watching her sleep, it wasn't hard to believe that a woman's face had once launched a thousand ships and started a war.

Three days max, McBride. That's all you get.

He reached for a gallon of water, one that he hadn't yet mixed with *suero*, the lemon-flavored electrolyte powder. Then he fished through his pack for the bandanas, wetted one, shed his shirt, and wiped the cool, wet cloth over his chest, throat, and face before tying it loosely around his neck, where it would help keep his body temp down.

He wetted the second bandana, then pressed it against Natalie's cheeks, throat, and forehead, smoothing her hair back from her face.

She stirred in her sleep, murmured something that sounded like his name, then her eyes drifted open. She looked up at him, still half-asleep. "So hot."

"Hell, yeah, it is. You should drink."

"I'm so tired of that electrolyte stuff." Her expression became a cute little pout. "What I wouldn't give for a glass of genuine Southern sweet tea the way my mama used to make it—black pecoe, real sugar, ice, no lemon."

"Let's see what I can do to cool you down." He poured more water onto the bandana, then gave it a gentle squeeze, letting the water drip into the divot between her collar bones. He caught the drops and spread them across her throat, then bent down and blew across her skin to make up for the lack of breeze.

"Mmm." She turned her head, giving him access to first one side of her throat and then the other. "That feels good."

Just as had happened under the bridge, her response aroused him. Only now, having already crossed the line into a sexual relationship, he no longer felt the need to deny himself.

He reached down, caught her T-shirt, started to pull it over her head.

She caught his hand. "But I'm all sweaty."

"So am I."

He drew off her shirt and felt that now familiar hitch in his chest at the sight of her. Her nipples were smooth and full from the heat, but the flush that rose in her skin as he looked down at her had nothing to do with the temperature. Blood rushed to his groin, even as the bruises that Zeta bastard had left on her breasts reminded him that he'd vowed to show her tenderness.

She was wide awake now, one hand resting against his chest, her other arm stretched above her head, her gaze following his every move.

He wetted the bandana once more, then squeezed it out, leaving a trail of droplets from her navel to her breastbone. He spread the droplets over her belly, across her rib cage, over her breasts. Then, as he'd done before, he blew across her skin.

She arched, sucked in a quick breath, her nipples puckering and drawing tight before his eyes, goose bumps rising on her skin.

It felt like such a luxury, just being with her like this— a few perfect hours after years of ugliness. Zach savored it, refusing to rush. He had no goals, no plans, nothing he wanted to do right now beyond giving Natalie pleasure.

Guided by her sighs, he kissed a lazy trail across her belly, stopping to taste her navel. He nipped at the pebbled tips of her breasts, then kissed their satiny undersides. He kissed the sensitive skin of her throat, licked her closed eyelids, teased her earlobe with his tongue, all the while raking her ticklish ribs with his fingertips. And then he couldn't help himself. He lowered his mouth to her nipples and suckled.

She slid her fingers deep into his hair, her body tensing and shifting beneath him, her sighs now moans.

"God, you're beautiful." It wasn't poetic, and it didn't express how he felt on the inside, but it was all he had.

He slid a hand beneath the waistband of her BDUs, popped the button with this thumb, and found his way inside her panties. He took time to stroke her smooth outer lips and to tease and tug on the delicate inner ones. Then, gathering her own wetness, he stroked her clitoris, felt it begin to swell. It was amazing to think that something so small could be so sensitive. One flick, and her hips jerked. Another, and she whimpered.

He lavished the little nub with attention until it was taut and her breathing was ragged. Then he slid first one, then two fingers deep inside her, the hot, wet feel of her sending a jagged bolt of need through him. But this was for her, not for him.

He stroked her deeply, taking care to catch her clitoris with each stroke, watching the rapture on her face as the tension inside her peaked—and broke. He kept up the rhythm, her vagina contracting in tight spasms around his fingers, her nails digging sharply into the skin of his forearm. Then slowly her grip relaxed, the quaking inside her fading to a soft pulse, his fingers drenched with the honey of her orgasm.

He withdrew his fingers, ran them along her lower lip, planning to taste her with his next kiss. But she caught his hand, drew his fingers into her mouth, and sucked them, her tongue swirling over them in a way that made his cock instantly hard.

Holy shit.

Okay, he hadn't been expecting that—but damned if it wasn't sexy as hell.

He leaned over her, taking what he could of her taste from her lips, delving into her mouth with his tongue, vowing to himself to take her with his mouth before this was all over and she was gone.

For a while—he had no idea how long—they kissed.

Then slowly, sinuously, she sat up, planted a hand in the middle of his chest—and pushed him onto his back. She surprised him again by straddling him. And what a sight she was, half-military, half-nymph. Her long hair spilled in tangles over her shoulders, dusky nipples peeking through the strands, her skin slick with sweat, the camo of her unzipped BDUs a striking contrast to her femininity.

"I love this muscle." She slid her hands along his obliques, making his belly jerk. "You're a beautiful man, Zach Black."

No one had ever said that to him before.

She leaned over and began to taste her way down his body, kissing his lips, his throat, his pecs, until she was running her tongue along his obliques just above his waistband. Without a word, she unzipped him, reached inside his boxer briefs to free his erection—and kissed the head of his cock.

Zach's entire body jerked.

She looked up at him, a hint of uncertainty in her eyes. "I'm probably not very good at this, but I want to taste you."

The idea of his erection in her mouth shorted out his brain.

"Okay," he said, stupidly.

Okay? Holy hell, McBride, you stupid idiot!

It was more than okay.

It was a fantasy come true wrapped in a wet dream.

She licked him, then took him into her mouth, her hand and lips working in tandem as she built up a rhythm, her tongue swirling around the aching, engorged head, catching him right where he was most sensitive.

Not very good at this? Where in the hell had she gotten that idea?

"Oh, angel. God, yeah!" He muttered something incoherent, caught her hair, and held it aside so that he could watch, the sight of her devouring him nearly sending him over the edge.

He fought to hold his hips still, but she seemed to understand what he needed, going faster, increasing the pressure, until his body shook, his groin throbbing, the ache almost unbearable. Then his balls drew tight and . . .

He lifted Natalie's head out of the way, orgasm hitting like a bolt of lighting, sheering through him as she finished him with her fist, hot ejaculate shooting from deep inside him and landing in pools on his belly.

And for a moment he couldn't move, his body floating.

Then he felt her snuggle up beside him, her fingers tracing designs through the rapidly cooling semen. He opened his eyes, watched her amuse herself. Then he reached down, caught her wrist, and in imitation of what she'd done, sucked her fingers into his mouth, tasting himself.

He gave it a moment, then met her gaze. "You taste better."

THEY EACH ATE an MRE after that, feeding each other tasteless bites of so-called food by hand. Then, still topless, Natalie curled up beside him, and they drifted off to sleep again. But by late afternoon it was so hot that no matter how many times Zach wet her down with the bandana, she couldn't sleep.

"Maybe we should just start walking again." She lay with her head on his outstretched leg, one of his big hands splayed on her bare belly, the casual intimacy of being physically close to him like this filling her with a kind of contentment she hadn't known for years.

Zach shook his head, pointing to the gallon of water he'd kept on hand. "We've gone through half a gallon today. If we'd been walking in this heat, we'd have consumed much more than that. We need to wait until dusk."

She must have let some of what she was feeling show on her face because in the next instant he tried to encourage her.

He stroked her hair. "I know it's hard. Just rest."

She let her gaze travel over the scenery. There were dry hills and mountains all around them, one of them much taller than the others. But, beyond empty water jugs, food containers, and other trash, there was no sign of human habitation. No fences. No buildings. Not so much as an outhouse. It seemed still, desolate, empty. And yet it wasn't empty at all. It was full of wildlife—not to mention people. And once the sun set, they would all come out of hiding.

Last night's close encounter with the drug traffickers seemed far away in the blazing light of the sun. But it had been real, and it might have turned deadly if not for Zach. And though she supposed she ought to be afraid—they still had two or three more nights out here—she wasn't. She might not know his real name, and she might not know what kind of trouble he was in, but she knew without a shred of doubt that he would do everything he could to protect her. She just hoped she wouldn't be too much of a burden.

"Where exactly are we? Texas? Arizona? The Sahara?"

"Arizona." He pointed. "Do you see that mountain? That's Baboquivari Peak. It's sacred to the Tohono O'Odham people. Right now we're in the southeast corner of the Tohono O'Odham reservation."

And it clicked.

She sat up, faced him. "That's what you told Kat, isn't it? Your secret message, all that gibberish. It was about this place."

He nodded, his lips curving in a lopsided grin. "More or less. I told her we were leaving Altar and that we were going to cross the border onto Tohono O'Odham land. I also hinted that she get in touch with the reservation's answer to the drug cartels."

"What would that be?"

"The Shadow Wolves."

* * *

NATALIE FELT SORE but well rested by the time they set off again, the sun setting behind a thick bank of pink and orange clouds to the sound of yowling coyotes. As she'd done last night, she followed behind Zach, watching where he stepped and doing her best not to get hurt, but her thoughts were still on their conversation from earlier.

Had Kat figured out the message? And if she had, were these Shadow Wolves out here trying to find her?

At first, the idea had filled her with a sense of relief to think that this nightmare would soon be over and she would be home again. And then . . .

Then Zach would return to the life that had almost gotten him killed. She would go back to the newspaper and the existence she'd known before she'd met him. And everything would be fine.

Except that nothing would be fine at all. Zach would be in danger, not only from the Zetas, but possibly also from law enforcement. And she . . .

She would miss him.

After six long years, she'd finally begun to feel again, and he was the reason why. It wasn't just the situation. It was *him*. It was Zach. She didn't understand it, couldn't explain it, but it was true. The idea of him walking out of her life made the bottom drop out of her heart. She couldn't go back to the way she'd been before—darker, emptier, and more parched inside than this desert.

That's up to you, isn't it, girl?

She supposed it was. She'd made herself a promise to live again, and she needed to keep that promise, no matter who was in her life.

And what will happen to Zach?

Would the two of them be processed like others who'd crossed the border illegally? Would they be detained, fingerprinted, questioned? How would they prove who they were without ID?

One thing was certain: If they were fingerprinted, and Zach had a criminal record, he would be arrested. She didn't want that to happen.

"What will these Shadow Wolves do with us when they find us?"

Ahead of her, Zach came to an abrupt halt. For a moment, she thought he'd stopped because he was irritated with her for asking a question. Then he crouched down, motioning for her to do the same, pistol in hand. She did, her pulse rocketing. It was in that same moment that she noticed it—an indescribably awful stench.

Zach seemed to be looking toward a stand of mesquite that stood off to their right. Her gaze followed his, and though she didn't have night vision goggles, she was just able to make it out—the shapes of human bodies strewn across the ground. "All dead."

Natalie was on her feet, hand covering her mouth, her stomach revolting at the sight, the smell, the shock of it.

Then Zach was there beside her. "Breathe! Don't you dare get sick. You'll get dehydrated."

He took her gloved hand with his and drew her along behind him, until the horrible odor had dissipated. Then he turned to her and wrapped his arms around her, tucking her head beneath his chin. "Sorry. I smelled them before I saw them. They were hidden by the mesquite."

"Wh-what happened to them?"

"Don't know. Couldn't tell." He held her tighter. "Whatever it was, it's not going to happen to you."

JOAQUIN SIPPED HIS coffee wanting this damned meeting to end. It was already ten o'clock and hotter than hell outside. If Natalie was out there somewhere . . .

"So you think they've crossed onto our land?" Ned Zepeda, commander of the Shadow Wolves, looked across the table at Marc and Kat, who sat close to Gabe holding their baby on her lap.

Kat had insisted on coming along, certain that she, as a Navajo, could help. Gabe had refused to let her go without him, and Marc had welcomed his company. As an extreme climber and skier, as well as a paramedic and a former park ranger, he was not only experienced with the outdoors, but also good with a gun and handy when it came to first aid.

And he had balls of solid rock, having sacrificed his left leg to save Kat's life. No one watching him would suspect he wore a prosthesis.

"Yes, sir, we do." Kat handed Commander Zepeda a copy of the transcribed code-talk message. "We were hoping you might be able to help us find her."

Zepeda studied it, his brow furrowing. His face was weathered by the sun, deep lines etched into his cheeks, making Joaquin wish he'd brought his camera inside. But that's not why they were here.

"Rossiter and I are both trained law enforcement, so we can handle ourselves." Marc pointed to Joaquin with a jerk of his head. "Ramirez is a photojournalist. He was with Ms. Benoit when she was taken. We'd like to ride along, or if you can't mount a rescue effort today, we'd like permission to rent or borrow a vehicle and head out on your land ourselves."

Still looking at the transcript, Zepeda shouted toward the hallway. "Eh, Chiago, get in here. You're going to want to see this."

Another officer—a tall son of a gun—walked into the room. Well over six feet, he looked like he was in his thirties. Dressed in a green military-style uniform, a pistol holstered on his hip, he looked at them through dark eyes that had seen their share of action. His dark hair was cropped short, his hard gaze moving over everyone in the room as if sizing them up, then softening when he looked at Kat and Alissa. "Yeah, Chief?"

Commander Zepeda repeated the story that Kat and Marc had just told him, then handed the transcript to Chiago. "Got any thoughts on this?"

Chiago frowned, read through it, then looked up at them. "I'll take you out. We'll get a team together. It's a big reservation, but we'll see if we can find her. But tell me again about this man you heard whispering in the background. Did you bring a file of that recording with you?"

CHAPTER 18

NATALIE WAS STILL dreaming when the first fat raindrop hit her cheek. That raindrop was followed by another—and a kiss on her forehead.

Zach ran his knuckles over her cheek. "Wake up, angel. We need to get out of here—and fast."

She opened her eyes, felt herself being hauled to her feet. She blinked, looked around, still groggy and confused. "Is it raining?"

Thunder crashed overhead.

"A monsoon has moved in. If we don't haul ass, we're going to get caught in a flash flood. Get your pack on, and let's leave this death trap."

And then she remembered.

They'd taken shelter early this morning at the bottom of a dry wash. He'd warned her that it was dangerous because they were in the middle of monsoon season and people died every year when the washes, which were dry most of the time, turned into raging rivers. But she'd been so tired that she'd barely been able to put one foot in front of the other, so he'd relented.

She grabbed her pack, shook it to dislodge anything that might have climbed into the harness, then slipped it on her aching shoulders. She hadn't come all this way to die in a muddy ditch. "Let's go."

Zach grinned, his stubbled face turning from rough to handsome as hell in a heartbeat. "Yes, ma'am."

By the time they reached the spot where they'd descended into the wash, it was raining hard, the fine desert silt turning to butter beneath Natalie's feet. Zach climbed out of the wash, and she tried to follow, but the bank was too slippery and too steep.

A flash of lightning. The crash of thunder.

She tried again, grabbing on to a clump of grass and digging hard with the toes of her boots, but she just wasn't strong enough to lift both her body weight and the weight of the backpack. Breathing hard, she felt herself sliding backward. Below her, the water was already ankle deep—and rising.

She hadn't been afraid before, but she was now.

"I can't do it!" She looked up only to be blinded by raindrops.

Zach was shouting something to her, but she couldn't hear it over the rumble of thunder and the rush of water and wind.

Again she tried, and again she slipped, the water up to her knees and tugging hard, threatening to pull her off balance.

Oh, come on! You can't drown in the damned desert, girl!

Then something hit her face.

A rope.

A loop had been tied on the end of it.

She didn't need to hear what Zach was saying to know what to do. She slipped it over her head and beneath her arms and held on tight, the current sucking at her feet.

And slowly Zach dragged her up the muddy embankment until she lay at the top, covered head to toe in mud and breathing hard.

Then he was there beside her. "You okay?"

She nodded, still trying to catch her breath, the shock of what had almost happened catching up with her. "I could've drowned."

"That was too damned close." He got her to her feet, lifted the rope over her head, then tucked a gloved finger beneath her chin and kissed her. Rain spilled over his face, catching in his stubble. "Let's get out of this storm."

She glanced over her shoulder and felt her knees go weak.

The place where she'd just been standing was now a deep, roiling current.

*   *   *

THE THUNDERSTORM LASTED for almost an hour, changing the landscape. Low-lying areas were now muddy marshes. The washes were brimming and impassible. And everywhere the fine desert silt was slick and muddy. This slowed them down considerably and left footprints that any idiot could follow. But it also made the journey more difficult for Natalie, her feet slipping with each step.

Zach slowed the pace, trying to find a dry place where they could rest until dark, some place that wasn't already occupied by snakes or arachnids trying to avoid the wet. He was about to explain to her why it would be okay in these circumstances to sit next to a spider, when he saw an outcropping of granite a bit farther up the hill to their right. He helped her up the slippery slope, then shooed away the bobcat that had taken shelter in a deep alcove on the north side of the outcropping. Larger than the space they'd camped in that first day, it would get them out of the wind and the rain and give them a safe place to rest until nightfall.

He took Natalie's hand and helped her inside, dropped his pack and then took hers. "Take your jacket off. It's drenched."

He shed his jacket, as well, then grabbed the woolen blanket. He drew her down beside him in the soft, dry sand and wrapped the blanket around both of them, hoping the wool would hold in their body heat and help them dry off. Being wet out here at night would put them at risk of hypothermia. And there was nothing like walking in cold, wet BDUs to chafe one's inner thighs. He could write a dissertation on that subject.

Petroleum jelly. You knew you'd forget something. Damn it, McBride!

The rain had rinsed off most of the mud that had coated her, her lashes wet, her hair sticking to her cheeks, droplets beading on her face. She huddled up against him, shivering. "Don't we have to get skin to skin for this to work?"

"Are you saying you want to get naked with me, angel?"

She smiled through chattering teeth, two little dimples appearing in her cheeks. "That's not what I meant."

"No? Too bad." He drew her tighter against him, wrapping

his arms around her, doing his best to share his surplus body heat.

For a while, they sat there, watching the rain fall, water spilling over the edge of their little shelter like a translucent curtain, partly concealing them from the world beyond. Gradually, her shivering subsided, and she began to relax into him.

"What did you want to be when you grew up?"

The question came out of nowhere.

"I wanted to drive a dump truck. Then I wanted to be a fireman. Then I wanted to be an astronaut. Then I wanted to be a football star. And then I went to college and had no clue what I wanted to do." He glanced down and saw her smiling. "What about you? Did you grow up wanting to be a journalist?"

She shook her head. "No. I wanted to be a vet and take care of horses."

"Really?" For some reason, that surprised him. "What changed your mind?"

"Math. I'm no good at it. I barely got through college algebra. I was much better at English, so I ended up majoring in journalism. I discovered I really loved it. Beau always told me he . . ." Her words trailed off into silence.

"Hey, it's okay. You can talk about him with me." Zach wasn't insecure enough to be jealous of a dead man. Besides, he had no claim over Natalie.

Two days at most, McBride.

He glanced down, saw a bittersweet smile on her face. "He always told me that journalism was my destiny because I was always asking questions."

That sounded like Natalie. "Did you meet him in college?"

She shook her head. "I met him the night I graduated from high school. I was from the Garden District and went to Louis S. McGehee High School—that's a private girl's school—and he was the football star at St. Bernard High School, a public school in Chalmette." Her accent grew stronger when she talked about her hometown. Zach found it almost irresistible. "I went out with some friends to celebrate—we were wearing matching pink gowns and wrist corsages—and a guy he was with started picking on me and plucking the petals off my corsage. Beau made him stop and apologize."

"It takes a lot of courage for a man to stand up to his male friends." Particularly when it revolved around how they treated women. "He sounds like a good guy."

"He was." She smiled, a sad smile. "I ran into him about a week later at a White Stripes concert at Tulane. He asked me out. We ended up dating throughout my three years of college—"

"Three years?" It had taken Zach five.

"I skipped a grade in middle school and graduated early from college due to advanced credits." She said this without a hint of arrogance. "I turned twenty-one the year of the storm."

Hadn't he known she was smart? "Sorry to interrupt."

"We dated through college, despite my parents' fears that he was just after their money. We were well off, and his family wasn't. They didn't like his accent, thought he seemed uncultured. But they eventually came around. He worked hard to earn their respect, and I think they saw the man he truly was. He turned down a football scholarship and worked his way through college. He'd just gotten accepted to law school when . . .

"We couldn't live together because that would have freaked my parents out, but we spent lots of time together. He proposed to me on my twenty-first birthday over champagne at Commander's Palace. He had a ring tucked in the pocket of his sports jacket. I was so surprised, and the ring was so beautiful— antique white gold with a one-karat diamond. He said he'd been saving his money since the night we met. I accepted his proposal and . . . In less than two months, he was gone and my folks, too."

Something twisted in Zach's chest at the depth of her grief. "I'm so sorry."

"They didn't like each other at first, but they died together because they all loved me."

"Don't you dare blame yourself, Natalie. It wasn't your fault."

But she didn't seem to hear him.

"Now the Chalmette I knew is gone. St. Bernard High is gone." Her voice quavered, and he knew she was near tears. "There have been so many times when I wished they hadn't found me in the morgue. I wasn't afraid anymore. I had blacked out. It would have been so easy to die. Then Beau and Mama and Daddy would still be here."

A part of Zach wanted to tell her not to think like that, but he understood that feeling only too well. It sucked being the one left behind.

She went on. "Sometimes I'm afraid I've forgotten the sound of his voice. I find myself wondering if I can remember his face without photographs. I kept my old cell phone—the one that had messages from him saved on it. I fell apart when I accidentally ran it through the washing machine and destroyed it. Somehow, it felt like I was losing him all over again. Isn't that ridiculous?"

"No, it isn't." He rested her head against his chest. "I may not have met Beau, but I know one thing for certain. He wouldn't have wanted you to waste a moment blaming yourself. If he loved you at all, he would want you to live a full and happy life without him."

She sniffed. "I'm sorry. I shouldn't have gone on like that. I haven't even told my friends at work about Beau or what happened during the storm. I didn't mean . . ."

"Hey, don't be so hard on yourself. It's a hell of a thing to have been through."

He wanted to say more than that. He wanted to tell her how sorry he was that life had thrown so much shit her way. He wanted to remind her that if it weren't for her, he'd be dead right now. He wanted to tell her that if it were simply a matter of crossing the river Styx and trading places with Beau, he'd be gone in a heartbeat.

But he didn't.

She drew back from him, wiping the tears from her face, clearly embarrassed that she was crying in front of him. But, hell, who could blame her?

"I think the rain's letting up."

THE RAIN DID, indeed, stop, and the sun came out. Within fifteen minutes the air was warm again. Feeling both embarrassed about having fallen apart in front of Zach and grateful that he'd listened, Natalie concentrated on the scenery. Pools of water shimmered in the light of the setting sun, tiny ponds and puddles drawing thirsty wildlife. She saw pronghorns and more javelinas, and she thought for a moment she'd spotted a mountain lion. And then she noticed something odd—the sound of running water.

She stood, walked out of their little haven and downhill around to the side of the rock outcropping, where she discovered a little waterfall. Only about ten feet high and no more than a foot wide, it spilled from a crack near the base of the stone, down the slope, where erosion had washed the sand away, leaving granite. But it had stopped raining almost twenty minutes ago, which meant that this must be . . .

"A spring." Zach's voice came from beside her. He stood beside her, rifle in hand, as always. "It probably taps an aquifer near the surface and only runs when there's been a downpour."

Then an idea came to her—a crazy, wonderful idea. "Is there any soap in that backpack of yours?"

"I think the first-aid kit has a small bar."

She turned on her heels and marched back uphill. "I'm taking a shower."

"You're . . . What?" He followed.

"I'm taking a shower." She opened his pack and began to rummage through it.

"Here, let me find it. You're going to mess up my system."

She stepped back, watching as he moved things carefully aside, withdrew the first-aid kit, then handed her a small bar of soap. "Thanks. I can't wait to feel clean again."

She made her way back down to the little waterfall and was about to undress, when Zach insisted that he check the site to make sure there wasn't anything there that could harm her. Once he was satisfied, she stripped, sliding out of boots and socks and her still-damp pants, T-shirt, and panties and setting them down on a dry rock.

She supposed she ought to feel self-conscious being naked in the open air like this, but there was no one there apart from Zach, and he'd seen it all before. She grabbed the soap and stepped through the sand into the stream of water. It wasn't as cold as she'd thought it would be, but it wasn't warm either.

Working quickly, she lathered her entire body, then rinsed

herself off, bubbles sliding downhill over stone. Then she tilted her head back and let the water wash her hair, the thought of being clean—if even for a moment—invigorating.

"Let me help."

Startled, she whirled about to find Zach standing gloriously naked, his clothes piled with an AK beside hers. He took the soap from her and worked some into her hair just at the base of the strands, gently massaging her scalp. Then he lathered her back, his hands moving in slow, titillating circles down to her buttocks. "Rinse."

She hadn't intended this shower to lead to sex, but his touch changed that. She faced him, took the soap from his hands. "Your turn."

She lathered him well, savoring the feel of hard muscle beneath soap-slick skin as she rubbed her hands slowly over his chest, belly, and upper thighs, aroused by touching him—and being touched by him. He palmed her breasts, played with her nipples, while she slowly spread lather over those abdominal muscles she loved, her fingers tracing the veins low on his belly before grasping his erection.

He groaned, dragged her hard against him. "God, Natalie, what the hell have you done to me? I can't keep my hands off you."

There was true desperation in his voice, and she felt a feminine thrill to know that she affected him so strongly. She yielded to his kiss, the rasp of his chest hair on her nipples making her ache for him. "Please! Now!"

He stepped away for a second, grabbed something from his pile of clothes. A condom. In a heartbeat, he had it out and quickly rolled it onto himself.

Then he reached for her, lifted her against him, the head of his cock nudging impatiently against her, seeking entrance. She wrapped her legs around his hips, held tight to his shoulders with one arm, then reached down to guide him inside her.

He filled her with a single upward thrust, making them both moan.

And then there was nothing but urgent need. He drove into her fast and hard, his hands clenching her derriere, his muscles tensing beneath her hands, the cords of his neck straining. She'd never done anything like this before, never felt anything like this—being held by a man while he moved inside her. All she had to do was hang on and take him, each thrust lifting her up, carrying her higher and higher.

Then her head fell back, and she heard herself cry out, orgasm washing through her in a surge of liquid gold, flooding her with pleasure.

But he was right behind her. He groaned through gritted teeth, thrusting into her once, twice, three times, his body jerking as climax claimed him.

For a moment he held her, both of them wet and breathing hard, time measured in heartbeats. Sunset spilled its rosy light across the landscape. The now familiar night chorus was just beginning, crickets starting up, a million frogs joining them, coyotes yipping excitedly in the distance.

Natalie's body seemed to sing with them, wild and free. She closed her eyes, vowing silently to do all she could to keep Zach from being arrested. Whatever mistakes he might have made, he was a good man through and through. How could she ever have mistrusted him? She pressed her cheek against his shoulder, let her fingers trail across his back, breathing in the rain-washed scent of him. "Am I getting too heavy?"

"No. Never." Slowly he withdrew and lowered her to her feet. "*Damn*."

She looked up to find him frowning. "What?"

"The condom." He held crumpled bits of wet latex in his hands. "It broke."

WEARING BORROWED BODY armor and carrying his camera, Joaquin stood next to a flooded wash, his gaze moving over the seemingly endless expanse of the Sonoran Desert. Natalie was out there somewhere, trying to make her way home. And he was going to find her. Or rather the Shadow Wolves were going to find her. He was just along for the ride.

Agent Chiago knelt next to muddy tracks beside the bank of the wash, reached out, and pulled something off a shrub, while the rest of his unit stood watch by the vehicles. "Whoever they were, they got caught napping during the thunderstorm. Looks like they had a hell of a time getting out, but they made it."

Marc's gaze followed the tracks. He was wearing his own Kevlar and carrying a rifle. "Two sets of tracks heading west-northwest."

A gun on his hip, Gabe followed the tracks a short distance. "They probably headed to higher ground to find shelter."

Chiago held up what looked like dark strands of hair. "This looks like it belongs to the same person as those strands I found before."

Joaquin reached and took them. "Yeah, this looks like it could be hers."

How did this guy see this shit? Chiago had been looking for tracks—what he called cutting sign—along the southern corner of the reservation, when he'd found a trail of bent grass, overturned rocks, and windblown indentations that he said were footprints. He'd even found a few strands of dark hair and a bit of blood on an ocotillo. They'd followed sign to what Chiago said had probably been a campsite, then continued on past a group of rotting corpses. Afraid Natalie might be among them, Joaquin had covered his nose and started to search, but Chiago had told them to forget it.

"They've been dead for a week or more," he said, before calling the bodies in to HQ.

The man's ability to track was like nothing Joaquin had ever seen.

Chiago followed the tracks to the base of a steep incline, then pulled out his infrared binoculars and scanned the darkening hillside ahead of them. "So, we're most likely looking for one female and one male, right? I think I found them." Then he lowered the binoculars. "We should, uh . . . give them a minute."

Marc grabbed the binoculars from him, then looked up in the same general direction. "What the . . . ?" He lowered the binoculars, a strange expression on his face that was something between rage and astonishment. "We should move now. What if he's forcing her?"

Chiago shrugged. "It looks consensual to me."

And then Joaquin understood. "You don't mean they're . . ."

"That's exactly what I mean." Marc lowered his voice. "If I find out he coerced her in any way, I'll kill that son of a bitch—whoever he is."

Gabe's gaze wandered over the hillside. "Not before I make him eat his balls."

"I'll help." Joaquin took the opportunity to ask Marc something he'd been meaning to ask for days. "When we get her back home, can you do me a favor?"

Marc nodded. "Sure. Name it."

"Teach me to shoot. I want to learn how to use firearms."

Both men looked at him, then looked at each other.

Marc's brow furrowed, but he reached out and clapped Joaquin on the shoulder as if he understood. "You got it."

CHAPTER 19

ZACH HAD JUST zipped his BDUs when he saw it out of the corner of his eye—the glint of starlight on gunmetal. "Natalie, get down!"

Wearing only her T-shirt and panties, she dropped to the sand.

Still shirtless, he grabbed his rifle and got into position, scanning the hillside below through the weapon's night scope. And there they were—a unit of Shadow Wolves. Judging from his height, the man leading them was Chiago.

Zach's first emotion wasn't relief—it was soul-deep disappointment.

It was over.

The thought hit him like a body blow, leaving a dull emptiness behind. He wasn't ready to let her go—not yet.

She was never yours to hold on to, McBride.

He got back to his feet, brushed the sand off his chest. "Better get your clothes on, angel. We're about to have company."

"Company?" She grabbed her BDUs and scrambled into them. "Drug runners?"

"There's a unit of Shadow Wolves making their way up the hill, rifles at the ready. It looks like we've been found."

"Really?" For a moment, she gaped at him, smiling. Then her smile faded, a shadow passing over her face. "You should run. Just leave me here and go. I know you can do it. You can get away. I won't say anything. I promise."

He drew away, removed his shoulder harness, and set it, with his two Glocks, aside. "Relax. I have no reason to run."

"But—"

"Natalie, listen to me. They are going to treat this like any other raid, so be ready. No one's going to hurt you, but they will come in strong. For all they know, I could be a trafficker or *bajador*, and you could be my accomplice. They'll want to secure the scene."

"Secure the scene?" She looked confused.

He knelt down and removed the Ka-Bar rig from his ankle. "We want to make this easy on everyone, so put down the AK. I'm just going to disarm and sit here on my knees with my hands behind my head. You might want to do the same, though I doubt they'll be as aggressive with you as they'll be with me."

"Zach, please go! I couldn't stand it if you—"

"Freeze! Federal agents!"

But Natalie did the opposite of freeze. She ran over and knelt down in front of Chiago, words streaming out of her. "I'm Natalie Benoit. I was kidnapped by the Zetas, and this man helped me escape! He's not one of them!"

If the situation hadn't been so serious, Zach might have laughed out loud. "Natalie, they're not going to hurt me."

"Put your hands on top of your head!" Agents swarmed into the little alcove, moving toward them, weapons drawn.

"He didn't do anything! He helped me escape!"

Zach leaned forward. "Natalie! Put your hands on your head!"

She finally did as he asked, but that didn't shut her up. She kept pleading with the officers not to arrest him.

And Zach realized that at least in one respect he'd been looking forward to this, because now he could finally tell her the truth about his identity.

In the next moment, he was being patted down.

But no one touched Natalie.

Then Chiago was there, kneeling down in front of her. "What's your name?"

"I-I'm Natalie Benoit from Denver, Colorado. I'm a reporter with the *Denver Independent*. I was kidnapped off a bus in Juárez, Mexico, and held captive by the Zetas until this man helped me escape."

Chiago turned to three men who'd just walked up behind them. Two were tall, and dark haired, one carrying an M4 like he knew how to use it, the other packing a sidearm in a hip holster. The third looked to be just under six foot, Latino, and armed with . . . a camera? The photographer.

Joaquin.

"Can you make a positive identification?"

"Marc? Gabe? Joaquin!" Heedless of the men with guns, she jumped up and ran to the newcomers, throwing her arms around Joaquin. "I was so sure you'd been shot!"

Her throat sounded tight, and Zach knew she was on the brink of tears.

"*Madre María*, it really is you. Thank God! I thought I'd never see my sweet *chula* again. I don't think I've ever been more afraid for anyone in my life."

Zach felt his teeth grind.

Then Natalie turned and hugged the one with the M4. "Oh, Marc, I knew you'd come. Thank you so much!"

He hugged her back, almost lifting her off the ground. "Hey, we take care of our own. No matter what happened, we're going to help you get through it. We're going to take care of you. Darcangelo would have come, too, but he didn't want to miss his manicure and back waxing."

For some reason, this made her laugh.

Then she turned to the one with the hip holster and sank into his arms. "Oh, Gabe, thank you! I don't know how I'll ever make this up to you all."

"I'm so happy to see you alive and in one piece." The guy kissed her on the cheek. "We're here to bring you home. Kat is in Sells waiting at the hotel with the baby. She's been worried sick about you."

"So she deciphered Zach's message."

Marc nodded. "She did—with some insight from Joaquin and me."

And Zach's jealousy melted away. Natalie was safe now. She was going back to her life, back to a circle of friends who clearly cared for her. He should feel relieved, happy for her, satisfied that he'd kept his promise and gotten her home safely.

Chiago bent down, looked Zach in the eyes. "Zach McBride, old friend, what in the hell have you gotten yourself mixed up in now? Let him up, boys."

ZACH MCBRIDE?

Natalie turned, looked at the man she'd just made love with not an hour ago. "So that's your real name?"

"Chief Deputy U.S. Marshal Zachariah McBride at your service, Ms. Benoit." He smiled, winked.

Behind her, Marc gave a snort, Joaquin whispering something that sounded like, "Yeah, right."

"Simmer down, boys," Gabe whispered. "We'll kill him later."

But her attention was on Zach.

"Sorry I couldn't tell you before. The situation was too volatile. I couldn't put your life or the operation at greater risk."

A deputy U.S. marshal.

Zach was a chief deputy U.S. marshal.

Instead of being impressed, she felt a surge of anger, and before she could stop herself, she slapped him across the face hard enough to turn his head. "You let me believe you were some kind of criminal—a drug thief, an arms smuggler, a mercenary!"

He shook his head as if to clear it, his gaze piercing hers. "You came up with that on your own. I told you that I wasn't what you thought I was. You didn't believe me."

So what if he was right? "I've been worried sick about what would happen to you when they found us. At least you could have told me you were some kind of good guy."

"I thought my actions proved that."

You haven't exactly seen me at my best.

His words came back to her, and piece after piece slid into place. Why he knew so much about the cartels and smuggling routes. How he knew where to cross the border. His dedication to keeping her safe.

Why hadn't she considered the possibility that he was law enforcement? It seemed so obvious now. "Are you really ex-military, or was that all just a story you made up to make me stop asking questions?"

The tall Indian agent stepped forward. "That's the truth. McBride used to be a Navy SEAL. He's one of three living men to have been awarded—"

Zach frowned. "Chiago, stop!"

"—the Medal of Honor for nearly dying while trying to save his team."

"You two know each other?" She looked back and forth between the two men.

"McBride trained with us for a while after joining the Marshal Service. He wanted to learn to cut sign."

"I see."

A former Navy SEAL. And a Medal of Honor winner no less.

The man standing before her—the man who'd protected her, who'd saved her life, who'd made love to her—was a true American hero.

It stunned Natalie, and yet it fit him so well. "I . . . I'm sorry I didn't believe you. It's just that the circumstances . . ."

"If I'd been in your shoes, I would've thought the same thing." Then he turned to Chiago—and started giving orders. "Until I say otherwise, there's a news blackout on Ms. Benoit's rescue and whereabouts. The Zetas were in full hunt-and-destroy mode, so I'd like to get her away from the border before we tell the world where she is. Besides, you don't want to have to deal with the brass at the Justice Department, and they're going to be very interested in this. Anyone have a dry jacket she can borrow? How far away are your vehicles?"

Natalie felt someone slide a jacket over her shoulders, and looked up to see Marc and Gabe exchange a knowing glance, Marc rolling his eyes for good measure.

"What is it?"

Gabe leaned down, whispered in her ear. "The U.S. Marshal Service is at the top of the law-enforcement pecking order, outranking everyone, even the FBI. They have jurisdiction no matter where they are."

Marc's gaze followed Zach. "I wish Darcangelo were here. He'd fucking hate this."

Natalie watched as Zach took control of the scene. Six

days of brutal torture. An arduous five-day escape. And he was completely in command.

NATALIE FELT LIKE the most protected woman in the world as they started downhill for the hour-long trek back to the Shadow Wolves' vehicles. Marc walked on one side of her, Gabe and Joaquin on the other, and Zach in front, a dozen armed Shadow Wolves fanned out around them. Yes, she was safe now, and she was grateful to be rescued.

But that didn't stop her from looking back over her shoulder at the little waterfall and feeling like she was leaving something precious behind.

ZACH USED HIS authority to arrange for Natalie to sit beside him on the long, bumpy ride to Sells. He knew her friends saw through it—for some reason the three of them seemed to want to kick his ass—but he didn't really give a damn. This might be his last chance to be close to her.

He climbed into the seat and fastened his safety belt, her small, cool fingers twining with his—and holding on tight.

He leaned down and spoke for her ears only. "What's wrong?"

She looked up at him, every emotion he was trying so hard not to feel written plainly on her face. "I'm scared. I'm so afraid I'll never see you again after tonight. Don't you dare leave without saying good-bye, Zach McBride."

"AND THAT'S WHEN you saw McBride in chains?"

Natalie nodded. "He was hanging blindfolded from the ceiling by his wrists, too weak to support his own weight. He was soaking wet and covered with red electrical burns. There was a cart with a big battery and two electrical cables . . . I don't think I'll ever be able to forget the sound of his cries. They almost killed him."

Agent Chiago wrote something down in his notebook. "Then what happened?"

Natalie had already given a written deposition, detailing

everything she could remember from the moment the bus had stopped. Now she was just answering questions. Zach had warned her she'd have to do this more than once. But she'd been through this whole experience once before—when she'd helped investigators piece together their case against the intern who'd tried to kill her. She'd known it wouldn't be easy.

"Then they . . . They held me, took off my shirt and bra and . . . One of the Zetas, the one with the scar on his face . . ." She pressed her hands into her lap to keep them from shaking, finding it hard to talk about this without breaking into tears.

Agent Chiago looked at her through brown eyes soft with compassion. "I know this must be hard for you. But we need to make sure we understand exactly what happened. Can I get you anything—water, soda, another cup of coffee?"

Natalie shook her head, trying to calm the sick feeling in her stomach. "They took off my shirt and bra, then the one with the scar . . . touched me. He was very rough. He left bruises. I couldn't understand everything he was saying, but I knew he was trying to make a deal with Zach—the location of the stolen cocaine in exchange for . . . me."

Chiago nodded. "How did McBride respond to this offer?"

Oh, God, was she going to get Zach into trouble? "He . . . He pretended to go along with it, trying to get them to unchain him so that he could fight them. He later apologized and told me he never would have hurt me. I believed him."

Chiago wrote something down, glanced through his notes. "You also stated that you watched him give a duffel bag of things he'd taken from the Zeta compound to a Mexican national in exchange for a car. Do you know what was in that duffel bag?"

Natalie shook her head. "Please don't ask me that. I don't want to cause trouble for him. He saved my life. I can't repay him by—"

"I understand your distress, Ms. Benoit, but the folks in Washington, D.C., are going to be mighty interested in this case. You can either answer my questions or wait for the Justice Department to knock on your door. And, hell, they might knock on your door anyway, knowing them. They like their frequent-flyer miles."

Natalie swallowed—hard. "Guns. Ammunition. He said

we'd be caught and killed for sure if we didn't get into a different car because that one had a Z on the license plate like all Zeta vehicles."

Chiago wrote more notes, then flipped back a few pages. "When you asked McBride why the Zetas had captured him, what was his answer?"

"He said he'd made a bad decision and to leave it at that. He said they were interrogating him and if they thought I knew anything, they'd torture me, too. He said they were going to kill him."

"How did you hear about the stolen cocaine?"

"The Zeta with the Santa Muerte tattoo told me about it. I asked why they were torturing Zach, and he said that Zach had stolen a shipment of cocaine. But Zach told me he didn't do it. He said the woman who *did* steal it had turned him over to the Zetas, making him her scapegoat."

"Did you believe him?"

Natalie closed her eyes. "I didn't know what to believe."

Forgive me, Zach. Please forgive me.

"I BEAT HIM with the steel handcuff, then kicked him a bunch in the stomach, then hit him on the head twice with a brick as hard as I could. I . . . I'd watched him kill Mexican journalists. I thought he'd killed my friend Joaquin."

Joaquin watched through a one-way mirror as Agent Chiago went through the details of Natalie's escape from the Zetas for a third time. He was sickened by the terrible things she'd had to endure—and stunned to think that she'd shot one man and beaten the shit out of another.

"She's is a lot tougher than she looks, isn't she? She had your back, buddy." Marc clapped Joaquin on the shoulder. "God, I wish I'd been there."

"Yeah, me, too. I wish Chiago would give her a break, though. He's questioning her like he thinks she's a criminal or something."

"No, he isn't. If you want to see what that looks like, go down the hall and listen to the conversation they're having with McBride."

Gabe stood, stretched, a cup of coffee in his hands. "What do you two think? You think McBride's dirty?"

Joaquin shook his head. "I don't know."

"I think he's telling the truth." Marc leaned back in his chair, arms crossed over his chest, a thoughtful frown on his face. He'd once worked as a DEA agent, so he knew more about cartel stuff than anyone Joaquin knew. "If McBride had been part of some kind of drug ring made up of dirty agents, he wouldn't have busted his ass getting her safely home. She'd already seen and heard too much. He'd have used her to escape—then he'd have put a bullet in her brain and let the Zetas take the blame. Everyone knew they'd kidnapped her. He could have killed her with no risk to himself."

Gabe walked up to the glass, his gaze on Natalie. "I hope he's the man he seems to be, because I think Natalie has feelings for him."

"You think? Shit, Rossiter, you're a damned psychic."

"Not just feelings." Joaquin had seen it in her eyes. "She might not realize it yet, but she's in love with him."

IT WAS MIDNIGHT before Agent Zepeda finished debriefing him.

That wasn't a debriefing, McBride, it was an interrogation.

Hungry and needing a shower, Zach walked down the dark, silent street to the hotel, thinking through what they'd asked him—and what he'd learned.

He'd known he'd be investigated, and he understood why. He'd been working a black bag op that had gone wrong, and they would want to understand *why* it had gone wrong. More than that, they would want to know exactly how he'd been captured, what had happened when he'd been imprisoned, and how he'd managed to escape and make it back alive. They had to know for certain that he wasn't compromised. Other people's lives depended on it.

It would help to have Natalie to back up the part of the story that concerned her. She'd witnessed the torture, seen him in chains, seen how badly hurt he'd been. She'd been

with him during his escape. Hell, she was the reason he'd
escaped. Her deposition would lend credibility to his. Not that
he expected trouble. This was standard operating procedure.
He was doing everything he was supposed to do under these
circumstances, and so were they.

He had reported in to D.C. the moment they'd arrived in
Sells. Pearce had been surprised to hear from him and had
immediately arranged for a helo to pick him up in Sells and
fly him to Tucson in the morning. From there, Zach would fly
to D.C., and then the real fun would begin.

Zepeda had already sent his own report, together with both
Zach's and Natalie's depositions and video files of their debrief-
ings, to the Operations Directorate at the Justice Department.
By the time Zach got to Washington tomorrow, Pearce and the
brass in the OD would have lots of questions for him.

He walked into the hotel's lobby, where he saw Natalie's
friends—Marc, Gabe, and Joaquin. Were they waiting for him?

Three sets of eyes turned his way, and the men stood.

Yeah, they were waiting for him.

Zach had heard about Joaquin from Natalie, but she hadn't
mentioned the other two. So he'd taken a few minutes to
dig up a little intel. Hunter was an undisputed badass—a
decorated Special Forces sniper, former DEA agent, ex-con.
He now worked as a SWAT sniper for the Denver PD. Rossiter was a former park ranger and paramedic who'd made a
name for himself in the world of extreme sports. Both were
married—a fact that had made Zach more willing to tolerate
their territorial attitude where Natalie was concerned.

You should be glad they're so protective of her.

Yes, he supposed he should be. But why did they seem to
think they had to protect her from *him*? Hadn't he just saved
her life?

"McBride." Hunter reached out his hand. "I just wanted to
thank you for all you did to help Natalie. When we heard the
Zetas had her, we thought we'd never see her again."

Zach took Hunter's hand, gave as firm a shake as he got.
"She deserves a lot of credit for that. She had to help me
escape before I could help her."

Rossiter stuck out his hand next. "She's a fighter, but we
know she wouldn't be here without your help. Thank you."

Then it was Joaquin's turn. He held out his hand, his emotions plain on his face. "I never would have been able to forgive myself if she'd been hurt. Thank you for doing what I couldn't do. Thanks for keeping her safe."

Zach knew it had been hard for Joaquin to say this. It would be hard for any man. "She never blamed you for what the Zetas did, and neither should you."

Joaquin nodded. "I tell myself that, but . . ."

An awkward silence filled the space between them.

"It was good to meet you all. I've got a plane to catch first thing in the morning." Zach turned to go, then stopped and looked back. "Natalie is a special woman. I'm glad she has such good friends. Take care of her."

"Oh, we will. Don't you doubt it." Hunter crossed his arms over his chest. "And while we're on the subject, we know your relationship with her crossed a line. We were there for about an hour before we moved up the hill."

It took a second for Hunter's meaning to sink in.

Son of a bitch.

That right there explained the territorial attitude.

Zach turned and faced Hunter head-on. "Natalie's well past the age of consent. She's smart enough to know what she wants—and whom."

Rossiter shook his head. "She'd just been through hell and was completely dependent on you for her life. A woman in that situation is bound to be vulnerable and easy to manipulate. You should've kept your pants on until you—"

Zach's temper flashed white-hot. "If you're suggesting that she was coerced in some way, then you don't know her very well. In fact, I'd be willing to bet that I know her better than you do at this point. If you all care so much about her, then why do none of you have a clue what happened to her during Hurricane Katrina?"

The three men stared at him, blinked.

Then as abruptly as it had come, Zach's anger faded. "I'd appreciate it if you didn't mention what you saw out there to anyone. Be gentlemen and keep it to yourselves."

Joaquin glared at him. "Like you were a gentleman?"

He has a point, man.

Hunter put a restraining hand on Joaquin's shoulder. "No

need to worry on that account, McBride. I'm not even going to tell my wife, because if I do . . . Well, let's just say that the I-Team women have a way of sharing one another's secrets."

Rossiter cleared his throat. "Kat knows, but she'll keep it to herself. She's that way."

Zach met each man's gaze in turn. "Thanks. I care about Natalie more than you know."

Then, feeling hollow, he turned and walked away.

CHAPTER 20

FRESH FROM A long, hot shower, Natalie finished drying her hair then slipped into the nightgown Zach had bought for her.

She hadn't known he'd packed her clothes until she'd come back to her room and found them sitting on her bed, a bit wrinkled but otherwise brand-new. To think that he had carried these things all the way from Altar . . .

At least she would have this reminder of him.

Fighting a looming sense of depression, she brushed her teeth, then drew down the covers. Emotionally exhausted but not sleepy, she was about to switch on the television, when someone knocked on the door. She stood, stared at the door, afraid to open it, afraid he'd come to say good-bye.

You can't just leave him standing there.

Pulse tripping, she crossed the room and opened the door. "Kat!"

"I hope I'm not bothering you."

"Don't be silly. It's so good to see you!" And it was.

They drew together in a tight hug, then sat on the bed like girls at a high school slumber party, Natalie in her nightgown, Kat in a red broomstick skirt and a white blouse, her long, dark hair pulled back in a silver barrette. But the topic of their conversation was much more sinister than anything Natalie could have imagined as a teenager.

She told Kat what had happened from the moment the bus

was attacked to the arrival of the Shadow Wolves, leaving out only the intimate details of her relationship with Zach. But sharing her story with Kat was different than sharing it with Agent Chiago. Giving a deposition was all about facts. This was about feelings, too.

By the time she finished, they were both in tears, a box of tissues sitting on the bed between them.

"When Julian told us that we probably wouldn't see you again, I thought I was going to throw up." Kat wiped tears from her cheeks. "I'm ashamed to say it, but I tried not to think about what they might be doing to you because I couldn't stand it. I prayed for you every day. We held a special sweat lodge to pray for you."

"Thank you." Natalie gave Kat's hand a squeeze, more touched than she could convey. "And thank you for cracking Zach's code. I had no idea what I was saying when I read that over the phone."

"Zach must be a very special man to do all that he did for you. Gabe tells me he's a former Navy SEAL, a Medal of Honor recipient, and a deputy U.S. marshal."

Natalie couldn't help but smile, a bittersweet ache in her chest. "He's . . . incredible. The pain he endured, the way he watched out for me, his ability to strategize, even the way he moves—I've never seen anyone who can do what he does. He put his life on the line for me."

"You did the same for him." Kat gave her hand a squeeze. "Breaking out of that filthy, infested cell, beating the heck out of that Zeta guard, setting Zach free when you could have left him behind—that was incredibly brave, too, you know."

Coming from Kat, this felt to Natalie like a great compliment.

"Zach is the brave one. What they put him through . . . If you had heard his screams . . ." She shuddered. "I only met him five days ago, but it feels like so much longer than that. Now he's going back to his life, and I'm going back to mine. And I'm going to miss him."

"You care about him. I can tell."

And then Natalie could keep it to herself no longer. "I . . . I had sex with him."

Strangely, Kat didn't seem surprised by this revelation.

Maybe it was obvious. Then again, Kat was very good at reading people.

Natalie went on. "Being with him is . . . amazing. But now he's leaving. And that really stinks because I didn't think I could even have feelings for a man."

Kat looked at her, puzzled. "What do you mean?"

"I was engaged once."

Telling Zach about Beau must have opened up something inside her. She found herself telling Kat about her life before the storm and how Beau and her parents had died and why, tears spilling down her cheeks.

"I loved Beau so much, Kat. For six years, I've spent every moment of my life missing him. And some part of me feels guilty not because I had sex with Zach, but because it didn't make me think of Beau. I want to move on with my life. I want to have love again. But I don't want to forget Beau."

For a moment, Kat said nothing.

"The Lakota have a special way of dealing with mourning. They spend a year acknowledging their grief, and then they hold a Wiping of the Tears Ceremony so that they can move beyond sadness. You haven't yet wiped away your tears." She picked up a tissue and with great tenderness dabbed Natalie's cheeks. "Moving on and finding love again doesn't mean you have to forget Beau. He will always be there, inside you, in your memories. Moving on only means that you wipe your tears away—and let yourself live and love again."

Natalie had never thought of it quite like that before. "Thank you."

"I'm glad you finally told me what it was that had broken your heart. I knew there was something, but you never talked about it. You're like a sister to me, Natalie. I'm happy I could be here for you." Then she put her hand on her belly and rubbed, and Natalie noticed something she hadn't before.

"Are you . . . Are you pregnant again?"

Kat smiled, nodding. "Thirteen weeks. I haven't said anything. With Tessa having problems, it doesn't seem right."

"Did you plan to have another baby so soon?"

Alissa was only nine months old.

"Gabe and I agreed to go the first ten years of our marriage without using contraception."

"No contraception at all? You could end up with . . . *ten* kids."

"Big families are common among traditional Navajo." Kat smiled, clearly amused by Natalie's surprise. "My grandmother gave birth to twelve children. My mother had eleven. I look at Alissa, and I see both Gabe and myself in her. It's hard to explain, but it feels to me that Gabe and I are truly joined together in her. How could I not want to have lots of children with him when I love him so much?"

"That's a beautiful way of looking at it, though I don't know that I would want to have ten babies even if . . ." And then she remembered.

The condom.

She'd completely forgotten about that the moment the Shadow Wolves had arrived. What if she got pregnant as a result? She started doing mental math, trying to figure out where she was in her cycle.

"What is it? Is something wrong?"

"No. I . . . Well, it's just that—"

There was another knock at the door.

Kat stood, tossing the tissue in the trash. "It's probably Gabe. I told him to come get me when Alissa woke up. She wakes up to nurse at night."

Remembering what she was wearing, Natalie walked to the door and opened it discreetly so that only her head was showing. But it wasn't Gabe who'd knocked.

It was Zach.

Clean-shaven, his hair still wet, he leaned against the doorjamb wearing a pair of jeans and a black shirt with its sleeves rolled up. He looked in, saw Kat. "Oh. You've got company. I don't want to bother you. I can come back."

He turned to go.

"No, no, it's fine. I was just leaving." Kat held out her hand. "I'm Kat James, Gabe's wife. *Ahéhee'*. Thank you for helping Natalie get home to us. You were the answer to many prayers."

Zach took her hand, looking almost embarrassed by her praise. "Yeah, well, I guess I was in the wrong place at the right time. Thanks for decoding that message. Was it difficult?"

"It was harder than I thought it would be, but I was happy to help. It made me feel like I was doing something. Good night, Natalie. I'm so grateful you're safe." Then Kat gave Natalie another hug and disappeared down the hallway.

His gaze met Natalie's. "Can I come in?"

ZACH COULD SEE she'd been crying. "Are you okay?"

She nodded. "Yes."

Liar.

"I'm sorry I slapped you."

"I probably deserved it." He ran a thumb down one tearstained cheek, his gaze taking in every feature on her sweet face. She looked up at him, both longing and fear in her eyes. The longing he understood. But the fear?

I'm so afraid I'll never see you again after tonight. Don't you dare leave without saying good-bye, Zach McBride.

He'd come to say good-bye—and to give her his contact information at the El Paso Intelligence Center so she could reach him if it turned out he'd gotten her pregnant. But now that he was here, now that he was with her, the words wouldn't come.

This is it, McBride. Say good-bye.

Fuck that.

He still had tonight.

He lifted her into his arms, some primitive part of him gratified by her surprised little gasp, then carried her the few short feet to the bed, lowered her onto the sheets, and stretched himself out above her. He claimed her mouth with his, kissing her with a desperation he'd never felt before, just being close to her dissolving the blackness that had gathered in his chest.

She came alive beneath him, sliding one hand into his hair, melting into him, her tongue carrying the minty taste of toothpaste into his mouth. And, oh, the girl could kiss. Whether it was her Cajun blood, something she'd learned from Beau, or her own special sensuality, she put her whole body into it, her breasts pressing against his chest, her hips undulating beneath him, her lips, her tongue, her teeth teasing him, defying him, forcing him to take control back from her again and again.

He dragged his mouth off hers, out of breath, his body shaking with the urgent need to be inside her. He took off his shirt, felt Natalie's hands slide over his bare chest. Then she reached for his zipper. But this was moving too fast. Too fast.

If all he had was tonight, then he was going to make it last.

He caught her wrists, brought her hands to his lips. "Slow down."

She gave a frustrated, breathless whimper, her lips swollen and wet, her pupils dilated, her hands clenched into fists.

Slowly, his eyes on hers, he drew her arms over her head and pinned them there, the little tremor that ran through her proof that she could handle a little gentle domination—and might even enjoy it.

Just one of the many parts of her you'll never get to explore, McBride.

He forced her onto her belly, then slid down the bed until his knees were on the floor and her feet were before him. He kissed her toes, pressed his lips to her soles, nibbled his way over her slender ankles. Then, pushing the nightgown up to her hips, he moved on to the silk of her newly shaved legs, kissing and nipping her firm calves, the sensitive skin at the back of her knees, her thighs.

He glanced up, saw that her arms were bent at the elbow and tucked in against her sides, her fingers clenching the sheets.

Just wait, angel.

With both hands, he pushed the nightgown up to her waist, the sweet, clean scent of her skin enticing him. He cupped her bare ass, squeezed, his gaze taking everything in. A man could see a lot from behind—the dimples just above her rounded buttocks, the dark cleft between her bare labia, her rosy inner lips just nudging out, begging him to taste her there. And he would.

But not yet.

Natalie shivered, undone by Zach's sensual assault, his lips hot against her derriere, her skin unbelievably sensitive as he kissed, nibbled, nipped, and licked her bottom. He bared her body as he went, his hands sliding over her skin, crumpling the soft silk. Goose bumps rose on her skin, spreading as he worked his way up, kissing and tasting her lower back, the curves of her hips, her rib cage, the length of her spine, her nape, the whorls of her ears.

He drew the nightgown over her head, kissing her shoulders,

her temples, her hair. Then she felt his fingers begin a long, slow glide back down her spine, finding their way between her buttocks to stroke her labia from behind.

A muscular leg encased in blue jeans nudged its way between her knees, forcing them apart. "I need room to work, angel."

She felt his gaze on her there, heard him groan, and knew he was aroused by what he saw. And *that* aroused her even more. He parted her, one hand caressing her bare bottom, the fingers of the other busy between her thighs, stroking her clitoris, playing with her inner lips, teasing her entrance until she was drenched and aching to be filled. But he seemed to be in no hurry to take the ache away.

She bit the sheets, her lower back arching of its own accord, raising her bottom to give him better access, her body begging him to enter. And then, when she thought she could take it no more, he slid two fingers deep inside her, stroking her, driving her out of her mind.

"You're so tight and wet." He whispered to her, his words heightening her arousal. "Your scent—it's like an aphrodisiac."

But just as the pleasure inside her began to crest, he stopped, forced her onto her back, and started all over again, kissing his way up her body, tasting, nipping, licking her scorched skin, suckling her nipples, the ache inside her unbearable. She trembled, her body tensing with each new kiss, her nerve endings overwhelmed by sensation.

Then he rose and stood at the foot of the bed, leaving her naked and burning, his gray eyes gone dark. His gaze on hers, he grabbed her ankles and dragged her toward him, pulling her to the edge of the bed. Her heart began to pound, the need to have him buried inside her overriding all else.

But rather than unzipping his pants, he knelt down, draped her calves over his shoulders, and buried his head between her thighs. Then he ran his tongue over her in one long lick. "You taste like heaven."

Her breath stopped, her entire body tensing, anticipation making her shiver.

"You have no idea how much I've wanted to do this." He lowered his mouth to her and groaned, his clever tongue finding her clitoris, his lips drawing the entire bud into his mouth.

And Natalie was lost.

She gave herself over to him, pleasure coiling deep in her belly as he licked her, nipped her, sucked her labia into his mouth, his fingers working magic inside her. She'd already been on the brink, this new onslaught of sensation pushing her right back to that golden edge. It was sweet, so sweet, hanging on the brink like this, nothing in her world but him and what he made her feel.

Little moans rolled from her throat with each exhalation, her fingers now clenched in his damp hair, her knees drawn back, the need to open herself for him, to give herself to him, instinctual. It felt so good, so incredibly good, pleasure twisting itself tighter and tighter inside her, a tense, shimmering knot. And then it broke.

She cried out, orgasm singing through her, sweet silver notes of bliss carrying her skyward, then leaving her to float in honeyed stillness.

Zach inhaled her musky scent, let it fill his head, her taste on his lips and tongue. He tried to memorize both, wanting to remember, wanting to carry something of her with him. He'd told himself that once life got back to normal and he was back at EPIC working the line again, his crazy need for her would fade and he would stop wanting her. But that was a damned lie. What he felt for her, it was . . .

He stopped himself, unable to go there. He was with her, and that was enough.

Natalie.

She was still now, her breathing deep and even, her face relaxed. Then, as if she knew he was watching, she opened her eyes and reached for him.

He stood, shucked his jeans and boxer briefs, and went to her, drawing her into the center of the bed. He settled himself between her thighs, brushed his lips over hers. "I didn't plan this. I don't have a condom with me."

"The last one broke anyway." She reached down, took his cock in her hand, and guided him to her.

His gaze locked with hers, he nudged himself into her, the shock of being inside her surging upward from his balls to his brain, making his mind go blank. She was hot and slick from her own orgasm, her muscles gripping him like a fist. He gave her a second to get used to him—or he tried to. But instinct was driving him to thrust, to pound himself into her, to go as hard and deep as he could.

Make it last, McBride.

He willed his body to relax, tried to sink into an easy rhythm, but she felt so good, her hips rising to meet his, her body arching upward, her throaty moans urging him on. Her hands slid up his biceps and over his shoulders, exploring his muscles, kneading them, testing them. Then she murmured his name and wrapped her arms around him, drawing his full weight down against her.

Natalie, sweet Natalie.

Skin against soft skin. A clash of lips and tongues. Hands seeking and caressing. She was everything he wanted. She was everything he couldn't have. But tonight . . . Right now . . . Here in this room, she was his.

God, she felt good. He'd stay like this forever if he could. Hell, yeah, he would. He'd stay right here inside this room, inside her, until her friends knocked down the door and shot him, until he starved to death, until hell froze over and melted again. But his male physiology wouldn't cooperate, his balls drawing tight, the first crest of an orgasm drawing near.

He shifted his position, riding her high, grinding against her with his pelvic bone and the root of his cock, trying to slow himself down, wanting to draw it out for both of them. He felt her tense, her breath coming in shudders, the tension building inside her, her nails digging into his skin. He kept the rhythm steady, refusing to rush her, giving her all the time she needed.

Her eyes went wide for a second. "Oh!"

Then she squeezed them shut, her head going back on a cry, her inner muscles contracting around him, delight shining on her beautiful face. And then . . .

Tears?

They slid from the corners of her eyes, down her temples. But he was too far gone now.

Shifting positions, he drove himself into her fast and deep and hard, his hips a piston. He couldn't stop himself, couldn't think, could only feel, her hands on his skin, her lips on his throat, her vagina gripping him, stroking him, sending him over the edge.

And then he could hold out no more. "Oh, angel, you're so . . ."

At the last second, he withdrew, but rather than coming into the cold and empty air, he felt her hand close around him. He groaned, the force of his release shaking him apart as he thrust into her fist once, twice, three times, spilling himself on her belly.

His head dropped to rest between her breasts as he caught his breath, her fingers sliding lazily through his hair. Then, contented down to his very soul, he kissed her tears away.

CHAPTER 21

THEY MADE LOVE twice more—again on the bed and then in the shower. Natalie wanted the night to last forever, but soon it was four in the morning and then six, time unstoppable, minutes slipping away, the sun already up.

She snuggled against his chest, running her fingers through his chest hair, savoring the scent and feel of him, knowing that the magic spell that had bound them together all night would soon be broken and that he would rise, dress, kiss her—and then walk out of her life.

How strange it was that a week ago she hadn't even known this man. She'd been a ghost then, drifting, hollow, numb. Then Zach had spoken to her out of the darkness, saving her, making her *feel* again, bringing her back to life. And now he was going to leave her world as abruptly as he'd entered it. What she didn't understand was *why*.

It had made sense when he'd been Zach Black the criminal. He'd told her that his life wasn't the kind a man shared with a woman. She'd taken that to mean that he was mixed up in bad things, dangerous things that could get him and those close to him hurt. And perhaps that is what he'd meant. Except that he was on the *right* side of the law.

He stroked her shoulder lazily with his thumb. "What are you thinking? There's a frown on your pretty face."

She wasn't sure she wanted to tell him, afraid her words

would spoil whatever was left of their time together. "I was thinking how much I'm going to miss you."

He kissed her hair and for a while said nothing.

Then at last he spoke. "Five days ago, I was ready to die. I was down to my last twenty-four hours, and I was ready to die. There was so much at stake—the whole operation. If the Zetas had known who and what I was . . . I was so afraid my mind would break before my body gave out. And then you were there, and everything changed. These past few days with you have been . . . There's no woman on earth like you, Natalie."

His words gave her hope.

She decided to risk it. "Back when I thought you were a criminal, I understood why we couldn't be together. But now that I know the truth . . . If we're both going to miss each other, why can't we keep seeing each other?"

He turned onto his side to face her, his gaze level with hers, one hand cupping her cheek. "It's not because I don't care about you, Natalie. It just wouldn't work. It wouldn't be fair to you. You deserve to have a man who can truly be a part of your life, someone who comes home for dinner every night, who has time to play with the kids, who can grow old with you. I'm not that man."

She could see in his eyes that he believed what he said. "Being a deputy U.S. marshal doesn't mean you don't get to have a life."

That did it.

He turned away from her, sat up, put his feet on the carpeted floor. "This *is* my life, Natalie. I spend most of my days south of the line. I'm rarely home. When I am, it's just to sleep, shower, refuel, and reload."

She slid her hand up his back and sat up, draping her arm over his shoulder to caress his chest, her chin perched on his shoulder. "Lots of women have husbands who work long hours. Women whose men are in the military go months—"

"It's not just that I'm gone all the time." He took a deep breath, as if steeling himself. "Another DUSM, a guy who'd worked the line for a dozen years, disappeared a couple years ago. Somehow his cover was blown. Do you know what the cartels did to him? They butchered him and left his face—just his face—in a goddamned pizza box on his family's front porch. His six-year-old son found it."

"Oh, God!" Natalie felt her empty stomach drop.

Zach turned to face her, his gaze hard, his jaw tight. "I know what happens to women and kids when their husbands and fathers are killed in action or go MIA. I won't do that to any woman, most especially not one who matters to me."

"Well, if your job is so damned dangerous, why don't you do something else?"

He laughed, shook his head. "Leave it to you to ask the tough questions."

Then he stood, still naked, and began searching for his clothes. "I tried being a regular civilian. I tried for nine long months. It didn't work."

"*Tried* being a civilian? What does that mean?"

Zach looked over at Natalie, wondering how they'd gotten onto this topic in the first place. He so did *not* want to go here.

"Some men come home from combat." He slid into his boxer briefs, adjusted himself, then reached for his pants. "I . . . I can't."

That's really all there was to it.

"I don't understand."

Of course, she didn't.

He zipped his fly, looked up to see her shimmying into her nightgown, paradise vanishing behind a film of silk.

You must be out of your fucking mind to walk away from her, McBride.

Maybe. But it would be worse for her if he stayed.

"There's something inside of me—it just doesn't work. I went away to war, but I can't seem to come back. I do all right out there where the adrenaline is high and the rules of engagement are clear—shoot to kill. But in the civilian world . . . You know what I spent those nine months doing? Drinking scotch and trying to get up the guts to eat my gun."

"Oh, Zach. I'm so sorry."

He couldn't meet her gaze, a tight feeling in his chest. He'd never talked to anyone about this outside of the VA, and it made him feel like a fucking weak loser to admit it to her. But after what she'd done for him, she deserved the truth.

"If I left the service and we started dating, you'd look at

me one day and wonder who in the hell I was, this pathetic *loser* who spends his days drunk and his nights in a cold sweat. Staying in the fight is the only way I know how to keep it together."

She crossed the distance between them and pressed her hand to his bare chest, her voice soft. "That's PTSD. I had to deal with it after the storm. But they can treat—"

He drew back, slipped his shirt over his head. "Yeah, they can treat it—with therapy where I talk to someone who really doesn't give a damn about what a weak piece of shit I am—"

"You are *not* a weak piece of shit. Don't even say—"

"—or with pills that dull my mind and leave my dick limp. But that's not curing it. I was a SEAL, for God's sake. I'm supposed to be one of the strong ones, not a guy who falls the fuck apart. At least this way, I do the world some good. I was there when you needed me, wasn't I?"

"Yes, you were." She stood there, all silk, sad eyes, and tousled hair, her arms hugged around herself. "After I saved your butt."

Caught off guard by her smart mouth, he chuckled. Then he drew a deep breath, not wanting this to end with anger, his insides in knots because of what he'd revealed to her—and because he didn't want to leave.

He reached for the complimentary pad of paper and pen that sat by the phone in every hotel room, and wrote down his contact info at EPIC and in Washington, D.C. He handed it to her. "Here's how you can reach me. If I've gotten you pregnant, I want to know. I'll support whatever you decide to do. You won't lack for money."

She looked up at him, her chin lifting. "I have money. My parents were wealthy, and I was their only child. If money is your only concern, then don't worry about it. I'll be fine."

He didn't like the way that sounded. "Whether you need my help or not, I have a right to know, Natalie."

Her gaze dropped to the floor. "If it turns out I'm pregnant, I will let you know."

And now it was time to say what he hadn't been able to say last night. Somehow the intervening hours hadn't made it any easier. He should never have let things cross the sexual line. It only made it harder for both of them.

He reached out, ran a knuckle over her cheek. "I'm sorry. I don't want hurt you. I never wanted that. These past few days with you . . . They meant something to me. You're the most amazing woman I've ever met. I won't forget you, Natalie."

She reached up, caught his hand, pressed it to her lips, then looked at him through eyes that shimmered. "I won't forget you either."

Regret cut razor-sharp into his chest at the sight of her distress. She was struggling with this as much as he was. For a moment, they stood in silence, fingers entwined.

"I'm going to find Cárdenas, and I'm going to bring him and his Zetas down. I promise you that." He probably shouldn't have told her that—mission secrecy and all.

She shook her head. "Promise me instead that you won't get hurt or killed."

He couldn't promise that, so he said nothing. "Good-bye, angel."

"Good-bye, Zach Black." Her voice quavered, her lips curving in a tremulous smile. "Watch your back. I might not be there next time to save you."

"Yes, ma'am." He gave her hand one last squeeze, then turned and walked away, her fingers releasing his one at a time, until his hand was empty.

THE TRIP BACK to Denver took a lot less time than Natalie had imagined. She packed her belongings in Kat's luggage, since hers had been in her hotel room in Juárez when she'd been taken. Then Agent Chiago drove her and her friends to the small Sells airport, where she thanked him with a kiss on his cheek.

He grinned, his eyes hidden behind Ray-Bans. "We were just doing our job. I hope you'll come visit the reservation again, Ms. Benoit, but under better circumstances. We have a lot we're proud of here in our operation."

From Sells she and the others were flown by helicopter to the Tucson International Airport, where a small private jet waited to carry them back to Denver.

As she climbed on board, Natalie was amazed at what her friends had done for her. She took a seat, feeling more like she was sitting in someone's living room than on a plane. "Thanks for arranging all of this. It's incredible."

They all stared at her.

"We can't take credit for this. How much do you think they're paying cops these days, anyway?" Marc sat and stretched out his long legs. "McBride set it up."

Gabe sat across from her. "He wants to keep the fact that you're back a secret until you're farther away from the border."

"Oh." She remembered him saying something about a media blackout when the Shadow Wolves found them. But a chartered jet? A helicopter ride?

"Got enough leg room there, Rossiter?" Marc asked.

"You bet. If not, I'll just make use of the overhead bin."

Kat shook her head, sharing a glance with Natalie, Alissa asleep in her lap.

But Natalie barely noticed the good-natured male ribbing, her gaze traveling over the luxurious cabin.

Then the flight attendant, a young woman about Natalie's age, came to offer them drinks. "We heard there was a special request for southern sweet tea. We've brewed some up just for this flight. Who asked for that?"

Stunned, Natalie could only stare. Then she swallowed the lump in her throat. "I . . . I did. Thank you very much."

The flight attendant took everyone's order, then returned with a cart of drinks including a big glass brimming with iced tea just the way Natalie's mother had made it—black pekoe with real sugar, not a lemon in sight.

Natalie sipped and savored, her eyes pricking with tears.

Thank you, Zach. Thank you so much. For everything.

She looked up to find her friends watching her. She tried to explain. "When we were in the desert, I got sick of that lemon electrolyte stuff and told him how much I wished I could have a big glass of real southern sweet tea."

Kat gave her a reassuring smile, and Natalie could see she understood.

"Yeah, I got sick of that lemon stuff, too." Marc made a sour face. "We drank that in Afghanistan and Iraq. Saves lives, but it tastes like shit."

Gabe made a "blech" sound. "That lemon stuff is obnoxious."

Marc looked over at him. "What do you know about the lemon stuff? You weren't in desert combat. You were a park ranger. I'm not dissing that. It's an important job. Someone has to keep the chipmunks in line. I've watched *Chip and Dale*. I know how sneaky those little bastards can be."

Gabe glared at Marc. "For your information, Hunter, I've climbed in the desert, done some mountain biking and canyoneering, and we drink the lemon shit."

Kat met Natalie's gaze again. "How long is this flight?"

Natalie savored her tea and tried to be cheerful. Everyone else was in high spirits because they were bringing her home again. And God only knew she was happy and grateful beyond words to be alive and on her way home. She had so much for which to be thankful.

But saying good-bye to Zach was one of the hardest things she'd ever had to do. It wasn't hard in a "beat the Zeta on the skull" sort of way or a "trek across the desert" kind of way. It had been hard on the most fragile part of her—her heart.

It had taken more strength that she'd realized she had not to cry when he'd walked away. He'd brought her back to life, showed her what it was to feel again. It hadn't seemed possible that he would leave her. She'd known that if she opened her mouth, something desperate and completely undignified would come out. So she'd stood there in silence and watched him go, her heart breaking—not just for herself, but also for the man who'd come home from one war only to find himself trapped in another, much more personal battle.

I'm supposed to be one of the strong ones, not a guy who falls the fuck apart.

Whatever had happened in the war had scarred him deeply. She'd seen herself how terrible his nightmares could be. He was trying so hard to be strong that he didn't even believe he deserved help. But did he really think that chasing men like Cárdenas could keep his demons from catching up with him?

At least this way, I do the world some good.

Oh, Zach!

They arrived in Denver shortly after noon. With no need to go through baggage claim, they went straight to ground transportation. Natalie didn't have her keys—God only knew where her purse had ended up—so she had to leave her car at the airport, riding with Kat and Gabe because her things were in Kat's suitcase.

They drove her home first. She retrieved the extra house key she kept hidden under a flowerpot and waited with Kat in the car while Gabe went inside to check her house.

She found everything just as she'd left it. The plants on the windowsill. The coffee mug she'd put in the sink the morning of her departure. That day's copy of the paper with a typo circled in red. There was no sign that the life of the person who lived here had just been turned upside down.

She carried Kat's suitcase up to her room, took her things out, and was about to come back downstairs when her gaze fell on the framed photo of Beau she kept on her nightstand. It was the last picture she'd taken of him, though of course she hadn't known that at the time. He was sitting on the beach at Waveland in Mississippi, hair wet, sand on his skin, a big smile on his face. She reached for the photo, studied it, then held it against her chest.

"He was good to me, Beau. He saved my life. You would like him."

She missed Zach so much already.

She set the photo down, ran her finger over Beau's image, then walked down the stairs, Kat's suitcase in hand. She found Gabe outside facing down two men on her walkway, one of whom carried her purse and luggage.

Gabe blocked their path. "You're not taking another step until I know who you are and what you want."

The men stopped, and one pulled out a badge. "I'm Deputy U.S. Marshal Larry Garrett and this is Frank Dearborn from the U.S. State Department. We're here to speak with Ms. Benoit and to return her belongings."

ZACH GOT ANOTHER cup of godawful coffee from the vending machine, this day stretching on forever. He'd gotten to D.C. around noon, and it had been a fun ride ever since. He'd been questioned twice. He'd been examined by a doctor, who'd treated his wrists, drawn blood, and X-rayed his ribs. And he was about meet with Pearce.

Something wasn't right. It wasn't what they were doing so

much as how they were doing it. Questioning him was just standard operating procedure, but they were treating him as if they believed he was crooked. He could see it in their eyes, feel it in the way they spoke to him. And for the life of him, he couldn't figure out why.

The door to Pearce's office opened, and two suits from the State Department stepped out, their gazes cold as they walked past Zach.

"McBride." Pearce stuck his head out of his office and motioned Zach inside.

In his midfifties, John Pearce had the look of a man who spent too much time behind a desk—gray hair, paunchy, ruddy complexion. Like everyone else in the political cesspool of Washington, D.C., he wore a suit and tie and enjoyed playing the game. But he'd always backed Zach up in the past, and he'd been a damned good marshal in his day.

"I've read the reports and depositions. I've listened to the audio. I've read the doctor's file. Sorry to hear about the broken ribs and the wrists." Pearce looked at him through pale blue eyes that gave away nothing. "You're damned lucky to be alive."

Zach couldn't argue with that.

"Here's the situation from our point of view." Pearce leaned back in his chair. "Gisella calls in to say you disappeared with cocaine you stole from the Zetas and tells us she's afraid for her life. Ten days later you reappear—with a high-profile kidnapping victim in tow—and claim that Gisella stole the coke and betrayed you to the Zetas. That's quite a story."

"Yes, sir, it is. It's also the truth."

"Here's the kicker. Two days ago, Interpol lost contact with Gisella. Yesterday, the *federales* found her body—or some identifiable pieces of it—in the middle of the street in downtown Juárez."

That explained the looks he'd been getting all day. Gisella had tried to cover for herself by implicating him—and now she was dead. Which only made him look worse.

"Cárdenas must have realized she'd deceived him and gone after her."

"You had no idea she was dead?" Pearce leveled his gaze at Zach.

"No. Of course, I didn't. At the time I was in the middle of the desert."

"It's damned lucky for you that you've got an alibi—and a very credible witness." Pearce frowned. "About this Benoit woman—do you think she'll be a problem?"

"What do you mean?"

"We sent the Denver guys in today to clarify for her and her editor what they may and may not print regarding you and her rescue. I'm wondering if she'll cooperate."

"She won't do anything that would endanger me or other DUSMs. I feel certain of that. She's not a headline chasing sort of reporter. You just need to explain it to her—and be ready to answer a lot of questions."

Pearce nodded. "I have to say this whole thing is likely to turn into an international shit storm. The Mexican government is already accusing us of ignoring their national sovereignty by deploying a black ops team within their borders to rescue Benoit without their permission, so the State Department's panties are in a twist."

Zach laughed. Black ops team? "That 'black ops team' was one half-dead DUSM and a young female reporter with a strong will to survive."

"Interpol thinks you stole the cocaine, arranged to have Gisella killed after she found out, and then got snagged by the Zetas."

Zach felt his temper spike. "And what do you think?"

"I believe you, of course, but we want the matter investigated thoroughly before you head back out on assignment again."

That had Zach on his feet. "What the hell does that mean?"

"Sit down, McBride. It's not all that bad. I'm sure it will be sorted out in the end. But in the meantime, you're being placed on paid administrative leave. You're not to leave D.C. until the investigation is concluded."

Great. "And how long will that take?"

Pearce shrugged. "A couple of weeks. A month."

A month was a long time to be doing nothing. Too long.

"It will give you time to recuperate from those broken ribs and rest up a bit."

Zach took a breath, trying to keep his temper in check. "Yeah. And in the meantime, Cárdenas—"

"Is not your problem. Come back tomorrow, and we'll pick up where we left off."

And Zach realized he'd been dismissed. He stood, walked toward the door.

"McBride, remember what my mother always said."

Zach looked back. "And what was that?"

"No good deed goes unpunished."

CHAPTER 22

THE NEXT MORNING, Natalie awoke to find a throng of reporters camped in front of her house and on her lawn, her driveway blocked by a Fox News van. The package of articles that Tom and Sophie had put together about her kidnapping and rescue had gone up on the Internet last night and was the focus of today's front page.

But Natalie had given all the interviews she was going to give. Tom and Sophie had interviewed her for most of yesterday afternoon, respecting the boundaries she'd put in place on the advice of Officer Garrett, to protect Zach. She didn't want anything she said to get him or any other DUSM hurt or killed.

Reliving the story, recounting the slaughter on the bus and the horror of being held captive by the Zetas, had left her shaken, making it hard to sleep last night. There was no chance she was going to open herself to that again. Besides, the focus ought to be on the journalists who'd been murdered, not the one who got away.

Ignoring the knocks on her door, she got dressed for work—a shirtdress of ruffled navy blue silk, pearl earrings, and navy pumps, then walked outside onto her front porch, where she read a statement, thanking people for their concern and prayers, expressing her gratitude to the U.S. and Mexican governments for their efforts to find her and ending with a special thank-you to the man who risked his life to save hers.

"Words will never fully express my gratitude for all you

did to get me safely home," she said, trying to stop the shaking of her voice. Then she looked straight into the CNN camera, hoping Zach would see it. "You are my hero."

Being on the other end of the microphone was more intimidating than she'd imagined, flashes like strobe lights, microphones and digital recorders mere inches from her face, the press of so many people on her property unnerving.

In the end, she called Kat who called Tessa who called Julian, who came to get her in an unmarked police car, clearing her driveway with flashing lights and a few blasts from his siren and pulling into her empty garage.

"How are you holding up?" he asked when she climbed into the car, his eyes hidden behind sunglasses, his long dark hair pulled back in a ponytail.

"Okay, I think."

He reached over, put a hand on her arm. "I read the articles, heard what Hunter and Rossiter had to say, and I'm blown away by what you did—Natalie the Ninja. And this McBride, too. The man knows his shit. I wasn't able to come to Arizona, but I've got your back here. If you need anything, you call me."

She gave him a smile. "Thanks, Julian. That's very kind of you."

He backed out of the driveway, tinted windows giving her some privacy as reporters moved in with cameras. Then he drove her to the airport, staying nearby while she picked up her car, then followed her back into the city, flashing his lights in farewell.

She had to wade through a crowd of reporters in front of the paper, then entered the building to the sound of applause, coworkers she didn't even know cheering as she made her way across the lobby to the elevator. Upstairs, the newsroom was filled with balloons and streamers, a bouquet of flowers at her desk along with dozens and dozens of cards mailed from all over the United States by people who'd heard of her kidnapping and had written to the paper, offering comfort, prayers, and even condolences, assuming that she was dead.

"We set them here because we told ourselves you would make it back to read them. And here you are." Sophie gave her a big hug, tears in her eyes. "I can't tell you how relieved we all were when Marc called and told me they'd found you."

"Thank you all so much for your help—and for this." She gestured toward the flowers.

Joaquin came up behind them. "I got something for you, Natalie. I drove all the way to Lakewood and back for these."

Natalie turned and saw him holding a large paper bag that had several grease spots on it. She didn't have to open the bag to know what it was. She recognized the mouthwatering scent. She'd been trying to find good beignets in Denver ever since she'd moved here. "Thank you, Joaquin. Where on God's green earth did you find these?"

"Went online, found a little Cajun restaurant in Lakewood off Union." He kissed her cheek. "I'm just so happy you're home."

"Beignets. That's a kind of Cajun fry bread, right?" Kat's smile let Natalie know she was joking. She knew what beignets were. "They smell wonderful."

"Excellent." Matt peered over the desk, a predatory look on his face. "I didn't have time for breakfast."

They sat together, enjoying the beignets with coffee, the conversation taking random turns. The Rockies' latest victory over the Dodgers. The new appliances Sophie and Marc had bought for their new house. The upcoming Quinceañera of Joaquin's oldest niece. The Denver metro area's current heat wave.

"You think this is hot?" Natalie shook her head. "Try the Sonoran Desert."

She found herself overcome by the strangeness of this ordinary moment—to be sitting here, drinking coffee and eating pastries with her friends when just a few days ago she'd thought she'd never see them again.

Then Holly came down the hallway wearing a fitted short suit—jacket, cream-colored silk top, shorts, strappy high heels, bright stripes of yellow eye shadow on her lids. She was the only woman Natalie knew who could pull off high-fashion clothes and makeup. Her flawless figure, striking face, and platinum blond hair helped, of course.

"You're back!" She skipped over to Natalie and gave her a hug. "I read the interview this morning. All I can say is— God, that smells good!"

"Please, try one," Natalie offered. "They're beignets. We

had these for breakfast every Sunday morning when I was a child."

Holly backed away, warily eyeing the beignets. "I can't. I can't."

"Oh, come on, Bradshaw." Matt put one on a paper plate and held it out for her. "One beignet won't make you fat."

Holly hesitated for a moment, then took the plate, picked up the powdered sugar–coated pastry, took a tiny bite —and moaned.

Then everyone's head came up, and Matt, who'd been half sitting on Natalie's desk, got to his feet. Natalie turned to see Tom walking toward them.

"Welcome back, Benoit. Let's bring the goodies to the conference room so we can get our meeting under way."

ZACH SAT IN one of the back conference rooms watching CNN, having just finished another so-called debriefing. No matter what channel he watched, she was there. She looked amazing for someone who'd been in the middle of the desert only yesterday evening—pretty dress, cute pearl earrings, calm, composed features. But he could tell she'd been nervous when she'd given her statement this morning.

He was so caught up in her face that it took him a moment to realize she was talking directly to him at the end.

"Words will never fully express my gratitude for all you did to get me safely home. You are my hero."

He was nobody's fucking hero.

He changed channels. Fox. MSNBC. The local news. But there she was again, looking directly into the camera, those beautiful eyes of hers gazing into his.

"You are my hero."

God, how he missed her. He'd had a nightmare about her last night—the same nightmare he'd had when they were at the hotel in Altar. He'd woken up covered in cold sweat. He'd started in on a bottle of whiskey, but then decided to go to the twenty-four-hour gym, where he'd worked out until his ribs ached and he'd been ready to puke.

Now, punchy on lack of sleep, he was back for a second day of answering questions, doing all he could to cooperate with the investigation. He wished he knew how it was progressing, but no one was telling him anything, not even Pearce.

"Zachariah?"

Fuck.

Zach recognized that voice. He switched off the television set, stood, and turned to face his old man. "What the hell do you want?"

It had been four years since he'd last seen his father face-to-face. But time had been good to the bastard. He stood there in a three-thousand-dollar suit, looking like an older and better dressed version of Zach, the resemblance undeniable. Though his hair was whiter than Zach remembered, the man looked strong and healthy as an ox.

He fidgeted with his tie. Was he nervous? That would be a first. "I heard what happened—how you were captured and almost killed, how you escaped and rescued that girl."

"That *girl* rescued me. And how do you know anything about this? Some of that information is classified."

His father gave him a wounded look. "You don't think I have my sources after thirty years of working inside the Beltway? I'm the ranking member of the Senate Armed Services Committee."

As arrogant as ever.

"So you heard what happened, and you came by to tell me how glad you are I wasn't killed. Is that it?"

"Partly. I also know you're being investigated, that some of the people here think you might have stolen cocaine from one of the cartels and murdered an Interpol agent."

Now it made sense.

"I can see why there are no reporters with you this time. Your son is in trouble. How embarrassing. And by the way, that really is classified."

"You're my son. My sources knew I'd want to hear about it."

Zach crossed his arms over his chest. "I suppose you're worried about how this might look in the media if word gets out that Senator Robert McBride's son was exposed as a crook. Well, you can relax, because I'm clean."

"That's not it at all." His father's voice rose a notch, the old man's temper kicking in. "I know you're innocent. I came to see if I could help in any way, cut through some of the red tape, help make sure the process goes smoothly."

And Zach felt his own temper rise. "You just don't get it, do you? You really believe that your elected position gives you rights the rest of America just doesn't have. Forget it. I don't need your help. I don't want your help. Justice will take its course. I trust the agency I work for to get to the truth."

"I've never understood you. You don't think that fathers out there everywhere do all they can to help their kids get ahead in this life? You think I'm the only one who tries to pave the road for my son?"

"You don't just pave the road. You manipulate someone into moving it so that it comes to my front door. Being a U.S. senator's son shouldn't mean that I get to live by a special set of rules. You're charged with making the laws. You need to respect them *more* than the average person, not less."

They'd been arguing about this since 9/11, when Zach had walked into the living room to overhear his father tell his mother that their son would never have to serve in the military because he was a U.S. senator's son. It had been the last straw after years of watching his father wade through one scandal after another. In disgust, Zach had joined the navy and applied for Officer Candidate School the next day.

His father shook his head. "You know, I thought maybe you'd matured enough—"

"Matured? Go to hell!"

"—so that we could have an honest conversation, maybe spend some time together. But you're just as pigheaded and unreasonable as you've always been. You know, your mother understood—"

"Don't you bring her into this!" Zach was in his father's face now, blood pumping hot in his veins. "My mother was an idealist who believed in everything she thought you stood for. It literally *killed* her to watch you turn into a crook. All your sleazy mistresses. The money you blew on—"

The blow took Zach by surprise. He rubbed his jaw, looked his father in the eye. "You better get the hell out of here, old man. If I hit back, it's going to hurt."

"I'm sorry! I'm sorry, Zach. I don't know what made me

do that. I've missed you. I came here to make amends, to help—"

"I said get the hell out of here. *Now.*"

His father turned and, with an angry look over his shoulder, stomped off.

Jaw aching, Zach sank into a chair and buried his face in his hands.

The moment Arturo heard the voice on the other end of the line, he broke into a sweat, beads of perspiration gathering on his forehead and upper lip.

"Are you watching the news?"

"*Sí.* Yes, I am. And I can explain—"

"Explanations are irrelevant. Besides, it's obvious what happened. You wanted her for your perverted little rituals, so rather than instructing your men to put a bullet through her head on the bus, you had them take her captive. Isn't that right?"

How dare this gringo speak of La Santa Muerte as if she were a perversion?

"*Sí.* I had them take her captive. I wanted to see the woman who was so dangerous that she frightened you."

"That was a grave mistake. We asked you to do something for us, and you agreed to do it. Board the bus, and kill her, along with the Mexican journalists. It would look like just another act of cartel-related violence. No one would think twice about it.

"But now, somehow, she's back in the United States, very much alive. That's very disappointing, Arturo. Very disappointing."

Arturo swallowed—hard. "I am sorry. She had help. A shipment of cocaine was stolen, and we caught the man who—"

"He didn't steal the cocaine, you imbecile. The woman you cut up and tossed in the street stole it. Or hadn't you figured that out yet?"

"She stole it?"

"Yes. Gisella Sanchez worked for Interpol. And that man you chained up wasn't a drug pusher. He's a deputy U.S. marshal and former Navy SEAL—a war hero no less. That pretty reporter you planned to rape—she turned out to be a lot tougher than she looked, too. She's the one who broke them out. You probably assumed it was the man, didn't you? That's what you get for being a chauvinist bastard."

Arturo heard all this, but only one part connected.

"U.S. marshal? SEAL? How do you know all of this?" His heart was beating so hard it hurt. Was he having a heart attack?

"That doesn't matter. You fucked up, Arturo."

"I can fix it. I will send my best man to Denver to—"

"No, Arturo, we don't trust you. Your incompetence sickens us. So we're going to take care of it ourselves. We wanted to have her eliminated down there to prevent any suspicion being cast our way. But since it's known that your men took her and were tearing your country apart looking for her, people will assume that you had her killed."

"If you think that is best." Arturo didn't tell him he'd put his own plans into motion the moment he'd seen that little *puta*'s face on television this morning.

"We do." There was a pause. "For the sake of our long association, we'll forgive—no, that's not the word—*overlook* your failure this time. But we need you to do something for us."

"What is that?"

"Spread word on the street that Los Zetas are crossing the border to finish the reporter."

That made no sense. "If I do that, won't the police put her under their protection, making it harder and riskier for you?"

"By the time the police mobilize, she'll already be dead. Action has already been taken. The pieces are moving. Just get the word out. Do it tonight."

Then the line went dead.

Arturo put the phone down and then, with shaking hands, he poured himself a shot.

Santa Muerte protect me!

"YOU'VE GOT IT, Syd." Natalie hung up the phone, glad her article was done and in the hands of the managing editor.

She'd spent the day writing an eyewitness account of the attack on the bus, her kidnapping, captivity, and escape. It wasn't something she'd wanted to do, but Tom had thought it would be good for readership. Rather than focusing on her own experience, she'd decided to use the article as a chance to pay tribute to the slain Mexican journalists, sharing what she remembered about each of them. Their home newspapers had generously donated head shots and other photographs, enabling her to put a face with each name. It had been especially painful to write about Sr. Marquez.

Marquez finished his prayers, then turned to me and apologized, as if he were to blame for the fact that he was about to be murdered. Then, he looked up into his killer's face. In the next instant, it was over, and he was gone, a bullet hole in his forehead.

Then, referring to Zach only as Mr. Black—a joke for his benefit in case he read the article—she'd managed to report on her hours in the Zeta prison, as well as the escape, without giving away sensitive information. She'd felt close to him, as if she were connecting with him, writing words about a shared experience, words that he might see and even appreciate.

He probably won't even read it, girl.

God, how she missed him! It put a constant ache in her chest, some part of her unable and unwilling to accept that she wouldn't see him again. More than once she'd found herself wondering what would happen if it turned out she was pregnant. Would he change his mind and come back? Would he want to see the baby, be a part of its life?

That's no way to win a man's heart, girl. Are you that desperate?

Quashing the thought, she gathered her things, took the elevator down, and walked out to her car, only to find a dozen or more persistent reporters staking out the front entrance. She thought for a moment about taking the back entrance, but slinking down the alley while gunshots still echoed in her memory held no appeal. So she lifted her chin and walked out the door.

"Thank you, but no comment," she said again and again, finally making it to her car. She unlocked the door, got inside, and quickly locked it again. Then slowly, she nudged the car forward.

And then out of the corner of her eye she saw him—Sr. Scar Face.

She gasped, jerked her head around, looking for him. But he was gone.

Or maybe he'd never been there. Writing the article had left her jumpy, reviving the terror for her. Perhaps she was just seeing things. Besides, how could he have gotten here so quickly?

The same way you did.

A chill shivered up her spine. She picked up her cell phone and called Julian.

CHAPTER 23

"I'M SORRY. WE'VE moved on. We're going to focus on letting our daughter heal, and we're not interested in talking to the press."

Natalie stared at the phone as the line went dead. "That's strange."

"What's strange?" Sophie looked up from a report she was reading, purple highlighter poised above the page.

"Before I went to Mexico, I had five families who'd agreed to be interviewed about what had happened to their daughters at the Whitcomb Academy. They were outraged and after blood. Now none of them want to speak with me at all."

"That is strange. Did they say why?"

"They said they'd talked about it and had decided that lots of press was not what their daughters needed. They want to move on and let their daughters heal."

"I suppose I can understand them feeling that way."

Natalie turned in her chair. "I can, too. But how do you go from begging to be interviewed to refusing to speak in a week?"

But Sophie was already buried in her report again.

Natalie ran through the facts of this investigation, trying to figure out whether she had enough for an article. She had already reported the basics. A soccer coach at Whitcomb Academy, a small private school for gifted and talented girls, had been using a picklock kit to get into girls' dorm rooms at night, where he had allegedly raped them. After one of the victims attempted suicide, the truth came out, and the parents went to the county sheriff.

The sheriff had moved quickly, arresting the coach on a host of felonies, and promising a full investigation. And then . . . nothing.

After two weeks of investigating the case, the sheriff let it go, and the DA dropped the charges against the coach for lack of evidence. Given that the evidence included semen samples on one of the girls' sheets, a picklock kit, and fifteen victims telling almost exactly the same story, this came as a surprise to everyone. But it had been good news for the coach, who'd promptly disappeared, leaving no forwarding address.

Understandably, the girls' parents had been outraged, some insinuating that the sheriff and the DA had been bought off or intimidated by the school's administration. Feeling that they had nowhere left to turn, the parents had come to the newspaper. Natalie had done some preliminary poking around, gathering police reports and tax documents for all the players. She had arranged to interview the families, but she'd gone to Mexico before she'd gotten the chance.

And now no one wanted to talk.

It looked like she would end up dropping the story.

She stretched, unable to stifle a yawn, wishing she could run out for another café au lait. Even though Julian and Marc had cleared her house and the Denver police had parked a surveillance team on her street, she hadn't slept well last night, every sound she'd heard making her jump. The ice maker. The AC kicking on. The creaking of her wooden floors. In her mind all of them became Sr. Scar Face. Then she'd imagined Zach was there, holding her, sleeping beside her, and she'd finally fallen asleep.

She'd been tempted more times than she could count to call him today just to make sure he was okay. She was so afraid her deposition had gotten him into trouble. If only his superiors in the Justice Department understood that he'd done what he'd done to keep her safe . . .

Oh, who was she fooling? She wanted to talk to him, wanted to hear his voice, wanted to know that he was okay. But if she called, she'd only make it harder on herself. He'd made it clear that he didn't feel capable of having a relationship, and she had too much self-respect to throw herself at any man.

Outside her window, gray clouds rose over the mountains, promising a late afternoon thunderstorm. Already the wind was picking up, branches swaying.

Don't we have to get skin to skin for this to work?

Are you saying you want to get naked with me, angel?

That's not what I meant.

No? Too bad.

Memories of another thunderstorm came back to her. It seemed like a lifetime ago that she'd taken shelter with Zach in that alcove and made love underneath the little waterfall. But in fact, it was just the day before yesterday.

Too much, too fast. Two worlds apart.

She grabbed her file and stood, then walked the short distance to Tom's office. He had a way of resurrecting investigations she thought were dead in the water. And if he thought she was wasting her time on this one, he wouldn't hesitate to tell her.

He glanced up, a shock of gray curls slipping over his forehead, reading glasses low on his nose. "Benoit."

She stepped into the mess that was Tom's office—newspapers piled everywhere, manila file folders with coffee stains, books stacked wherever there was space, and on the wall above his head, a poster with his favorite quote, from George Orwell: *In a time of universal deceit, telling the truth is a revolutionary act.*

"I think this Whitcomb Academy investigation is at a dead end, but I wanted to run through it with you first."

"Let's hear it."

She refreshed his memory about the facts of the case, then told him what had happened with the girls' families today. "I feel like there's something there, but I can't find a way to crack the nut. I'm not even sure where the nut is."

He frowned, clearly thinking it through. "So the alleged victims and their families won't talk. The school won't talk. And the sheriff and DA won't talk."

"Yes, that's about the size of it."

"What about the perp?"

"He skipped town the day after they let him out of jail. His neighbors said a moving van showed up and cleared out his apartment. No forwarding address."

"I assume you've already gotten everyone's tax records."

Natalie nodded. "The sheriff's, the DA's, the administrator's, the alleged perpetrator's, as well as all of the school's public records for the past five years. There was nothing that seemed suspicious to me, but then I admit I'm not a tax genius."

"You could fax those documents to that forensic accountant we keep on retainer and see what she finds. She knows all the tricks. If anyone is playing games, she'll be able to spot it."

Natalie stood. "Thanks. That's what I'll do."

He turned back to his work. "When in doubt, Benoit, follow the money."

"DID YOU KILL Agent Gisella Sanchez?"

"No." Zach sat with a blood pressure cuff on his right arm, two pneumographs strapped around his chest, and galvanometers on the first and third fingers of his left hand.

He had agreed to take a polygraph test in hopes that it would speed the investigation along. He knew he was telling the truth. He needed to convince them of that fact so that he could get back to work.

So far the experience had been tedious rather than intimidating, perhaps because he knew he was innocent. They'd brought in the FBI's top polygraph expert, a small bald man whose thick glasses gave him the appearance of a mad scientist—or Mr. Magoo.

"Whom did you pay to kill her?"

"No one. I had nothing to do with her death."

"How was she killed?"

"I have no idea."

"Did you and Agent Sanchez work together to steal cocaine from the Zetas?"

"No."

"Was it your idea to steal the drugs?"

"I didn't steal the coke."

"Did you have sexual relations with journalist Natalie Benoit?"

"Yes." Zach felt his pulse spike. "Are you going to ask me if it was good?"

So, somehow Pearce knew about him and Natalie. Chiago's report must have been very thorough. They would use questions like this—questions to which they already knew the answer—to monitor his responses. It gave them a better idea of how his body responded when he told the truth and when he lied.

But, of course, he was telling only the truth.

"Did you have sexual relations with Agent Sanchez?"

"Good God, no."

On it went for two long hours. They asked him variations on the same questions again and again, Pearce no doubt watching from the other side of the one-way mirror. Zach was about ready to tell them that he was finished with this bullshit, when the examiner finally turned off the machines and removed the blood pressure cuff.

"How long till we have the analysis?" Zach pulled off the galvanometers himself.

"Just a few days." Thin fingers unfastened the pnueumographs. "Be careful. That's delicate equipment."

Done being probed for the day, Zach left the building, headed to his small apartment, and dressed for a run, hoping to burn off the tension, frustration, and anger that had been building inside him since he arrived in D.C. First, the investigation. Then the old man's surprise visit.

You sure know how to have a good time, McBride.

It was early evening, but still warm and humid. Tucking his cell phone into his shorts pocket, Zach set out for the National Mall, running down Independence Avenue past the U.S. Botanic Garden to Third Street and left on Madison Drive. He set a fast pace, focused on his breathing, threading his way through pedestrians, bicycles, people without noticing them, his mind filled with random images.

Gisella smiling and handing him a Coke. Endless darkness and pain. Natalie looking pleadingly up at him while that Zeta bastard groped her. Carlos and his gold chains. His father's angry face and flying fist.

Then his thoughts began to change.

Natalie removing his blindfold, setting him free. Natalie asleep beside him in the shade, her face flushed from the heat. Natalie naked and beautiful beneath him. Natalie reading a statement on national television, looking into his eyes.

You are my hero.

Ribs aching, he slowed to a walk. There was no point in running himself to death. He wasn't going to get her out of his mind any time soon.

He'd read her first-person account of her ordeal this morning, catching it online just before he'd left home. He couldn't imagine that it had been easy to write, her compassion for the Mexican journalists and the terror she'd felt evident in every word. He'd gotten a chuckle out of her alias for him, as, no doubt, she'd intended. But what had struck him as he'd read the article was her writing. She wasn't just a good reporter. She was a talented writer, her words describing her experience in a way that put the reader there beside her.

Of course, Zach *had* been beside her for most of it, and reading the article had brought him to the rather amazing realization that their trek through the desert had been the most fun he'd had in a very long time.

You are sick in the head, frogman.

He was about a block from his apartment when his cell buzzed. He drew it out and saw that the number was restricted. "McBride."

"It's Farrell calling from EPIC."

Farrell was a DUSM who spent his time tracking down fugitives from the United States who'd crossed into Mexico. What would make him call?

"Go ahead."

"Word on the street is that men working for Cárdenas have crossed the line and are on their way to Denver to take out that pretty reporter of yours. I thought you'd want to know."

Cárdenas had never sent his men more than a few miles across the border, and he'd never killed anyone who wasn't involved with the narco trade. For him to kill a U.S. national deep inside the United States . . .

"Are you sure about this?"

"Heard it myself from a Juarense cop today. Watch your back."

The line went dead.

"Son of a bitch!" Zach didn't have Natalie's cell phone number programmed into his phone or tucked away in his jock. He dialed information. "I need the cell number for Natalie Benoit in Denver, Colorado. It's an emergency."

He headed back toward his apartment at a jog.

NATALIE ORGANIZED THE stacks of paper she'd printed out, put them in paper clips, and tucked them into a file folder. Inspired, she'd decided to download everything she could about the Whitcomb Academy that had to do with money—its major donors, its major corporate sponsors, its board of directors, its board of trustees. Then she'd printed a list of everyone who'd contributed to the sheriff's and DA's last re-election campaigns.

She would spend tonight reading through what she had. If she found nothing suspicious and if the forensic accountant found nothing amiss, she would drop the story tomorrow and pick up something else.

Natalie made her way down to the front entrance. Gil Cormack, the paper's security guard, had gone for the day. She'd thought about asking him to walk her to her car, but she'd stayed a bit too late. She stopped and scanned the parking lot, but didn't see anyone. Then she opened the door and stepped outside.

The wind nearly blew the files she was carrying out of her grasp. Overhead the sky was gray, thunder coming from the west. From the looks of it, they were about to get a downpour.

She had almost reached her car when she heard the faint ring of her cell phone. She fished it out of her purse, struggling to hold on to her files. "Natalie Benoit."

"Natalie, it's Zach. I need . . . call . . . Hunter and wait . . ."

"Zach?" She hadn't been expecting a call from him, and all at once hopes that she'd hidden away came rushing back. "Can you speak a bit louder? I'm in the parking lot on the way to my car, and it's really windy here."

"I said . . . back . . . them there. Listen . . . it now."

"Hold on a minute. I'm at my car now. Let me just get inside. Then I'll be able to hear you." She stuck her key in the lock, just as a gust came and tossed the manila folder with its carefully organized pages into the wind. "Oh, damn it. Hang on, Zach."

She bent down, picked up paper as fast as she could, gusts and eddies swirling some pages under the car next to hers, tossing others across the row. She ran, bending down, purse in one hand, cell phone tucked between her jaw and ear, Zach still shouting something to her.

"Marc and . . . wait inside!"

Wait inside?

"Wait inside? Inside my car?" She'd just gone around to the other side of the car next to hers, when a big gust of wind blew the door of her car shut.

Her car exploded.

She saw the fireball, felt the heat, felt herself falling backward.

And then she felt nothing.

ZACH HAD JUST stepped inside his own front door when he heard the blast and then . . . nothing. Natalie's phone was dead.

A car bomb.

Christ, no!

Fear hit him with the force of a body blow, making his heart burst, driving the breath from his lungs, turning his knees to rubber.

He dialed 911, told the person on the phone that a car had just exploded in a parking lot in front of the *Denver Independent* in Denver, Colorado. Answering the dispatcher's inane questions, he packed a bag, careful to remember his passport, his badge, and his two service weapons. Leaving D.C. now would end his career, but he didn't give a damn.

"Look, I'm in Washington, D.C. I was on the phone with a friend when I heard an explosion, and now her phone is dead. I'm a deputy U.S. marshal, and I'm telling you a car bomb just went off. Get someone—"

"Denver emergency dispatch reports they've gotten several calls about it. Fire, police, and ambulance are already en route."

Zach hung up, finished packing, changed his clothes, and was out the door, hailing a cab the moment his feet hit the sidewalk.

"Get me to the airport as fast as you can."

But Zach knew that no matter how fast he went, it wouldn't be fast enough. It was a three-and-a-half-hour flight to Denver, and he didn't even have a ticket. By the time he made it to Denver . . .

Please let her be alive. Please let her be safe.

"Wait inside? Inside my car?" she'd asked.

That's not what he'd said, but that's what she'd heard. He'd told her to go back inside the paper, to call Hunter or Rossiter, and to wait there until they arrived. He hadn't even had a chance to warn her about the Zetas.

Wait inside? Inside my car?

And then her car had exploded.

Let her be alive! God, please let her be safe!

He never should have left her.

Blackness seeped into Zach's chest, eating at him like acid, leaving a gaping hole where his stomach had been, cold sweat beading on his forehead.

His prayers meant nothing.

He'd had lots of training in demolition as a SEAL. He knew the kind of explosives the Zetas typically used—high-tech, sophisticated, military grade. If they had rigged her car to explode when she sat in the driver's seat, then Natalie was already dead.

CHAPTER 24

JOAQUIN WAS STANDING with the others in the ER waiting room sipping the last of his coffee when McBride walked in. He wanted to deck the bastard. "Well, look who's here."

Heads turned.

Hunter, still wearing his full SWAT uniform, glared. "Great timing, McBride."

"Marc!" Sophie chided softly.

Rossiter got to his feet. "Glad you could make it."

McBride didn't seem to notice their sarcasm—or maybe he just didn't care. To be fair, the man looked like hell, his face gray, his eyes haunted. "How is she?"

Darcangelo crossed the room and held out his hand. "Detective Julian Darcangelo, Denver PD. You must be McBride. I'm surprised to see you here with the media circus outside. I would think you'd want to keep a low profile now that every reporter in America is looking for Mr. Black, Natalie's hero."

Some hero.

Natalie had saved McBride's ass, and he'd paid her back by taking advantage of her in the desert and then leaving her to face these Zeta bastards alone.

McBride accepted Darcangelo's hand, gave it a few wooden shakes. "How is she? The online news reports said she was alive but—"

"You think you can just walk in and out of her life?" Hunter wasn't letting it go.

Good for him.

McBride stepped up, looked Hunter right in the face, a muscle clenching in his jaw. "Not now, Hunter, for Christ's sake!" Then he looked around at the rest of them. "Can someone please answer my goddamned question?"

Joaquin tossed the empty coffee cup into the trash. "I was the first to reach her. She's in one piece but unconscious. The blast knocked her backward, and it looks like she hit her head on the pavement. She's got some cuts from flying glass."

McBride took two steps and sank into a chair, resting his face in his hands.

Joaquin looked at Hunter, who glanced over at Gabe, the three of them sharing a guilty look. The guy was obviously shredded over this.

Kat, who'd been quiet until now, stood and went to sit down beside him, slipping an arm around him. "All we've been told so far is that she's stable but unconscious and that they're doing another MRI to make sure she doesn't have trauma to her brain."

"Thank you." McBride drew a breath. "I was on the phone with her when it happened. I told her to go back inside and call Hunter because I'd gotten a tip that the Zetas had come to Denver after her. But it was too windy—"

"Thank God for that wind." Joaquin tried to keep the anger out of his voice. Kat was a better judge of people than he was, and if she trusted McBride . . . "It scattered some papers she was carrying, so she was on the other side of the car next to hers when the bomb went off."

"My team was investigating the scene until the feds showed up." Hunter sat down next to Sophie. "It looked to us like the blast was directed upward into the driver's seat. The roof of her car was blown about a hundred feet into the air and landed on the other side of the parking lot. If she'd been sitting inside the car . . ."

McBride stood. "I need to see her."

Sophie shook her head. "Sorry, but they won't let any of us back yet. I've tried."

McBride drew out what looked like a wallet. On the front was a silver five-point star with an eagle in the center. "They'll let me back."

He stood and walked across the waiting room to the main ER entrance and the check-in desk. Then he showed the woman at the desk his badge and ID. "Chief Deputy U.S. Marshal Zach McBride here to see Natalie Benoit."

She looked at his badge, then picked up the phone and called someone. Joaquin watched as a nurse in green scrubs appeared and ushered McBride back through the electronic double door. "Well, I'll be damned. Gotta get me one of those shiny badges. Think they sell them on the Net?"

"You three could try to be kinder to him." Kat glared at them. "He risked his life to get Natalie safely home, remember? He obviously cares about her. Sometimes men are just bullheaded."

The tone of her voice left no doubt that she was referring to them, not McBride.

Darcangelo grinned. "Guys, I think you've just been told."

"Natalie, can you hear me?"

Warm lips pressed against her forehead.

At the familiar sound of that voice, her pulse gave a kick. It was . . . "Zach?"

She must be dreaming.

"Yeah, angel, I'm right here." Fingers gave her hand a squeeze.

He'd come back. He'd come back to her.

Relief, warm and sweet, flowed through her but got lost in forgetfulness. Time seemed to drift. A confusion of words and feelings. She heard a woman whimpering in pain and realized that she was the one making that sound. "My head . . . hurts."

"You've got a bad concussion." Zach's voice again. "They're going to keep you in the hospital until they're sure you're okay."

A concussion? In the hospital?

They'd been in the desert. There'd been a thunderstorm, and then the waterfall. But hadn't they made it back to Sells? Yes, they had. Marc, Gabe, and Joaquin had been there with the Shadow Wolves—Agent Chiago and the others. So why was she in the hospital?

Zach was talking to someone. "Can she have something for pain?"

"The doctor is going to want her fully conscious first so he can evaluate her."

"Then you'd better get him in here. I don't want her to suffer."

"I'll page him."

Again, she tried to open her eyes, her head throbbing. "Zach?"

"I'm here." He stroked her hair. "I'm not going anywhere."

At this news, she felt a dark cloud lift off her. He'd come back to her.

But how had she landed in the hospital? "What . . . happened?"

"What do you remember?"

It was so hard to think. "The hotel . . . You left. You left me."

"Yeah. I went back to D.C. Do you remember going home to Denver?"

Going home?

Yes, she'd gone home to Denver. She'd flown on a private airplane. Zach had done that for her. And he'd done something else, too.

"Southern sweet tea. You did that. Thank you."

"You're welcome. Can you remember anything after you arrived in Denver?"

There'd been reporters outside her house. She'd given a statement, gone to work, written about what had happened in Mexico. Joaquin had brought beignets. But that was just the first day. She'd gone to work the second day, and no one had wanted to be interviewed. She'd gotten tax documents and faxed them to the forensic accountant, then gotten her stuff together to go home. And then . . .

She opened her eyes, saw Zach's face, his gray eyes clouded with concern. "I remember leaving the newsroom but . . . nothing else."

"You don't remember anything after that? Leaving the building? My calling you on your cell phone? The wind?"

She tried to think, tried to remember, pain making her confused. Zach calling her on her cell phone . . . the wind . . . Fear welled up inside her, nameless but overwhelming. "I can't . . . remember. Please tell me. What happened?"

"Your car exploded. Someone—likely the Zetas—rigged it with explosives."

Her car had exploded?

She had no memory of that at all, and for a moment she thought he'd made it up. But the look on his face told her he wasn't joking. "A car bomb? Am I . . ."

And the fear was back.

She wiggled her toes, raised a hand, saw it had all its fingers, then felt her face.

"You've got a few cuts from flying glass, but you're okay—thank God." He ran a knuckle over her cheek. "The wind apparently blew some papers out of your hands, and while you were chasing them, a gust blew your car door shut, detonating the bomb."

Natalie listened, almost too stunned to speak, while Zach recounted the past several hours, from the moment he'd gotten the phone call tipping him off to the moment he'd arrived at the hospital. She'd almost been killed. If it hadn't been for Colorado's wind storms, she would be dead right now.

She found herself holding tightly to Zach's hand. "I-I thought I saw Señor Scar Face—that's what I call the Zeta who tortured you. I thought I saw him out of the corner of my eye yesterday. But when I looked, he wasn't there. I called Julian. He and Marc cleared my home and put a watch on my house last night. I thought I had imagined seeing him, but he must have truly been there."

"Seems like it."

And then it hit her.

"If I'm not safe from Cárdenas and his men here, where—"

He cupped her cheek, looked into her eyes, his gaze soft. "Hey, don't you worry. That's why I'm here. I'm going to make sure you're safe. You just rest."

But then the doctor was there. He sent Zach outside in the hallway and examined her, shining a flashlight into her eyes, asking her questions, making her squeeze his fingers, getting her out of bed with a nurse to spot her so he could check her balance. The throbbing inside her skull was so much worse when she stood. By the time she'd crawled back into bed again, she had what felt like a migraine.

She lay back in the bed, eyes closed, the pain overwhelming, then felt warm fingers take hers, a hand gently stroking the hair from her face.

"We'll get her some morphine now." That was the nurse.

"Just a few more minutes, and you'll feel a lot better." Zach's voice soothed her.

"Don't leave me, please." She hated how needy she sounded, but she couldn't help it. She was afraid and in pain, and she *did* need him.

"I'm not going anywhere. Just rest."

Then the nurse came and injected something into her IV. She felt a warm sensation in her arm. Almost instantly, her pain slipped away.

Holding on to Zach's hand, so did she.

ZACH WATCHED NATALIE'S eyes drift shut, unable to take his gaze off her.

He'd never been more afraid in his life than on that long drive to the airport when he'd believed she was dead. By the time he'd reached the United ticket counter, the online news reports claimed she was alive but en route to the hospital. Terrible images had come to his mind, images of men torn apart by IEDs in Iraq, mangled limbs, charred bodies.

But here she was, in one battered but beautiful piece.

Zach wasn't a religious man. He'd seen things in combat that defied the existence of a caring, compassionate god. But to see her, alive and whole, felt like a miracle.

IGNORING PEARCE'S REPEATED calls to his cell phone, Zach left a sleeping Natalie with Sophie, Kat, and a pretty, pregnant blonde who'd kissed him on the cheek and introduced herself as Tessa, Darcangelo's wife. He walked out to the private ER waiting room, where he found Joaquin gone and Hunter, Darcangelo, and Rossiter with their kids.

It looked like a nursery. Two preschoolers sat on the floor playing with blocks, one a little girl with dark brown curls and big blue eyes, surely Darcangelo's daughter, the other a little boy with sandy brown hair and green eyes who was the spitting image of Hunter. A little girl with strawberry blond hair toddled unsteadily along the edge of the furniture not far from Hunter's protective reach, while Rossiter cuddled a sleeping baby girl with coal black hair.

Zach stopped in his tracks, the sight throwing him off. He didn't like babies, didn't care for children. Or at least he didn't think he did. But these little ones were so damned . . . *cute.* Little bits of sweetness, each one of them was tiny and helpless and utterly innocent. Some part of him—some part he wanted to disown—gave a big, unmistakable "awww!"

What the hell is wrong with you, McBride?

He'd known the three men were married. He supposed Natalie might have mentioned they had kids, but he hadn't paid attention to that part. But seeing Hunter in his SWAT uniform holding a pacifier . . .

And what will happen to his kids if he gets killed in the line of duty?

The men looked up.

Darcangelo stood. "How is she?"

"The doc checked her MRIs and evaluated her and says it's a bad concussion. They gave her some morphine, so she's sleeping. She was pretty coherent, though she can't remember the explosion."

Hunter's little girl lost her grip on the edge of a chair, plopped down heavily onto her diapered bottom, and began to cry, her precious little face the very image of distress, her tiny world temporarily shattered.

Hunter picked her up, kissed her. "It could have been a lot worse."

"You said it, Hunter." Rossiter gently settled his sleeping baby in her car seat and covered her with a small blanket decorated with Indian designs. "That was too damned close."

Which reminded Zach of the bone he had to pick with the three of them. "She said she told you she saw one of Cárdenas's men yesterday. Why didn't you get her off the streets entirely or at least put a watch on the newspaper?"

"Okay, that's fair." Darcangelo took a step in his direction. "But why didn't you tell us that you were after Cárdenas for murdering Americans on U.S. soil? We'd have taken what she reported yesterday much more seriously if we'd known Cárdenas was capable of that."

"Not sure how you got that bit of info. My mission was classified."

Hunter got to his feet, daughter in his arms. "If you thought there was any chance he would strike at her here in Denver, you should have told us. We'd have done everything we could to protect her. Instead, you flew off to D.C. and left her here to face this alone."

Guilt churning in his chest, Zach reined in the urge to get in Hunter's face. The man might not like him, but he was Natalie's friend. And then there was the baby in his arms. The sweet little thing had quit crying, her head resting against her daddy's Kevlar while she sucked her thumb, itty-bitty tears on her chubby cheeks.

Jesus, McBride!

He met first Hunter's gaze, then Darcangelo's. "The Zetas have never hit anyone farther north than El Paso and Nogales, and the U.S. nationals they've killed have all been mixed up in the drug trade. If I'd thought for a moment he would send his men to Denver, don't you think I'd have taken steps to protect her myself?"

"I don't know." Rossiter gave him a cold look. "Seems to me you were more concerned about getting back to D.C. so you could cover your you-know-what and save your career."

"My *career* is probably trashed. I was supposed to stay in—"

From behind him, a woman spoke. "This is what I love to see—different branches of law enforcement at each other's throats. It gives the bad guys the head start they need, which in turn gives us all job security."

Zach turned and looked straight into the eyes of a woman with short blond hair. In her late forties or early fifties, she was more than six feet tall, her body trim and fit, her tweed jacket and tailored slacks giving her a smart look. Beside her stood a younger woman, also wearing a pantsuit.

"I'm Teresa Rowan, U.S. marshal for Colorado. This is one of my deputies, Michelle Reyes." She held up a badge case, flipping quickly from a gold badge to her government ID. "You know, Reyes, the thing you have to remember when working with men is that they're very emotional. For example, these guys are on the same side, trying to protect the same woman, but they have to fight about it like dogs trying to decide who's the alpha." After this verbal blow to the balls, she turned to face them again. "But guess what, gentlemen—I'm the alpha."

And she was.

Zach had no doubt why she was here. She'd come to take him into custody and fly his ass back to D.C. But he had news for her. He didn't give a damn who she was. He wasn't leaving until he knew Natalie was safe.

She met his gaze. "Is there somewhere we can talk in private, McBride?"

"Look me in the eyes and tell me—did you steal the cocaine?"

Zach met Rowan's gaze, her steel blue eyes devoid of emotion. "No."

"Did you have anything to do with the Interpol agent's death?"

"No. It happened exactly like I said it happened. She almost got *me* killed."

"Okay then."

Zach stared at her. "That's it? Now you trust me?"

"After two decades on the job, I've gotten pretty good at judging people." She smiled, tapped a manicured fingernail on the sleeve of her jacket. "Besides, I've read the reports, seen the tape. I believed you before I set foot in this hospital."

That was a nice surprise. "But let me guess—you're here to tell me I have to get on a plane back to D.C. and that if I don't—"

She shook her head. "No. I'm here to ask you to help me protect Ms. Benoit."

Now Zach truly was surprised—and intrigued.

"We can't enroll her in WITSEC." Rowan's brow furrowed, deep lines forming on her forehead. "She doesn't fit the parameters for witness protection. But she is a journalist, and protecting journalists can fall to the Justice Department under certain circumstances. We've done it before."

Zach nodded. "The shooting of that radio talk-show host

in Seattle. The editor in Idaho who was being stalked by white supremacists."

"I can see you read the company newsletter." She gave him an approving grin. "I've claimed jurisdiction on this case. The Denver PD knows it. FBI knows it. Trouble is, my people aren't used to dealing with cartel violence. I need your expertise."

"What do you have in mind?"

"Make Ms. Benoit vanish. You'll get the support and resources you need from my office. Then help me get these Zeta bastards out of my state." There was emotion in her voice when she spoke those last words—the first Zach had sensed in her.

"There's one little problem. I'm currently the subject of an internal investigation in Washington. Pearce and the brass at the OD won't be happy about this. He ordered me to stay in D.C. until the investigation was complete."

"Fuck Pearce. I'll deal with him. I was appointed by the President. If Pearce doesn't like how I work, he can take it up with the White House."

Zach was really starting to dig this chick. "I'll need a team—people I can trust."

"ANSWER TO *HIM*?" Hunter gaped at Rowan. "You've got to be kidding. I want to help Natalie in any way I can, but—"

"Then say yes." Zach had expected this response.

He'd given the men a good twenty minutes in private to talk about it with their wives, knowing that the women would want to weigh in before their men agreed to take on the added responsibility and risk. And the risk was real. The women knew this. He could see it in their eyes, in the grave way they watched their men, in the way they held their children, in the way they looked at him, as if trying to decide whether they could trust him.

It's one hell of a position you've put them in—choosing between a friend's safety and that of the men they love.

Rowan stared Hunter down. "McBride knows he can trust you three. If you don't agree, he'll have to find others to back him up. I've already run background checks on you.

Darcangelo, I'm familiar with your deep cover work against sex trafficking during your years with the FBI and your record with Denver vice. When you brought Alexi Burien down, I was impressed. Hunter, you ran into some trouble in the DEA, but that's behind you now. Chief Irving says you've done good work for him. You still hold the U.S. military record for long-distance sniper kill. Earned yourself a Bronze Star in Afghanistan, didn't you?"

Zach had known this, but his faith in these men had nothing to do with their skills and everything to do with their loyalty to Natalie. The first rule of defeating the cartels was working with law enforcement and government officials who couldn't be bought, and Zach knew that none of them would sell Natalie out to Cárdenas.

Rowan went on. "Rossiter, your law enforcement record is outstanding, and though you've been out of the game for a while, you've got more than your share of guts."

"You've already talked to Chief Irving about this?" Darcangelo asked.

Rowan nodded. "He's pledged his full support."

Darcangelo frowned. "I thought special deputies have to be approved by DEA if there are illegal drugs involved."

Rowan gave a dismissive wave of her hand. "What drugs? This is a case of organized crime striking at a U.S. citizen, a journalist. It's about the free press, not drugs. Look, I know you FBI boys carry a deep grudge against the Marshal Service, but I really don't give a damn. And I know, Hunter, that you and McBride didn't start out on the right foot and the idea of working under him probably makes your teeth grind. But it's time to put your big boy pants on. Either you're in, or we're wasting our time."

Looking more than a little uncomfortable at this dressing down, Hunter, Darcangelo, and Rossiter raised their right hands, while Rowan quickly swore them in. She turned to Reyes. "Make sure they get badges."

Then she met Zach's gaze. "You've got your team. It's up to you. Make her disappear, McBride."

Unable to suppress a grin at Hunter's and Rossiter's irritation at suddenly working under his command, he nodded. "Yes, ma'am."

CHAPTER 25

NATALIE LAY STRAPPED to a gurney, a bright blue sky passing by overhead as DUSMs disguised as medical staff rolled her feet-first across the rooftop helipad to the waiting chopper. They were hot-loading her, the helicopter's rotors already running, drowning out the nurses' shouts. The helicopter was a small one, the name LifeFlight painted in bright red against a royal blue background on its shell. Its side door opened as they drew near, hands reaching out to grab the handles of the collapsed gurney as she was quickly and carefully lifted up and brought on board.

The gurney was strapped into place, then the door shut beside her.

"Hang tight, angel." It wasn't a flight nurse who spoke, but Zach, his voice raised above the drone of the rotors. "We've got a thirty-minute flight."

He sat back onto the flight seat beside her and strapped himself in, Kevlar visible beneath his bright blue flight nurse jumpsuit, an assault rifle beside him that looked like it ate AK-47s for breakfast.

The sound of the rotors became a high-pitched whir, and the chopper lifted off, the floor seeming to fall away from beneath her, making her gasp, her head suddenly lower than her feet.

A hand stroked her cheek—Zach reassuring her that everything was fine.

She'd been discharged this morning, a dull headache, memory loss, and a few nicks and cuts all that remained of her injuries from the explosion. She didn't need to be strapped to a gurney in a medical helicopter, but Zach had decided it was the safest way to get her out of the hospital. U.S. Marshal Teresa Rowen, whom Natalie had met this morning, had grounded all air traffic over Colorado for ten minutes, so there would be no one else in the sky when they took off. The chopper pilot was a DUSM, not a LifeFlight employee. No flight plan had been filed, and once they were away from Denver, they'd fly below the radar. Even if the Zetas somehow realized Natalie was on that helicopter, they wouldn't be able to follow her.

"You okay?" Zach called to her, his brows bent in a concerned frown.

She nodded, forcing a smile onto her face.

She wasn't sure she knew what "okay" was any longer. If "okay" meant she was thankful to be alive, then, yes, absolutely, she was okay. If it meant she was grateful that Zach was with her, then she was definitely okay. If it meant she was no longer afraid . . .

She didn't know if she'd ever feel safe again. If the Zetas could plant explosives in her car right here in Denver, what couldn't they do? Despite assurances from Marshal Rowan, Zach, and the others that the Zetas wouldn't get another crack at her, she couldn't shake the feeling that something terrible was going to happen. Her friends told her it was just post-traumatic stress from all she'd been through these past ten days—or perhaps the psychological impact of her head injury. She hoped they were right.

She still didn't remember the explosion, and the neurosurgeon had told her that she probably never would, her short-term memory having been damaged by the blow. Not that she *wanted* to remember. The photographs Joaquin had showed her of the flaming shell that had once been her shiny black Lexus had been more than enough.

It's going to be fine. Everything is going to be fine.

She drew a deep breath, her gaze seeking out Zach, who was checking his watch. She knew they had a tight schedule. First they were flying her to a little-used military airfield where they would meet up with Marc and Gabe. Then they would drive to the undisclosed location that would be her home for as long as it took to ensure that the Zetas were no longer a threat to her—weeks, months, years.

Julian was already there, handling security, including the installation of the cryptographic private network that would enable her to communicate safely with the newspaper. Until this was over, e-mail and her encrypted cell phone would be the only ways she had to stay in touch with her friends, for their sake as well as hers. If the Zetas discovered who her friends were, it could potentially put all of them in danger, too.

Natalie would rather hand herself over to Cárdenas right now and be done with it than allow any of them to get hurt or killed.

She looked up again, to find Zach holding the assault rifle, his gaze fixed on the ground below, everything about him radiating readiness for action. Her mind flashed to the memory of him sitting beside her in the Zetas' car wearing that skintight marijuana T-shirt and loading an AK-47, his face beaded with sweat, his jaw dark with stubble.

You haven't exactly caught me at my best.

He'd been wrong about that. The contrast between his appearance then and now might be sharp, but it was only skin-deep. What she'd seen in Mexico was a deputy U.S. marshal who'd withstood torture and deprivation doing everything he could against terrible odds to safeguard his mission and save her life.

If that wasn't a man at his best, what was?

He was doing the same thing now—except now the odds were stacked in his favor. This was Colorado, not Mexico. He had the resources of the U.S. Marshal Service behind him, with all the tech and weaponry he needed. And he had help.

Everything is going to be okay. It's going to be okay.

Whether it was the drone of the rotors, the motion of the helicopter, or the lingering effects of her concussion, she was soon fast asleep.

NATALIE AWOKE WHEN Zach unbuckled her from the gurney. "Have we landed?"

"Yeah. Right on time." He helped her sit up. "Easy now."

Then he turned the thick handle on the door and opened it. Hot air rolled in, the tarmac heated by the summer sun. The mountains had disappeared, which meant they must have brought her to the far eastern part of the state. Other than that, she had no idea where she was.

It was a good four feet to the ground, but before Natalie could move, Marc and Gabe were there, both armed and wearing Kevlar beneath ordinary street clothes. They reached for her and lifted her to the ground.

"Can you walk?" Marc looked like he was about to pick her up.

Natalie held up a hand to stop him. "I'm fine."

The two hurried her across the tarmac to an unmarked police car that was idling nearby, holding her between them. She glanced over her shoulder, and caught a glimpse of Zach removing the flight nurse jumpsuit.

"Don't worry. He's coming." Marc gave her a wink.

Then Marc opened the back door of the car, put a hand on top of her head, and guided her inside, Gabe sliding in beside her.

"Buckle up." Gabe gave her a warm smile, his seat belt fastening with a *click*.

A second later, the doors were all shut and locked, Marc in the driver's seat and Zach in the passenger seat.

And Natalie's sense of dread returned.

For the first time since she'd known them, the guys weren't bickering. They weren't joking. They weren't insulting one another. Other than the occasional reassuring word to her, they were absolutely silent.

You're in trouble deep, girl.

"WE'RE BACK IN Denver."

Zach glanced over his shoulder, saw the confusion on Natalie's face as she realized where she was. She'd fallen asleep again, proof that she was suffering the effects of the concussion perhaps more than he'd realized. "We're not trying to sneak you off to Timbuktu, but to get you someplace secret and secure."

They had worked around the clock since Rowan's visit to the hospital yesterday to arrange things—transportation, housing, security. Zach had been pleasantly surprised by the skill of his new special deputies. The three of them were pros, and they worked like a team, united by friendship, their concern for Natalie, and perhaps even their loathing for him. But that was okay with Zach.

They didn't have to like him to do their jobs.

Though he had no military training, Darcangelo had more years in federal law enforcement than Zach and was every bit his equal when it came to organizing security. Of the three of them, he seemed to dislike Zach the least.

Probably because he didn't catch you having sex with his wife's friend when you were supposed to be watching over her.

Hunter's Special Forces and SWAT experience had proved valuable. The man had gone so far as to scope out from a sniper's perspective the possible lofts where Natalie might stay, making sure that no one would be able to take a shot at her from anywhere in the city. That's how they'd ended up in the penthouse and not at the first two lofts Zach had considered.

And Rossiter's . . . *unique* talents had come in handy, too. He was a solid law enforcement officer, but he had a special skill for defying gravity. When Zach had wanted to check the roof of the penthouse for possible places to install a private satellite dish, Rossiter had simply climbed the flagstone wall as if he were Spider-Man, eliminating the need to find a ladder. Zach had been astonished when he'd seen that the man had a prosthetic leg.

"Don't be impressed," Hunter had muttered. "It'll give him a big head."

With the help of some of Rowan's men and resources, the four of them had pulled things together in record time. Because Natalie wasn't eligible for enrollment in WITSEC, there were a lot of steps they'd been able to skip. No need to establish an identity, find her a new town, or launch her into a new career. She wasn't leaving her life behind for good. Once Cárdenas was in custody or dead—and Zach now had a strong preference for the latter—she would be able to go home again.

He glanced over his shoulder once more, his gaze drawn

inexorably to her face. Then he saw Rossiter watching him over the top of his sunglasses, a knowing look in his eyes.

Caught in the act. Eyes front, McBride.

Zach turned his gaze back to the road ahead.

There would be consequences as a result of his coming here, and not just in Washington, D.C. He was finding it damned hard to treat this like a job. This morning in the hospital, he hadn't been able to keep himself from touching her, holding her hand, drawing her into his arms. Now he could barely keep his eyes off her, the idea of being alone with her for the foreseeable future far too satisfying.

But he was on assignment, and that meant putting some professional distance between them. Would she understand that? Would she understand that they couldn't pick up where they'd left off in Arizona?

Do you understand that, McBride?

Of course, he did. He was officially assigned to protect her and get the Zetas out of Denver, and he couldn't focus on either of those things if he was busy getting her naked and doing the horizontal tango.

Then why did you buy a new box of condoms?

Well, the ones he'd bought in Mexico had been too small, and he wanted to be safe rather than sorry.

Wrong answer.

If he were smart, he wouldn't have to worry about being safe *or* sorry. But then where Natalie was concerned, he'd been anything but smart or safe. And, strangely, he wasn't one bit sorry either.

And that's really the problem, isn't it?

Yeah, it was.

He'd never felt this way about a woman—out of control, shaken up in body, mind, and soul. She was as necessary for him as the breath in his own lungs. He'd gladly rip out his beating heart to keep her safe. But he wouldn't be able to do his best for her if he couldn't keep his mind and his hands off her. And afterward, when this was over . . .

He'd had the courage to say good-bye and walk away from her once. He wasn't sure he could do it again. But if he cared for her . . .

If he cared for her, if he truly cared for her, that's exactly what he'd have to do.

Hunter turned right at the next light, heading west toward Riverfront Park, prompting Zach to pull out his encrypted cell phone and call Darcangelo. "ETA five minutes."

Natalie stared up in disbelief as the car turned toward the underground parking garage at the most exclusive address in Denver—the Glass Tower. "I'm staying here?"

Newly built, it rose twenty-three stories high, all shining, silvery glass. They'd run an article on it in the paper's Lifestyle section. Even the smallest lofts sold for a million dollars.

"It's got unparalleled security." Gabe pointed. "Watch this."

The car drew up to what looked like an automated ticket dispenser, like the ones at city-owned parking lots. In the front seat ahead of her, Marc rolled down his window, reached out, and pressed the pad of his left thumb to what looked like a square plastic button. The moment he touched it, the plastic button glowed red.

Zach turned to look back at her. "Biometric technology. The pad is keyed for our fingerprints. No one who's not in the system can enter. If anyone tries to hack it, the thing shuts down and sets off a security alarm."

In front of them, the steel garage door rose. Julian walked out, his eyes hidden behind sunglasses, the gray sports jacket he wore over his black T-shirt almost certainly concealing weapons. He walked toward the street, passing them as if they weren't there, not even acknowledging them.

"He's making sure we weren't followed," Gabe explained.

The car rolled into the well-lighted garage, the door coming down behind them, leaving Julian outside.

Natalie looked around at the expensive vehicles parked here, each parking spot marked with a number, probably an apartment number. But Marc didn't park the car. Instead, he drove around to the back to what looked like a large freight elevator. Then he stepped out and pushed his thumb against the button—another biometric scanner. The doors opened just as he climbed back inside the car, and he nudged it forward.

"We're driving the car into the elevator?" Natalie had never imagined such a thing. But the elevator was more than big enough.

Zach nodded. "We're keeping you off security cameras so that not even building security knows you're here."

"Wow." That's all she could really think to say.

The elevator doors closed behind them, and Natalie felt them moving quickly upward, the motion leaving her dizzy. In less than a minute, the elevator car stopped and the doors opened.

Zach climbed out and pushed the round red HOLD button.

Beside her, Gabe unbuckled his seat belt. "We're here."

While Marc and Gabe took the elevator back down to the garage to park the car, Natalie followed Zach along a tiled hallway, passing an ordinary elevator meant for people. At the end of the hallway was a wide double door with the brass number 2400 on it. They must be on the top floor.

Zach pressed his thumb against a biometric pad beside the door, and it opened with a quiet click. "Welcome home."

Natalie stepped inside—and found herself in the pages of a magazine.

Sunlight streamed through floor-to-ceiling windows on the west side, French doors open to a patio with a breathtaking view of the mountains. And she realized this wasn't just a loft, but the penthouse. She was in the penthouse of the Glass Tower.

"This belongs to the U.S. Marshal Service?" No wonder there was a deficit.

Zach laughed. "No. I'm renting it under an alias. I want you to be safe, but also comfortable. You might be stuck here for a while."

Being stuck here didn't seem so bad—especially not if Zach was with her.

To her left was the living room, with wood floors and furniture in earth tones of cream, sage green, and a soft sky blue, a large painting of golden aspens in snow drawing the colors together, a gas fireplace beneath it. To her right stood an open kitchen with stainless-steel appliances, the refrigerator flush with the wall, the countertops made of white granite. Beyond that was a dining room graced by a long oak table and matching chairs, a modern take on the chandelier hanging above the table's center.

Between the kitchen and the living room was a flight of stairs, the banister of polished oak. She took the stairs, but was hit by another wave of dizziness halfway up, her headache worse. She leaned against the rail, drew in deep breaths.

A hand rested against her back. "You okay?"

"Just a little dizzy."

"Better take it slowly then."

With him beside her, she took the remaining few stairs and found herself in a hallway. To her left, above the living room, was the master bedroom, a king-sized bed set on a platform against one wall and covered with a fluffy white down comforter. The bed was flanked by nightstands and surrounded by matching chairs near the windows and a chest of drawers against the far wall. In the corner was a second gas fireplace, its mantel made of polished oak. And on the mantel sat her framed photograph of Beau.

Natalie walked over to it, picked it up, turned back to look at Zach. "How . . . ?"

"We moved some of your things here last night. I thought you'd want that."

"Thank you. That was very thoughtful of you." She held the photo against her chest for a moment, something familiar in the chaos that had become her life.

She set the photo down, walked to the closet, found her clothes hanging neatly inside. Then she turned and saw it—the bathroom. "Oh, my stars!"

The floors, walls, and countertops were made of a gray-veined marble, the tub deep and elliptical. *Big enough for two.* The shower was one of those with multiple showerheads, one overhead, three on each side, all adjustable. Twin sinks sat before twin oval mirrors. Small recessed lights shined down from the ceiling like stars, fluffy white towels hung from silver towel racks.

She walked through the room, ran her fingertips over the cool marble, then looked out the single square window onto the city below. "This is unbelievable, Zach. Thank you."

"We're not done with the tour yet."

He led her back out in the hallway to a small room that was her office, her laptop and files sitting on a wide oak desk. "We're using VPN to allow you to connect with the newspaper, but I'll explain that later. Let me show you the gym."

He started back down the stairs, but Natalie had noticed another room upstairs. She walked over to it, saw a double bed with a duffel bag full of weapons on top of it, some shaving things set on the dresser. So he planned to sleep in here, away from her.

She hadn't expected that. Nothing in how he'd acted toward her had given her any reason to expect that. And her spirits, which hadn't been high to begin with, sank.

She turned to find him watching her.

"Nothing has changed between us, Natalie. We can't be together. It will just make things harder for both of us if we sleep together. I've been assigned to protect you and help get the Zetas out of Colorado, and I need to stay focused. What happened in the desert—"

"Let me guess—it stays in the desert." She walked past him and down the stairs, trying not to let him see that what was left of her world had just crumbled.

ARTURO WANTED TO laugh. He wanted to gloat. He wanted to rub it in their faces. Instead, he sent a prayer of thanks to La Santa Muerte, fighting to keep the joy out of his voice. "She is not so easy to kill, this Natalie Benoit."

The bastard sons of whores had planted explosives in her car, but the wind had detonated the bomb, leaving her alive and almost uninjured. Even worse, she had disappeared, evading their best attempts to track her and finish the job.

"She told the cops she saw one of your men outside the newspaper. From her description, it must be your nephew, José-Luis."

Arturo stopped, shifted the phone to his other ear, the laughter dying inside him. "José-Luis? Perhaps . . . I don't know where he is. *Sí.* Yes, he is there, I think."

A low chuckle. "We know he's there, Arturo. If his presence were to blame for our failure, we'd have sent him back to you in pieces. Instead, it's convinced every cop and agent in Denver that the Zetas are there on the streets hunting for her. Nice work."

Arturo could hear the mocking tone in his voice. The stupid *cabrón*.

"The good news is that we may have use for your nephew. And for you. How soon can you meet us in Denver?"

CHAPTER 26

ZACH FINISHED READING the forensics report on Natalie's car, rage on slow boil in his gut. "It wasn't a VBIED. The trace amounts of C4 are too low for that, and the blast didn't crater the pavement. They wanted to kill her. They weren't interested in destroying anything else."

He'd decided to take advantage of the fact that Natalie was asleep to hold a briefing with the men. Now that they'd gotten her safely here, it was time to start the next phase of the operation—finding and eliminating the Zetas. He looked up from the page to find the others still reading.

"Agreed." Darcangelo met his gaze, nodding. "The blast was carefully channeled upward—the work of a pro."

"You think it was a tilt fuse?" Rossiter asked, still reading.

"That's what the Zetas typically use," Zach answered. "The victim gets in the car, starts driving, and the car's motion rocks the fuse, sending the mercury to the other end to close the circuit and set off the explosion. It's a way to make sure the victim is in the vehicle before detonation."

"And she would have been right where they wanted her, if not for the wind." Hunter shook his head, set his copy of the report down on the coffee table. "This fucker Cárdenas—what's his obsession with her?"

"She's the one who got away." That was Zach's best theory at the moment. "He has what I guess you'd call a death fetish.

His men kidnap young women and bring them to him. He rapes them, brutalizes them. Then, when they're almost dead, he sacrifices them to La Santa Muerte, getting his ultimate thrill as that last breath leaves their bodies. We know this because one of his victims wasn't as dead as he thought she was. Tourists found her in the desert. She was sixteen."

Rossiter looked up from the page, his gaze hard. "And that's what this sick son of a bitch had planned for Natalie?"

"Yeah." It turned Zach's stomach even to think about it. "One of the Zetas told her that Cárdenas planned to enjoy her and then sacrifice her."

"I really want to get my hands on this *chingadero*, show him a few things about pain he might have forgotten." The tight set of Darcangelo's jaw told Zach that he wasn't kidding.

"I doubt he'll set foot north of the line, especially now. He has people do his dirty work for him, like his nephew José-Luis Quintana." Zach handed out color printouts of Quintana's face, having gotten an ID on him late this afternoon from Interpol. "This is the man Natalie saw in the newspaper parking lot—the man who assaulted her."

Darcangelo looked up. "And who tortured you."

Zach nodded, shoving those memories aside.

"So what is this La Santa Muerte?" Hunter pronounced the name with uncertainty. "Is this a real Catholic saint?"

"No." Zach and Darcangelo answered at the same time.

"It's a narco-saint," Darcangelo added.

Zach deferred to Darcangelo, let him explain it, his own thoughts drifting back to Cárdenas and his motives. By planting those explosives in Natalie's car, the Zetas had done something they'd never done before. They'd tried to kill someone who wasn't mixed up in drug trafficking—and they'd come deep into the U.S. to do it.

What had driven them to act?

Maybe this was revenge for the humiliation Cárdenas had suffered when she and Zach escaped. Perhaps she was the first woman to escape him in quite that way. Maybe this was about the cocaine Zach hadn't stolen. God only knew what Gisella had told them before they'd killed her. Or maybe Cárdenas was trying to keep a vow to his favorite sick icon.

But if that were true, why not try to reacquire Natalie and carry out his original plan?

Zach shook his head in frustration and tossed the report onto the coffee table. He wouldn't find the answers he needed in its pages.

Hunter watched him. "What is it?"

Zach leaned back, stretched his arms out along the back of the leather sofa. "Something feels off about this. I can't quite explain it, but it's not like the Zetas to strike this deep into the U.S. or to try to kill someone who isn't into the drug trade. Zebras don't change their stripes."

"Zebras don't, but maybe Zetas do." Hunter shrugged and met Zach's gaze head on. "Just because you couldn't predict it and were therefore unable to prevent it doesn't mean it didn't happen."

Zach ignored Hunter's gibe. "I can't shake the feeling that Cárdenas's interest in her has to do with something she's working on at the paper. I looked through her files when we moved them—"

"You looked through my files?" Natalie's voice came from behind them.

Zach looked over his shoulder to find her standing at the base of the stairs, wearing purple plaid pajamas, looking both sexy and unmistakably pissed off, her hair tousled, her gaze boring through him, her lips a grim line.

"*Shit.*" That was Rossiter.

Hunter gave a low whistle. "Dude—you looked through her files?"

Darcangelo stood. "I think it's time for us to go."

"YOU CAN'T JUST look through a reporter's files no matter who you are." Natalie poured hot water into a mug, set the kettle back on the stove, and pushed past him to reach for a bag of Darjeeling.

"In case you've forgotten, there are men out there who are trying very hard to kill you. I'm trying to figure out why so I can keep you safe."

Turning her back on him, she dropped the tea bag into

the water, picked up the mug, and walked to the table, so angry she could spit. "Even if we were investigating the same thing—which we are *not*—you'd have to get a court order before I'd be compelled to share the files with you."

"A court order? You really expect me to waste time getting a court order when I'm trying save your life?"

"No." Of course, she didn't. "But I *do* expect you to ask."

If he'd been her lover, she wouldn't have been as angry. But he'd made it clear he wasn't, that he needed a degree of professional distance from her now. If professional distance was what he needed, she would give it to him.

"I wasn't trying to sneak behind your back or violate your space. You were in the hospital at the time."

"Then you should've waited. You wouldn't want me snooping through your files, would you?" She looked down at her tea, realized she'd forgotten sugar and milk. She stood and walked back into the kitchen, avoiding his gaze.

"That's different. I'm a federal operative. I have access to classified information, secrets that could get people killed, stuff no one is allowed to see."

She whirled about to face him. "And I'm a journalist. My job is—"

Dizziness swamped her. She reached for the counter, granite cool beneath her palm as she fought to not faint.

Strong hands caught her shoulders, held her steady. "You need to calm down and take it easy."

"Don't touch me." She drew away from him, hugged her way along the counter, then sank into a chair, her head still spinning.

"What did you want?"

"What do you mean?" She didn't understand.

"When you came back this way—what did you come for?"

It took her a moment. "Milk and sugar."

He brought both, together with something else she'd forgotten—a spoon. He set all three in front of her.

"Thank you." No matter how angry she was, she couldn't forfeit her manners.

"You're welcome." He sat down across from her. "This isn't about me looking through your files. It's about what I said this afternoon. It's about the two of us."

His words cut through her anger, left her perilously close to tears. Fighting to hold herself together, she stirred milk and sugar into her tea, then set the spoon aside and held the warm mug between her palms.

"When I woke up in the hospital and saw you there, I thought . . . I thought you'd come back for me, that you'd changed your mind." She'd thought that maybe her brush with death had made him realize he cared about her enough to stop running and to face his PTSD. But the explosion hadn't changed a thing. He was still running. "But you're just here to do a job. You didn't come back for me. You came for the Zetas."

"You know that's not true." There was a defensive edge to his voice, and she could tell she'd hurt him.

"Since you're on assignment now, maybe you should be out on the streets instead of babysitting me." She sipped, burned her tongue. "Maybe someone else with less experience dealing with the Zetas—another DUSM or maybe one of your new special deputies—should stay here with me, while you hunt down this Quintana."

"I'm here and not on the streets because I don't trust anyone else to keep you safe. I *am* here for you, Natalie. I care about you more than you know. But I've already told you—it won't work."

This admission only made her more upset. He said he cared about her, but he wasn't willing to give the two of them a chance.

"Why won't it work? Because you saw some terrible things in combat and have nightmares? I have nightmares, too, Zach. I lost everyone I loved in a single day. We all have our demons."

He shook his head, his gray eyes going hard. "You wouldn't understand."

Forgetting her tea, she stood. "I thought you were the bravest man I ever met, but I guess I was wrong. You're a big chicken, Zach McBride. You can face the scary stuff like torture, killers, and bullets, but when it comes to things that can't really hurt you, like memories, like the past, you can't stand your ground."

Fighting another spell of dizziness, she hurried upstairs to her bedroom, shutting the door behind her.

*   *   *

Zach walked upstairs toward Natalie's room to check on her. It had been a good three hours since she'd dropped that bomb in his lap and disappeared. At first he'd been mad as hell and glad for the space. Then suppertime had come and gone without a sound from her, and he'd begun to worry that perhaps she wasn't sulking.

Head injuries had a bad way of surprising people.

He rapped with a knuckle on her door. "Natalie?"

No response.

He grasped the doorknob and quietly opened the door. And there she was—lying on her side, sound asleep on her bed. He took a few silent steps, moving closer, wanting to see for himself that she was breathing. And she was. Her lips were parted, her breathing deep and even, her dark hair fanned out behind her. He exhaled, relieved, then noticed the tearstains on her cheeks.

Aw, hell.

The angry storm that had roiled around inside him all evening ebbed, and he found himself wanting to lie down beside her and hold her until she woke up. But he couldn't do that, not if he wanted to be able to live with himself afterward. Instead, he stood there, watching her sleep, an ache in his chest that wouldn't go away.

Zach had just finished his morning briefing with Rowan and was making himself an omelet when he heard Natalie coming down the stairs.

She shuffled into the kitchen, looking tousled and confused, the flannel of her purple plaid pajamas wrinkled. She stared at the clock, then looked at him. "Did I just sleep sixteen hours—or just four?"

"It's tomorrow." Surly from lack of sleep—and lack of progress in finding Quintana—he said nothing more.

He'd had another nightmare last night, worse than before. It had started out in Afghanistan like it always did, but then he'd found himself in Mexico, forced to watch while Quintana mauled and tortured Natalie, her screams turning his blood to ice. He'd woken, chilled to the bone and craving a bottle of Jack, but the loft was dry as a nunnery. So he'd made his way to the gym, gone for a punishing uphill run on the treadmill until he'd gotten the dry heaves. Then he'd showered and tried to sleep, but couldn't.

He found it strange that he was having nightmares while on assignment. Usually, work kept the dreams at bay. Maybe those six days of torture had done a number on his already fucked-up mind. Or maybe being near Natalie was throwing him off balance. Either way, he needed to get a grip.

Natalie made her way past him to the fridge, opened it, looked through the offerings inside. "It looks like someone already made groceries."

Okay, McBride, you have to admit that was damned adorable.

Hell, yeah, it was. You could take the woman out of New Orleans, but you couldn't take New Orleans out of the woman.

Some of his dark mood lifted. "You want an omelet?"

She shut the fridge door and peered into the skillet, where sliced ham, green pepper, onion, and mushrooms simmered in a bed of scrambled egg. "That looks yummy. I don't want to take it if it's yours."

"I'll make another one." He flipped the omelet in half, then turned it over. "Coffee's already brewed."

She poured herself a cup, then added milk and sugar. By the time she'd put the milk away, her omelet was done. He slid it onto a plate, carried it to the little breakfast nook together with a fork, then went back to chopping ham and veggies for his own.

"Toast?" He grabbed a loaf of whole wheat.

"Yes, please. And thanks."

He popped two slices in the toaster, then grabbed three more eggs from the refrigerator and cracked them into a bowl, tossing the shells into the sink.

"You said you looked through my files." She hadn't sat down to eat yet, but stood across the kitchen from him, coffee mug in hand.

"I glanced through them. I didn't have time to study them."

"I could go through them with you if you like. They might make better sense that way. I can't fathom how they could be tied to the Zetas in any way, but if you think it's important . . ."

It wasn't an apology, but then he probably didn't deserve an apology. Still, he appreciated the fact that she wanted to work with him on this.

"It might be important. Hard to say."

"Can we make a deal then? I'll show you my files if you let me look at what you have on Cárdenas."

He started to object, but she talked over him.

"I'm not asking so that I can report on it. In fact, we can say this is strictly deep background, off the record. I just think it might be helpful to your investigation if both of us were familiar with both sides of this."

He thought about it for a moment, weighing the risks against the possible benefits. He glanced over, met her gaze. "It's a deal."

"I JUST DON'T see what sexual assaults at a Denver boarding school could have to do with a Mexican drug cartel." Natalie finished arranging her documents in neat piles on the coffee table, almost painfully aware of the man who sat beside her.

It didn't help that Zach had left his shirt unbuttoned, exposing that amazing body of his. Even the fact that he hadn't showered seemed to make it worse, the natural scent of his skin arousing her, his tousled hair and the stubble on his jaw giving him a manly, earthy look. But there were also dark circles beneath his eyes and lines of fatigue on his face. Had he had another nightmare?

She regretted what she'd said to him last night—or at least she regretted the way she'd said it. He was a hero many times over, a man who'd sacrificed so much for the sake of his country. He didn't deserve to be called "chicken."

And yet the heart of what she'd said felt true to her. He had an easier time facing down men with guns than his own memories, and those memories he couldn't face were holding him back, depriving him of companionship, laughter, love.

Just like your grief over Beau held you back.

No. For him it was worse. She hadn't believed herself capable of love. He didn't seem to believe he deserved it.

Fighting to stay focused, she gave Zach an overview of her investigation, then left him to read through the stories she'd written so far, along with police reports and other documents, while she took a shower and shaved her legs. She dried her hair, put on a bit of makeup, then dressed in clothes he'd bought for her—linen pants and a violet V-neck tank top. She couldn't wear them without thinking of their time together in the desert. Would he have the same reaction?

Are you trying to catch his attention, Benoit?

Maybe. Was there anything wrong with that?

She came back downstairs to find him sipping his coffee, his gaze fixed on the soccer coach's mug shot. "Find anything?"

He shook his head, looked up, his gaze sliding over her, his eyes going dark. "Nothing yet."

"What are we searching for anyway?" She went into the kitchen, poured herself another cup of coffee.

His voice—and his gaze—followed her. "Most of the time when cartels kill it comes down to protecting their business. In other words, money."

"So money really *is* the root of all evil." She poured cream into her coffee, added a teaspoon of sugar, and stirred, then walked back into the living room. "I sent everyone's tax documents to a forensic accountant. If there's anything strange going on with their tax returns, she'll spot it. I expect to hear from her soon."

"Good idea." There was a note of appreciation in his voice. "If anything pops, I'll have Rowan search their financials."

She sat across from him, a nervous trill in her belly. "So where do we start?"

"Let's take a step back here and look at the big picture. Either your abduction is related to this investigation, or it's not. If it *is* related, then someone had something to hide that your investigation threatened to reveal, something that was connected in some way to the Zetas. If it's *not* related then what we're dealing with here is Cárdenas trying to kill you in an effort to avenge his ego."

"Because I escaped?"

"Because you escaped."

Natalie thought about this, tried to wrap her mind around

it. "I just can't see how anyone at Whitcomb could have ties to the Zetas. It's a very exclusive school—lots of girls from wealthy families whose ancestors probably came over on the *Mayflower*. Isn't the simplest scenario more likely? Cárdenas looked on the SPJ website to see which Mexican journalists were on the tour, saw my photo, and decided to kidnap me for his sick little ritual. Now he's angry because I got away."

Zach frowned. "Yeah. Maybe this is a waste of time, but I still can't believe that Cárdenas would reach all the way up to Denver to try to kill you unless he had a bigger motivation than that. He's a narcissist, to be sure, and we know your escape had him tearing apart his own country to find you. But he's also a businessman. Trying to kill an innocent American woman deep in her homeland—that's a bad move for *so* many reasons."

"What do we look for then?"

"Let's determine who stood to lose the most from your investigation and focus on them."

She shrugged. "Well, that's easy. The district attorney. The sheriff. If either one of them were caught dropping the case for bribes, their careers would be over. There's the alleged rapist himself. He would've spent the rest of his life in prison if he'd been convicted. The school. It's bad PR when students get raped by a coach. Whitcomb Academy would probably have lost a lot of revenue if the coach had been convicted."

He looked into her eyes, his lips curving in a lopsided grin. "Ever think of being a cop?"

"Good heavens, no! I'm a journalist, and that's scary enough."

"Yeah, no shit. Okay, let's go through them one by one." His smile gone, he picked up the alleged rapist's mug shot. "They never look like rapists, do they?"

"THIS IS LOCO. You know that, don't you? You're going to get yourself killed, amigo, and me along with you."

Joaquin watched street names as his cousin, a member of the Latin Kings gang, drove him deep into the barrio, the Glock 9mm he'd bought two days ago heavy in his pocket. "No one is going to get killed."

"This man you are after—he's connected to a cartel."

"I know. Los Zetas."

Jesús glanced over at him, a look of disbelief on his face. "Then you must be loco. These *chingaderos*—they kill for fun."

"He hurt and tried to kill a friend of mine—a woman."

Comprehension dawned on Jesús's face. "This is about that reporter who got kidnapped in Juárez."

"I'm not going to let him hurt her again."

"This is bullshit. We're going home." Jesús flipped a U-turn in the middle of traffic, drawing angry honks and curses.

"Stop!" Joaquin jerked the wheel hard to the right, forcing his cousin to the curb.

Jesús slammed on the breaks. "Are you trying to kill someone?"

As a matter of fact, it *had* crossed Joaquin's mind. "Just show me where he is, and then leave. You don't even have to get out of the car."

Jesús looked genuinely afraid, sweat beading on his forehead, sliding past the little five-point crown tattooed on his temple. "If you get killed, your mother and mine will blame me. So you'd better stay alive, eh?"

"I promise."

Jesús turned the car around again, drove a couple of blocks north, then pulled over to the curb. "You see the flophouse behind us? Word is he's living upstairs with a hooker. Third window from the right."

Joaquin studied it with the help of the passenger-side mirror. "Drop me off down the street. Then go home."

Ten minutes later, Joaquin lay on a rooftop across the street, watching, his camera and the Glock ready. One hour went by. Two. Three. It was hot on the rooftop, the late afternoon sun beating down on shingles that reeked of tar.

And then he saw him—a man who looked just like the man in the police sketch, a jagged scar stretching along his jawline on the right.

Joaquin focused the shot, clicked, and clicked again as the man disappeared into the flophouse, then reappeared at the window.

Joaquin clicked away, focusing in tightly with a telephoto lens on the bastard's face, catching the address of the flophouse.

It took a moment before he saw that the man was looking in his direction.

He moved the camera away from his face, looked up, and realized that the sun was glinting off his camera lens. "Shit."

That's why you're not a secret agent, Ramirez.

Pulse picking up, Joaquin reached in his pocket, grabbed his cell phone, dialed. "Hey, Darcangelo. I think I found our man—that Zeta with the scarred face. Yeah. The only problem is, I think he found me, too."

By the time Joaquin looked back at the window, the Zeta had disappeared.

CHAPTER 27

"HE'S COMPLETELY MIA—no forwarding address, no land-line, no calls made on his cell phone since the day he moved out. Same thing with his credit cards—no recent charges. He's got two accounts with a total of fifteen grand cooling in the bank, and he hasn't touched a dime. His parents and brother say they've had no contact."

Natalie sat in the shade of the awning on the rooftop patio, sipping southern sweet tea, barely aware of Zach's phone conversation with Rowan, her gaze riveted to the dossier he had put together for her on Cárdenas. There were hundreds of pages, most stamped "CLASSIFIED" in big, red letters, some with photographs, all describing the actions of a man who could only be described as evil.

Cárdenas had been arrested on suspicion of rape at the age of sixteen, rape and murder at seventeen, and numerous counts of drug trafficking at eighteen. Arrest mug shots showed a skinny, angry boy with hate in his eyes and a smirk on his face. By the time he was twenty, he'd been arrested almost a dozen times, and the smirk had become a fixed sneer. He had reason to scorn the police. They'd arrested him again and again, but the charges had never stuck. According to background notes, his father had paid handsomely to keep him out of prison, buying off judges, cops, witnesses.

It was his father's money that had opened doors for him when he'd joined the *federales* at the age of twenty-one. The arrests had stopped, and he'd risen through the ranks, eventually joining a newly formed elite team created to combat drug trafficking throughout Mexico. By the time he was in his mid-thirties, the Pentagon and the State Department had invited him and other members of his unit—known as Los Zetas—to come to a special training facility in Virginia called the Americas Institute for Tactical Training (AMINTAC), a U.S.-funded school for Latin American law enforcement and military officers, designed to teach them advanced tactical skills.

Cárdenas had filled out by then, no longer a skinny teenager. Tall with a heavy mustache, he seemed to like posing in his uniform, gun in hand. There were more than a dozen photographs of him standing with U.S. military and intelligence personnel, a broad smile on his face, his hair cut in a mullet, aviator-style Ray-Bans covering his eyes.

You think you're so cool, don't you, Cárdenas?

Even the sight of him sickened Natalie.

The concept behind AMINTAC was to help democratic governments keep the peace and counter organized crime. But keeping the peace was apparently not what Cárdenas had had in mind.

Not long after he'd returned to Mexico, DEA memos showed that some agents had begun to suspect the Zetas of selling the drugs they confiscated from cartels, using weapons and tactical training provided by the United States to carve out their own drug empire, slaughtering cartel members—and anyone else who got in their way. And then things had really gotten ugly.

U.S. agents began to suspect Cárdenas of playing a role in the disappearance of young women around Ciudad Juárez. Hundreds of girls and women had been found dead in and around the city, all of them victims of sexual violence, all of them battered, their bodies brutalized. Some had been as young as fourteen. None had been older than thirty.

Such terrible suffering. So young to die.

Natalie couldn't bring herself to look closely at the photographs. She'd seen some of them the day before she'd been kidnapped—horrific images of young women lying naked and dead in the desert.

That could have been me.

She forced her emotions aside, read through several reports about Cárdenas that focused mostly on the organization of the Zetas and their drug operation. But some of the reports indicated that Cárdenas was a suspect in at least some of the femicides. Then he'd ordered the death of an American on U.S. soil, a former business associate who'd become an informant for the DEA. Zeta snipers had shot the informant through the window of his El Paso home, killing him in front of his wife and children.

That's when the U.S. Marshal Service had taken over.

Natalie had no trouble distinguishing Zach's reports from the others. His neat handwriting. His sharp, declarative sentences. His ability to separate facts from conjecture and organize both.

That's when she found it—the report on the sixteen-year-old girl tourists had found lying more dead than alive in the desert.

As soon as she realized what she was reading, Natalie tried to turn the page. She didn't want to know what it said. And yet she couldn't stop herself.

It was perhaps the most chilling report she'd ever read, the young victim describing her ordeal in detail. How she'd been kidnapped and stuffed in a trunk on her way home from working late at one of the *maquiladoras*. How Cárdenas had brutally raped and beaten her over a period of days, until she'd wanted to die. How he'd brought her into a little chapel and had raped her for hours in front of an altar dedicated to La Santa Muerte. How he'd strangled her, calling her beautiful, his face inches from hers as she slowly lapsed into unconsciousness.

Oh, God! That's what he would have done to me.

And then it was too much.

Natalie stood, pushed past Zach, who was still on the phone, and raced to the nearest bathroom, where she threw up her lunch, her body shaking, her blood gone cold, an image of the Zeta with the tattoo on his arm fixed in her mind.

Él te sacrificará a la Santa Muerte.

He will sacrifice you to La Santa Muerte.

Trembling, she flushed the toilet, got unsteadily to her feet, and rinsed out her mouth, splashing water over her face, still feeling nauseated.

"Natalie?" Zach's voice came from beside her. "Are you okay?"

She nodded, reached for a towel, and turned to find him watching her, a concerned frown on his face. "I'm . . . I'm fine."

"The hell you are! You're white as a sheet." He touched his wrist to her forehead, apparently feeling for fever.

"I'm not sick. I was reading the dossier and . . ." Tears blurred her vision. "Oh, Zach, what he did to that sixteen-year-old, what he did to all those girls. It's beyond horrific. It's what he would have done to me, isn't it?"

The answer was on Zach's face, in his unflinching gaze. He drew her into his arms and held her. "That can't have been easy to read."

Natalie sank into the shelter of Zach's embrace. "You knew. When we were locked up, you knew exactly what he had planned for me. You told me the truth."

I imagine he'll rape you repeatedly over a period of days or maybe even weeks and then sell you or kill you.

There was no way Natalie could have understood what he'd meant. The reality that young girl had survived was so much worse than anything Natalie's imagination could have conjured, even locked in the dark of that arachnid-infested cell.

"Shhh. Try not to think about that now." He stroked her hair, the warmth of his body chasing the ice from her blood. It was the first time he'd held her since he'd drawn the line between them, and she wanted it to last forever. But it didn't.

All too soon he released her and stepped back. "Are you sure you don't want to go rest for a while?"

Natalie swallowed her disappointment, wiped the tears from her cheeks. "No, thank you. I'll be fine. And thanks."

He stepped aside, let her walk past him and out of the bathroom. "That was Rowan on the phone. She sent some DUSMs to see whether the company that helped the soccer coach move had his new address. Turns out they never met him. They were paid in cash—an envelope of bills left in the apartment. And they didn't move his shit into a new home. They delivered it to the Goodwill—every bit of clothing, every dish and spoon, every piece of furniture."

Natalie willed her mind to focus on what Zach had just

told her. "Was he in such a hurry to leave town that he left everything behind?"

Zach opened his mouth to speak, but was interrupted by his cell phone. He drew it out of his pocket. "Hey, Darcangelo. What's up?"

Natalie watched as Zach's expression changed first to astonishment and then anger.

"You are fucking kidding me! I'm on my way." He hung up, shoved the phone in his pocket, and strode toward the living room.

She hurried after him. "What's wrong?"

"Your friend Joaquin took it upon himself to track down Quintana on his own, but Quintana spotted him."

The blood rushed from her head. "Is Joaquin—"

"He's fine—or he will be until I get ahold of him."

What had Joaquin been thinking? Was he trying to get himself killed?

"Quintana got away?"

"No. They got him. I don't know the details." Zach turned into the kitchen, grabbed his keys from the counter, and shoved a belt badge over the waistband of his jeans just above his left hip.

Natalie's fear for Joaquin gave way to a surge of relief. They'd caught Quintana. Maybe this was over. Maybe this was the end.

Oh, thank God!

Only when Zach walked to the front door did it dawn on her that he was leaving.

"Where are you going?"

"Denver PD. They've put him in isolation at the city jail. I'm going to lead the interrogation."

"But I'll be—"

"You're safest here. Don't leave the loft for any reason. You can call me using your new cell phone if you need me. Otherwise, you know the rules—no phone calls except on the encrypted cell and no e-mail that isn't sent through the encrypted address. I'll be back as soon as I can."

She stood there, watching as he opened the door and stepped into the hallway.

He turned back toward her. "This is the biggest break

we've gotten so far. Quintana is Cárdenas's right-hand man, his nephew. If I can get him to talk . . ."

Natalie nodded. "Go."

Then the door closed, and she was alone.

JOAQUIN SAT IN the hallway, still a bit stunned, his jaw aching where that bastard Quintana had punched him.

"I want him in full restraints in Interrogation Room One." Darcangelo told Denver Police Chief Irving—the man who, until Darcangelo had been deputized, had been his boss. "No trips to the bathroom, no water, no phone calls—nothing until McBride gets here and approves it."

"Your wish is our command." Irving turned to the officer next to him, every year of his three decades as a cop showing in the lines on his face and the heavy bags beneath his eyes. "Do what the deputy marshal says, Sergeant Wu."

Wu nodded, a suppressed grin on his face. "I'm on it."

Darcangelo clapped Irving on the shoulder, the two men offering a sharp visual contrast—one young and athletic with long dark hair held back in a ponytail, the other middle-aged with a belly that protruded over his belt, his gray hair buzzed into a crew cut. "Irving, I'm going to put in a good word for you. You've been very cooperative."

Even though it hurt, Joaquin couldn't help but laugh.

Darcangelo turned on him, jabbed a finger in his face. "I don't want to hear a thing from you, Ramirez. I'm still not sure whether I should arrest you, kick your ass myself, or buy you a drink."

"Maybe all three." Hunter appeared with an ice pack in his hand and McBride at his side. He tossed the ice pack to Joaquin. "I still think you should see a doc."

"I'll be fine." Joaquin pressed the ice to his jaw.

He probably deserved to get his ass kicked. He definitely deserved to get arrested. How *stupid* could he be, letting the sunlight catch his lens like that? If the cops hadn't gotten there in time . . .

McBride stopped in front of him, looked him over. "You're damned lucky to be alive. I'm just glad I didn't have to tell

Natalie you'd gotten yourself killed. Later, you and I are going to have a very serious conversation."

Then McBride turned to the other men. "Now, where is the son of a bitch?"

Darcangelo turned and walked down the hallway, McBride and Hunter following him, their voices trailing back. "Are you sure you're up for this, bro? This asshole tortured you for six days and tried to kill Natalie. If it's too personal—"

"Worry about him, not me."

"You're not going to hit him, are you?" That was Hunter, the tone of his voice suggesting that perhaps McBride *should* hit Quintana.

"That would be illegal, wouldn't it? No, I'm not going to hit him. I'm going to kick the living shit out of him."

Irving looked at Joaquin, shook his head, the weariness in his eyes brightened by just a hint of amusement. "Christ."

WHILE DARCANGELO AND Hunter watched from the other side of the one-way mirror, Zach entered the interrogation room and found Quintana staring upward as if counting ceiling tiles, looking bored. "*¿Te acuerdas de mí?*" *Do you remember me?*

Quintana met his gaze, smiled. "We miss you—my little stinger and I."

Ignoring the taunt, Zach crossed the small room, dragged Quintana to his feet, and drove his fist into Quintana's gut hard enough to bend the bastard double and knock the breath from his lungs. Then he grabbed Quintana by the hair, jerking his head up, forcing Quintana to meet his gaze. "If anything happens to Señorita Benoit, I will make you watch while I feed your balls to my dogs."

Never mind that he had no dogs.

Quintana struggled to breathe, his lips twisting in a painful grimace that became a grin. "Like I made you watch . . . when I played with her perfect tits?"

Pulse thrumming, Zach willed himself to step back, knowing he was a heartbeat away from losing control and killing a man in his custody. He turned himself to stone, let himself go cold. "We have so much to talk about—like the explosives you planted in Señorita Benoit's car."

"I have nothing to say to you, except this." Quintana fixed him with his gaze. "In the end you will fail. Your enemy follows no rules, while you are bound by many."

It was going to be a long night.

NATALIE CLICKED ON yet another private school's website. This one—a boarding school outside of Colorado Springs— had an endowment of a little more than a million dollars, with almost twice the number of students that attended Whitcomb Academy. She jotted down a few notes about it, then sat back on the sofa and stretched, her neck and shoulders stiff from so many hours at the computer.

The forensic accountant had contacted the paper today with the results of her analysis. Although she'd found nothing wrong with anyone's tax records, she'd been surprised by the amount of money in Whitcomb Academy's endowment, as well as the rate at which the fund had grown. She'd taken it upon herself to look up schools similar to Whitcomb across the country and hadn't been able to find one that boasted a seven-hundred-forty-five-million-dollar endowment. She'd sent her findings to Natalie via e-mail.

It's no smoking gun, to be sure. In fact, it might be nothing. But I thought I'd mention it anyway.

Natalie had spent the evening reading the report and doing her own search of private boarding schools. She'd gotten the same results. There wasn't another boarding school in Colorado or across the country that could compare with Whitcomb when it came to the wealth of its endowment. In fact, Whitcomb exceeded even some private colleges. Did the school have a lot of wealthy donors or did the money come from—

Behind her, the clock on the mantel struck two a.m., making her gasp.

Get a grip on yourself, girl!

She drew a deep breath, blew it out, trying to relax.

As late as it was, she ought to quit working and go to bed. But she'd tried that once already, and she hadn't been able to sleep. Every time she'd closed her eyes, she'd seen images of murdered girls, their bodies violated, twisted, broken. She'd given up at midnight and decided that if she was awake she might as well work.

Not that she was getting anywhere.

A wealthy boarding school where teenage girls had been raped. A serial rapist/killer drug lord who wanted to kill her. The Whitcomb investigation and Cárdenas had two things in common—sexual assault and lots of money. But that was surely just coincidence. The Zetas hadn't raped those schoolgirls, and she and Zach had yet to uncover any ties between Cárdenas's money and Whitcomb.

She clicked on the school's website again, randomly scrolling through pages, stopping to look through the photo album, a slideshow of smiling young women that reminded her of her days at McGehee. What happy days those had been, with Mama and Daddy still alive, her world intact, Beau still in her future . . .

Her thoughts trailed off as she looked at the photograph in front of her, an image of a girl accepting an award on stage, a bright smile on her face as she shook the hand of one of the school's administrators. No, not an administrator. The caption identified him as Edward Wulfe, the president of the school's Board of Trustees.

Though Natalie had never met the man, she knew she'd seen him someplace before. He was tall, with a head of salt-and-pepper hair, his features nondescript, his smile bland—not the sort of face that stood out. And still she remembered him from somewhere.

You probably saw him right here in this photo the last time you searched the school's website.

Her tired brain tied in knots, she closed her laptop, stood, and carried her empty teacup to the kitchen sink. Still unable to face the darkness of her bedroom, she walked back into the living room. Beyond the wall of glass stretched the twinkling lights of Denver, the sight somehow comforting, friendly, warm. She dimmed the lights in the loft, then walked to the French doors and stepped out into the cool air.

She didn't feel so alone out here amid the sounds of traffic and the glittering lights. She walked to the edge, looked out at the city beyond, two million people living their lives, most of them asleep. Denver didn't roll up the sidewalks at sunset, but its nightlife couldn't compare to that of New Orleans, where the parties went on—

"Natalie?"

She gasped, and whirled about to find Zach standing in the doorway.

"Jesus!" He shook his head. "You scared the crap out of me. I walked in, saw the lights off and doors open. Are you okay?"

"I'm fine." She squelched the surge of joy she felt to see him standing there. He wasn't home to be with her, after all. He was simply back on duty. "How did it go? Is it really him?"

He stepped out into the darkness, closing the distance between them with slow strides. "It's him all right. Rowan's men found weapons in his hotel room but no traces of explosives. He isn't talking. I left him in lockdown under the guard of two DUSMs. I'll have to try again tomorrow."

"How's Joaquin?"

"He took a couple of body blows and a fist to the jaw, but he'll be fine—until the four of us get time to kick his ass. He's lucky DPD got to him as quickly as they did." Zach stopped just a few feet away from her, close enough to reach out and touch her, if he wanted to. But he didn't. "What are you still doing up?"

"I . . . I couldn't sleep. That dossier on Cárdenas . . ." She saw on his face that she didn't need to explain.

For a moment he looked like he was going to reach for her, like he wanted to hold her. Then a muscle clenched in his jaw, and he looked away, his fingers curling into fists, his gaze far away. "It's late. We both need sleep. Let's talk in the morning."

He ushered her back inside, locking the doors behind them.

ARTURO LOOKED OUT the window, hating everything about this town—the dry air, the altitude, the people. He couldn't wait to go home to Mexico. There, he lived like a king. Here, he was subjected to intolerable rudeness and humiliation.

Behind him, his host conducted business with one of his minions. "Is the GPS tracker in place on McBride's vehicle?"

"Yes, sir. We should have the first upload in a couple of hours."

"Excellent. We'll know exactly where they're hiding. By tomorrow night, this should all be over—and our friend Arturo will have learned a valuable lesson."

It was on the tip of Arturo's tongue to tell his whoreson of a business partner to fuck a goat, but he kept his silence.

There was no man on earth who frightened him like Edward Wulfe.

CHAPTER 28

ZACH LAY ON his belly with his face in the dirt, desperately thirsty from blood loss, the pain in his back excruciating. The sat phone was smashed, but that didn't matter. He'd completed the call. Support was on its way. Mike, Chris, Brian, and Jimmy would be okay.

From down in the valley came the sound of three M4s and one HK MP5. They were still alive, still fighting. He might not make it out of here, but they would.

Give 'em hell, boys.

And then he saw.

At least eighty enemy combatants snaked down the mountainside across from him headed straight for the men, all of them armed with AKs. They would come up behind his element and catch them by surprise. The guys would be caught in a cross fire by an enemy that outnumbered them and had the high ground. By the time support arrived, it would be too late—for all of them.

Zach reached for his rifle, determined to send as many Taliban fighters to hell as he could, only to find his hands chained above his head. He couldn't move.

There in front of him, two Zetas held Natalie while Quintana tore off her clothes, Natalie's desperate screams drowning out the Taliban gunfire. How had she gotten here? He'd thought she was safe. He'd thought she was home.

"Natalie!" He tried to free himself so he could get to her,

blood pouring down his arms from his lacerated wrists, pooling at his feet, electric cables perilously near.

"*Chichis perfectas,*" Quintana said. Perfect tits.

Then Brian's wife, Debbie, appeared beside him, dressed in black, baby in her arms. "You didn't save my husband. You won't save her."

From the valley behind him came the blast of an IED, the explosion followed by the cries of dying friends.

"Zach!"

His hands suddenly free, Zach lunged for Quintana, determined to get the fucker off her, his hands closing around the bastard's neck.

And then inexplicably, he found himself staring into Natalie's frightened face. She lay on the floor beneath him, clutching at the hands that squeezed her throat. A man's big hands. *His* hands.

"*Jesus Christ!*" Zach jerked back from her and landed flat on his ass, his mind caught somewhere between his nightmare and the horror of what he'd almost done. Cold sweat beaded on his skin, his body shaking uncontrollably, the sound of screams and automatic weapons fire still echoing through his mind.

She sat up, coughed, a hand raised to her throat. "It's okay, Zach. I'm okay. It was just a bad dream. I heard you cry out, and I came to—"

He staggered to his feet and headed downstairs toward the dark kitchen, wearing nothing but boxer briefs. He grabbed the unopened bottle of Jack he'd bought on his way home, his only thought to get himself away from her, away from the nightmare in his head. Without bothering to turn on the lights, he twisted off the cap, brought the bottle to his lips, and took a deep drink, whiskey burning its way down his throat to his empty stomach.

"Zach?" She stood there in that damned silk nightgown, watching him through eyes filled with concern, his own personal angel of mercy.

But he didn't deserve her mercy, not after tonight.

"It's obvious I can't handle this assignment. I'll ask Rowan to task someone else tomorrow morning."

"But I don't want that. I—"

"Go to bed." He pushed past her, walked through the living room, then opened the French doors and stepped out onto the rooftop patio. Cool night air hit him in the face. He raised the bottle to his lips again, his heart still beating too fast, the image of his hands around Natalie's throat making his stomach churn.

She came up behind him. "Does that really help?"

"Depends on how much I drink." He laughed—a dark sound—then took another swallow. "Leave me alone, Natalie."

"No. You don't need to be alone. You've been alone with this for too long."

Something inside him wanted to lash out at her, to say or do something that would drive her away. But he held his tongue, bit back his rage.

"You're hurt." The tone of her voice was soft, gentle, the tone a person used to soothe a wounded animal. "Sometimes the scar isn't on the outside. Sometimes it's on the inside where no one else can see it. Believe me, I know."

"Stop!" He ground the words out through gritted teeth. He didn't want her to see him like this again—weak, pathetic, broken. Why couldn't she understand that? "Just leave me the hell alone! Please!"

"I can't." Her palm, soft and warm, pressed against the skin of his bare back, making every muscle in his body tense. "After the storm, I died inside. I lost everyone I loved in a single hour, and it hurt so much that something inside me shut down. My life was cold and dark and empty. But you made me *feel* again. You brought me to life, Zach. Do you think I can turn my back on you when you're hurting like this? You're the strongest man I've ever known, but sometimes even heroes need help."

Zach started to raise the whiskey bottle again, but his arm wouldn't move. His muscles had gone rigid, his body shaking, a strange burning in his eyes. Then his vision blurred, and he felt it—something hot and wet on his cheeks. Was he crying?

Oh, Christ!

He couldn't stop it, couldn't stop, something inside him cracking, a choked cry ripping its way out of his throat. His knees gave, and he sank into a chair, helpless to combat the maelstrom inside him. The harder he fought, the more it dragged him down.

But then Natalie was there, holding him tight, her slender arms around his shoulders. He let her take the bottle from him and held on to her like a drowning man, surrendering himself to her along with whatever was left of his pride.

Slowly, the horror began to seep away—but not the shame. He was a grown man, a former SEAL, for Christ sake! He was being comforted by a woman he was supposed to protect, a woman who'd survived her own hell, a woman whose neck he could just as easily have broken a few moments ago.

You're a fucking pussy, McBride. If the guys could see this, they wouldn't even recognize you.

Natalie set the bottle of whiskey aside and cradled Zach's head against her chest and held him, a hard lump in her throat. He was such a strong man, such a man's man. He probably hadn't shed a tear since he was a little boy. But he was crying now, real tears, his body shaking with the effort to suppress them. And it broke her heart.

"I tried! God, I tried! I tried to save them!" The words burst out of him, his voice ragged, tinged with despair.

She remembered what Agent Chiago had said about Zach and how he'd earned his Medal of Honor. He'd come close to being killed while trying to save his team. That must be what this was about.

"Aw, Jesus!" He drew back from her, shot to his feet, and took a couple of steps, wiping his face with his hands, clearly enraged with himself. And for a moment he stood there, ramrod straight, sucking in lungful after lungful of air.

Natalie held back, gave him his space, afraid she'd pushed him too far.

"I led a five-man team into the Hindu Kush mountains in Nuristan province in Afghanistan." His voice was flat, lifeless. "We'd gotten a tip from an informant about caves where Taliban combatants had hidden a cache of weapons and explosives. Our objective was to find the caves and to destroy the cache. But the informant turned out to be a Qaeda agent. Instead of finding caves, we were ambushed."

He grabbed a chair, sank into it, avoiding her gaze.

"We fought our way free. Chris, Mike, Jimmy, Brian, and

I had been together since BUD/S. We were a team. It's like we read each other's minds. No matter what the odds or what the situation, we . . ." A faint smile played on his lips, then faded. "We retreated, tried to make our way to the extraction point, but we got boxed into a canyon by enemy fire—five of us against more than a hundred of them. We took cover as best we could. I . . . Ah, hell, I can't believe I'm talking about this."

Natalie sat across from him, waiting, giving him the time he needed.

He drew a breath, went on. "I tried to call for extraction, but I couldn't get a clear signal. I knew that someone had to climb to the rim of the canyon to make the call, but that meant being exposed to enemy fire. They all had wives and kids. I didn't."

"So you took it upon yourself." How like the Zach she knew to risk his own life to save others.

"I was their commanding officer. It was my job to bring them back alive. It was my *job*. And there was no one at home waiting for me to return."

That sounded so terribly lonely. "What about your parents?"

He shook his head. "My mother had died a few months earlier of a rare heart infection, and my old man . . . We barely spoke to one another. The SEALs, my team—that was my family."

Natalie knew what it was like to lose one's entire family. She waited, fairly sure she knew where this story was going.

"I climbed to the rim of the canyon. Made it almost to the top before I got hit. Caught an AK round in the back. I managed to hold on, hauled myself over the top, made the call. I could hear the men's weapons firing. I knew the guys were still alive. Six Black Hawks were in the air and on their way. If they could just hold on another twenty minutes . . ." He held out his hand, reaching for the bottle.

Natalie picked it up, passed it to him.

He drank, seeming to swallow his own emotions along with the alcohol, his face becoming an expressionless mask, his gaze focused on nothing. "I was thirsty from blood loss and needed water. I reached for my pack and saw a group of Taliban fighters making their way down the slope across from me, headed for my team. They didn't see me. I grabbed my rifle, emptied the magazine, and reloaded. But I couldn't move fast enough. I didn't get all of them. They tossed a couple IEDs into the hollow where the men were hiding. I listened to my team die, heard their cries, Brian screaming . . ."

Tears trickled down Natalie's cheeks, her heart aching for him. Yes, she'd lost her parents and the man she loved, but she hadn't been there to watch and hear them die. She couldn't even bear to imagine that.

"I blacked out. When I came to, I was in the hands of a medevac unit. The rescue I'd called for turned out to be my own. The navy patched me up and shipped me stateside to recover."

Then Zach's mask began to crumble. "I arrived the same week as their bodies. I went to their funerals at Arlington. I watched while their wives cried and their kids sat there looking confused and . . . and asking about Daddy."

His voice broke, and for the first time since he'd started telling Natalie his story, his gaze met hers. "*I* was the one who was supposed to die that day. They were supposed to come home."

"It's not your fault, Zach. You did more than most men—"

Ignoring her, he stood, walked over the railing, and looked out over the sleeping city. Natalie followed, unsure what to do or say. And for a time they stood there in silence, his jaw clenched, his body shaking again, a look of raw anguish on his face.

He took another drink. "After Brian's funeral, his wife, Debbie, came up to me, carrying their youngest. I'd known her since she and Brian met. I was the best man at their wedding. She . . ."

He paused, drew a deep breath. "She called me a coward, told me . . . that I'd left her husband and the others to die, that I'd climbed out of that canyon to save my own ass. 'You should have died,' she said, 'not my husband.' I tried to explain but . . ."

His voice trailed off.

Natalie watched him, saw the torment on his face, and found herself wanting to smack poor widowed Debbie. Did he actually believe her? Yes, he did. He'd gotten so tangled in his grief that he truly believed he'd failed his friends.

Oh, Zach!

She rested her hand against his arm, the need to comfort him overwhelming. "Debbie didn't mean what she said. That was her grief talking. She doesn't really believe that, and neither should you. You know what really happened that day. You know you did all you could to save them. For God's sake, you almost died!"

But her words didn't seem to reach him. "A few years later, the White House called. The President told me I'd been awarded the Medal of Honor. I asked him why. I let my team down. They died. I lived. There's nothing honorable in that."

He turned, sat back against the railing. "I went to the ceremony anyway. I felt like such a fucking fraud. My old man was there. As a U.S. senator, he'd have been on the guest list anyway, but he was running for reelection. Even though we hadn't spoken since my mother's death, he showed up with a media entourage, turning it into a goddamned photo op in hopes of winning votes."

"I'm sure he was proud of you." What parent wouldn't be?

Zach shook his head. "I joined the navy over his objections. I overheard him tell my mother that their son would never have to serve in the military even if the draft were reinstated, because he was a senator. I was disgusted. I signed up the next day. I wanted to show him that being a senator's son didn't mean I was entitled to sit on the sidelines in safety while other men's sons and daughters went to war. At the time, he was furious, but that didn't stop him from trying to take advantage of the limelight later. I left the medal on the table and walked out."

"You left the medal there?" How terribly sad to think he'd given up something so precious, something he'd earned through blood and pain. "What happened to it?"

"I have no idea." He shook his head as if it didn't matter. "God, I'm such a weak piece of shit. I'm sorry you had to see this."

She could see the shame on his face, tearstains on his cheeks. "What I saw tonight was a wounded hero, a warrior who served his country when others would have chosen an easier path, who willingly risked his own life to save his men, but who can't forgive himself for being the one to survive."

"You don't understand." He glared at her, then walked back toward the doors.

"Oh, yes, I do," she called after him, her voice trembling, that lump back in her throat. "I know what it's like to be the one left behind. I know what it's like to lose everyone you love in a single day. I know what it's like to blame yourself, to wonder if they'd still be alive if only you'd done this instead of that. But you can't waste your life wishing you'd been the one to die."

He turned to face her, stopped, anger on his face. "I don't know what you're talking about. You're confusing your situation with mine."

"No, I'm not." She walked over to him, looked up into his eyes. "You told me that when you came back from the war you thought about killing yourself—or is there some other meaning for the phrase 'eat my gun'?"

He opened his mouth to speak, but she cut him off, spurred on by a sudden surge of insight. "You didn't join the marshal service just to drown your demons in adrenaline. You did it because some dark and desperate part of you is *hoping* to die in a hail of bullets like they did so you can prove to yourself that you're worthy, that you're *not* a coward. Look me in the eyes and tell me I'm wrong."

But Zach couldn't look her in the eyes. Her words had struck hard. He felt the anger leave him, along with breath and will and any defenses he'd had left. He made it inside to the sofa, then sank onto the cushions and buried his face in his hands.

"Zach?" She sounded worried. "Are you okay?"

Hell, no, he wasn't okay. He'd come close to strangling her, had done some serious damage to a bottle of whiskey, had broken down in front of her and cried like a baby, and had just had the skin peeled off his psyche. How could he be okay?

Welcome to rock bottom, McBride. How does it feel?

Pretty shitty, actually.

She knelt down before him, her hands soft against his shoulders. "Zach, please. Say something. Tell me I'm wrong. Tell me to go to hell if you want."

"Why would I do that?" He raised his head, reached out to smooth a strand of hair off her cheek, looked into her worried eyes. "You're right. You're right about all of it. I would fix it if I could, Natalie. I just don't know how. I don't know how."

She gave him a sad little smile. "You don't have to figure that out alone."

He shook his head. "I'm done with therapy. I won't go—"

She pressed her fingers to his lips. "I'm not talking about therapy. I'm talking about you and me."

It took him a moment to understand. "After tonight, can you really say you want to get involved with me?"

"Oh, Zach, look at us. We're already involved. You just keep running from it."

He squeezed his eyes shut, turned his head away. "You deserve better, Natalie."

"I was right. You *are* a big chicken." She took his face between her palms, forced him to meet her gaze. "I love you, Zach McBride. You're not alone in this anymore. You fought the Zetas for me. I'm going to fight for you—even if the one I have to fight is *you*."

Breath left Zach's lungs in a rush. He stared at her, wondering if she'd lost her mind. "I'm not worth—"

"We'll take it slow." She drew his face down and kissed him. "One day at a time." She kissed him again. "One hour at a time." Again she kissed him. "One kiss at a time."

He closed his eyes, gave himself over to her kisses, fairly certain he was too dead inside, too empty, too wrung out for what she seemed to have in mind. But her mouth was sweet, her tongue insistent.

Heat. A spark. Desire kindled.

He opened his mouth to her, let her shape the kiss, her lips never leaving his, even when her clever hand slid inside his briefs and stroked him to life. Then she hitched her night-gown up to her hips, climbed onto his lap, and settled herself over him, her gaze holding his as she took him inside her.

Mingled moans. Whiskey and pheromone. Burning need.

Zach's heart pounded, not from the horror of his nightmares this time, but from desire, life surging hot and strong through his veins, his breathing hard and fast, every nerve ending in his body alive.

His tripping pulse. Her cries. A quicksilver rush of bliss.

And Zach was reborn inside her.

She sank against him, out of breath, boneless, and he held her, kissing her hair, stroking the silk of her skin, breathing her scent. Then he lifted her into his arms, carried her upstairs to her bed, lay down beside her—and fell into a deep, dreamless sleep.

"We've got them, sir."

Arturo's head came up from the porn video he was watching on his laptop.

One of Wulfe's men came in, carrying a file, which he set down on the coffee table in front of Wulfe. "Here are the schematics of the building. It will take some time for us to learn which loft they're in. We're already working on it, checking to see which units were available last week that are no longer available today."

Wulfe set down his newspaper, picked up the file, and scanned its pages, his head tilted back to allow him to see through his bifocals. His hair was mostly gray now. He was getting old. They were all getting old. "Excellent work."

"The building has top-flight security—twenty-four-hour guards, video surveillance, biometric scanners encoded with thumbprints."

"Figure out who is helping McBride on this case, who besides McBride has access to the building. Then all we'll need to do is collect a thumb." Wulfe set the file down, his gaze meeting Arturo's. "You see the difficulty you've caused, Arturo? Now some poor idiot is going to lose his thumb—and his life—because you couldn't get the job done in Mexico."

Arturo felt his face burn.

CHAPTER 29

ZACH WOKE THE next morning to find Natalie curled up against him, her head resting on his chest, one of her legs tucked between his. The sheets were tangled around their legs, leaving the creamy curve of her hip bare. He watched her sleep, his body relaxed, his mind blissfully empty.

A part of him hated himself for breaking down like that in front of her again. This time he'd fallen completely the hell apart. He'd cried, for God's sake, shed actual freaking tears. What kind of man acted like that?

But Natalie hadn't turned away from him in disgust. She hadn't been repulsed by him. Just as she'd done in Altar, she'd caught the pieces of him, held them in her arms, then helped him put himself back together.

I love you, Zach McBride. You're not alone in this anymore. You fought for me. I'm going to fight for you—even if the one I have to fight is you.

He didn't know what he'd done to deserve that, to deserve love from a woman like Natalie. She was right when she'd called him a chicken. He was afraid of so many things. Losing himself to nightmares and alcohol. Failing at his mission and letting Cárdenas kill again. Being unworthy of the trust his country had placed in him.

But what frightened him most at this moment was the very real possibility that he'd fallen in love with Natalie.

He stroked her hair, made room for her when she snuggled

deeper into his chest, cherishing the feel of her soft body against his. And for a moment he let himself imagine that this was how every day of his life began—with her sleeping naked beside him, the scent of sex still lingering on their skin, a feeling of contentment inside him. They'd get up, make love in the shower, have breakfast together, kiss each other good-bye, the promise of home getting them through the day.

And then that night, or one just like it, you'd come home in a body bag—or a pizza box. Great idea, McBride.

God knew he didn't want to do that to her. She'd already lost everyone she loved. And yet most of the DUSMs he knew had families. Was it so wrong to work a dangerous job and to have a family, too?

Being a deputy U.S. marshal shouldn't mean you don't get to have a life.

Isn't that what Natalie had said to him in Altar?

He tried to imagine himself as a husband, a father. It didn't seem as impossible as it had even a week ago. Of course, the only condom he'd worn had broken, which meant that he might already be on his way from here to paternity, whether he could imagine being a father or not.

What are you going to do if you've gotten her pregnant, buddy?

He wasn't going to worry about that now.

He looked down at her beautiful face, a tangled knot of emotions swelling inside his chest—longing, protectiveness, doubt, possessiveness, hope. He held her tighter, the feel of her precious. And for a time, he lay there, listening to her breathe, inhaling the stillness, wishing he could stay like this forever.

But, of course, he couldn't. He needed to check in with Rowan, find out where she planned to transfer Quintana, and get back to interrogating the son of a bitch. He glanced over to check the alarm clock, his gaze falling on Natalie's photograph of Beau.

A good-looking young guy with dark brown hair, a solid build, and an easy smile, Beau looked into the camera, unaware that his life was about to end, the love he felt for Natalie unmistakable in his eyes,

Zach understood why Beau had braved the flooded, debris-strewn streets of New Orleans to come for her. He knew what

Beau must have felt when he'd heard that she'd almost been murdered—shock, seething rage, a bone-deep need to protect and comfort her. And he knew that Beau's last thought must have been of her.

Zach met Beau's gaze, found himself whispering to a dead man. "I'd die for her, too."

NATALIE WOKE TO the delicious feeling of kisses trailing down her back, Zach's big hand caressing the bare curve of her hip. "Mmm."

"You're finally awake." His hand slid in delicious circles upward along her side and around front to cup her breast. His skilled fingers teased her nipple, pinched it, tugged it, his touch sending sparks deep into her belly. "Good."

She could smell on his minty breath that he'd already been up and had brushed his teeth. She wanted to do the same. Reluctantly, she drew away. "Hold that thought."

She climbed out of bed, walked naked into the beautiful marble bathroom, the tiles cool against her feet. She grabbed her toothbrush and quickly brushed, holding her hair back as she rinsed her mouth. She finished, set her toothbrush aside, then turned toward the door—and froze.

Still naked, he stood in the doorway, his gaze sliding intimately over her, his erection standing against his belly, his testicles hanging full and heavy beneath. There was something deeply primal about his aroused body, about the heat in his eyes, about the way he watched her.

He walked slowly toward her. "Do you have any idea how beautiful you are?"

Beautiful.

That's how she would describe *him*—beautiful, erotic, so powerfully male.

She met him halfway, rose on her tiptoes, and kissed him, her arms sliding behind his neck. He groaned, his tongue greeting hers.

And then she got an idea—a silly, naughty, exciting idea. Suppressing her own laughter, she deliberately turned them in a slow-motion waltz until her back was toward the door. Slowly, she stepped back from him, smiled up at him from beneath her eyelashes—then turned and ran.

She dashed toward the bed, jumped in, and scuttled to the far side, looking back to find him watching her, a predatory gleam in his eyes now. Excitement shivered through her, the thrill of being pursued making her pulse trip.

"Where do you think you're going?" He walked in slow strides toward her, his muscles shifting. "You can't get away from me. You know that, don't you?"

Quashing the giggle that welled up inside her, she drew back against the headboard, curling her legs beneath her, covering her bare breasts with her hands, her heart pounding harder as he drew near.

"Why are you covering yourself?" He stopped at the edge of the bed. "I'm going to see it all, touch it all, taste it all. I'm going to do whatever I want with your sweet body, and there's nothing you can do to stop me."

Then he lowered himself to one knee on the mattress.

With a squeal, Natalie leapt from the bed, but she didn't make it far. A strong arm caught her around her waist and drew her back onto the bed. She fought just hard enough to make him use his strength, turning onto her belly, trying to crawl away.

"You think this will stop me?" He laughed, a dark masculine sound. "Save your strength. You're going to need it."

His weight pinned her to the bed. Powerful thighs pressed against her hips as he straddled her from behind, forcing her legs tightly together. He caught her wrists, drew her arms behind her back, one of his hands holding them there while the other grasped one of her buttocks, spreading her, exposing her to his view.

It was a position of utter submission, one that gave him total power over her and left her no means to resist.

But she wasn't willing to surrender yet. She twisted and writhed, the thrill of being overpowered more arousing than she could have imagined. Then she felt the head of his cock rub against her labia. Liquid heat gathered inside her, her body longing for him, even as she pretended to resist.

"I can see everything—those sexy, bare outer lips . . . the

pink edges of your sweet inner lips . . . And this . . ." His thumb brushed over a part of her no man had ever touched, the sensation both alarming and arousing, and for a moment she was afraid he planned to penetrate her there.

She gasped, shocked.

But he didn't enter her there. Instead, he nudged the thick head of his cock between her labia and thrust deep, his groan drowning out the sound of her whimper.

With her legs held together like this, there seemed to be no room inside her. She could feel every inch of his steel-hard cock as he moved, from the engorged head that almost touched her cervix, to the thick base that stretched and stroked her sensitive entrance, to the taut skin of his testicles as they brushed her labia.

She moaned, bit a pillow, lost in the heat of these intense, new sensations. She'd never believed all that G-spot hype, never believed that a woman could climax through penetration alone. But now she knew she'd been wrong, his thrusts caressing some secret place inside her, the ache unbearable and sweet.

She whimpered and panted into the pillow, desperate for release. She wanted to raise her bottom, to spread her legs, to do something to bring the sweet torment to an end, but she couldn't move. Helpless to do anything but take him, she was left hanging on the edge of an orgasm that seemed to hover just beyond her reach.

Then, when it seemed she could take no more, the tension inside her drew to its full height like a great shimmering wave and crashed over her, carrying her helplessly along as it surged through her, drowning her in pleasure.

She cried out, arching back, Zach's sure strokes making her pleasure last until she lay, weak and panting, her face against a pillow.

He released her wrists and withdrew from her, pressing kisses along her back. Then gently he turned her onto her back, catching her legs and settling himself between them. It was then she realized he hadn't yet come, his erection lying hard against her.

But when she opened her eyes, it wasn't lust or playfulness she saw on his face, but a look of tenderness and torment, his brow furrowed, his gaze soft, his lips parted, his breathing still fast.

He smoothed the hair off her face, his gaze traveling over her features. For a moment, she thought he had something to tell her. But when at last he spoke, it was only to say her name. *"Natalie."*

He adjusted his hips, nudged himself slowly inside her, and the pleasure began again. But this time he took it slowly, his gaze never leaving her face, as he brought her to a second shattering climax, his groans mingling with her cries as he at last claimed his own release.

AFTERWARD, THEY TOOK a long, hot shower together, getting water all over the marble floor, Zach feeling more alive and more at peace with himself than he had in years. While Natalie dressed and made breakfast, he checked in with Rowan, who told him Quintana was being transferred to a more secure federal facility—this one run by ICE, Immigration and Customs Enforcement—within the hour. He'd be available for interrogation by early afternoon.

Zach found Natalie setting the table, the scent of her cooking making his mouth water. She was wearing a short denim skirt that showed off her legs, together with a lacy V-neck tank top that made the most of her beautiful breasts, her dark hair still damp, her sweet face free of makeup.

She glanced up and smiled, those adorable dimples appearing in her cheeks. "Hungry?"

He held her gaze, grinned. "Starving."

Her cheeks flushed pink. "I hope you like eggs Benedict. I made sausage, grits, and fresh coffee."

"Mmm." He sat, unable to take his gaze off her while she poured the coffee then sat across from him.

How in the hell had he gotten so lucky? She was smart, brave, beautiful, sexy as hell, had a playful side in the bedroom—and she could cook. No man deserved all that in one sweet package, let alone him.

Don't question it, McBride. Just go with it.

He took a bite of the eggs and another. "Delicious."

She smiled, clearly pleased. "I'm glad you like it."

He jabbed his fork at what looked like a thick, white pool of Cream of Wheat. "So this is grits?"

"You've never had grits?" She gaped at him. "How did you get to be thirty-three years old without ever tasting grits?"

Amused by her reaction, he scooped some onto his fork and tasted it, nodding in approval. "Tastes like . . . corn?"

"That's what it is—a corn mash or corn gruel."

So the mystery of grits was solved once and for all.

They ate their breakfast slowly, talking about everything and nothing at all, the moment so like Zach's fantasy from early this morning that it was like waking to find himself living in his own dream. But dreams rarely lasted.

He washed the last bite of eggs down with a gulp of strong black coffee, then glanced at his watch. "They're transferring Quintana to the ICE facility outside town this morning. I'll go in this afternoon to continue interrogating him."

The sunshine left her face, her expression anxious, shadows in her eyes. "Will you be gone late?"

He reached over, took her hand. "If you want me to arrange for someone to be here with you while I'm away, I can do that. I don't want you to be afraid."

She shook her head. "It's not that. Okay, well, it's partly that. But also, I just hate to think of you being anywhere near him. I don't know how you keep from beating the tar out of him after what he put you through."

"It's not easy." Then Zach told her about yesterday's fruitless interrogation and how he'd allowed himself one punch to the bastard's gut before reining in his rage. He didn't tell her what Quintana had said to him. "Sometimes I want to forget that I'm supposed to be one of the good guys. If I ever get my hands on Cárdenas . . ."

He let it go, the subject clearly upsetting to her.

"Tom called while you were on the phone. He wants to know what I'm working on. I had to tell him I didn't have anything. That's the first time that's happened."

"He doesn't expect you to put out the same amount of material while all of this is going on, does he?"

She picked up her coffee. "I guess I could try to work something up about the forensic accountant's report, even though she—"

"You heard back from her?" Zach didn't know anything about this.

Natalie looked over at him. "I didn't tell you?"

He shook his head. "I guess you didn't get a chance."

"She didn't find any smoking guns, but she says the school's endowment is very high for a private high school. And she's right. I poked around the Internet and couldn't find another private girls school in Colorado or anywhere else for that matter that came anywhere close to it."

"That's why you were logged onto the school's website last night."

"I was trying to figure out where the money came from, looking for major donors, hoping to compile a list you could check for ties to the Zetas—or that's what I started doing." Her lips curved in a sad smile. "I got caught up looking at photographs. They have a slideshow of photos that reminded me of my years at McGehee."

Zach stood and walked into the kitchen to refill his coffee cup. "That list of donors is good thinking. I'll definitely run it. In the meantime, I'll see whether Rowan wants to assign someone to dig into the school's endowment. She's not as convinced as I am that the school is tied into this. Are you done with that dossier on Cárdenas or do you—"

Glass shattered behind him.

He turned to find Natalie staring at nothing, her eyes wide and startled, the plates she'd been carrying in shards on the wood floor. "Natalie, are you—"

"That's it! That's where I saw him!" She met his gaze. "Find the dossier! That's the connection!"

HER HANDS SHAKING, Natalie turned the pages in the Cárdenas dossier, looking for one particular photograph. "I know it's here! I saw it! Why didn't I remember—"

Zach took her hands, held them in his. "Breathe, Natalie. It's okay."

She drew a deep breath, calmed by the reassurance she saw in his eyes, her heart still beating hard. With his help, she went through the pages one by one again, more carefully this time, until she found it.

A younger Cárdenas stood in the foreground holding some kind of assault rifle, wearing aviator-style sunglasses and a broad smile on his face. In the background, also smiling, stood another man, a bit older. Both were dressed in camouflage, a military vehicle parked behind them.

Natalie pointed toward the man in the background. "That's him. It has to be."

"That's who?"

"You'll see." She reached for her laptop, typed Whitcomb Academy into her browser, misspelling it three times in her haste. "Damn!"

Finally, she made it to the school's website and launched the slideshow she'd watched last night. The photographs drifted by one at a time—happy girls playing volleyball, camping, working in a science lab, studying in a library. And then . . .

"See. That's him." She paused at the photograph of the girl receiving her award, pointing to the image of Edward Wulfe. "Look at him. He's older, yes, but it's the same person. Look at the gap between his front teeth. Look at the helmet hair. And his face—so bland, so plain. That's why I couldn't remember."

"Give me that." Zach took her laptop, looked back and forth between the two images. "I'll be damned. You're right."

"He and Cárdenas must be using the school to launder drug money."

"That's a good guess." Zach set her laptop down on the coffee table and set the dossier beside it. He stood, drew out his cell phone, and dialed. "McBride here. I need everything you have on one Edward Wulfe and his past association with the Americas Institute for Tactical Training, often abbreviated AMINTAC. That's Wulfe—Whiskey-Uniform-Lima-Foxtrot-Echo . . . Yeah, thanks. As fast as you can."

He disconnected, walked toward the patio, and stood looking out at the city, his leather shoulder holster making a dark X against the white of his shirt. And for a time, he just stood there.

She stood also, his silence making her uneasy. "What is it?"

"Just something Quintana said yesterday." Zach turned toward her. " 'Your enemy follows no rules, while you are bound by many,' he said. Now I know what he meant by that."

"Tell me."

Zach turned to face her, his expression grim. "AMINTAC is the bastard offspring of the Department of Defense and the Central Intelligence Agency. If Wulfe worked for AMINTAC, he's almost certainly former CIA. He knows all the tricks, has access to all the latest technology, not to mention connections and inexhaustible cash. We are in such deep shit."

Natalie felt chills shiver down her spine.

Zach's phone rang. "That's Rowan's office, calling to tell me Wulfe's file is missing or encrypted." He answered. "McBride . . . What the fuck? How did that happen? . . . God-*damn* it!"

Natalie's mind swirled with a thousand terrible possibilities. Something had happened to Julian, Marc, or Gabe. Zach had been removed from the case by the people in Washington who'd been investigating him. Wulfe had hacked into the USMS system, found out where she was, and was on his way with Cárdenas to kill her.

By the time Zach ended the call, her pulse was racing. "Wh-what is it?"

He met her gaze, black rage on his face. "A U.S. marshal convoy was hit on its way from the Denver jail to the ICE detention facility. Rowan's chief deputy was shot and killed. Four other DUSMs were wounded in a shoot-out. Quintana has escaped."

CHAPTER 30

"DO YOU THINK Rowan is compromised?"

Zach had been asking himself this same question. He looked over at Darcangelo and shrugged. "My gut says no, but Quintana's escape happened on her watch. Nothing is impossible. I think we should proceed under the assumption that she or someone close to her is working for Wulfe."

Hunter frowned, peeling off his body armor and dropping it on the floor near his feet, exposing the Glock he wore in a hip holster. "That means you're shit out of tactical support."

"It means that, for the time being, I'm relying almost entirely on you three." Zach met each man's gaze.

Natalie entered the room carrying a tray laden with a coffeepot, five mugs, a small pitcher of cream, and a bowl of sugar, and set it down on the coffee table, making eye contact with Zach briefly before walking back to the kitchen.

He lowered his voice, hoping she wouldn't hear. News of Quintana's escape and the slain and injured DUSMs had upset her greatly. She was terrified—and not just for herself. What he was about to say wouldn't make things any easier for her.

"You all signed on thinking we were dealing with the Zetas. But the game has changed. There's no doubt in my mind that taking on Wulfe could expose both you and your families to significantly greater risk. I won't think anything less of you if you want to turn in your badges and take care of your own."

Three armed men glared at him.

"Sorry, McBride." Hunter stretched his arms across the back of his armchair as if to say he wasn't leaving any time soon. "You're not shaking us off that easily. Besides, Natalie *is* one of our own."

Rossiter grabbed a cup and poured himself some coffee. "I've sent Kat and the baby to the rez, so I've got nothing better to do than hang with you losers anyway."

"We've already taken steps to protect our families." Darcangelo peeled off the black sports jacket that hid a shoulder holster and a SIG Sauer, his concealable body armor barely noticeable beneath his black T-shirt. "Let's just get the job done."

And just like that, they moved on.

"You've already warned Joaquin?" Zach asked, as Natalie entered the room and settled herself on the couch beside him. He reached over and threaded his fingers through hers, wanting to offer her whatever comfort he could. The guys noticed, but wisely they kept their teeth together. "Given the role he played in capturing Quintana, it's not farfetched to think the Zetas might want to retaliate."

Hunter nodded, aiming a reassuring smile at Natalie. "I've assigned a couple of cops I trust to keep a watch on him, but the Latin Kings are watching over him, too. He's armed, and I've given him some basic instruction. He's a natural. That kid shoots almost as well with a forty-five as he does with a camera."

"Good." Zach rose, walked to the standing dry erase board he'd asked Hunter to pick up, and rolled it to the center of the room where they could all see it. "Let's piece this together from the beginning and see where it takes us. Natalie, if you could fill in some of the blanks for us regarding your investigation, that would help."

"Yes, of course." She looked relieved to be asked to play a role.

Zach could understand that. No one wanted to feel helpless.

He stuck the photo of Cárdenas and Wulfe at the top far left. "So it's 1983, and Cárdenas wants to be a cop. His family's money has kept him out of prison so far, and he thinks maybe he'll do better if he's the one with the uniform and the gun. He joins Los Zetas, an elite law enforcement group, rises through the ranks, then gets into AMINTAC, where he meets Edward Wulfe, who at the time is working for the Agency."

Darcangelo looked up at the photo, coffee mug in his hand. "Cárdenas goes back to Mexico a better killer with better weapons and better technology than the *federales*. He's gotten a taste of real power, and he *likes* it. There's not a lot of money to be made in police work, and his instincts run to rape and torture anyway. Slowly, secretly, he and his men go to work for one of the bigger cartels."

"I studied this when I was with DEA." Hunter leaned forward, resting his elbows on his knees. "The Zetas started small, carrying out hits and raids against the enemies of the Oaxaca Cartel while still pretending to uphold the law. They were still catching drug smugglers and impounding contraband, so no one knew. Then almost overnight, they annihilated the Oaxaca Cartel, claiming their territory. It was a brilliant strategy. With the other cartels weakened from their constant raids and arrests, and the Oaxaca Cartel gone, the entire balance of power shifted."

"I bet it did—right into Cárdenas's offshore bank accounts." Rossiter rested his boots on the coffee table, his denim shirt falling open to reveal the shoulder holster he wore over a white T-shirt beneath. "But how does Wulfe come back into the picture?"

"That's easy." Zach took over. "Cárdenas and the Zetas are still pretending to be cops when the Berlin Wall comes down. The Cold War ends, and Wulfe now finds himself nearing retirement. Could be that he's made good money over the years selling classified information to the Soviets. By the early nineties, with the Soviet Union gone, he turns to illegal arms and drugs sales to keep raking in the jack."

Darcangelo seemed to consider this. "Wulfe would've been in a position to follow Cárdenas's career, even if they weren't in touch. He would have known that federal agents suspected the Zetas of being crooked. And he would have known when the Zetas finally hit out on their own."

Zach wrote the dates on the board—1989–1991. "Hell, maybe it was Wulfe's idea. He sees Cárdenas trying to fit in as an officer of the law and makes a suggestion. 'You'd make a lot more money—' "

" '—and be a lot more powerful—' " Hunter added.

" '—if you went over to the other side.' "

"Coming from the CIA agent who trained him, that would've felt a lot like getting permission, wouldn't it?" Rossiter looked around at them.

Zach nodded. "Sure, it would."

Darcangelo went on. "So they reestablish contact, come to some kind of agreement. Maybe it's guns, explosives, and tech for drugs and teenage girls. Maybe Wulfe handles U.S. distribution in exchange for a cut of the profits. Who knows? Regardless, they become rich men, the Zetas dominating much of Mexico and Wulfe living the genteel life of a retired millionaire here in the U.S."

Zach turned to Natalie, found her listening attentively. "You suggested it yesterday. Wulfe uses the school to launder the money. What better way to do it than through an institution that receives grants, bequests, and anonymous donations. When did Whitcomb Academy open?"

"In 1993."

Darcangelo looked over at Zach, understanding in his eyes. "The school—that's where Wulfe is most vulnerable. Intercept a shipment at the border, and all you end up with is contraband and low-level smugglers who know their lives depend on keeping their mouths shut. They probably have no clue who Wulfe is. The loss to the Zetas is minimal, and another shipment is on its way in a matter of days. But the school is where Wulfe funnels his share of the money. It's his Achilles' heel."

Zach's pulse picked up, just like it always did whenever a case came together. He looked over at Natalie again. "When you began to investigate the school, they panicked. They didn't want you digging through their records or bringing any kind of negative attention their way. That soccer coach—I bet he didn't run off to start a new life. My money says he's dead. Then they decided to take you out, too."

She shook her head. "It was my idea to go to Mexico, not theirs. I signed up for that trip in January, long before I'd even heard of Whitcomb Academy."

"Exactly. It was the perfect setup." But Zach could see she wasn't following him. "They could put a hit on you here, but then they'd have a murder investigation. And although they're pretty good at covering their tracks, killing you—a journalist—would mean bringing additional scrutiny to whatever stories you were covering. They couldn't risk that. But if you were killed while in a foreign country, shot by a paramilitary cartel known for its brutality and hatred of journalists—well, that's just a tragic incident, one that has nothing to do with the school."

He saw on her face the moment she understood.

Her face drained of its color. "You're saying they wanted to kill me, but when they saw I was going on the SPJ trip, they decided to wait until I was in Mexico so that no one would be able to connect it with the school. They would stop my investigation, and no one would think twice about it."

"That's my best guess. They studied you, saw you were going to Mexico, and decided to let Cárdenas handle you in his own sick way. But they underestimated you, angel. You did something they never could have imagined. You escaped, forcing them to strike at you again here in Colorado."

Zach was right. He felt it in his bones.

But she wasn't listening.

She stood, her breathing rapid, her voice almost panicked. "All those people—poor Sr. Marquez, Ana-Letitia, Sergio—they died because of me? *I* brought that down on them? Oh, God!"

Then she turned and fled up the stairs.

"Well, I'd say you handled that with great sensitivity."

"Go to hell, Hunter!" Zach stood there, staring after her.

"You first."

NATALIE SAT IN front of her open bedroom window, looking out at the bruised sky, flashes of distant lightning heralding the approach of a late-afternoon thunderstorm, a chilly wind filling the sheer, white drapes like sails. Not that she really noticed any of it, those endless terrible minutes on the bus running through her mind again and again.

"*¡No! Por favor, no—*"

Pop!

"I am sorry, Miss Benoit."

"No, don't—!"

Pop!

"Natalie?"

She gasped, startled out of her thoughts.

Zach stood just inside the doorway to her room. "Are you okay, angel?"

She didn't know how to answer, so for a time she said nothing. "It seems really obvious now when I think about it. The look on that Zeta's face when he saw me—he wasn't smiling because he thought it was funny watching me trying to protect Joaquin. He recognized me. It was there in his eyes. I just didn't see it."

Zach stood behind her now. His hand slid gently beneath her hair to cup the nape of her neck. "It's not your fault, Natalie. You didn't pull the trigger. You're a victim of this crime, just like the journalists who were killed."

"But if I hadn't gone on that trip—"

"Don't torture yourself like that. The Zetas probably took advantage of the conference to do a little multitasking, taking out multiple targets at once."

"I watched them die. Poor, sweet Sr. Marquez. He was terrified, but he still had the courage to look into his killer's face. And do you know what? He apologized to me. Just before they shot him, he apologized as if it were somehow his fault that he was about to be murdered in front of me."

"I know. I read your articles."

"You did?" She turned her head, looked up at him, surprised.

He nodded, his lips curving in a smile. "You're a talented writer, Natalie. I don't think anyone could read what you wrote and not be touched by it."

It felt good to hear him say that. "Did you see my little press conference?"

"How could I not? It was on every news channel. You called me your hero." Then he knelt down beside her, pressed his forehead to hers, and looked into her eyes, his hand against her cheek. "But, Natalie, you're *my* hero. You got me out of that Zeta hell. You saved my life. You were strong when you needed to be strong. Don't you dare blame yourself for something you didn't do, something you were powerless to stop."

His words felt like absolution, and yet . . .

She shared her darkest fear. "I don't want anyone else to die. If you or any of the guys get hurt or killed . . ."

She'd sat there this afternoon, surrounded by the strongest men she knew, each one of them armed to the teeth and wearing body armor, but instead of feeling safe, she'd felt terrified—for them. After what had happened to those poor DUSMs today . . .

"We're doing everything we can to prevent that." He stood and sat across from her. "We made a lot of progress today."

"You came up with some compelling scenarios, but they're based entirely on circumstantial evidence."

He gave her a cocky grin. "Not for long, angel. Rowan is procuring a federal warrant for the school's financials. I guarantee you we'll find bogus donors, anonymous donations from offshore accounts—that kind of thing. Darcangelo is in my office trying to crack the encryption on Wulfe's file. Hunter and Rossiter left to get a helo ready in case we need to leave here quickly. I'm going to go to work finding Wulfe. We'll get the job done. In the meantime, you need to eat something."

"I'm not really hungry."

He frowned. "Do you think . . . When will you know whether . . . ?"

So he couldn't even say the word. That disappointed her. "When will I know whether I'm pregnant? I should get my period in about a week. Are you worried?"

"I just wondered if that's why you weren't hungry." Then he smiled. "Darcangelo's wife called. She had a test that showed she's carrying a boy. Darcangelo couldn't quit grinning."

That was the first good news Natalie had heard in what felt like forever. "That's wonderful! And the baby's okay?"

"Apparently."

From down the hallway came Julian's voice. "Hey, McBride, I made a copy of the file. I'll try to crack it at home and give you a call later."

"Sounds good. Thanks." Then Zach frowned and glanced toward the window.

Fat raindrops were falling now, the wind whipping the drapes about, dark clouds obscuring the city. A flash of lightning. Thunder.

He stood, crossed the room, and closed the window. "Looks like we're in for one hell of a storm tonight."

Natalie shivered.

ARTURO SAT IN the back of the first van, a battered AK-47 in his hands, thinking of ways to kill Wulfe. After all they'd done together, the stupid *chingadero* ought to have welcomed him as a brother. Instead, Wulfe had done nothing but humiliate him since he arrived. And now he'd gone too far.

While Wulfe sat in his new luxury hideout, Arturo was being forced to take part in this pathetic little action as if he were one of Wulfe's underlings. It was clear that Wulfe wanted to pin the Benoit whore's death on Arturo and his organization. More than that, he wanted to rub Arturo's face in his failure.

"You made this mess. You're going to help clean it up," Wulfe had said. Then he'd motioned to his men. "You follow their orders, do you understand, Arturo? You still have so much to learn."

Arturo would avenge this insult. If only he'd had time to speak with José-Luis, but they hadn't been given a moment alone together, and now his nephew was waiting this out with Wulfe.

"The gate's coming up." One of Wulfe's men pressed his fingers to his earpiece, listening. "It's a dark blue Chevy Impala. The vehicle has exited the garage. It's turning the corner."

They'd parked a couple of blocks away so that the cops who were protecting the Benoit bitch wouldn't see them and grow suspicious.

"It's him. He's alone, and he's taking the bait. Go!"

The bait was one of Wulfe's female operatives with a fake belly to make her look *embarazada*—pregnant. The target's wife was blond and pregnant, and they felt certain the target would stop to help a woman who made him think of her.

Arturo had to admit that part was clever, even if he hated

the idea of women carrying guns and pretending to be men. It was unnatural.

The van drove quietly and slowly around the corner, and up ahead, Arturo saw a man with a dark ponytail get out of the Impala and walk over to the woman, who stood beside her own car, hand on her fake belly, staring down at a flat tire.

"Look at that overgrown Boy Scout."

Wulfe's men laughed, pulling ski masks down over their faces.

The van drew closer, the target looking over his shoulder once. He saw the van, watched it for a second.

"Easy now."

Apparently not perceiving it as a danger, the target turned back to the woman and motioned toward the car's trunk. The blonde waddled to the trunk and opened it. The target bent over, picked up a lug wrench and stood upright again.

Arturo felt the van speed up, his heart beating faster.

It went—how did the *gringos* say?—like clockwork. The target turned around, lug wrench in hand, just as the blonde pointed a suppressed handgun at his chest and fired. Five shots to the chest dropped him onto the pavement, where he lay still.

Their faces covered, their hands in nitrile gloves, Wulfe's men jerked open the van's door and jumped out, one of them carrying a pair of bolt cutters. Two of them lifted the man's big body and shoved it into the trunk, while the third cut off his left thumb. Then they shut the body inside the trunk and climbed into the van, the blonde following them in.

Having no modesty at all, she kicked off her heels, pulled her dress over her head, and unfastened the shoulder straps that held her fake belly in place. It fell to the floor, leaving her wearing a wet tank top and shorts. "I am fucking *never* getting pregnant. That shit is uncomfortable."

The men laughed.

Puta estupida. The stupid whore.

She quickly dressed in pants, a shirt, and body armor, sliding a ski mask over her face. Then she grabbed a rifle. She was going in with them? A woman?

The van moved forward, turned the corner, and drove up to the protected entrance of the tall glass building. The man who held the bloody thumb, passed it forward to the driver, who rolled down his window and carefully pressed the pad of it to the scanner.

An electric buzz. A green light. And the garage door began to move.

"We're in."

CHAPTER 31

ARTURO FELT HIS heartbeat quicken as they reached the penthouse. But it wasn't from excitement. It had been many years since he'd taken part in a hit. A man of his standing shouldn't have to get his own hands bloody. He had others to do wet work. He'd tried to stay down in the van, but Wulfe's underlings wouldn't let him. They shoved him from the van, calling him "old man" and "coward." When he'd asked for a ski mask, they laughed at him.

"Remember to smile for the cameras," that bitch of a woman had said when they stepped into the elevator.

Arturo hoped she eventually found herself in Mexico. He would enjoy breaking her and watching her cower before the altar of Santa Muerte.

The elevator opened, and they moved out, Arturo keeping to the rear as they quietly got into position around the door to the penthouse, his pulse pounding, but not just from nervousness. Now that he was here, it excited him to think that McBride and Benoit were on the other side of this door. They thought they were safe, that they'd gotten away from him. But they hadn't.

Oh, how he wanted to watch Benoit suffer! He wanted to see her face twist with fear when she saw him. He wanted to hear her scream and beg. He wanted to look into her eyes the moment she realized Death had found her at last.

"Remember, we need the DUSM alive. Wulfe wants to

know what he knows." The man in the lead drew the bloody thumb from his pocket once more, pressed it against the biometric scanner, then dropped it onto the floor.

A quiet buzz. A click.

The door opened.

¡Protégeme, Santa Muerte! Protect me, Santa Muerte!

Rifles raised, they surged inside, Arturo hanging back. If anyone were going to die today, it would not be him.

He'd expected them to walk in to find the two of them fucking, watching television, or eating food. Instead, the apartment was dark, silent, the only light coming from the big windows to their left, flashes of lightning giving the place a strange, ghostly feel. He squinted, his eyes unprepared for the darkness, his heart beating faster.

Something wasn't right.

He took a step back, felt something jab him in the back.

"Move it, Grandpa," a male voice hissed from behind him.

The boy Wulfe had placed in charge of them gave the hand signals for three of them to head to their right through the dark kitchen, while the rest were to follow him up the stairs. They fanned out—just as the room exploded in gunfire.

Rat-ta-ta-ta ta-tat! Rat-ta-ta-ta-ta-tat! Rat-ta-ta-ta-ta-tat!

Grunts. The thud of bullets hitting flesh. Bodies falling.

Arturo dived behind the sofa, lay flat against the floor, heart slamming. How had that *pendejo* McBride known? How had he known they were coming?

Rat-ta-ta-ta-tat! Rat-ta-ta-ta-ta-tat! Rat-ta-ta-ta-ta-tat!

A woman's scream. Groans. The coppery scent of blood.

Then came the bang and flare of a flash grenade, followed by the tromp of boots on the stairs as Wulfe's men attempted to overrun McBride.

Arturo took advantage of the distraction to crawl to the other end of the couch, getting himself out of the line of fire.

Pop! Pop! Pop!

Shots fired from a suppressed pistol. Grunts and gasps as men fought hand to hand. A choking sound.

And then . . .

Silence.

A flash of lightning. A peal of thunder. Rain pounding glass.

"Cárdenas, you sick son of a whore, I know you're hiding down there."

McBride!

Cárdenas felt his mouth go dry.

This man had survived six days of torture without breaking. He'd killed five of Cárdenas's best men. He'd escaped every trap Cárdenas had set for him in Mexico. He'd just killed six of Wulfe's CIA operatives in less than five minutes.

And now Cárdenas was alone with him.

CLUTCHING AN ASSAULT rifle to her side, Natalie lay on her belly on the slick rooftop, soaked through to her skin, strong gusts threatening to push her over the edge. She thought she'd heard gunshots, but it was hard to tell over the roar of the storm, lightning flashing just overhead, thunder seeming to make the building shake. Or maybe that was just her shivering.

Please be safe! Zach and Julian, please be safe!

The moment he'd gotten Julian's horrifying text message, Zach had jerked open her window and helped her climb onto the roof, tossing a rifle, a spare magazine, and his cell phone up to her, and telling her to call for help, then going back inside to wait for Wulfe's men alone. She'd called Marc and Gabe immediately, shouting over the storm, and they'd told her they were on their way together with SWAT and an ambulance for Julian. But that had been an eternity ago.

Where were they?

Hurry please! Julian and Zach need you!

She pushed wet hair and water out of her eyes, peering through the rain toward the rooftop patio, keeping an eye out for bad guys.

"I doubt they'll think to look on the roof, but if they do, they'll have to step onto the patio to reach you," Zach had told her. "Shoot to kill."

And she would, without hesitation.

But no matter how hard she blinked, she couldn't keep the rain out of her eyes. Teeth chattering, she got to her hands and knees, tried to crawl closer to the patio, gasping and falling flat again as a powerful gust caught her, pushing her across the roof like a hydroplaning car. She lay there for a moment, heart hammering, then she looked up into the gray and sodden sky.

"I-I'm from N-new Orleans!" she shouted, her words vanishing in the gale. "I-I survived H-hurricane Katrina. Th-there's nothing y-you can throw at m-me that I can't h-handle! Y-you're nothing but a puny th-thunderstorm!"

Then she did the only thing she could do.

She held on—and prayed.

HIS GAZE FIXED on the stairs, Zach took a minute to catch his breath, his hand pressed against his aching ribs. Just his luck to get kicked there again. He wiped the sweat out of his eyes, saw streaks of blood on the back of his hand. Shrapnel from the flash grenade must have nicked his face. Well, that wasn't the only place he was bleeding. His right shoulder had been creased, but it was nothing serious.

You're good to go, McBride.

Wulfe had sent seven operatives. And now all but one of them— Cárdenas—was dead. Or dying, he corrected himself, as the man whose throat he'd been forced to cut finished bleeding out, his eyes rolling back in his skull, his body convulsing.

Zach wiped the blood off his knife, stuck it back in his ankle rig, then popped a fresh magazine into his M16 and got to his feet, still astonished that Cárdenas was here. The bastard hadn't set foot on U.S. soil since his days at AMINTAC. He must want Natalie more than Zach had realized. But was he still alive, waiting for a chance to use the AK Zach had seen in his hands, or had a stray round killed him?

And where the hell was the cavalry?

Warned by Darcangelo's text message, Zach had helped Natalie onto the roof and asked her to call for backup—and an ambulance—the moment she'd gotten to a safe position. Of course, for all Zach knew, there could be a hundred police sirens blaring in the streets below. He couldn't hear a damned thing over this thunderstorm.

Hang on, angel. It's almost over.

Zach grabbed a couple of flash grenades off the belt of

the man he'd just killed—now officially dead—and made his way carefully toward the stairs.

From down below, he could just make out the sound of someone breathing. Quietly, he moved down the stairs, his back to the wall. When he was near the bottom, he tossed the first grenade, closing his eyes and turning his face away from the blast.

BAM!

A flash of light. Smoke.

He jumped to the bottom of the stairs and rushed at Cárdenas, who held up the AK and fired blindly, one steel-core round grazing Zach's left thigh, the others going wild. He kicked the weapon out of the bastard's hands, then drove his boot into Cárdenas's gut and pressed the barrel of the M16 against his skull.

"Lie flat on your stomach! Do it!" A part of Zach wanted to tear Cárdenas apart, but he was supposed to be one of the good guys. "Arturo César Cárdenas, you are under arrest for the distribution and sale of schedule one narcotics, human trafficking, the murders of U.S. nationals on U.S. soil, the kidnapping and attempted murder of American journalist Natalie Benoit—and a whole lot of other sick shit."

He said the words in English and in Spanish, then worked quickly, cuffing and Mirandizing Cárdenas, stripping him of his weapons, cell phone, shoes, then double-checking to see whether any of the others in the room were still alive. They weren't.

He cleared the hallway, the stairwell, and the elevator, stopping when he saw a bloody *something* on the floor near the door.

Darcangelo's thumb.

He picked it up and carried it inside, where he quickly wrapped it in a paper towel and put it in the refrigerator. In the living room, Cardenas struggled to get to his feet. Zach walked over to him and raised the Glock. "Stay down!"

"So where is my little *puta*?" Cárdenas looked over his shoulder at Zach. "Did you enjoy fucking what was mine?"

Zach crossed the room, nudged the toe of his boot beneath Cárdenas's chin, and forced the son of a bitch's neck back, looking down into his eyes, M16 still in hand. When he spoke it was with years worth of disgust and loathing. "She was never yours. Like all women, she belongs to herself. You will *never* lay a hand on her. So shut the *fuck* up!"

There was genuine fear in Cárdenas's eyes now.

Good.

Zach took a step back. "If you want to chat, why don't you tell me about your relationship with Edward Wulfe. You met him at AMINTAC, and you've been doing business with him since at least 1993. So what is it? Drugs? Arms? Both?"

"Why don't you ask me?"

Zach whirled, dropped to one knee, and fired, hitting another black-clad figure in the chest, but not before the men standing on either side of Wulfe fired at him. He felt a round strike his temple, and then . . .

The next thing he knew, he was tied sitting upright, duct taped to a chair from the kitchen table, the pain inside his skull so intense he could barely think.

"Can you hear me, McBride?" Wulfe stood before him, looking into his face, his own bland face devoid of expression. "That was a nonlethal round—a rubber bullet. It was necessary to neutralize you without killing you. I have a few questions."

Still stunned, Zach fought to hold up his head. "Fuck. You."

Nearby, Cárdenas struggled with his cuffs and shouted in Spanish. "José-Luis, you stupid bastard, get over here! Help me out of these."

"Show some dignity, Arturo," Wulfe said. "Help your uncle, Mr. Quintana."

Zach's stomach sank as Quintana crossed the floor, about to free the man he'd tried so long to capture.

Hunter, Rossiter, where the fuck are you?

But rather than cutting the plastic cuffs off Cárdenas's wrists, Quintana racked the slide on a shiny, new Beretta. A gift from Wulfe?

"¡No! ¡No! Tu eres el hijo de mi hermana, mi propio sobrino! No se puede—" *You are my sister's son, my own nephew. You can't—*

Oh, but Quintana could. And he did.

The blast cut Cárdenas's plea short, leaving him dead on the floor.

"Tear this place apart. Find the girl, and bring me all documents, files, hard drives, flash drives—anything that might compromise our operation."

With that command, Wulfe's men began to search the loft.

"¡MADRE DE DIOS! There she is!" Joaquin pointed to the small figure clinging to the rooftop below them. Wearing a short denim skirt and a tank top, she lay flat on the slick rooftop, hugging a rifle to her side, rain and hail pelting her, the wind whipping her wet hair and clothes. "The wind. It's pushing her toward the edge!"

He raised his camera and started shooting.

"I see her." Hunter looked out the copter window beside him, wearing full SWAT body armor, Rossiter and three handpicked SWAT officers beside him. "Hang on, Natalie. We're almost there."

Joaquin had heard the call go out over the newsroom police scanner—officer down, another caught in a firefight, civilian trapped on the roof of the Glass Tower, helicopter rescue needed—and had driven straight to the airport, hoping to get in on the action. He hadn't known that Julian was the injured officer or that Natalie was the stranded civilian until he'd seen Hunter and Rossiter, their faces grim.

He still couldn't fucking believe these bastards had cut off Darcangelo's thumb. He hoped McBride killed every last one of them.

"If we can get this bird to hover above her, I'll rappel and send her up," Rossiter called up to the pilot. He was already roped in, harness around his waist, a pack of paramedic supplies on his back.

"Are you kidding? I'm catching gusts of sixty knots." The pilot worked the cyclic, sweat on his face. Joaquin focused on his worried facial expression, adjusted for glare from the window and clicked. "See that obstacle indicator rod with the red flashing light on the roof? The wind is whipping it all over the goddamned place. If I get too close, it will hit the helo or the propeller, and it will be lights out for all of us."

"You know what they say," Marc said to the SWAT guys behind him. "Planes want to fly. Helos want to crash."

The man laughed, but Joaquin didn't like the sound of that. The camera came down.

He looked out the window at the rod and at Natalie, who now looked over her shoulder up at them, her soaked hair plastered to her face. "You can't just leave her there. Rope me in. I'll go down if no one else—"

Hunter grabbed his shirt, drew his face close. "We're *not* going to leave her there. We just have to find a way to get to her that won't get us all killed."

And Joaquin realized Hunter was as upset as he was at the idea that they might not be able to reach her.

"Have you got a thing for her, Ramirez?" Rossiter organized the rope between his legs and crossed the small, cramped space to stand near the door, checking his harness and straps. "Hate to break it to you, but she is crazy in love with McBride."

Joaquin glared at him. He would never in a million years admit to anyone that he'd signed on to the Mexico trip hoping the time away would start something between him and Natalie. "I just think she's been through enough, you know?"

Rossiter nodded. "That is a true fact."

The nose of the chopper dipped to give the pilot a better view, Natalie below them and to their left. She tried to get up on her hands and knees, then got caught in a gust. The wind pushed her several inches. She flattened herself out again, her fingers splayed wide, seeking friction on the slick surface.

"Shit!" Hunter paled. "Oh, sweetheart, don't do that again."

The pilot looked down at her. "I'll try to hold it here. Be quick."

Rossiter checked his straps again, then picked up a coil of rope and draped it over one shoulder. "Just lower me down. I'll stay with her and listen in on my earpiece. When you move in, I'll be in position to enter through one of the upstairs windows or perhaps the patio."

Hunter raised an eyebrow. "You'll be a team of one."

"I can handle that."

Hunter gave him a slap on the shoulder. "Okay, rock jock, we'll do it your way. Just keep her safe. She's your number one priority."

"Got it."

Then Hunter and Rossiter frowned, sharing an ominous glance, both pressing a finger to their earpieces.

Hunter explained. "SWAT reached the vehicle with the flat tire. They opened the trunk and found lots of blood, but they haven't found Darcangelo. They say it looks like he pushed the backseats down and climbed out on his own."

Then the pilot called back to them. "It's now or never."

Hunter helped Rossiter open the door, wind and rain spilling in.

Having almost forgotten that he was supposed to be taking photos, Joaquin shifted position, adjusted his settings, and started clicking off shots, as the winch slowly lowered Rossiter through the air toward Natalie. But Rossiter had gone only about a dozen feet when the helo lurched, making the rope swing like a pendulum, out over the street, then back over the roof.

The pilot struggled to regain control, holding the cyclic in a death grip, his knuckles white. "I can't hold this. I've got to get us out of here!"

Hunter spoke into his mouthpiece. "Rossiter, the pilot says we have to go. We're winching you up. We'll have to try another—"

"What the fuck is he doing?" one of the other SWAT guys asked.

Joaquin lowered the camera, missing the shot of the century as Rossiter unbuckled his harness and let himself fall, backpack and all, to the roof. He landed more or less on his feet, then pitched forward onto his abdomen and started crawling toward Natalie, rope still over his shoulder, the heavy, rubberized soles of his SWAT boots apparently offering enough traction to keep him from slipping.

"Son of a bitch!" Hunter stared. "I fucking *hate* it when he does shit like that. That man has a supernatural relationship with gravity."

"Yeah." That was all Joaquin could manage, his mouth dry, his stomach somewhere down on the street below.

"That fucker's crazy!" The pilot's face was white as a sheet.

"It's the bionic leg," Hunter muttered. "Just stabilize this bird and help me find a way to get us onto that rooftop patio."

"You're crazy, too," the pilot mumbled.

Then the chopper moved forward, gaining altitude and speed, heading into the wind, leaving Rossiter and Natalie behind.

HEART STILL POUNDING, Natalie watched over her shoulder, barely able to breathe as Gabe moved toward her, slowed down by the periodic gust. It probably took him less than a minute to reach her, but it felt like an eternity. "Y-you're n-nuts!"

"You're welcome." He grinned, covering her body with his, his weight pinning her to the rooftop, offering some warmth and stopping the backward slide she'd been fighting for what felt like hours now. Then he drew off his pack and pulled out what looked like a climbing harness. "Now, listen up. Here's what we're going to do."

CHAPTER 32

"WHAT WAS THAT?"

Through a haze of pain, Zach listened to the muted thrum of the helo's rotors as it disappeared in the distance, hoping to God that Natalie was safely aboard that bird.

Every man in the room looked up.

"They're on the roof." Wulfe motioned to two of his men. "Get rid of them."

Two men ran out onto the patio, squinting against the rain, heads craning to get a good look at the roof, assault rifles in hand.

Zach's pulse spiked. If she was still up there . . .

God, let her be gone!

Zach fought to keep his fear off his face. "You're out of time, Wulfe. You've lost. Your only hope is to get the hell out of here while you can. Hey, maybe Quintana will let you stay on his couch. You should ask him."

Wulfe looked down at Zach, his calm façade impenetrable. "Oh, don't worry. My men will take out the officers on the roof. The streets of Lower Downtown are flooded, cars stalled everywhere, so it's going to take the rest of SWAT a while to get here. Then they'll want to evacuate the building, study the problem, come up with a plan. Do you know what SWAT stands for? Stand, Wait, And Talk. We have some time."

Flooded streets?

So that's what was keeping Hunter and Rossiter.

"My lucky day."

Wulfe smiled. "I don't want to kill you, McBride. Of course, I must, but I regret that. You're a true hero. Ah, yes, I see it surprises you that I value such qualities. But I do. You're a former SEAL, a Medal of Honor recipient. Men with your strength, skill, and dedication are rare. You're worth a hundred of my men."

Zach gave a snort. "Forgive me if I don't see that as a compliment."

Wulfe's smile grew thin. "If Arturo hadn't been so inept, you'd still be out there, doing your job. But he allowed himself to be manipulated by the Interpol operative into believing you'd stolen cocaine. Then he had his men kidnap Ms. Benoit rather than simply terminating her on that bus, as I'd ordered him to do. Naturally, you felt obliged to help her, led by your cock, no doubt. And here we are."

So Wulfe had ordered Cárdenas to kill Natalie. Cárdenas must have seen her photo online and let his lust for her get the better of him. He'd had his men kidnap Natalie, planning to carry out Wulfe's orders—but only after he'd used her in his sick way.

"So Los Zetas usually do what you tell them to do?"

Wulfe's chin went up. "I *am* Los Zetas. I made them powerful, wealthy. Cárdenas was one of a handful of men who've run the organization for me."

That was an interesting bit of information.

Zach hoped he lived to share it. He stalled for time. "What made you sell out, Ed? Do you mind if I call you Ed? Was it money? Power? Did someone at the Pentagon sleep with your wife?"

But Wulfe ignored the taunts. "Make things easier for yourself. I have no desire to see you suffer, so spare yourself unnecessary pain and answer the questions."

Zach laughed. "Maybe that rubber bullet scrambled my brains, but I don't see how answering questions that betray my mission so that I can be killed sooner and die with a guilty conscience makes anything easier for me."

Wulfe leaned in. "Where did you send Ms. Benoit?"

"Disneyland."

"Who knows about my connection to the Zetas?"

"The U.S. Marshal Service, SWAT, my dentist, Oprah—"

"How did you know we were coming? Clearly, someone tipped you off."

"That guy." Zach pointed with a jerk of his head toward one of Wulfe's minions. The man looked uncertainly at Wulfe, taking a step backward. "He texted me just before you stepped into the elevator."

Without a word, Wulfe stepped aside for Quintana, who moved in, holding the severed cord from an electrical lamp in his hand. Cut from the lamp's base, it was still plugged into the wall, the bare wires capable of delivering raw current that was far more powerful than the truck battery and excruciatingly painful.

Zach met Quintana's gaze. "Don't you ever get bored with this?"

Electricity poured through him like liquid agony, setting every nerve on fire. His body arched, his muscles going into spasms, a cry tearing itself from between his clenched teeth.

Then Quintana stepped back, leaving Zach shaking, breathless, wanting to puke. Strangely he found the pain easier to bear now than he had two weeks ago. Perhaps it was just that he'd been through this before. Or perhaps it was the fact that his pain was buying time for the woman he loved.

Why hadn't he told her? Why hadn't he told Natalie he loved her when he'd had the chance? It would've taken only a few seconds. What the hell had he been afraid of?

And all at once it hit him—regret as deep and wide as the ocean.

Natalie.

If he died today, she would never know what she meant to him. If he died, he would never even get a shot at building a life with her, of knowing what it was like to come home every night and find someone waiting for him. Hell, he wouldn't even know whether he'd gotten her pregnant.

Then don't die, McBride.

Right.

He raised his head and looked into Wulfe's eyes, ready to answer at least one question. "Do you really think you can kill us all? SWAT knows. Denver PD knows. The newspaper knows. The Marshal Service and FBI know. All of my documents and hers have been uploaded to encrypted accounts. If you kill us, someone else will follow. It's over, Wulfe. Turn yourself in, and I'll argue for leniency."

Wulfe's nostrils flared—an adrenaline response. He stepped aside and motioned Quintana forward again.

Zach gave a weak laugh. "What did I do? I answered your question, offered to help you out, and you fry me for that? You know what, Ed? You suck."

Just then the two men who'd run onto the patio returned. "There's no one on the roof, but SWAT is down in the street. They've set up a staging area around the block and have all the entry points to the building covered."

No one on the roof.

Thank God!

Relief washed through Zach, a balm for the lingering pain, both physical and emotional. He might not live through this day, but Natalie was safe.

Quintana moved in on him.

WET AND CHILLED to the bone, Natalie slipped through the bathroom window, having had more than her fill of heights. She reached for the floor with her bare feet while Gabe slowly lowered her down, then she stood there shivering. He followed her, his feet landing silently on the marble floor.

The room had been torn apart, the shower curtain slashed, the shelves emptied, skin cream, shampoo, and conditioner dumped on the floor. Beyond the door, bodies lay in the hallway, blood on the walls and floor. Was it Zach's blood?

Her stomach churned.

From the living room, she could hear men's voices. She strained to listen and thought she heard Zach.

Or maybe that was wishful thinking.

Was he hurt? Was he even still alive? And what about Julian?

"They've already searched here, so I think you'll be safe. Get into the bathtub. The steel will halt most stray rounds." Gabe unfastened her harness and pressed a pistol into her hands. "Use this for self-defense only. Don't come out until I tell you it's safe. Not a sound!"

Natalie nodded and did as he asked, her limbs stiff from the cold. She'd gained a new respect for Gabe today. Realizing that Wulfe and his men had probably heard him hit the roof, he'd quickly put her in a harness, roped her in, then fixed the rope around the base of the lighted metal pole that warned airplanes away and dangled her—yes, dangled her—off the edge, more than two hundred feet of air beneath her.

Then, while she hung there, dizzy, her heart in her throat, he'd crept along a narrow steel ledge with no protection, to keep an eye on the patio, waiting for Wulfe's men, who had, indeed, come out to check, to go back inside. When they'd gone, he'd made his way back to her, then used the rope to rappel to the bathroom window.

A man's agonized cry silenced her thoughts.

Zach!

She squeezed her eyes shut, a sick feeling swelling inside her at the sound of his suffering. It had been hard enough to hear when they'd been in Mexico and she'd barely known him. But she loved him now. To know they were hurting him . . .

From beside the tub, she heard Gabe speak quietly into his mouthpiece. "They're going to kill him! Let me help him!"

Zach's cry fell into silence.

A man's raised voice: "For the last time, McBride—where is she?"

This was followed by a moment of silence—and then another agonized cry.

They were torturing him over her.

She opened her eyes, looked up at Gabe. "I have to do something!"

"If you care about Zach, then stay here and stay alive!"

"I can't stand to hear him suffer! You don't know what you're asking of me!"

Gabe leaned in until his face was inches from hers, his gaze hard. "Yes, I do."

And Natalie remembered that he'd been forced to listen, drugged and bounded, while a murdering sociopath had brutalized Kat. Now she understood just how terrible that had been for him. She might have said something had he not turned away from her, whispering fiercely into his microphone, his fingertips against his earpiece.

"I'm giving you two minutes, then I move whether you're here or not. Fuck you, Hunter! You're not my boss. He is, and they're fucking killing him! Stand by? Christ! Hurry the fuck up!"

From downstairs came another rending cry.

"I've got two officers up there who are injured, maybe even dead, and I've got another officer and an innocent woman who are in danger of becoming dead, and you refuse to fly? What the hell kind of pilot did DPD stick us with?"

"One who seriously needs to grow a pair," Joaquin muttered under his breath, unable to hide his contempt. He shot a few frames as Marc moved in on the chopper pilot, towering over him with his six-foot-plus frame, the helicopter sitting idle in the sodden park grass behind them.

"I'm just the traffic guy. I help bust speeders on the open highway. With all the skyscrapers, those buildings all so close together, the wind." The pilot backed up, crossed his arms over his chest, and tucked his hands into his armpits. "It's not safe to fly."

"I'm a helicopter pilot." A SWAT officer who'd been standing nearby held out his hand. "Clifton from Boulder County SWAT. I can get us up there."

Marc shook the man's hand. "What kind of experience do you have?"

"I did six years with Army Airborne flying missions in Afghan—"

"Good." Marc slapped him on the shoulder. "I want four volunteers ready to fly in two minutes. Let's do some combat-style snipe-and-rappel with this bird."

"You can't take my chopper!" The pilot stood glaring, red-faced, at Marc. "I'm responsible for this machine."

"Not any longer." Marc pulled out his badge case, showed the ID, then flipped to the shiny star. "Special Deputy U.S. Marshal Marc Hunter. I'm commandeering the use of your helo."

The pilot's face grew even redder, then he turned and stomped away.

Joaquin met Marc's gaze. "I think you enjoyed that."

"You're damned right I did." Marc grinned.

But his smile couldn't mask the worry in his eyes.

COLD SWEAT SPILLING down his temples, Zach fought to catch his breath, his heart beating erratically, flailing in his chest. Another blast like that and he was a goner.

Quintana shook his head as if his heart were no longer in his work. He turned to Wulfe, speaking in a heavy Spanish accent. "He's not going to break. I've been through this with him. Kill him now and go—or bring him with us and let me find his weakness."

"*She* is his weakness, and she isn't here. I'm betting he put her on the roof, and that chopper we heard was SWAT retrieving her." Wulfe drew a deep breath. "You're right. There's no further point in this. Finish him."

Zach let his contempt for Wulfe show. "You don't have the courage to kill me yourself? Can't even pull a trigger. You're pathetic."

Wulfe looked down at him, seemed to hesitate, then gestured to Quintana, who stepped forward, a smile on his face, wires in his hand.

Zach watched Wulfe walk toward the door. "You're a coward, Wulfe."

Over thunder of his own pulse, he heard the whirring of an approaching helo. Everyone, including Quintana, turned to look. One of Wulfe's men ran out onto the patio and looked skyward, making a full circle, eyes on the sky, before turning back to Wulfe and shrugging his shoulders. "I don't see it!"

Quintana faced Zach again.

Zach looked into the eyes of the man who was going to kill him.

I love you, Natalie. I'm sorry I didn't tell you. Forgive me.

It all happened in slow motion.

Quintana reaching out with the wires. Sunset breaking through the clouds. The hulking form of a helo rising up from below to hover just off the rooftop patio.

And then there was only pain.

* * *

"Hold it right there. I've got Quintana in my sights."

Joaquin didn't dare to breathe. He'd never seen anyone be so calm with so much at stake. Hunter lay motionless on his belly on the chopper floor, sniper rifle aimed toward the wall of glass at the other end of the patio.

On either side of him, four SWAT officers knelt, ready to rappel.

The helicopter bobbed in the wind. Up a few feet. Down again. Over.

"Hold it. Hold it."

Time itself seemed to stop, Joaquin's heartbeat louder than the chopper's throbbing rotors. Then . . .

BAM! BAM!

The rifle seemed to fire itself. Hunter hadn't moved at all.

"Go!" Hunter shouted.

The chopper rose, turned slightly, and hovered over the patio.

Hunter and the four volunteers dropped like spiders down thick, nylon webs, friction making the ropes whine. They landed on their feet and dispersed along the edges of the patio, heading toward the door. Assault rifles fired.

Rat-ta-ta-ta-ta-tat! Rat ta-ta-ta-ta-tat! Rat-ta-ta-ta-ta-tat!

It took Joaquin a moment to realize that the bullets were headed their way. His friends were going into danger, and once again he wasn't with them.

Without thinking, he drew his camera strap over his head, grabbed on to one of the ropes, and, ignoring the pilot's shouts, slid to the patio.

"Stay down and don't make a sound!"

With those words, Gabe left her. Natalie pressed herself against the bottom of the tub, her pulse tripping, hell breaking loose around her.

The heavy drone of a helicopter. Zach's strangled cry. Burst after burst of automatic weapons fire. Men's shouts.

Rat-ta-ta-ta-ta-tat! Rat-ta-ta-ta-ta-tat! Rat-ta-ta-ta-ta-tat!

Unable to stop herself, she raised her head just enough so that she could see above the rim of the tub.

Gabe had just shot a man, the body lying in a heap at Gabe's feet. He raised the rifle again, crouched against the wall, glaring back at her. "Stay down!"

From the distance there came one last burst of gunfire—a high-caliber pistol.

BAM! BAM! BAM!

And then . . .

"Face down! Hands behind your head! Do it!" That was Marc's voice.

"Clear back here." A voice Natalie didn't recognize.

"Clear up here." That was Gabe.

"Where's Wulfe?" Marc again. "I saw him in here. Son of a bitch! He's gone!"

She waited to hear Zach's voice, waited for him to ask about her.

"Hey, Rossiter," Marc called, his voice grave. "Get down here!"

Natalie leapt from the tub, stepped over the body of the man Gabe had killed, and ran down the stairs—then stopped, stunned by the carnage. Black-clad bodies lay strewn about, blood in pools on the floor. Furniture was shredded, bullet holes in the walls. Lying in the middle of the room was Quintana, shot in the head. And nearby . . .

Head bowed and shirtless, Zach sat bound to a kitchen chair by silver duct tape, which Marc and Gabe were tearing off in handfuls. Even from a distance she could see the burn marks on his skin.

"Zach?" Natalie's stomach fell.

"Ease him down." Gabe held Zach's head while Hunter helped lower Zach to the floor. Then Gabe pressed two fingers to Zach's carotid artery. "He's got no pulse. I think he's in V-fib. Hunter, get the AED out of my pack. And someone call LifeFlight."

No pulse?

The breath left Natalie's lungs, her heart seeming to stop, legs with no strength left in them somehow carrying her across the floor. And then it all became a blur.

Marc tearing through Gabe's pack. Gabe starting chest

compressions. SWAT officers cuffing and patting down survivors.

"Zach?" Tears stinging her eyes, Natalie knelt beside him, touched her hand to his cheek, to the deep bruise on his temple, to the hair that lay across his brow. "Zach? Please don't die! Don't go! I love you! I love you so much!"

She didn't hear Gabe tell her to move, didn't realize what was happening until she felt arms surround her, Marc pulling her back.

"Clear!"

Gabe pressed the AED paddles to Zach's still chest.

Zap!

Zach's body jerked.

Gabe felt for a pulse again, his expression grim. "One more time."

Marc held Natalie back as the defibrillator charged.

Gabe pressed the paddles to Zach's chest once more. "Come on, McBride. You're young and strong. You can pull through this."

Zap!

Once again, Zach's body jerked.

And then . . .

Gabe pressed his fingers to Zach's throat. "I'm getting a pulse."

"Oh, thank God!" Natalie pressed a hand against her lips, trembling with relief.

"It's weak, but it's there." Gabe ripped open a package of nitrile gloves and slipped them on. "I'm going to get a couple IVs going, get some fluids in him. We need to get him to the ER as soon as possible. He's alive, but I can't guarantee he'll stay that way. There could be trauma to his heart or other internal organs."

"Thank you, Gabe. Thank you both." Natalie took Zach's hand, bent down, pressed her lips to his forehead. "Can you hear me, Zach? We're going to take good care of you. Just stay alive."

JOAQUIN WALKED IN off the patio to a scene he would never forget. Bodies and blood everywhere. And there in front of him, Natalie, still soaking wet, bent over McBride, her hands stroking his face, her cheeks streaked with tears.

Natalie looked up, saw him. "Joaquin?"

Then Marc was on his feet. "Jesus H. Christ! I really *am* going to kick your ass. How the hell did you get in here?"

"Same way you did." But with blisters. He hadn't been wearing gloves, and the rope had done a number on his palms.

"Stay the hell out of the way—and no photos!"

He nodded, then looked over at McBride. "Is he going to make it?"

It was Rossiter who answered, his gloved fingers busy inserting an IV needle into McBride's arm. "I think so."

Joaquin stepped over Quintana's body, proof of Hunter's skill with a sniper rifle. He found a throw on the couch that wasn't bloodstained, carried it over to Natalie, and draped it over her shoulders, certain she must be cold.

She glanced up. "Thank you." Then her gaze returned to McBride.

Out of the corner of his eye, Joaquin saw movement near the door. He tensed, looked up—and his jaw dropped.

Hunter pivoted, pistol out. "Darcangelo?"

Covered in blood, his face pale, Darcangelo slumped against the doorjamb. "It takes a while to climb . . . twenty-four flights of stairs . . . with a round in your shoulder . . . and no thumb. Anyone seen it . . . lying around?"

In an instant, Hunter was at Darcangelo's side, helping him to the floor. "Easy does it, buddy."

"Make yourself useful, Ramirez." Gabe stuffed a plastic carton of gauze, a folded emergency blanket, and a package of nitrile gloves into Joaquin's hands. "Take these to Hunter, then see if there's anything in the fridge or freezer you can use as an ice pack on his hand. Hunter, get him out of his shirt and body armor. Apply direct pressure, and keep him warm. I'll come start an IV as soon as I can."

Joaquin did as he was told, carrying the supplies to Hunter, who already had Darcangelo out of his shirt and was stripping off the bloody and pitted armor. There, on the right side of the vest was a blackened and bloodstained hole.

One of the rounds had penetrated.

Darcangelo looked up at Hunter, his face and lips unnaturally pale. "Wulfe was surprised to see me. Drew on me. I recognized him. Fired. Killed the son of a bitch."

"Wulfe is dead?" Hunter and Rossiter asked at once.

Having no idea who this Wulfe was, Joaquin hurried into kitchen and opened the fridge and freezer, looking for something that could serve as an ice bag. There on the shelf was . . . His stomach did a flip. "I think I found your thumb."

"Leave it there," Rossiter called to him.

Joaquin grabbed a bag of frozen peas from the freezer and carried it over to Hunter, who now sat behind Darcangelo, supporting him and pressing a handful of gauze squares over the bullet wound in his shoulder, the emergency blanket covering them both. "Here you go, man."

Hunter took the frozen peas and laid the bag over the already bloodstained gauze that covered Darcangelo's maimed hand.

Darcangelo winced, gritted his teeth. "Want to tell me why . . . you're sitting here cuddling me, Hunter?"

"Rossiter says I have to keep you warm. He thinks you're in shock or some shit." Despite his words and the tone of his voice, there was real worry on Hunter's face.

"Great. Thanks." Darcangelo's head fell back to rest against Hunter's vest, the big guy's strength clearly spent.

A muscle clenched in Hunter's jaw. "Hey, don't mention it—ever."

And that, Joaquin decided, swallowing the lump in his throat, was true friendship. Somehow his camera found its way back into his blistered hands, and he started shooting.

ZACH SAT ON the rim of the canyon, Mike, Chris, Brian, and Jimmy beside him. Like him, they were wearing civilian clothes, and for a moment Zach wondered why they were all out of uniform.

"Why are you still here, bro?" Jimmy asked. "Do you like this place?"

"No," Zach answered. "I'm here because of you guys." Wasn't that obvious?

Brian laughed. "We left a long time ago."

Mike gave him a jab in the side with his elbow. "If you're

waiting here for us, you're wasting your time. We only came back to check on you."

There was something Zach needed to say to them, words that wouldn't quite come to him that he needed to get out. "I'm . . . sorry."

It was the only thing he could articulate.

Chris clapped him on the shoulder. "There's no reason to be sorry, McBride. It wasn't your fault. It was never your fault. We knew it then. We know it now."

Relief, sweet and pure, flowed through him. It was as if an unbearable weight had been lifted from his shoulders. He felt so . . . light.

The four of them stood.

"We need to get rolling." Jimmy reached down, helped Zach to his feet.

"Where are we going?" Zach looked around at the landscape. It didn't look like Afghanistan now that he thought about it.

Mike shook his head. "Oh, no. You're not coming with us."

Brian pointed. "You need to head that way."

But Zach didn't want to say good-bye so soon. "Can't you stay for a while?"

Chris shook his head. "It's time to move on."

They exchanged man-hugs, the back-slapping ritual making Zach smile, a bittersweet ache in his chest. It had been so long. Why couldn't they stay?

"Take it easy, McBride," Jimmy said, reaching out for a final handshake.

"See you around, frogman." Chris gave him a mock salute.

"We'll never forget you, bro." Mike slugged him lightly in the shoulder.

Brian met his gaze. "You were the best of us." Then he, too, turned and walked away.

Zach watched them go, sadness seeping through him like a chill as they disappeared in the distance.

Then he turned and looked in the direction they'd pointed. He started walking, but the path was obscured to the point where he could barely make out the trail, the landscape shifting in front of him. Then there was a voice—a woman's voice. She was calling him, guiding him.

"Zach, stay with me. Can you hear me?"

He opened his eyes and found Natalie looking down at him, tears in her beautiful eyes, anguish on her sweet face. "Natalie? Are you . . . okay?"

Through her tears, she smiled. "I will be now."

CHAPTER 33

NATALIE STAYED WITH Zach and Julian while they were transported by helicopter to University Hospital, Marc and the others remaining behind to finish the job and answer questions from federal investigators. Zach was admitted into intensive care for tests and monitoring, while Julian was rushed into surgery, where a team of doctors hoped to remove the bullet from his shoulder and reattach his severed thumb.

Despite her objections, Natalie found herself shooed into the waiting area. It was only then that the horror of the past two hours hit her, leaving her weak and shaking. She struggled not to cry, getting herself a cup of coffee, hoping it would ward off the chill that had taken hold inside her. People stared at her damp clothes, bare feet, and wet, tangled hair, but she didn't care. Let them try to hang on to a slippery roof twenty-four stories in the air during a thunderstorm while evil men tortured the man they loved, and see what they looked like afterward.

"Natalie?"

Natalie turned toward the sound of her own name. "Tessa!"

The two women hugged.

"You're ice-cold. Your clothes and hair are damp. Bless your heart!" Tessa drew back, slipped her sweater off her shoulders. "Wear my cardigan."

Natalie slipped into the warm blue cashmere, touched that Tessa would consider her comfort when she must be terribly worried about Julian and desperate to know how he'd been hurt. "Thanks."

They found a quiet corner and Natalie told her what had happened—or what she knew of it, which wasn't all that much. She stopped when she got to the part about dead bodies and blood. "I'm not sure I should be telling you any of this, with the baby."

Tessa put on a brave smile. "The little guy is fine, and Julian will be, too. Chief Irving says Julian stopped to help a pregnant woman with a flat tire, and she shot him."

Natalie hadn't heard that. "I wondered what had happened."

It would take some kind of deception to get the best of a man like Julian.

Tessa's smile crumpled. "What sickens me is knowing that he was thinking of *me* when he stopped to help her. He's a good man with a soft heart, especially when it comes to women. And it almost got him killed."

Natalie took Tessa's hand. "I'm sorry, Tessa. I didn't want anyone to get hurt."

"It's not your fault." Tessa gave her hand a squeeze. "Julian does a dangerous job. I've known that since I met him, and it's part of why I respect and love him. We'll get through this. We'll all get through this. At least he's alive."

And Natalie wondered if she'd be able to respond with half as much grace if she were in Tessa's position.

THE HOURS DRAGGED by as Natalie and Tessa waited, sharing a quiet dinner in the hospital cafeteria and getting to know each other in a way they hadn't before. Holly and Kara came with a change of clothes, shoes, and a makeup kit so that Natalie should freshen up and have something dry to wear. Then investigators arrived to interview Natalie, followed by the media. Hospital security took Natalie and Tessa to a private waiting room upstairs to keep the media from pestering them—except for their own paper, of course.

Tom sent Matt to cover the shoot-out, as he was the only member of the I-Team available. Kat was still on the rez. Sophie was home with her own kids and babysitting Tessa's daughter. Comfortable only reporting the facts, Natalie told

Matt what she could—which was far more than any other media outlet would be able to report.

"Good God, Natalie," Matt said when she finished. "If you don't get a Pulitzer out of this, I will personally kick the committee's ass."

Then he left, headed back to the newsroom for a late night of deadline reporting.

"Tessa Darcangelo?" A doctor in surgical garb stepped into the room, his green surgical mask around his neck.

Tessa's face went white. She stood. "I'm Tessa."

The doctor came over, shook her hand. "Your husband's lost a fair amount of blood, so we transfused him. We were able to remove the bullet, and that injury should heal well. He'll have stiffness and pain in his shoulder for a time, but the bullet hit muscle, so there was no injury to the structure of the joint itself."

"Thank goodness! What about his thumb?"

"We've reattached it. There's blood flow. But we won't know for some time how much function or sensation he'll have. He's awake and in recovery now, so if you'd like to see him—"

"God bless you! Yes, I'd love to see him." Then Tessa turned, took Natalie's hand, and gave it a squeeze. "I hope they bring good news about Zach soon."

Natalie smiled, hoping the very same thing. "Go be with your husband."

It was almost midnight by the time doctors came for Natalie with the welcome news that none of the tests showed permanent damage to Zach's heart—and that Zach had been asking for her.

"Oh, thank God! When can I see him? I'd like to stay with him tonight."

"Only family are allowed back into the ICU."

And so she lied. "I'm his wife."

Back in the ICU, she found Zach asleep, his naked body covered only at the groin, by a towel. Electrodes were attached to his chest and side, IVs in his left arm, an oxygen tube beneath his nose. There were red blotches on his torso, dressings on his right shoulder and left thigh where bullets had grazed him—proof of how much he'd risked and how much he'd suffered to protect her.

She took his hand, pressed a kiss to his cheek. "I'm here, Zach. I'm going to stay right here beside you."

IT WAS A combination of fluorescent light and a woman's sweet voice that woke him.

Zach opened his eyes, found Natalie sitting next to him, her gaze fixed on the heart monitor screen, worry and exhaustion lining her pretty face. "Angel."

She looked down at him, her lips curving in a sweet smile. "How do you feel?"

"Not too bad . . . for a dead guy."

Her smile vanished. "Don't even joke about that."

"Sorry." He glanced around. "I thought they were moving me out of ICU."

She stroked his cheek. "Not till later this morning—and only if your heart keeps beating like it should."

His tests had come back normal, no sign of organ damage, external burns only. He was one lucky son of a bitch, and he knew it.

He reached up and ran a knuckle down her cheek, needing to touch her. "How can you look so beautiful after all you've been through?"

"I don't." Her smiled returned. "They're just giving you good drugs."

"You're the most amazing woman I've ever known." He slid his fingers into her hair, savoring the silky feel of her dark strands. "I love you, Natalie."

There. That didn't hurt, did it, McBride?

Her eyes widened, and she looked down at him, searching his eyes as if trying to see whether he truly meant it. "Zach, I—"

"Shh." He pressed his finger to her lips. "When I realized I was going to die, the only thing I could think about was you and what an idiot I'd been for not telling you how I felt about you. I think I've loved you from the moment you lifted that awful blindfold off my face. I opened my eyes, and there you were, the bravest, most beautiful woman I've ever known. You set me free, Natalie. In so many ways, you set me free."

Tears glittered in her eyes. "I was so afraid I'd lost you!"

He drew her down to his chest, held her. "When you're up to it, tell me what happened and how you got back inside the loft. I thought they'd carried you off in that helo. I was so relieved to think you were safe."

When she had finished her story, he found himself smiling. "My angel, up on the roof, shouting at the thunderstorm, telling it what to do with itself. Sounds like I owe Rossiter big-time. I'm sorry I had to put you up there. I really had no choice. If I'd put you inside a closet, they'd have found you— if a stray round hadn't killed you first. Even rounds from a handgun can pierce walls, and—"

"Hush, you. Don't you dare apologize. You kept me safe, kept me alive." She bent down and kissed him, her lips warm and soft.

Again and again she kissed him, and Zach knew that she, like he, was reveling in the feeling of being together, safe and alive. He slid his fingers deeper into her hair, teased her tongue with his, the feel of her beside him calling him back to life.

"Ahem."

They both looked toward the entrance to his room—in the ICU there were no doors—and saw his favorite nurse, a tall big-boned woman named Chris who looked like she could probably bench-press him.

"You had several ectopic heartbeats, so I thought I'd come check on you, see how you were doing. Now I see the cause."

Natalie looked at the nurse, guilt and regret on her face. "Ectopic heartbeats?"

Chris smiled. "That's medical jargon for when your heart skips a beat. It's completely harmless. You can go back to kissing your husband. Just keep it above the waist, okay? We don't offer *that* kind of intensive care here." Then Chris walked off, laughing at her own joke.

Zach looked up at Natalie. "Husband?"

That guilty look came over Natalie's face again. "I told them that so they'd let me stay here with you last night. I hope you're not angry. I don't think they really believed me, anyway. No ring."

That was something he planned to change.

He wasn't ready to ask her yet. There were still too many loose threads in his life. He needed to tie those up, consider the offers that were on the table, and choose what he thought would be best—for both of them.

Natalie looked down at him, a playful smile on his face. "So, kissing me makes your heart skip beats, does it?"

"That's hell-to-the-yeah, angel. Now kiss me again."

THEY MOVED ZACH out of the ICU just after lunch.

Natalie walked beside him as they wheeled him down to a medical ward, feeling lighter than she had since this entire ordeal began. For the first time in more than two weeks, she wasn't afraid for her life—or for the lives of those she loved.

It was over. As impossible as it seemed, it was finally over.

She'd just gotten Zach settled in the new room, opening the blinds to let in the sunlight, when Tom called on the hospital's landline, wanting to know when she planned to come into the office. She hadn't even been thinking about work.

"We've got a big story that's just waiting for you to get it into print. You fought hard for this one, Benoit. Don't let the other papers take it from you."

"I'll be in shortly." She hung up, then turned to Zach, who'd heard her side of the conversation. "I don't want to leave you here alone."

He reached over, took her hand. "Don't worry about me. I did my job so that you'd be safe to do yours. Besides, I don't think I'm going to be alone."

In the doorway stood Rowan with two DUSMs. She entered, the two men behind her. "Ms. Benoit. McBride."

"I want to thank you for all you did to protect me." Natalie held out her hand, shook Rowan's. "Whatever rules Zach may have broken, he did it to save my life. Don't be hard on him."

Rowan smiled. "You're welcome. And don't worry about McBride. The guys in D.C. might be idiots, but I've got his back. By the way, we found this on the bottom of your car, McBride." She held up a strange long box with magnets on one side and an antenna sticking out of the one end.

Natalie had no idea what it was, but Zach seemed to.

"Son of a bitch. A GPS tracker."

"We figure they watched the cop shop after Quintana was brought in, waited for you to arrive, then popped it on your car. You led them right to you. All they needed then was a thumb." She handed the device to one of the men. "And there's more. Wulfe rented a condo in the Glass Tower under a false name the day prior to the attack. My guess is that's where he was headed when Darcangelo stopped him. We found food, weapons, and cognac stockpiled there, along with Quintana's jail uniform and cuffs. If things went wrong, Wulfe apparently planned to hide out there, while we searched heaven and earth trying to bring him in."

Natalie could see Zach's mind working, understanding dawning on his face. "That's why he and Quintana appeared out of nowhere. And that's why he was so cool when SWAT moved in. He didn't need to get out of the building. He had a cozy hidey-hole waiting for him."

"Exactly. So you see, McBride, I didn't give you away. Oh, don't try to deny you had your doubts about me. From the moment Quintana escaped, I knew you'd wonder if I was dirty. I can't explain how they knew when we were moving Quintana, but before this is over, I will. Still, I can't blame you for suspecting me." Rowan met Natalie's gaze. "It's all in the report you're about to request from my office, Ms. Benoit."

Natalie smiled, liking this woman more by the minute. But she couldn't stay. She leaned down and kissed Zach. "I'll call to check on you. If you need anything, call me, okay? Don't let them hassle you. See you tonight."

Then she left the room and hurried down the hallway. She needed to go home, take a shower, then get to the office.

But first, there was someone else she needed to see.

SHE WENT TO Julian's hospital room, only to find it crowded when she walked in. Tessa was there, of course, but so was almost everyone else—Sophie and Marc, Gabe, Joaquin, Kara and Reece.

"I hear the doc gave you a thumbs-up on your surgery," Marc was saying.

"Sophie, your husband's mouth is talking again." Obviously on pain meds, but still alert and in good humor, Julian lay bare-chested in his bed, the head of his bed raised, multiple IVs in his right arm. There was a thick surgical dressing over his right shoulder and four dark bruises on his chest where bullets had struck his body armor. His left arm was heavily bandaged, his thumb in the extended position.

"Did they tell you how long you'll have to stay in the hospital?" Gabe asked. "You're not the kind who likes to lie around twiddling your thumbs."

"But, hey, they're saying you have a chance at full recovery," Reece added. "That's nothing to thumb your nose at."

Julian rolled his eyes, apparently resigned to being teased.

"Oh, for goodness' sake, stop with the thumb jokes!" Tessa objected, the slight smile on her face proving she was as amused as she was irritated.

It was Julian who saw her first.

"Hey, Natalie, come on in. How's McBride?"

"They just moved him out of ICU. It looks like he's going to be okay."

Natalie shared what the doctors had told her—that the shocks had basically shorted out the electrical impulses in Zach's heart. Only Gabe's intervention had saved his life. Fortunately, there seemed to be no permanent damage.

Sophie gave Natalie a hug. "Thank God! I'm so glad he's going to be okay."

"How are you?" Natalie asked Julian.

"Doing well, all things considered." Then he looked at Marc and Gabe. "I told you double plating was worth the cost."

Sophie looked sternly at Marc. "You're getting double plating in your vest today. I don't care how much it costs."

They talked for a good half an hour, Julian explaining how he'd been shot, how he'd come to in the trunk of the car with his thumb missing, and how he'd managed to send Zach a warning by text message, knowing what must be about to happen.

"That message saved our lives, Julian." Natalie gave his right hand a squeeze. "I don't know how to thank you—any of you—for what you've done for me and Zach."

Julian gave her a weak smile, his face pale. "Seems to me you just did."

"I was happy to help." Marc winked.

"You made it easy, Natalie." Gabe grinned. "You're one tough chick."

"I hope the woman who shot my husband has a run-in with karma," Tessa said.

Julian turned to Tessa. "Didn't I tell you? She's dead. When they started bagging the bodies, I saw her face. McBride must've gotten her in the first wave. And don't worry—she wasn't really pregnant."

"Well, I feel better." Tessa frowned. "Or maybe I don't. It doesn't feel right to be happy because someone's dead."

The room fell silent.

It was then that Joaquin decided to share the gift that he'd brought with him. "I have something for you all."

He reached into his camera bag and drew out an envelope holding prints he'd made this morning of photos from yesterday's action. He opened the envelope and drew out the photos one by one, handing them first to Natalie, who passed them on. He said nothing, letting the images speak for themselves.

Natalie clinging to the rooftop, looking pleadingly over her shoulder toward the helicopter. Gabe being lowered down in a rescue attempt. Gabe crawling across the rooftop toward Natalie. Flooded streets, stranded cars. The helicopter sitting idle while Marc yelled at the pilot. An overhead view of the SWAT staging area. Marc aiming his sniper rifle at Quintana, as calm and cool as steel. SWAT volunteers storming the loft.

And then came the photos he wasn't supposed to have taken.

"Oh, Joaquin!" Natalie whispered.

It was the photo of Marc and Julian. The lighting had been perfect, catching the texture of their skin, the subtlest details of their faces, exposing their emotions. Julian lay, bloodied and shirtless, against Marc's chest, his eyes closed, pain etched on every feature of his face. Marc looked down at him, pressing gauze to the bullet wound in his shoulder and an ice bag to his hand, his expression fierce, a mix of anger, concern, and—there was no other word for it—*love*.

Natalie stared at it, then looked up at Joaquin, passing it on. "This is amazing. These are Pulitzer quality, Joaquin."

"Unbelievable." Reece looked up at him. "They make me

feel like I was there, give me an appreciation for how terrible it truly was."

Joaquin drew out one more—an image of Natalie smiling through her tears at Zach, who had just opened his eyes, Gabe focused intently on starting an IV.

Natalie stared at it, tears shimmering in her eyes. "Thank you."

As the photos made the rounds, Joaquin watched, taking in people's reactions. He saw the glance of acknowledgment that passed between Marc and Julian, the tears in Tessa's and Sophie's eyes, the appreciation in Gabe's and Reece's, and he knew his images had revealed a deeper truth about their friendships and the ordeal they'd just endured than they could have expressed themselves.

"You have a gift," Julian said at last, handing back the photos. "Anyone can be trained to shoot a gun. But what you do, Ramirez—it's art."

And for the first time since Mexico, Joaquin felt at home in his own shoes.

For Natalie, the next few days passed in a blur. Zach was released after three days in the hospital and stayed at her place. They hadn't discussed it. Natalie had simply brought him home, and he'd stayed, moving what he had in, his toothbrush, razor, and shampoo taking up space beside hers in the bathroom, his clothes in her closet, his body in bed beside hers at night.

Officially on medical leave, he was supposed to be taking it easy, but he had a somewhat different idea of what that meant than she did. While she worked long hours at the paper putting together a series of articles about Wulfe, Cárdenas, and Whitcomb Academy, he installed a security alarm, new window locks, outdoor security lights, and a special lock for her sliding glass door.

She was at the paper one afternoon, interviewing Rowan for the fourth time, when Zach appeared in the newsroom.

"Did you hear?" she asked when she got off the phone. "They found the soccer coach's body in the county landfill. It was badly decomposed but . . ."

It was then she noticed the expression on his face.

"I've been called back to D.C.," he said. "It seems Pearce and the others at the OD have a few more questions before they can put the investigation against me to rest. I need to clear my name once and for all, Natalie."

She nodded. "Of course."

They said good-bye in the conference room, sealing their farewell with a long kiss.

"Please call as often as you can. I'm going to miss you, Zach Black."

He ran his thumb over the curve of her cheek. "I'll miss you, too, angel."

NATALIE'S SERIES, SET off by Joaquin's stunning photos, caused an uproar from the first installment through the third. But it wasn't over when the series was completed. She worked late every day, staying with the story, as one development led to another.

Three other members of the school's Board of Trustees were arrested for knowing about the bogus donations and failing to report them. The sheriff and district attorney resigned after the school's financials proved they'd gotten payoffs in exchange for dropping the investigation. Congress called for an investigation of AMINTAC, while the Department of Defense remained stoically silent.

While she interviewed congressmen, Pentagon brass, and Mexican government officials, other reporters wanted to interview her. She gave a couple of interviews to local papers, but balked when the TV talk shows showed up. Then an agent called, offering to help her get rich if she decided one day to write a book about her experience.

Though she felt great satisfaction at exposing Wulfe and Cárdenas—and everyone who had worked with them—the excitement of big headlines, interviews, and book offers meant little to her. She lived for the moments late in the evening when Zach called and the two of them shared their day.

In the middle of it all, Natalie started her period, the knowledge that she wasn't pregnant leaving her deeply disappointed.

One week became two. Two weeks became three, and still her spirits didn't lift. It was then she realized she needed some *real* time off—no SPJ seminar this time, but a bona fide vacation. She called Zach, told him her plans, then bought a plane ticket to New Orleans.

There was something she needed to do.

ZACH OPENED THE cemetery's elegant iron gate and walked through the rows of marble tombs, feeling a hitch in his chest when he spotted her. He stopped in his tracks and just watched her. It had been three weeks since he'd last seen her, and damned if she hadn't become even more beautiful.

You are so lost, McBride.

Yeah, he was completely and utterly lost—in her. And he loved it.

He hadn't been exaggerating when he told her in the hospital that she'd set him free. She'd seen him at his best and his worst, and she'd accepted all of him without question or condemnation. And when he'd broken, the guilt he'd carried with him for so long spilling out, she'd been there to put the pieces of him back together again. She was his absolution, his redemption, his salvation.

She had changed him. The man who'd told her not long ago that he didn't want to be a father had been surprised by how disappointed he'd felt when she'd told him that she wasn't pregnant. It had taken a few days for him to decide that it was probably for the best. It would give them some time just to be with each other. Natalie was only twenty-seven. They had plenty of time left to start a family.

He walked toward her, savoring the sight of her. She didn't know he was here in New Orleans. When she'd told him her plans, he'd known he wanted to see the city with her, to hear her stories, to get a glimpse of what her life had been. So he'd told Pearce he was done, and he'd hopped on the next plane. When he hadn't found her at her hotel, he'd known he'd find her here. Hadn't he just visited Arlington two days ago to check in on Mike, Chris, Brian, and Jimmy?

Wearing a sleeveless dress of dark blue, she sat on the

retaining wall in front of the tomb where her parents and Beau rested together. Three fresh bouquets of red roses lay propped against the marble. And she was saying something . . .

Go wait on a bench, and leave her in peace, McBride.

He was about to walk away and find somewhere to park his ass, when he realized she was crying. He moved closer.

"I know you'd both love him. He saved my life. Did I mention he's a Medal of Honor recipient? And, Mama, he's so handsome. I wish with all my heart the two of you could've met him."

Zach realized she was talking to her parents about *him.* Something warm stirred in his chest. And no matter how wrong it was for him to stand there listening to her private conversation, nothing could drag him away now.

She reached out and ran her fingers over the name "Beauregard Latour," her voice quavering as she spoke. "I love you, Beau. You were everything to me, and I will always treasure my memories of our days together. But I can't live on grief. I know that's not what you'd want for me anyway. I never thought I'd fall in love again, but I love him so much. Wherever you are now, I hope you can be happy for me."

Zach felt an ache behind his breastbone—for her, for Beau, for lives needlessly lost. But the past was gone. "Natalie?"

At the sound of her name, Natalie looked—and saw Zach standing not ten feet away. Her pulse tripped, joy surging through her. "Zach!"

"When you told me you were coming here, I decided to surprise you."

"Well, you certainly did that." She laughed, wiping the tears off her face with a tissue. "You must think I'm crazy to be out here talking to a tomb."

He shook his head and started toward her, looking sexier in his gray sports jacket, T-shirt, and jeans than any man had a right to. "No, I don't. I find it touching."

He drew her into his strong arms, holding her tight, his scent surrounding her. Still, she couldn't help feeling embarrassed. "You overheard what I was saying?"

He brushed his lips over hers. "Don't let me interrupt you. I came here to be with you and see the city through your eyes—and that means paying my respects to your parents and to Beau, doesn't it?"

Too touched for words, Natalie nodded, threading her fingers through his and drawing him over to the tomb.

Zach ran his fingers over her parents' names and Beau's. "I wish I could have met them."

Her throat was so tight that she could only whisper, "Me, too."

For a time they sat on the retaining wall in front of the tomb, holding hands in silence.

It was Zach who spoke first, telling her how he'd visited his friends' graves in Arlington and had then taken time to track down Debbie, Brian's widow, to see if he could help her in any way. When he'd finally found her, he learned that she'd been married to Mike's younger brother for almost three years.

"She apologized for what she said to me at Brian's funeral, said it had haunted her for years."

"I knew it must have." Natalie made a mental note to forgive the woman. "I'm so glad you can put that to rest."

"Also, I've been cleared of any wrongdoing by the brass at the OD. In fact, I think Pearce would have literally kissed my ass if I'd asked him to. He offered me a desk and a big salary, but I turned it down. It just so happens I've got a better offer."

"Oh?" Something about his tone of voice made her nervous.

"Rowan has asked me to serve as her chief deputy, and I've accepted. The money's decent. It will be a lot less dangerous than working the line, and I won't be away from home nearly as often." He looked into her eyes. "There will be time in my life for a wife and a family."

Natalie's heart skipped. "Are you . . . are you asking me to marry you?"

Zach got down on one knee. "I know I'm not the easiest man to be around, but I'm not the person I was when you met me. You told me we could take life one kiss at a time. But that's not enough for me now. I don't want one kiss—I want a thousand. I want to live, Natalie, and I want to love you. I want to be the father of your children. I want to make the most out of every sunrise and sunset. Life is short and fragile. I don't want to waste another moment on fear and regret."

Without breaking eye contact, he took her hand. "I love

you, Natalie. I love you with everything I am. Will you marry me?"

Natalie glanced over at the tombstone that bore Beau's name, then met Zach's gaze, the love he felt for her warm in his gray eyes. She had to swallow the lump in her throat before she could answer, tears of happiness blurring her vision. "Yes! Yes, I'll marry you, Zach."

He let out a shaky breath, and she realized he'd been nervous. Then he reached into his pocket and drew out the most beautiful diamond ring she'd ever seen. In the center was a princess-cut blue diamond with white solitaires on either side. He slipped it on her finger. "The diamond reminded me of the color of your eyes. I hope you like it."

"Oh!" She stared at it, astonished. "It's beautiful."

He drew her to her feet, took her into his arms, and kissed her—a long, slow kiss that told her how much he loved her in a way words could not, one big hand working its way up her spine till his fingers tangled in her hair.

Heart thudding, she smiled up at him. "Another nine-hundred ninety-nine to go."

"Then we'd better get back to the hotel." He grinned. "Besides we've got a lot of practicing to do if we want to get good at making babies."

"Let's hurry." It had been three weeks, after all.

Then, hand in hand, they walked out of the cemetery—and into a new beginning.

EPILOGUE

Two months later

"I CAN'T TAKE my eyes off you."

Natalie looked up at her new husband as they claimed the first dance, surrounded by friends. "You're pretty amazing yourself."

Dressed in a black Armani tux with a gray silk vest, gray silk tie, and crisp white shirt, he looked more edible to Natalie than the four-foot-tall cake they'd cut and left to their guests to devour.

The wedding had gone off without a hitch. They'd rented a manor in Estes Park amid stands of golden aspen, selected a cake, flowers, and a dinner menu, and then left it up to the manor's staff to put it all together. That had given Natalie the time she needed to find the right dresses for herself and her bridesmaids. She'd gone with a white silk Oscar de la Renta with sheer beaded sleeves and a mini-train, while her bridesmaids had chosen empire-waist gowns in a deep burgundy red, a style that would accommodate Tessa's and Kat's growing bellies. Natalie had spent her spare time with Zach hunting for their dream home. They'd found what they wanted—a sunny five-bedroom house with granite countertops, a big sunken tub, and indoor and outdoor fireplaces—in the mountains west of Denver and would move in once they got back from their honeymoon in France.

Zach nuzzled her temple. "I cannot wait to go to our room. I'm going to take off this beautiful silk dress—and whatever sweet things you're hiding beneath it—and spend the entire night making you scream."

"Is that a promise?"

"Damn straight it is."

From somewhere behind them, Joaquin's camera flashed. He was the official wedding photographer.

Natalie felt a flutter in her belly, anticipation beginning to build. "And how are you going to do that? How are you going to make me scream?"

He nuzzled deeper. "With my fingers, my lips, my tongue, and," he whispered into her ear, "with my cock."

She felt a familiar ache between her thighs. "How much longer do we have to wait before it's polite to leave? Everyone seems to be having such a wonderful time. I think Rowan's tipsy."

Zach glanced over at his new boss and chuckled, the smile on his handsome face lighting up Natalie's heart. "I think we should at least stay for the first hour."

He looked so much happier these days, less troubled, younger. It wasn't that the nightmares were gone. He still had bad dreams once in a while, but they were growing less frequent, and he wasn't turning to alcohol afterward. When dreams woke him, Natalie would hold him, and they would talk or make love, and he would sleep again.

"I am so lucky to have you in my life." He looked into her eyes, his voice rich and resonant.

She smiled, feeling loved. "Have I ever told you how much I love your voice?"

"My voice?" He looked amused.

"Yes, your voice. It's the first part of you I met, remember? You spoke to me out of the darkness. For a time, that's all you were—a voice holding me together."

He kissed her forehead. "I'm not going to let anything like that happen to you again. You're going to live out your days as the cosseted and cherished wife of a chief deputy U.S. marshal. What do you think of that, Natalie McBride?"

It helped that Natalie had left journalism. She wasn't going to work freelance. She wasn't going to write a book about her ordeal in Mexico. She was going to stay at home, cooking meals, baking pies, and making sure their life together was comfortable. When Zach came home from a hard day's work, she wanted to be there for him, not coping with her own stress and fatigue. She knew some women would object to her decision, but this was her life, and she was going to live it as she chose.

"That makes me very, very happy." She drew Zach's lips down to hers.

And, forgetting about the music, forgetting that they were supposed to be dancing, forgetting about the friends who watched and the camera that flashed, they kissed long and slow and deep.

SAVORING THE SIGHT of the woman he loved out there having fun, Zach stood near the bar with his groomsmen as they watched their wives dance together. The women showed off their sexy dance moves for one another like women did when they danced with other women, belting out the lyrics to Sister Sledge's "We Are Family" with no hint of inhibition. Next, the DJ played Madonna's "Papa Don't Preach," during which Tessa and Kat seemed to have great fun exhibiting their pregnant bellies. Then Sophie burst into giggles over something Holly said, wobbling slightly on her heels.

"Yeah, she's had a bit too much to drink." Hunter grinned. "Don't worry. I'll take advantage of her later."

"You have to get your wife drunk to get her in bed with you?" Rossiter asked, mock surprise in his voice. "Sorry to hear that."

"Up yours, Rossiter." Hunter took a drink. "And who said anything about bed when I got my old Chevy out front?"

"Thanks for the warning." Darcangelo made a face. "We'll make sure to give that relic a wide berth when we leave. If I saw your hairy ass bouncing up and down in the backseat, I think it would give me nightmares."

Hunter chuckled. "Or turn you on."

"In your dreams." Then Darcangelo turned to Zach. His left hand was still in a cast, but his thumb was healing well. "So, McBride, how long will it be before there's a little Zach or Natalie junior around to fight over toys with our kids?"

Rossiter grinned. "We hear you're, uh . . . practicing. I just have to say that some of us get it right on the first try."

"That's called 'lack of self-control,' Rossiter," Hunter said.

Darcangelo laughed. "Look who's talking. Who got his woman pregnant while he was still running from the law? Oh, yeah. That was *you*, Hunter. No, don't look at me like that. Tess and I were married before I got her pregnant. That's more than either of you can say."

Hunter and Rossiter looked at each other, grinned, then knocked their beer mugs together and drank.

But Zach was confused. "How did you hear that we're 'practicing'? I thought that was a private joke between me and my wife."

Hunter leveled a grave look his way. "They're women, and they're journalists. No secrets. Get used to it."

"Thanks for the warning." Zach took a drink of stout, then answered the question. "We're waiting till next year. I want this first year with her. So much has changed for both of us. Sometimes, I don't believe it's real."

He saw understanding in each man's eyes.

Darcangelo clapped him on the shoulder. "You did well. Natalie is a class act."

"I don't think I've ever thanked you all for what you did." Maybe it was the champagne and the beer, but Zach had to say it. "Each of you risked your own life and the happiness of your wife and children to help Natalie. You saved her life, and mine. I'll never forget that."

Hunter met his gaze. "I told you, McBride. We take care of our own. You'd do the same for us."

Darcangelo nodded. "For once, Hunter, you and I agree."

"To friends." Zach raised his glass. Then he smiled, chuckling. "And to the women none of us deserve."

The men laughed, shouting out their agreement, beer mugs clinking.

HOT FROM DANCING, Natalie took a sip of cool champagne.

"Mmm, I love the sight of my husband in a tux." Sophie nibbled on the olive from her martini. "Makes me want to rip his clothes off."

Holly smiled. "I love the sight of all of your husbands in tuxes. Anytime you want to share, just let me know."

"Poor Julian." Tessa put a hand against her lower back. "When I get home, all I'm going to want is a back rub and sleep."

Natalie gave Tessa a nudge. "Julian is so crazy in love with you, I don't think he'll be disappointed."

"I think I must be the only woman in the world who feels sexier when I'm pregnant." Kat took a drink of bottled water. "I want sex all the time now."

"No, you're not the only one." Kara sipped her chocolatini. "My labors with Caitlyn and Brendan were brought on by sex."

"So was mine with Alissa," Kat confessed.

Natalie found herself looking forward to the day when she would be part of this sisterhood of women who'd given birth. Then she caught sight of Zach toward the back of the room. He seemed to be arguing with a man whose face Natalie couldn't see. He grabbed the man by his jacket and marched him toward the foyer.

"What is it?" Sophie followed the direction of Natalie's gaze.

"I don't know. Trouble of some kind." She hurried after her husband, arriving just in time to see Zach step out the front door, pushing the man ahead of him.

"You weren't invited," he was saying.

"I shouldn't need an invitation. I'm your father."

Natalie stopped in her tracks. *His father?*

"How did you get in?"

"I told them I was the groom's father, and they let me in."

"So you bullied your way through the door. You need to leave."

"You're not going to introduce me to that beautiful young woman you married?"

"I told you when Mom died that I didn't want to see you again."

Natalie knew why Zach didn't want to be around his father, knew his father had mistreated his wife and his elected office. But something about this situation tore at her, and she found herself hurting for both men—the father who seemed to want to be reconciled to his only living relative and the son who had been disappointed so many times that he'd lost all respect for his father.

Then Zach's father's voice took on a resigned tone. "Why do we do this? Why do we always fight? That's not why I came here. I wanted you to know I'm not the man I was, Zach. I left the senate. I resigned."

"What?" Zach sounded stunned. "Why?"

"I wasn't doing anyone but myself any good. I realized it was time for me to leave. I'm no leader. I'm not a hero. You showed me what a hero really is."

Zach had only begun to take this in when he saw Natalie standing in the foyer, her face flushed from champagne and dancing.

She came to stand beside him. "Is something wrong?"

"No. My father was just leaving."

Her gaze shifted from him to his father. She graciously held out her hand. "I'm Natalie, Zach's wife."

Zach's father's face split in a wide smile. "Hi, Natalie. I'm Robert McBride. I'm so pleased to meet you. You've very beautiful—and very brave, from what I've read."

"Thank you, Mr. McBride. That's very kind of you. Do you mind if I speak with Zach for just a moment?"

Uh-oh, McBride. It's your wedding night, and already you're in trouble.

Zach let Natalie draw him deeper into the foyer, leaving his father on the manor's front steps. "He wasn't invited, Natalie."

She turned, took his hands. "I know he wasn't. If you want to send him away, that's your decision. He's your father. I'll support you, no matter what you choose. I just wanted to say that it took courage for him to come here, knowing he wasn't welcome. It would have been easier for him to stay away."

Zach looked into Natalie's eyes, just being near her taking the edge off his anger. "He says he resigned, left his senate seat."

"People change." Then she seemed to hesitate.

"What is it?"

"He's not immortal, Zach. One of these days, he'll be gone, along with any chance you have to mend fences. We've put the past behind us, haven't we? Maybe he's here because he wants a new start, too."

It was on the tip of Zach's tongue to say he didn't want to mend fences with his father, but he could see in her eyes that this mattered to her. Was that because she'd lost her parents?

He drew a deep breath, tried to let his anger go.

"Okay." With her hand in his, he walked back to the door, to find his father still standing on the steps, looking old and alone. "Listen, Dad, I—"

"You want me to leave. Fine. I'll go. But first . . ." He reached into his pocket and drew out a box. "I brought you something. This belongs to you."

Expecting to find a piece of jewelry or other object that had once belonged to his mother, Zach released Natalie's hand, took the box, and opened it, the breath leaving his lungs when he saw what lay inside. "You . . . you saved this?"

Natalie peered into the box, gasped. "Oh, Zach!"

"Of course, I did. I'm sorry I drove you away from the ceremony. I shouldn't have brought the media, but I was so damned proud of you, son." His father's voice broke. "I meant to give this to you last time I saw you in D.C., but I got so angry that I forgot. It's yours. Keep it. You earned it."

Zach stared at his Medal of Honor. Until he'd laid eyes on it, he hadn't realized how deeply he regretted leaving it behind. In a very real sense, it was all he had left of Mike, Chris, Brian, and Jimmy.

He ran his finger over the silk neckband, touched the thirteen white stars, then traced the anchor and the design in the center of the five-pointed star, where the goddess Minerva raised her shield to drive away Discord.

Struggling to contain his emotions, he looked up, saw his father walking away. "Dad, stay."

His father turned. "Is that what *you* want, or just your pretty bride?"

Natalie reached out her hand. "It's what we both want. Come in. Let's introduce you to our friends."

From behind him came Darcangelo's voice. "We've lost the bride and groom. What's going on? Trouble?" Then Darcangelo's head peered over Zach's shoulder. "Holy shit. Is that . . . ? Whoa."

"Put it on, McBride." That was Hunter.

"Well, I don't know if—"

"Let your bride put it on you, Zachariah." His father stepped through the door.

Taking a deep breath, Zach turned, surprised to find most of their wedding guests crowded into the foyer, the music playing to an empty room behind them.

"Put it on, McBride! You earned it!" That was Joaquin.

His shout was joined by others.

His pulse thrumming, Zach nodded to Natalie, who lifted the medal out of its box with hands that seemed to tremble, then walked behind him, her fingers fastening the neckband in place. He smoothed the medal so that it lay flat, then looked down to see it lying against his tie, the gold star shining.

The foyer erupted in cheers and applause.

He looked down to find Natalie watching him, her eyes sparkling, a smile on her beautiful face. "You're my hero."

HER HEAD TICKLING from champagne, Natalie kicked the door to the bridal suite shut with her foot, her arms around her husband's neck as he carried her over to the bed.

"Thank you," he said as he set her on her feet. "Thank you for stopping me from sending my dad away."

"I didn't stop you from doing anything." She walked behind him and carefully removed his Medal of Honor, setting it down on top of the antique chest of drawers. Such a beautiful medal, earned at such a price. She didn't think she'd ever forget the sight of him standing there, medal around his neck, their friends cheering for him. "You made up your own mind."

He chuckled, reaching up to remove his tie. "Nice try, but I was there, remember? I would have sent him packing if you hadn't come along."

"I think everyone liked him." She sat on the bed, kicked off her heels. "He's a very charming man."

"I'm sure his dozen or so mistresses agree." He sat on a nearby chair, drew off his shoes and socks. "But I don't want to talk about him any more."

"What would you like to talk about?"

"I don't want talk at all." He stood, shucked his jacket and vest, then walked toward her with slow steps, his shirt half-unbuttoned, the glimpse of sexy man chest it gave her enough to make her pulse skip. "Right now I have more important things to do with my tongue."

His words sent a shiver of anticipation down her spine.

She stood, turning her back to him so that he could unzip her dress, the silk falling into a puddle around her ankles. She heard his quick intake of breath, felt a thrill to know he liked the lingerie she'd chosen to titillate him. She stepped out of the dress, then turned to face him, her blood going hot as his gaze raked over her, taking in the white lace corset, panties, and garters she wore, a telltale bulge appearing behind his zipper.

"We'll have to get you out of those panties, angel. I'm going to need full access." He reached behind her, slid his hands beneath the sheer fabric and over the bare skin of her bottom. "The corset, stockings, and garters can stay—for now."

The moment her panties were off, he toppled her backward onto the bed. "I love you, Natalie McBride. You are everything to me."

"I love you, Zach Black." She looked up at him from beneath her lashes, let her hunger for him show. "Now keep your promise. Make me scream."

And he did.

GLOSSARY

BDUs—Battle dress uniform, commonly used for military fatigues or cammo

BUD/S—Basic Underwater Demolition/SEAL, i.e., basic SEAL training

DUSM—A deputy U.S. marshal; pronounced "DOO-zum," and sometimes used as a pejorative term

EPIC—El Paso Intelligence Center, home to fifteen government agencies, including the U.S. Marshal Service and the Drug Enforcement Agency

klick—A military measurement of distance; one klick is equal to one kilometer or about 0.62 miles

maquiladoras—Factories used by U.S. and multinational corporations to manufacture goods inexpensively in other countries

The OD—The Operation Directorate in the U.S. Department of Justice

surf torture—Being forced to remain in cold water for prolonged periods of time, a strategy used by the navy to weed out those without the resolve and strength to be SEALS

suppressed firearm—A gun equipped with what most people call a "silencer"

USMS—United States Marshal Service

VBIED—Vehicle-borne improvised explosive device, i.e., car bomb

working the line—Working as law enforcement along the U.S./Mexico border

Turn the page for a special preview of
Virginia Kantra's next Children of the Sea novel

FORGOTTEN SEA

Coming June 2011 from Berkley Sensation!

CHAPTER 1

THE MAN ON the boat stripped half naked, exposing a lean golden chest and muscled arms.

In the parking lot across the street from the dock, Lara Rho sucked in her breath. Held it as he dropped his shirt to the deck and began to climb.

The top of the mast swayed, stark against the bold blue sky. Her stomach fluttered. *Nerves?* she wondered. Recognition? Or simple female appreciation?

The sun beat down, forging the water of the bay to a sheet of hammered gold. The air inside the car heated like an oven.

Beside her in the driver's seat, Gideon stirred, chafing in the heat. His corn silk hair was pulled into a ponytail, his blue eyes narrowed against the glare. "Is he the one?"

Lara leaned forward to peer through the windshield of their nondescript gray car, testing the pull of the internal compass that had woken her at dawn. They'd driven all morning from the rolling hills of Pennsylvania through the flat Virginia tidewater, wasting precious minutes in the traffic around Norfolk before they found this place. This man.

Are you the one?

She exhaled slowly, willing herself to focus on the climber. He certainly looked like an angel, hanging in the rigging against the bold blue sky, his bronze hair tipped with gold like a halo.

"I think so." She bit her lip. She should *know*. "Yes."

"He's too old," Gideon said.

Lara swallowed her own misgivings. She was the designated Seeker on this mission. Gideon was along merely to support and defend. She wanted her instincts to be right, wanted to justify their master's faith in her. "Late twenties," she said. "Not much older than you."

"He should have been found before this."

"Maybe he wasn't meant to be found before." Her heartbeat quickened. Maybe she was the one meant to find him.

"Then he should be dead," Gideon said.

The brutal truth made her shiver despite the heat. Survival depended on banding together under the Rule. She was only nine when they brought her to Rockhaven, but she remembered being alone. Hunted. If Simon Axton had not found her . . .

She pushed the memories away to study her subject. He must be forty feet above the gleaming white deck. Snagging a rope at the top of the mast, he fed it to the two men waiting below, one old, one young, both wearing faded navy polo shirts. Some kind of uniform?

"He's been at sea," she murmured. "The water could have protected him."

It could do that, couldn't it? Protect against fire. Even if the water wasn't blessed.

"I don't like it," Gideon said bluntly. "You're sure he's one of us?"

She had felt him more with every mile, a tug on her attention, a prickle in her fingertips. Now that she could actually see him, the hum in her blood had become a buzz. But it was all vibration, like listening to a vacuum cleaner in the dark, without shape or color. Not only human, not wholly elemental . . .

"What else could he be?" she asked.

"He could be possessed."

"No."

She would know, she would feel that. She was attracted, not repelled, by his energy. And yet . . . Uncertainty ate at her. She had not been a Seeker very long. The gift was rough and raw inside her, despite Miriam's careful teaching. What if she was wrong? What if he wasn't one of them? At best she and Gideon would have a wasted trip and she'd look like a fool. At worst, she could betray them to their enemy.

She watched the man begin his descent, his long limbs fluid in the sun, sheened with sweat and sunlight.

And if she was right, his life depended on her.

She shook her head in frustration. "We're too far away. If I could touch him . . ."

"What are you going to do?" Gideon asked dryly. "Walk up and ask to feel his muscles?"

There was an idea. She gave a small, decisive nod. "If I have to."

She opened her door. Gideon opened his.

"No," she said again. She needed to assert herself. Gideon was five years older, in the cohort ahead of hers, but she was technically in charge. "I can get closer if you're not standing next to me."

A frown formed between his straight blond brows. "It could be dangerous."

She had chosen their watch post. They both had scanned the area. It was safe. For now. "There's no taint."

"That's not the kind of danger I'm talking about," Gideon muttered.

She disregarded him. For thirteen years, she had trained to handle herself. She could handle this.

She swung out of the car, lowering her sunglasses onto her nose like a knight adjusting his helm, considering her strategy. Her usual approach was unlikely to work here. This subject was no confused and frightened child or even a dazed, distrustful adolescent.

After a moment's thought, she undid another button on her blouse. Ignoring Gideon's scowl—after all, *he* was not the one responsible for the success of their mission—she crossed the street to the marina.

It was a long, uneven walk along sun-bleached boards to the end of the dock.

The man descending the mast had stopped halfway down, balanced on some sort of narrow crossbeam, staring out at the open sea on the other side of the boat.

She tipped back her head. Her nerves jittered. Surely he wasn't going to . . .

He jumped. Dived, rather, a blinding arc of grace and danger, sending up a plume of white water and a shout from the younger man on deck.

She must have cried out, too. The two men on the boat turned to look at her, the young one with a nudge and the old one with a nod.

The one in the water surfaced with an explosion of breath, tossing his wet hair back from his face.

Cooling off? Or showing off? It didn't matter.

He stroked cleanly through the water, making for the swimming platform at the back of the boat.

Show time, she thought.

Pasting a smile on her face, she walked to the edge of the dock. "Eight point six."

He angled his head, meeting her gaze. She felt the jolt clear to her stomach, threatening her detachment. His eyes were the same hammered gold as the water, with shadows beneath the surface.

"Ten."

She pushed her sunglasses up on her head. "I deducted a point for recklessness. You shouldn't dive this close to the dock."

He grinned and grabbed the ladder. "I wasn't talking about my dive."

Heat rose in her cheeks. No one under the Rule would speak to her that way. But that was what she wanted, wasn't it? For him to respond to her while she figured out what to do with him.

"I'm flattered." This close, she could feel his energy pulsing inside him like a second heart. She tried again to identify it, but her probing thought slid off him like a finger on wet glass. He was remarkably well shielded. Well, he would have to be, to survive this long on his own.

She cast about for a subject. "Nice boat."

He shot her a measuring glance, hauled himself out of the sea, water streaming from his arms and chest. "Yeah, she is."

She tried not to goggle at the way his wet shorts drooped on his hips, clung to his thighs. "How long have you had her?"

"She's not mine. Four of us crewed her up from the Caribbean for her owners."

"So you're staying here? In town."

He shook his head. "As soon as she's serviced, I'm on to the next one."

Apprehension gripped her. She arched her brows. "You're still referring to the boat, I hope."

He flashed another grin, quick and crooked as lightning. "Just making it clear. Once I line up another berth, another job, I'm gone."

"Then we don't have much time," she said with more truth than he knew.

He stood there, shirtless, dripping, regarding her with glinting golden eyes. "How much time do you need?"

Her heart beat in her throat. Her mouth was dry. He thought her interest was sexual. Of course he did. That's what she had led him to think.

"Why don't we start with coffee," she suggested, "and see what happens."

He glanced at his companions, bundling sails on deck. "Drinks, and you've got yourself a date."

Lara swallowed. She had hoped to be back in Rockhaven by nightfall. But a few hours wouldn't make that much difference to their safety. She wanted desperately to succeed in their mission, to prove herself to the school council. She rubbed her tingling fingertips together. If only she could touch him . . . But they were separated by more than four feet of water. "Five o'clock?"

"Seven. Where?"

She scrambled to cull a name from their frustrating foray along the waterfront earlier in the day. Someplace close, she thought. Someplace dark. "The Galaxy?"

His eyes narrowed before he nodded. "I'll be there."

Relief rushed through her. "I'll be waiting."

JUSTIN WATCHED HER walk away, slim legs, trim waist, snug skirt, nice ass, a shining fall of dark hair to the middle of her back. Definitely a ten.

"Hot." Rick Scott, the captain, offered his opinion.

"Very," Justin agreed.

Her face was as glossy and perfect as a picture in a magazine, her eyes large and gray beneath dark winged brows, her nose straight, her mouth full-lipped. Unsmiling.

Why a woman like that would choose a dive like the

Galaxy was beyond him. Unless she was slumming. He picked his way through the collapsed sails and coiled ropes on deck. Which explained her interest in him even after she'd learned he wasn't a rich yacht owner.

The stink of mineral spirits competed with the scent of brine and the smells of the bay, fish and fuel and mudflats.

"The hot chicks always go for Justin," Ted said. "Lucky bastard."

Rick spat with precision over the side. He was tidy that way, an ex-military man with close-cropped graying hair and squinting blue eyes. "Next time you send the halyard up the mast, you can climb after it. Maybe some girl will hit on you."

A red stain crept under the younger crewman's tan. "It was an accident."

Justin felt a flash of sympathy. He remembered—didn't he?—when he was that young. That dumb. That eager to please. "Could have happened to anybody."

He'd made enough mistakes himself his first few months and years at sea. Worse mistakes than tugging on an unsecured line.

He wondered if the girl would be another one.

Dredging the disassembled winch out of the bucket of mineral spirits, he laid out the gears to dry. He was working his way north again like a migrating seabird, following the coast and an instinct he did not try to understand. The last thing he needed was to get tangled up on shore.

"*I'll be waiting*," she'd said in that smooth, low voice.

He reached for the can of marine grease. Maybe she could slake the ache inside him, provide a few hours of distraction, a few minutes of release.

Mistake or not, he would be there.

THIS BAR WAS a mistake, Lara thought.

The Galaxy was four blocks from the waterfront, off the tourist path, in a rundown neighborhood of shaded windows, sagging porches, and chain fences.

She perched in one of the dingy booths, trying to watch the room without making eye contact with the sailors and construction types straddling the stools at the bar.

Or maybe not.

At least in these seedy surroundings, no one would question if she and Gideon helped one slurring, stumbling patron out to their car later that night.

Over the bottles, a TV flickered, competing with the glow of the neon signs. MILLER. BUD. PABST BLUE RIBBON. The air stank of bodies and beer, a trace of heavy cologne, a whiff from the men's room down the hall. She folded her hands in her lap, her untouched Diet Coke leaving another ring on the cloudy table.

"Is it hot in here, or is it you?"

She looked up to find two sailors flanking her table. "Excuse me?"

The larger sailor shifted closer, trapping her into the booth. "You're too pretty to be sitting here alone. Mind if we join you?"

She wasn't alone. Gideon watched from an ill-lit corner, his attention divided between her and the door.

She straightened on the sticky vinyl seat. "I'm waiting for someone."

"I don't see anybody." The sailor—hovering drunkenly between cheerful and offensive—nudged his companion. "You see anybody, T.J.?"

T.J.'s blurred gaze remained focused on Lara's breasts. "Nope."

"Let me buy you a drink," the first guy said.

"No, thanks," Lara said firmly.

"There you are." A male voice, deep and smooth, broke through the noise of the bar and the wail of the jukebox. Somehow the sailors shifted, and there *he* was, tall and lean and attractively unshaven, looking perfectly at ease among the Galaxy's rough clientele.

It was him. Her quarry from the boat.

Her heart, her breath, her whole body reacted. Her fingertips tingled. Well, they would. She was attuned to him, to his energy.

He grinned at her. "Miss me?"

"You're late," she said.

Twelve minutes. Not enough to abandon her mission, but enough to pinch her ego.

"Come on, baby, don't be mad. You know I had to work." The newcomer's eyes danced, and she realized abruptly he was acting, playing a part for the sailors who still hemmed her into the booth. He lowered his voice confidingly. "Thanks for keeping an eye on her. She gets . . . restless if I leave her alone too long. If you know what I mean."

Lara kept her mouth shut with an effort. The shorter sailor guffawed. His companion shifted his weight like a bull, hunching his shoulders.

"I should pay you back," the newcomer continued easily. Man-to-man, she thought, making them like him, make them side with him, diffusing the tension. He moved again, angling his body so smoothly she almost didn't see him slide his wallet from his front pocket.

Feet shuffled. Something passed hands. The sailors nodded to her and then ambled back to the bar.

Lara narrowed her eyes. "Did you just give them money?"

"I bought them a round." His grin flashed. "Why not?"

"You *paid* them to go away," she said, torn between outrage and admiration. She couldn't imagine Gideon—or Zayin or any of the Guardians—dispatching an opponent by buying him a drink.

"Think of it as supporting our troops." He met her gaze, his own wickedly amused. "Unless you'd rather we pound each other for the privilege of plying you with alcohol."

"Of course not. Anyway, I already have a drink, thank you."

He eyed her glass and shook his head. "Place like this, you order beer. In a bottle. Unless you want to wake up with something a hell of a lot worse than a headache."

He turned to signal the waitress.

Lara appreciated his concern. But his caution would make her task more difficult. Her fingers curled around the handle of her bag on the seat beside her. Maybe it wouldn't be necessary to drug his drink, she thought. Explanations were out of the question. He wouldn't believe her, and they might be overheard. But surely she could rouse something in him, a response, a spark, a memory.

Assuming he was one of them.

Perhaps she should offer to feel his muscles after all.

The thought made her flush. "I don't even know your name."

"Justin." No last name.

"Lara. Lara Rho."

She started to extend her hand, but at that moment he caught the waitress's eye and the opportunity to touch him was lost.

Lara swallowed her disappointment.

The waitress, a hard-edged, hard-eyed blonde who looked like she'd rather be somewhere else, left the knot of locals absorbed by the game on TV. "What can I get you?"

"Two Buds," Justin said.

The waitress looked at Lara. "ID?"

"Of course," she said, reaching for her purse.

Axton insisted they do their best to abide by human laws, to blend in with their human neighbors. She pulled out her perfectly valid Pennsylvania driver's license, hoping Justin would do the same, eager for any hint to his identity, any clue why he hadn't been found before now.

He smiled at the waitress. "Thanks."

The blonde cocked her hip, pulled a pen from her stack of hair. "Anything else?"

His grin was quick and charming. "I'll let you know."

Oh, he was smooth, Lara thought as the waitress sashayed away.

"So, Lara Rho." He stretched his arms along the back of the booth, his knees almost-not-quite brushing Lara's under the table. "What brings you to Norfolk?"

You.

Bad answer.

"Um." She inched her foot closer to his across the sticky floor, hoping that small, surreptitious contact would give her the answers she needed. "Just visiting."

"For work? Or pleasure?"

Her toe nudged his. A buzz radiated up her leg, as if her foot had fallen asleep.

Deliberately, she met his gaze. "That depends on you."

His tawny eyes locked with hers. The tingling spread to her thighs and the pit of her stomach.

"I'm done working," he said.

Her mouth dried at the lazy intent in his eyes. "Won't they be expecting you? Back at the boat?"

"Boat's been delivered and I got paid. Nobody will care if I jump ship." He smiled at her winningly. "I'm a free man."

She moistened her lips. "Isn't that convenient."

No one would miss him if he disappeared tonight.

Her heart thudded in her chest. All she had to do was identify him as one of her own kind, the nephilim, the Fallen children of air.

From his corner, Gideon glowered, no doubt wondering what was taking her so long.

If only she were more experienced . . .

The waitress returned with their beer, two bottles, no glasses.

Lara gripped the slick surface and gulped, drinking to ease the constriction of her throat.

"Let's get out of here," Justin invited suddenly.

"What?"

He reached across the table and took her hand, wet from the bottle. An almost visible spark arced between them, a snap of connection, a burst of power. Shock ripped through her.

His eyes flickered. "You pack quite a punch."

So he felt it, too. Felt something. Hope and confusion churned inside her. She dampened her own reaction, feeling as though her circuits had all been scrambled. The air between them crackled, too charged to breathe.

"I . . . You, too."

Her heart thudded. *He was not human.*

Or only partly human. His elemental energy beat inside his mortal flesh.

But he was not nephilim either. She didn't know what he was.

His energy was not light, but movement, swirling, thick, turbulent as storm. It swamped her. Flooded her. She clung to his hand like a lifeline, focusing with difficulty on his face.

". . . find someplace quiet," he was saying. "Let me take you out to dinner. Or for a walk along the waterfront."

"What are you doing?" Gideon demanded.

Lara flinched.

"Who the hell are you?" Justin asked.

Gideon ignored him. "Are you *trying* to call attention to yourself?" he asked Lara.

Lara tugged her hand from Justin's, her mind still stunned, her senses reeling from the force of their connection. "You felt that?"

"They could feel you in Philadelphia," Gideon said grimly. "Shield, before you get us both killed."

Justin's eyes narrowed. "Look, buddy, I don't know who the fuck you think you are, but—"

Gideon gripped Lara's elbow. "We're getting out of here."

Justin rose from the booth. "Take your hands off her."

"It's all right," Lara said quickly. She struggled to pull herself together. "I know him."

Justin's mouth tightened. "That doesn't mean you have to go with him."

"Try and stop her," Gideon invited.

Lara shook her arm from his grasp. "That's enough," she said, her voice sharp as a slap.

Gideon met her gaze. "Your little energy flare just gave away our location. This place will be crawling in an hour. We need to leave before they get here."

Lara's throat constricted. "What about him?"

"Is he one of us?"

Not fully human. Not nephilim either.

"No," she admitted.

"Then lose him. He's not our responsibility."

He was right. She was still new to her duties as Seeker, but the Rule of the community, codified over centuries, was clear about their obligations to keep and preserve their own kind. And the dangers of getting involved with those who were not their kind.

Yet . . .

"Give us a minute," she said.

Gideon's face set, cold and rigid as marble. "Five minutes," he acceded. "I'll wait for you outside."

Where he could guard the entrance and scan for danger. She nodded.

With another glare at Justin, he left.

"Are you okay?" Justin asked.

"Fine," she said firmly, whether it was true or not. Why had she felt the pull of his presence if she wasn't meant to find him?

"Listen, it's none of my business," he said. "But if this guy is giving you a hard time . . ."

His willingness to look out for a stranger shamed her. Especially since she was about to abandon him to his fate.

"Nothing like that. We work together," she explained.

He looked unconvinced.

"What about you?" she asked.

He frowned. "What about me?"

Who are you?

What are you?

"Will you be all right?" she asked.

"I think my ego will survive being ditched for another guy." The glint in his eye almost wrung a smile from her.

She bit her lip. Their enemies would be circling, drawn by that unexpected snap of energy. She already had to account for one mistake. She couldn't afford another.

Besides, he was not one of them.

He would be safe. He had to be.

"Right. Well." She slipped her purse strap onto her shoulder. At least now she didn't have to drug his beer.

"Take care of yourself."

As she slid out of the booth, he stepped back, lean and bronzed and just beyond her reach. "You, too."

She walked away, reluctance dogging her steps and dragging at her heart.

JUSTIN WATCHED HIS plans for the evening walk out the door with more regret than he had a right to. Her tight butt in that slim skirt attracted more than a few glances. Her fall of dark brown hair swung between her shoulders. The woman sure knew how to move.

He shook his head. He'd known she was slumming when she came on to him that afternoon. Presumably she was going back where she belonged, with Mr. Tall, Blond, and Uptight.

He hadn't lost anything more than half an hour of his time. So why was there this ache in the center of his chest, this sense of missed opportunity?

He took a long, cold pull at his bottle, his gaze drifting over the bar. He'd been in worse watering holes over the past seven years, before he got his bearings and some control over his life. Worse situations, in Puerto Parangua and Montevideo, in Newark and Miami. He drank more beer. He fit in with the surly locals and tattooed sea rats better than pretty Lara Rho and her upscale boyfriend ever could. But he didn't belong here. He belonged . . . The beer tasted suddenly flat in his mouth. He didn't know where he belonged.

He set down his bottle. He didn't want to drink alone tonight. And he didn't want to drink with the company the Galaxy had to offer.

Careful not to flash his roll, he dropped a couple of bills on the table and walked out.

Nobody followed.

Outside, the sky was stained with sunset and a chemical haze, orange, purple, gray. The day's heat lingered, radiating from the crumbling asphalt, sparking off the broken glass. He headed instinctively for the water, free as a bird thanks to the coworker boyfriend with the ponytail, trying to figure out what to do with the rest of his evening.

Or maybe his life.

Beyond the jumbled rooftops at the end of the street, he could see the flat shimmer of the sea. He passed a homeless guy huddled in a doorway, clutching a bottle, watching the street with flat, dead eyes. Something wrong there. He kept his arms loose and at his sides as the pawn shops and tattoo parlors gave way to warehouses and razed lots.

His neck crawled. Alley ahead. Empty. Good.

He lengthened his stride, taking note of blank windows and deserted doorways. Good place to get jumped, he thought, and angled to avoid the dirty white van blocking a side street.

He heard a thump. A grunt.

Not his problem, he reminded himself. None of his business.

A woman's cry, sharp with anger and alarm.

Shit.

He circled the van, shot a quick look down the street.

And saw Lara Rho backed against the brick wall of an empty lot with a couple of rough guys circling her like dogs.